The Sequel
Volume 2

Dina Rae

Solstice Publishing - www.solsticepublishing.com

The Sequel

by Dina Rae

Chapter One

"*Engel, engel*!" shrieked a little, blonde boy dressed in jeans and a flannel shirt.

I did not yet have a chance to process what had just happened. My body tingled and wobbled as I sat up in a small glass enclosure. My memories flooded back. Glenn Lucasek rescued me from the middle of nowhere and brought me to the *They Are Here* (T.A.H.) Institute inside of the Ruby Mountains. I agreed to continue the time travel experiment that Glenn and Jay McCallister started. Now I was inside of a different capsule with a screaming boy only steps away. Instinct told me to move. He might have attracted unwanted attention.

I didn't know what '*engel*' meant, but I suspected it might have meant 'angel' in German. The little boy, somewhere around eight years old, was definitely European, and maybe even Aryan. His words sounded German, and his flaxen hair and pale blue eyes only added to my theory. My race was still a mystery.

My dark complexion, dark eyes and black hair made it clear that I was not a local. The fact that I had just appeared out of a time machine had to have startled him. He might have even thought I was from another planet.

I opened the metal latches. The glass door of the capsule swung open. I stepped outside of the capsule. I stood inside of a rustic animal stall. The smell of manure, the dirt floor littered with hay, and the high beamed ceiling could only mean one thing, I was inside of a barn. I had only been to a farm once. My second set of foster parents had taken me to their parents, or my temporary grandparents, for the weekend up in northern California. This was similar, but cleaner.

The little boy's screams had escalated into full blown hysteria. He backed slowly away from me for the door. I walked a few feet away from the capsule. From a different vantage point, I saw how the machine was cleverly concealed behind a clutter of barrels, stacks of hay, and hanging hooks that held large tools.

I stood in between a couple of barrels. The boy was in the doorway, crying, yet refusing to lose sight of me. He looked more confused than scared. Someone, perhaps his parents, dabbled in the science of time travel. Why else would they have a capsule hidden in this barn?

The barrels smelled like stale beer. Was this a brewery too? I wanted to explore, but worried about the boy and whoever else lived on the farm. I was afraid of abandoning the capsule. It was the only way I knew how to get back home.

The boy finally turned around and ran out of the barn. Relief swept over me. I had some time to check out my surroundings. Through the other set of doors on the opposite side of the barn, I saw horses, cows, goats and sheep scattered throughout the pasture. Beyond the pasture and the animals was a fence which I assumed must border some sort of crops. There were a few other out-buildings, probably for storage. A silo and another barn were seen in the distance.

On the other side of the barn where the boy had just exited was a gravelly dirt road that led to a large farmhouse. The house looked dilapidated, even abandoned, as it sat ominously on top of a hill looking down at the barn.

The boy ran to the house. Soon he would come back with more company. My time was short.

The road to the house was a mystery. I wasn't sure if the marks were from the wheels of a carriage or a car.

Was I in the twentieth century? I still had no idea as I looked for more clues.

My calm and collected manner turned sour as I searched for controls for the time machine. They had to be nearby. I found none. There had to be a power source. I fiddled around with some of the gadgets inside of the capsule. Nothing. I regretted not asking Glenn for more information, and disappointed that he forgot to offer it.

I missed Eric. He had to be sick with worry. Did he even know I was alive? The last time we were together was when he took me home, and then sat in his car waiting. I just wanted my computer and my green crystal pendant.

Claude Kazinsky entered my mind. His name filled my head with fantasies of revenge. He would pay once I returned. Then there was Glenn. He needed my sequel to help his scientists unlock extraterrestrial secrets of DNA. As Jay first pointed out, I was subconsciously encoding it within my novel. My sequel probably had more coding. Both our novels had spelled out the DNA sequence of a gene that led to time travel. This gene enabled us to alter our physical bodies into particles and travel throughout time. Could there be even more to the code?

I wasn't sure what happened inside of Glenn's capsule. Once it had begun to spin, I couldn't see my appendages; in fact, I couldn't see anything. I felt partially asleep, weightless, like I was floating into another dimension. Someone or something was pulling me somewhere.

Jay had been the pioneer in this new way of travel. Only weeks later, he died. He supposedly drowned, although Glenn mentioned that Jay was murdered. Was it because of Jay's discoveries? All of it was still in the conspiracy stage. All I knew for sure was that Jay was dead, and so was my chance at having a family.

I knelt on the floor and felt around, searching for some kind of secret control box or even a door to a control room. There had to be a centrifuge or something. After surveying a third of the barn, I found nothing. Tears that seemingly came from nowhere suddenly streamed down my face. Was I stuck here forever?

I nervously put my hands in my pockets and felt the gold and silver coins with my fingers. The one hundred dollar bill with the 2017 date on it was intact. Interesting. Money also traveled through time. I could only guess that I could bring other objects to and from my time travels.

The little boy was on his way back to the barn. I saw him from the doorway. He watered the animals' trough with a bucket. Back and forth, back and forth, he filled a bucket from the pump, and then dumped it into the trough. These people had a time capsule in the barn yet watered their animals with a pump. Odd to me. Again, I tried to put a date on my trip. The boy put on quite a show, but there was no chance that he forgot about me coming out of the capsule.

I crouched down behind a barrel. He entered the barn and hesitantly looked around. Maybe he was too scared to move away from the entrance. He left once again and headed toward the house. With him gone, I could continue looking for the power source.

The soft, dirt floor of the barn seemed to vibrate. The centrifuge had to be close. The noise was a low, dull sound that I could only hear when concentrating. I looked through each animal stall, only finding more troughs, hay and buckets. There was no manure in any of the stalls except the one which housed the time capsule. I assumed it was put there as part of the camouflage. The barn was too spotless to be functioning. Either the boy was some kind of clean freak, or the animals didn't live in this building. I kept looking out the entrance for the boy.

Sunlight streamed through the barn and the temperature was crisp. I guessed the time to be around midday. The trees and grass were green. Was it spring time? I thought of the boy's screams again...*engel*. I was definitely not an *engel*. Assuming that I was in Germany, what did I know about Germany? Not much. Glenn and his scientists at the institute showed me how my chromosome was shaped like a swastika. I thought of Hitler and World War II, but that was the extent of my knowledge. I didn't blend in with twentieth century Germans. My dark features made me look Mexican, or American Indian, or even mixed race. Could I be taken captive and thrown into a concentration camp? I needed to find the time machine controls fast.

After a thorough intake of the barn's inventory, I became even more convinced that this barn was a decoy. Was the boy aware of the capsule? He had to know something. Could he have built it?

Across the soft dirt floor was a yellow cable. I followed its path, hopeful it led to the time capsule's controls. The yellow cable traveled upward toward a lofted area of the barn. I followed it, climbing a ladder up to the second story.

The loft jutted out halfway across the square footage of the barn's main floor. Far against the wall by a small window was a burled, wooden writing desk. The desk's brass pulls were in need of a good polish. The window by the desk was too high for me to see out of, but added lots of light. The yellow cable ran across the floor and ended inside of a wall outlet next to the desk.

I walked across the floor and the boards squeaked. There was a stack of papers underneath a paperweight on top of the desk. Something about the paperweight made my heart thump.

I stood over the papers and trembled. The paperweight was too familiar. Moldavite. It was the crystal that was given to me by the nuns of the orphanage, the crystal I had once believed was left to me from my mother. It was the crystal that had brought Jay and me together.

As I held the large rock in my hand, a soft breeze got control of the papers and blew them onto the first floor of the barn. I would gather them later.

The rock was the size of my fist, uncut, unpolished, and beautiful. The greenish-yellow color glowed once it was in my hand. I suddenly heard voices outside in the distance. *Engel* was the only world that I recognized. The harsh accents once again sounded German. One voice belonged to the boy and the other voice came from a woman, perhaps his mother or sister.

I put down the crystal and hid in between two of the extra bales of hay while sliding a third bale over my body. I heard both the boy and the woman getting closer. Then I heard a click. A rifle? The ladder that led to the loft was making the floor vibrate. Someone was close by. Was this how it was going to end? Death in another era?

I heard heavy breathing, but then the sound went away. After several minutes, I exhaled for the first time, convinced that the boy and woman must have left. The bale that lay on top of me was thrown to the side. A barrel of a shotgun was pointed at my head.

Chapter Two

1970
Broom Lake, Nevada

General Robert Andreas read the letter from Kate four more times and then tucked it into his wallet. Retirement was only six months away. Money was not an issue. His nest egg, family inheritance, and frugal lifestyle would give him security and comfort for the remainder of his life. At seventy years old, time was closing in. Despite his age, he wasn't ready to buy a house and putz around in the garden. The defense industry had been knocking on Andreas's proverbial door with lucrative job offers for years. Nothing was official, but most of the airmen at his base assumed he would soon be a civilian.

Andreas looked every bit his age. Lines were etched in deep around his brown eyes, forehead, and thin mouth. His salt and pepper hair turned white, but he still maintained a lithe, muscular body on his tall frame. He never did quit smoking, despite the growing cancer warnings put out by numerous medical associations. The cigarettes had yet to make their mark on his health.

It was 1970, and the world had greatly changed, yet Broom Lake oddly remained the same. Broom Lake had grown substantially bigger. The Air Force added more hangars, runways, and buildings. Security had tripled. Airmen were stationed miles away from the base's perimeter.

Social issues of the day called for more women to fill high-ranking military jobs. Living on the base for the last few decades had kept the general out of touch. He believed fiercely in equality and knew the military needed to change some of its outdated policies. But change had always come with a big set of headaches.

Andreas needed more separate buildings to accommodate the rising number of women within the air force. Construction workers in and out of the base attracted attention. Security tightened up. The base's secrecy led to many UFO conspiracy theories that occasionally made headlines.

Andreas estimated one hundred and twenty people knew about Broom Lake. Only half of them worked there on a full-time basis. These full-time airmen, airwomen, and engineers were accredited with creating and perfecting the world's most advanced aircraft. The futuristic jets looked like they belonged in the twenty-first century. These advancements only led to more ongoing UFO conspiracies.

Once upon a time, Andreas had been in charge of putting a shattered UFO back together. That was the first and last extraterrestrial craft that Broom Lake had seen. Andreas had heard through the grapevine that a new base in Idaho had been where all of the unidentified space crafts were now sent. He wished he was still in that loop.

Despite the change of UFO location, Broom Lake still attracted the most suspicion. The public always pointed to Broom Lake for housing the world's UFOs. He had to laugh. If only the world knew the truth about the base. He was still in charge of Operation Chrome, the hybrid baby program that he and his team of Nazi geneticists had started after the war.

The underground cage they once used for four captured aliens was converted into another wing of underground laboratories. Operation Chrome was invisible in everything, including funding. Top families who were interested in raising an Advanced Being baby had to pay. The base hadn't used public funds in years, keeping them off the books in Washington.

Karl Jaeger, Frederik Richtor, and Hans Schmidt surpassed the world's most brilliant doctors by light years. They still held a monopoly on genetic advancement. As promised so long ago, the doctors were allowed the same freedoms of all American citizens. Andreas sometimes had them followed every time they left the base. They occasionally consulted with the private sector in their genetic findings. The information they shared had to always be approved by the brass in Washington. The corporations who were given genetic secrets were the same ones who generously donated to key members of Congress.

The doctors enjoyed their freedom. Oddly, they never seemed to abuse it. The only thing that seemed to matter to them were their hybrids. The doctors were now into their sixties. Time was no longer a luxury. Andreas never understood their obsession and never trusted them. He lost control of their experiments long ago.

Andreas sat at his old metal desk and stared out the window. The last couple of decades had run smoothly. Doctor Kate Costello's letter hit him like a block of granite. She reminded him of his shortcomings. He thought about his ex-wife and his two daughters who slipped away. Kate gave him a second chance at something more than his career. He used her as a scapegoat without ever looking back.

Andreas knew that Kate had nothing to do with the missing baby or the Advanced Beings' escape. The tapes he found proved it. The A.B.s had always been in control. Their leader used a laser from his hand and cut right through the thick Plexiglas wall of the cage. Their captivity had been an illusion from day one. He never told anyone. Kate and the other engineers were the perfect patsies.

Six months until retirement. Were the sacrifices worth it? That was the million dollar question Andreas asked himself every day. Even with his top security clearance, he still was not sure about the purpose of the experiment. He imagined that the babies were being groomed for something big. A sinking feeling that he had for years told him that Operation Chrome would not make the world a better place.

Andreas didn't want to live as a civilian. Although he was no longer mesmerized by the pomp and glory of the military, his career gave him a purpose. Retirement would be even lonelier than his life at Broom Lake. He missed Kate. Her letter sounded as if she landed on her feet. He should have been happy for her. She found a new career, fell in love, and even had a family. He wasn't happy, just jealous. Should he call her? Was it too late?

The sentimentality evaporated as Andreas's thoughts shifted gear. He thought about Michael Bolantano dropping off one of their hybrids and leaving one of the crystals behind.

Fifteen minutes and two phone calls later, Andreas learned that Kate Costello lived in London and worked for a luxury automaker. She married a physics professor, Doctor Jacob Osbourne, and had a daughter named Lori Osbourne. Kate was extraordinary in every way. Brilliant, beautiful, kind, and ambitious-a woman he betrayed.

Michael Bolantano, an officer Andreas had once pegged as ambitious, had advanced one ranking over the last twenty years. He went from a captain to a major. He still had some time. Andreas thought Bolantano was somewhere in his late forties, maybe early fifties, but the major seemed disinterested in moving up the totem pole. He became more and more aloof, withdrawn, and burnt out.

Kate's letter only confirmed what Andreas had observed. Whatever Bolantano's motives, treason was treason. Andreas did not see betrayal as part of the bright man's constitution. Was someone paying him? Bolantano didn't seem too interested in money. Was he being blackmailed? Could Bolantano have been one of the fathers? Andreas never did get a clear answer of whose sperm was fathering these babies. Was it morality? An orphanage had many depressing elements to a child's upbringing. Why would he risk their emotional happiness knowing that they could be raised by the world's most influential people with every opportunity imaginable? On the other hand, the orphan would be free, not under obligation or studied like a rat.

Should Andreas just ask Bolantano? They were never close. He couldn't see the major opening up to him on a whim. More proof was needed. Again, he needed to talk to Kate. He *wanted* to talk to Kate.

Slowly, Andreas dialed each digit in the number he had tracked down through his connections. His heart raced. She sent him the letter. *She initiated this*, he thought. *She invited me to call.*

One ring. *What if she tells me to go to hell?*

Two rings. *What if she invites me to England?*

Three rings. "Hello?"

There was no mistaking her deep, no-nonsense voice, the voice of a leader, not a follower.

"Kate, it's me, Robert."

There was a pause which lasted much longer than Andreas liked. The silence caused his stomach to flip. Maybe this was a bad idea.

"Kate?" The general was the first to metaphorically blink in this conversation, not liking the surrender of power. That was the very least that he deserved. This letter, this story she sent him could be some kind of set-up/payback for almost ruining her life.

"Yeah. You sound the same. Your voice, it brought back a lot of memories," Kate said.

"I know. I was a real son of a bitch. Not the knight I pretended to be. I truly am sorry. Sorry about a lot of things. Lots of regrets."

Kate paused again and said, "Oh, I've forgiven you a long time ago. Had to, or would have ended up a bitter old biddy. God was good to me. Brought a man into my life and gave me a daughter."

"God?" Andreas asked, surprised to hear Kate using a religious reference. Science had always been her god.

"My late husband insisted on it. Turned me into a believer," Kate answered.

After seeing aliens and a spaceship, thought Andreas, *how could God even be a possibility?* But he kept his mouth shut. Maybe she needed to believe in something greater than Operation Chrome. "I'm tossing around retirement. Lamphrey is itching for me to go. I'm sure he's not the only one who wants me out. Maybe it's time. I'm too old for this shit." He heard her chuckle. "Much has changed since you left."

He heard the scoff in her voice. She never *left,* he had her removed.

"Listen, Robert, like I said in my letter…"

"Kate, please, not over the phone."

"I have something for you," Kate said.

"Be there tomorrow."

"But I can send…"

"Kate, I'll be there tomorrow. Unless…"

"No. Maybe it's time to bury the hatchet. See you then."

Andreas hung up the phone and booked a hotel room in London, telling his secretary he was taking a last minute vacation. He then booked the next commercial flight. He was not used to flying with a crowd, but didn't want any questions. He'd been to London before, but never for pleasure. His intelligence contacts told him where Kate lived and worked.

Kate earned a huge salary from Hanover Auto, an English automaker. He wasn't sure exactly what she did, but Hanover was into all kinds of products. Their high-end cars were only a small part of the company. In essence, they were more of a defense contractor. Andreas's sources said that Kate designed car engines and the gadgets that came with them. Andreas was sure she did much more. She was very much part of the James Bond culture. Her husband, Doctor Jacob Osbourne, was a well-respected physics professor at Imperial College. He was five years younger than Kate and recently died of a heart attack. Andreas wasn't sure how they had met, but assumed they shared an interest in physics and found each other in similar circles. Andreas knew almost nothing about her daughter, Lori, only that she was eighteen years old.

While flying as a passenger on the commercial jet, the general had a lot of time to think. He wished he was there for his two daughters. He wished he could start over with Kate. Her daughter should have been his. He was truly alone. He had once been religious, but then the evils of war and the discovery of aliens seemed to cancel out his beliefs.

As Andreas reclined in the first class leather seat, he thought about Operation Chrome. It all began when Andreas went to war to save the world from Hitler, but Hitler was only one of many monsters who had set up shop in Europe. Andreas found Doctor Josef Handel, another monster who happened to know a great deal about extraterrestrials and genetics. He had Andreas track down two more Nazi doctors for help. The three men had unlimited funds and a chance to play Frankenstein in America. Their first round of babies was just reaching adulthood. What were the babies capable of?

Andreas grabbed his carry-on bag and checked into the hotel, only minutes away from Kate's flat. Her work was a twenty minute walk in a different direction. He freshened up and changed his clothes from a pair of tan dress pants and a golf shirt to jeans and a different golf shirt.

London was cold, rainy, and gray, which was typical weather for the early spring. Andreas was used to the Nevada heat and only brought a lightweight windbreaker. The five minute walk made him shiver and feel even more vulnerable. He stood in front of Kate's flat which sat on a tree-lined street of other large brick and limestone buildings. Posh. Not over the top, but obviously she, her late husband, and daughter were living an upscale lifestyle. Again, he tried to be happy and not jealous. He went up the few stairs and then knocked on the black lacquered door. It was Saturday late morning London time and he told her he was coming.

A woman with a gray and white bobbed hair cut answered the door. Her eyes were hazel, a lighter hue than Andreas remembered, bright, filled with curiosity and intelligence. Her fair skin was softly lined and her curvy frame had thinned. He'd know her anywhere. Still beautiful. A tear rolled down his cheek and he turned away. Crying was always considered a weakness by him and he didn't want her to see.

"Please come in," Kate said and opened the door.

"I am sorry to be so vague on the phone, but I have my reasons." Andreas paused and took a deep breath. "You, you are still beautiful. Haven't aged a bit." He awkwardly gave her a hug that she wasn't expecting.

Kate blushed. "You lie. And you look the same. Still the distinguished general I met so long ago."

"Now you lie."

They both laughed, and then there was a pregnant pause.

Andreas couldn't stand the silence and searched for something to say. Back to the business at hand. "Uh, well, thank you for writing me about Michael. You know he hasn't exactly risen up the ranks. He's a major now, but that seems as far as he wants to go. Not sure what his angle is. He was and is very private…"

"Oh dear, where are my manners? Please come in the kitchen and I'll put a fresh pot of coffee on. Never got used the tea here. It's so cold and damp outside. You look frozen. And I bought some scones this morning," Kate said as she led him through the main hallway of the home.

Andreas took notice of the large, opulent rooms filled with beautiful furnishings. The inside of the house was even nicer than he expected. Again, twangs of jealousy stabbed away at his heart. She didn't need him, never did. There was a picture on the wall of her, her husband, and daughter. A picture of her as a wife and mother. Life had marched on for her, yet stagnated for him.

As Kate made the coffee and set out the scones, she asked, "Did you ever meet anyone special?"

"No."

"I'm sorry."

Andreas helped himself to a plateful of scones. He was starving. In between bites he said, "It's my fault. You know that better than anyone. This job, the power, all of it is about to end. Now I realize what I sacrificed."

"You must have some incredible job offers waiting for you," Kate said as she sat down and poured them each a cup of coffee. No milk or sugar. She still remembered how he took his coffee which made him feel good.

"Yes, I've had some offers. But what does it matter. I have no one, no legacy, in fact my entire operation is top secret so I won't even make the history books, hardly anyone knows about it. No one will cry for me at my funeral, much less attend."

Andreas saw the pity in Kate's eyes and wished she hated him instead.

Kate tried to make light of it. "Well, I see you brought an orchestra of violin players with you. Poor General Andreas." Her feeble comment cheered him up and he smiled. "Choices. I've made some poor ones myself. But we got to play the hand we're dealt."

Another moment of silence. At least he had food and coffee to fill the moment. "You know, Kate, you're right. I accept my failures. One of my biggest, if not the biggest, is not standing beside you, marrying you. I'll admit, I wish we had a kid, but then I already have two kids that I don't even see. So maybe it's for the best. I hope you forgive me."

Another awkward pause. Kate looked at the floor. Andreas sensed she also had many regrets. "Well, it's just too late for any of this. We're too old to beat ourselves up. Finish your scones and let me take you to the orphanage Lori works for. You can meet Lori, see the baby, the stone necklace, and a picture from the security camera."

Andreas threw on his light windbreaker and prepared to freeze. Kate bundled up for the chilly weather. She looked at his jacket and shook her head. "Here, take this hat and these gloves." He gratefully took them, feeling odd about wearing her dead husband's things.

"Thanks. I'm sorry about your husband. Heart attack, about ten months ago, right?"

"Ah, yes. At least that is what the doctor said. Come, let's go."

Something in the way that Kate said the word doctor made Andreas raise an eyebrow. Did she suspect foul play? He decided to let the question pass. "So, the orphanage is close?"

"Yes, it's only a few blocks from here. You know, Robert, if you were smart…"

"So, you're saying that I'm dumb?"

Kate laughed. "If you were smart, you would have had those Nazi doctors figure out a way to live forever instead of messing around with babies."

"Why? Then I'd have to feel sorry for myself forever. Nah, what fun would life be knowing that death is no longer a problem." They walked for several minutes in silence. He sensed there was something more going on in her life that she was reluctant to talk about.

Kate smiled. "We are here. Come meet my daughter."

They walked across a busy street and then through a locked gate. About fifty yards back was an old building with a large yard that had been transformed into a children's park. Andreas assumed they were entering the backway. They walked straight for door.

Inside the orphanage was a reception area which looked like it once been a doctor's clinic. The walls were bright primary colors and there were small tables everywhere, set up like a classroom. Two young women were behind the counter wiping down plastic toy blocks.

"Robert, meet Lori. Lori, meet Robert," said Kate to one of the young women. The other young woman gave Kate a look. "Oh, and Jackie."

Handshakes were exchanged. Jackie walked off with a basket of blocks to the play area. Lori was a dead ringer for Kate.

"Mum, are you alright?"

Kate gave her a look that mothers give daughters when they don't want to talk about certain things.

"Very well then. General Andreas, my mother has told me much about you. I know that you are here about the baby. Please, let me show you. He's beautiful." Lori had a charming English accent.

The general followed her beyond the counter and separating wall into the nursery area of the orphanage. There were four newborns. Lori stopped in front of the nearest crib.

"This boy was brought here ten days ago. Here." She went into a drawer marked "Daniel" and handed Andreas a necklace with a green-yellow crystal.

He sighed. "That's definitely our crystal."

"And here. This is a still from the security camera." Lori reached back into the drawer and handed it to Andreas. "You're not going to take him back, are you?"

"No. Not today. But for the moment, please don't allow anyone to adopt him, not yet." Lori nodded. "He belongs to the U.S. government, but he's much safer here." Andreas looked at the photo. It was definitely Michael Bolantano. "Can I keep this?" Andreas asked about the still photo. Lori nodded. "Where did he drop the baby off? Your gate was locked when your mother and I entered the building."

Lori led him to another entrance. "This is actually our main entrance. The one you came through is the back entrance. This building takes up a double corner lot so you can exit and enter it from three busy streets. I am assuming this man knew that. He must have been staking out the place. The security cameras are hidden; so, he probably didn't know he was being taped."

"Thank you, ladies."

"So, this is treason?" asked Lori, her hazel eyes shining bright.

The question made Andreas feel uncomfortable and he shrugged.

"Thanks, Lori. See you at home," Kate said as she ushered Andreas out of the orphanage. They walked back to her flat.

"Sorry, my daughter is full of curiosity and doesn't know how to mind her own business."

"No, it's exciting stuff, especially for an eighteen year old. I get it," Andreas said as they strolled. "She's beautiful. Looks just like you."

Kate blushed. "Robert, I know this is none of my business, but why are they still making these hybrids?"

"They are being groomed for something big, even bigger than my security clearance." He smiled. "I have some ideas, but nothing concrete. I will tell you this-we, meaning the U.S., are not the only ones who have interacted with A.B.s. I think all of this has something to do with a race, much like the space race or nuclear arms race, except this one is about extraterrestrial intelligence. Again, this is only a guess. I want to talk to Michael. He must have his reasons for doing this, but Lori is right. This is technically treason. Maybe he has been taking orders from someone else. I'm going to catch some Zs and then fly back. I've taken up too much of your time already." They stood in front of Kate's flat.

"Stay. We can have dinner tomorrow. I'll show you some of London during the day," Kate said.

Andreas wanted to stay more than anything, but he had no right. He never felt so raw before. "Kate, I will take a rain check on that invitation. Once I'm retired..."

"If you retire," she interrupted and then smiled.

"Okay, *if* I retire, I'd love to come back and visit."

Kate had a peculiar look on her face. Was it sadness? She looked into his brown eyes and said, "Please retire soon."

They hugged goodbye, this time the hug was not so awkward. The general went back to his hotel with the crystal and photo.

Chapter Three

Present Day
Nevada

Glenn Lucasek and Doctor Chuck Wu witnessed Maya disappear from the time capsule. Both men's jaws dropped to the floor in amazement. First Jay McCallister and now Maya Smock went into the unknown. The think tanks that Glenn and Jay put together had officially proven the possibility of time travel. They had suspected long ago that time travel was not just about physics. Genetics played a primary role.

A special gene found in both Jay and Maya allowed their bodies to breakdown into light particles while travelling. Their bodies would solidify back to normal once they were transported. Glenn's scientists had known time travel was possible. Advanced Beings travelled throughout the fourth dimension for millions of years. Most physicists put all of their energy into designing the machine. Doctor Lori Blacksmith figured out that the machine was only part of it. Genetics played just as an important of a role.

Once the capsule was empty, Glenn immediately grabbed the timer. Jay came back fifty-seven minutes later. Jay thought he was gone for much longer, estimating half of day. Time of the past was different to the future. Glenn wondered how long Maya would be gone. Were both of them dropped off in the same time period? The same location?

The T.A.H. Institute was filled with excitement. Chuck left the time capsule room often called the round room to gather up other staff members and champagne. They needed to take a moment to celebrate. Glenn toasted with the group, but would have preferred to crack out the bubbly after Maya was back and safe.

"To all of you," Glenn said. "I just wish we were waiting for Jay. His life was taken away right after discovering this...this miracle. At least he left us his sister. May she lead us to the secrets of time travel and much, much more."

"To Maya," the dozen staffers chanted as they raised their plastic cups.

The mood became much more somber. Jay had been dead for less than a week. It should have been Jay on another trip, or even he and Maya together. Glenn held back his tears. There wasn't time to grieve.

The bottles of champagne were emptied in a few hours. Still no Maya. Worry set in. Most of the doctors drifted out of the round room. Some went to check on the equipment and some examined the inside of the capsule. There wasn't a hair, fingerprint, or skin cell. It was as if Maya had never set foot inside of the capsule.

Several more hours passed by. Most of Glenn's crew retired for the evening. Some new staff members came in during a shift change. It was almost midnight. Maya had been gone for over eleven hours. Glenn sat faithfully by the time capsule, occasionally getting up to enter the adjoining room. The small room was used as a mini-kitchen, a break room, an office, and a storage unit. He turned on the computer and replayed the tape that captured Maya's disappearance inside of the capsule. His head hurt from the champagne and lack of food. Guilt only added weight to his headache. Was Maya even alive? The young woman had everything to live for. And now, he wondered if he had accidentally killed her.

Glenn took a bottle of water out of the mini-fridge, sat down in front of the computer and surfed the Internet for distraction. One of the top news stories caused him to drop the bottle.

Best-selling author Maya Smock was reported missing yesterday evening. The twenty-two-year-old author and heir to the McCallister fortune was last seen in her home by her husband, Claude Kazinsky, and her friend, Eric O'Reilly. Two masked assailants forced her into her white Lexus SUV and took off yesterday evening. The gender and race of the assailants are unknown. Any information on Maya Smock's disappearance, please call the Las Vegas police.

Ah shit, thought Glenn. He had some calls that he forgot to make. The first was to Eric O'Reilly. He promised Maya that he'd call the man. What would he say? *I convinced Maya to try out our time capsule. She's been gone for almost twelve hours, and might be dead...* He really screwed up.

He should have been a better friend to Jay. He should have made him get top-notch security along with a string of body guards. Now he made the same mistake with Maya. He let her walk out of T.A.H. one billion dollars richer with no security at all. Hours later she was kidnapped. Glenn had just filed her divorce papers. This might have prompted Claude to act. Maya believed he wanted her dead. Ironically, Claude just might get what he wanted. If Maya was dead, Glenn would be at fault.

Glenn shuffled through the papers and found the number Maya had written down for Eric. He didn't know the man, but going by Maya's taste in men, he wouldn't like or trust him. Maybe he was wrong. For all he knew, Eric could have been in on Maya's attempted murder. But a promise was a promise. She trusted Eric and loved him. She wanted to leave Claude for him. That had to be enough.

Two rings. A man picked up. "Hello?"

"Eric?" Glenn asked.

"Yes."

Glenn fidgeted with the paper. "Listen very carefully to me. Are you alone?"

"Who is this?"

Glenn heard anger in his voice and understood. "Please, are you alone? I am a friend of Maya's."

"I'm alone enough. What do you want? Money? I can come up with some. Please don't hurt her. I'm leaving the police station now and am in the parking lot. You probably know that..."

"I am not watching you. Just get in your car. Shut the door and turn on the engine. Go. Make sure you are not followed." A minute passed. Glenn heard the hum of the engine and the shifting of soft movements.

"Okay. I'm approaching the main strip and no one is following me. Now explain," Eric said.

"Maya is alive. She thinks Claude tried to kill her," Glenn said.

"But I found him tied up..."

"Maybe that was all for show. Maybe not. But he certainly had motive. All of this will be cleared up soon once she comes back." *Shit*, he thought. Wrong choice of words.

"Huh? Comeback? From where? Who the fuck is this?"

"A friend of Maya's and now a friend of yours. I will call you again. Just know this-someone shot Maya and dumped her in a lake in the middle of nowhere. She somehow saved herself. She's not what you think." Click. *That didn't go so well*, Glenn thought.

Chapter Four

Present Day
Las Vegas, Nevada

The plan seemed to be intact. Maya's dead body was somewhere by her beloved T.A.H. Sam and Allie would soon be on their way back to Vegas. And with some luck, Eric, who should have been Claude's worst nightmare, inadvertently became his alibi. Mission accomplished. Soon he could collect on murdering his wife. So why wasn't he happy? Maybe he would be happy once everything was over.

Claude thought about his father. He would have been so proud. The man was a true-blue sociopath. Killing, robbing, raping, and hurting anyone in his way was the way he lived his life. He beat Claude's mom to a pulp, almost killed her as she stood in the doorway the day he left. Claude peeled her off the floor and dragged her into the hospital. Yes, today would be a proud day for dear old dad. Claude would have got a pat on the back and then a barrel stuck in back of the head, demanding that Claude hand every cent over. Claude had no idea where the man was or even if he was alive.

Claude's mother was different. She was a never-ending vortex of want and need. But today she, like his dad, would have been proud. Force and violence were not her style. She preferred guilt, mind games, and psychological drama as her favorite weapons of manipulation. He hated both of them for everything they did and everything they didn't do. Hatred didn't save him from becoming just like them. Two murders, one in the name of jealousy and now one in the name of greed, were now on his conscious, but he knew that he was just getting started. Sam and Allie might be next.

Claude wished he could travel back in time, just one day, and start over. This feeling of regret was new. It was a hollow feeling. He didn't like himself at this moment. He was taught that money was the only thing that really mattered. His decision to become a literary agent disappointed and shocked both his mother and Sam. They had figured him to be a high finance conman. Claude now realized the literary world was his cry for help and an attempt to break free. Yet it led him down the road to avarice.

Claude knew he had been losing his mind for several years, but getting help was not on his calendar. Now he wanted help. Guilt throbbed throughout his body. He didn't feel any pain when he killed Jay. That was justice for taking his wife. But Maya was different. She was crazy, sexy, and vulnerable all at once, not to mention incredibly talented. He took her for granted and now she was gone, gone by his accountability. He almost wished Sam would call and tell him that he and Allie fucked the whole thing up.

Claude spent the entire night at the police station with Eric, both in separate rooms giving separate statements. Claude saw Eric cry like a baby. Claude forced out a few tears, not to be out done. He wasn't completely faking grief for the police. There was something oddly sincere. His tears were on the verge of turning into hysteria, which he quickly stuffed inside. He needed to be in control. The police would automatically suspect him. Once Eric got through with his tale of their rocky marriage and therapy sessions, he might even get arrested.

Claude believed Eric was an honest man. Had the table been turned, he would have probably lied and made

Eric look guilty. But Eric told the police the truth from his limited perspective-the house was in disarray and Claude was tied up to a chair. He further substantiated Claude's story by telling the police that two people with masks drove off with Maya in Maya's car.

Then came the big one. "Mister Kazinsky, according to Mister O'Reilly, you and Maya were only seeing a therapist because you were suicidal. According to Mister O'Reilly, Maya Smock was seeking a divorce. Were you aware she had a divorce lawyer?"

"Ah, no." Claude knew that she wanted a divorce. He received an attachment from her lawyer only hours before she came home. He hoped that his surprised expression looked genuine.

"You seem surprised," said Detective Chavez. He was young for being a detective. He wore a cheap suit, too tight on his large frame, perhaps on purpose to reveal his muscles. The man was a very good-looking Hispanic who looked more like an aspiring actor. There was a look of skepticism in his dark brown eyes. "Her lawyer filed online only hours before she was abducted."

"Detective Chavez, I had no idea. You can call Doctor Fidell. He's a marriage counselor here in town. I thought we were working it out." Claude forced out a stream of tears.

"Mister O'Reilly confirmed the divorce and even claims that he and Maya had plans, relationship plans. In fact, she was leaving you for him. She only went home to get a few things and then..."

A ton of bricks had just landed on his head. *Things... What did she need to get?* Claude drowned out the rest of what the detective said. "Listen, I don't know why she came into the house. I was tied up by two people wearing masks. They sat in my house for a few hours, waiting for her to come home. Eric saw all of that." Claude's indignation was over-acted. He needed to know what was so damned important to Maya. *Her computer had the sequel saved on the hard drive. That was worth a few million dollars, but then she had just inherited over a billion and change...*

"Mister Kazinsky, we cannot hold you, but don't leave town."

Once he was released from the police station, Claude rushed home and scoured the house, finding Maya's computer in the bedroom. He fired up the laptop. On the desktop was her sequel, *The Master Plan.* He clicked on it, surprised that she had not installed a password for protection. Her mother's crystal, which she used to wear every day, was also lying on the counter of the dresser. The computer and the necklace were what she came home for.

Before reading the novel, Claude thought about his brother. Their plan was simple: Step 1-Make it look like a kidnapping and then take off in Maya's car. Step 2-Ditch the car close to the body. This would help the police find her body. Step 3-Take off in Sam's Buick which should have been picked up along the route. Step 4-Head back to Las Vegas and wait it out. Four steps. Easy.

Sam should soon be calling and talking in code. *I heard on the news* meant everything went down perfectly. *Why would anyone want to hurt you or Maya?* meant the plan hit a few road bumps. *Maya's gone?* meant watch your back, we are all going down. Claude checked his phone to make sure the battery was fully charged. No new messages.

He stared at the title page on the screen of Maya's new laptop. Did she buy this fancy computer? Was it a gift from Jay? Claude knew Maya as well as anyone could know her. She was an enigma, but did have her moments of pattern and predictability. She just inherited a billion dollars and an alien empire, yet according to Eric and the cops she insisted on stopping back at home to pick up her stuff. *Oh, Maya, why was this so important? I actually thought you were coming home for good, and not running out on me. I wished you never came home, never walked straight into our trap.*

Claude laid down on the bed and tried to sleep, but the wheels inside of his head kept turning. He grabbed the laptop and opened up the new novel. Two hours later he was halfway through with reading the seven hundred pages. There were irregularities, odd sentences, and overused words. He began highlighting these oddities with the mouse. There was definitely a pattern. Thirty to forty of the same words were constantly used. All of them began with A, T. C, or G. Claude grabbed her first novel off of the book shelf. Minutes later, he found the same pattern in her first novel.

"Maya, what went on in that pretty head of yours?" Claude mumbled as he flipped through more pages of first novel. Suddenly, Claude put the book down and reached for his phone and Googled "A", "T", "C", "G". DNA sites popped up. *What the hell? Page numbers. Could that have something do with this?*

Claude began recording what page numbers the same familiar words kept appearing within the novel. He noticed a pattern of multiples of eight just like her sequel. Maya deliberately had the publisher publish her first novel in a certain format despite changes the editor wanted to make. *What did this have to do with Jay?* A million questions ran through his mind.

Claude continued to look for patterns from both novels until the sun came up. He finally stopped for a quick snack and cup of coffee. It was almost seven thirty in the morning and he still hadn't heard from Sam. The phone rang. He lunged for his cell, hoping everything happened according to plan.

"I heard on the news that Maya is missing."

It was Sam. Relief took away the two-ton monkey on his back.

Sam then said, "I'm here for you. Just about to leave L.A. Do you mind if I bring my girlfriend?"

That was code for *I am on the way to your house with Allie.*

Chapter Five

1970
Broom Lake, Nevada

Andreas was back at Broom Lake a couple of days after leaving for his supposed vacation. He rarely took off any personal time, and was sure it caused many officers to gossip. His airmen could talk all they wanted. He needed an explanation from Bolantano as to why he was stealing government property, stealing babies. Andreas was never close to the man, but respected him. His actions were undoubtedly treason. Why would he risk everything?

Of all of Andreas's airmen, Bolantano was the least he'd expect to pull this off. Bolantano was always aloof and mysterious. Early in his military career Bolantano was quite ambitious. Operation Chrome seemed to squash that dream. Their experiments with embryos seemed to cause Bolantano to withdraw.

Andreas had forgotten the man's background, but knew he had once been very religious. He pulled Bolantano's file. *Ah, yes*, Andreas thought. Bolantano had a degree in theology from Saint Xavier University, and then served seven years as a priest in Chicago. Once Hitler rose to power, Bolantano quit the church and enlisted in the Air Force, passing all the required tests with flying colors. His faith hadn't stopped him from serving valiantly with Andreas during World War II. Michael never let his morality get in the way of carrying out his orders. So, what made these babies worth risking his career, even his life?

Bolantano would soon be fifty-two years old, eligible for retirement. He was still young enough to find someone, even have a family. Yet he had no plans for moving up the ranks or retiring. The babies had to be the only reason he was still around. His position gave him access.

Andreas thought of telling his protégé, General William Lamphrey, about the missing babies. It would soon be his problem once Andreas was retired. But something about Lamphrey had always made Andreas wince. Besides having a reputation for being a cutthroat and a kiss-ass, he carried himself as a Nazi. The newly promoted general still had a full head of flaxen hair. His icy blue eyes were void of emotion much like the eyes of the Nazi doctors Andreas had recruited so long ago. Lamphrey's lust for power surpassed the most eager of all beavers. He was the perfect robot for the military. The general chose to keep Lamphrey close instead of making an enemy.

Despite Andreas's reservations, Lamphrey never gave him a reason to distrust him. He proved himself to be faithful and loyal for two decades. Like Andreas, Lamphrey chose the military over his personal life during his rising career. Both men married, had children, and then divorced. Like Andreas, Lamphrey was in his early forties when he was promoted to general. He was also alone. His career was even brighter than Andreas's. The young man was a hero in World War II, along with an accomplished pilot in several covert Air Force missions in Korea. He had risen to legendary status. Andreas would not be surprised if Lamphrey became Chairman of the Joint Chiefs of Staff one day. If the young man had a political bug, then even the presidency was possible.

In the same hangar that Kate and three other engineers had once put together a shattered spaceship, Andreas saw Lamphrey inspecting one of the fighter jets. He was about to tell him about Bolantano, but then changed his mind. Andreas walked outside, lit a smoke and shuffled around the warehouse that still served as headquarters to Broom Lake. He inhaled three cigarettes, one after another, waiting. Bolantano pulled up to headquarters in a Jeep.

Andreas approached. "Can I talk to you for a few minutes?" Andreas asked with a phony smile. He saw a glint of fear in Bolantano's deep brown eyes for a split second.

"Yes, Sir." Bolantano got out of the vehicle and saluted.

"At ease." Andreas said, and then directed him into the warehouse. The building still housed the same worn-out furniture as it did so long ago. Andreas had never gotten around to buying new furnishings.

They walked into Andreas's office. "Michael, sit down. Let's drop the titles today. We're just two men having a chat." Andreas sat behind his cheap, metal desk and Bolantano took a seat across from him in a rickety old wooden chair.

Andreas folded his hands and did his best impersonation of someone's old, kind-hearted grandfather. "Alright, then, I'll cut to it. I went to London and found out that you were there recently."

Bolantano didn't flinch.

Andreas watched him stare at a cheap clock on his desk. The clock was one of the only items in his office that could be considered as home décor. "I know, Michael. I know all about the babies. Why?" Bolantano changed his focus to the concrete floor. "C'mon, man-up." Andreas slammed one of the still photos that Kate's daughter had given him onto the desk. "Care to explain? Once I'm gone, Lamphrey will be running things. You know damn well that he won't care why you're stealing babies. And you know what? Twenty years ago, I probably wouldn't have given a shit either. Stealing, kidnapping, whatever you want to call it, is unforgivable. It's treason. Punishable by death. But today is your lucky day, for now. Today I actually give a shit. So, what's going on with this little baby project that you are running?"

Bolantano looked the general straight in the eye and said, "Did you know that I once was a priest?"

Andreas nodded. "I reread your file. But until this morning, I had forgotten about your past. Still believe in God? Is that why you kidnap babies?"

"Don't mock what you don't understand, Sir. Evil is all over. Different kinds of evil compared to war, but evil nonetheless. My prayers were not being answered. And then Hitler came to power and I thought that I might be able to make a difference. I just wanted to be a hero like you. Hell, you must have known that. When we found those Jewish prisoners...Well, you were the ultimate Superman. I didn't understand why you took back that monster who you now call Jaeger. What was his real name? Handel? It doesn't matter much now, only to the Nazi hunters and all of the families of the people who he killed. But then you brought in more monsters. You must know the rumors. Your star geneticists were cloning their *Fuehrer* in Argentina. They had access to Hitler's body, his live body, because that's where he lives."

"Michael, that's rumor and not fact. Hitler killed himself. He and his wife Ava Braun committed suicide."

Michael scoffed. "We both know that's a lie. You recruited demons, the most wicked... I thought you were a good guy. Watching those wolves create life as if they were gods...it just about broke me. My soul was at stake."

Andreas froze and stared into Bolantano's deep, troubled eyes trying to determine how much of this was true and how much of it was bullshit. So far, he had no reason to think the man was lying. He knew exactly how Bolantano felt. The guilt got heavier with each passing year. A long pause followed.

"Michael, please go on."

"Alright, I took the first baby from the lab on the same night the A.B.s escaped with the spaceship. A friend, and I don't want her involved, helped me just the one time. We left the baby at an orphanage in California. I suddenly felt a surge of redemption, as if I could save these beings from whatever they were bred to do. You know as well as I do that their fates are sealed once they are placed with one of those families. You've see them. They grow wicked, like their adopted parents."

So, Michael was a religious zealot... Andreas didn't respond, but he knew about the families who were adopting the babies. There were the Rothhavens, English bankers who controlled the International Monetary Fund, and then the Bartletts, a political dynasty of almost two centuries of nonstop generations of senators, congressmen, and governors. Andreas then thought of the Devereaux family, who ran one of the biggest pharmaceutical companies in Europe. The Lansatti family, who had a secret monopoly on oil, gas, and electricity within the western world. The powerful list of elites went on and on. Why did these privileged families even want the babies? Most of them had several children of their own. It wasn't as if these families could not conceive. These families were the reason Broom Lake was still in operation. They quietly bankrolled the entire genetics research program, keeping it off the books.

"These babies have opportunities that you and I will never have no matter how heroic we were during war. They have everything they could ever want or need, a real chance to make the world a better place," Andreas murmured.

"Yeah, yeah, heard that a few million times. Why do these families want them so bad?" Michael asked.

"I'm asking the questions, not you. How many did you steal? Weren't the German doctors even suspicious?" Andreas blew out a breath and rubbed his hand over his face, reaching for his pack of smokes.

"I stole five babies in three years before Richtor caught me. I kept a chunk of that crystal found with the spaceship and had it broken down into smaller stones. I then had them set in silver, complete with a chain. Each baby was dropped off at an orphanage with a necklace. My hopes were that maybe, just maybe, they would find each other and know that they came from the same place. They might have a sense of their origins and figure out that they were different. General, did you even think that some of the older ones might be on the verge of losing their minds? For your information, I still believe they are God's children. I am giving them a normal life."

"Five babies? What are you saying? The doctors know about this? Did you stop and then start back up again?" Andreas asked, unclear as to why Richtor didn't report Bolantano. He, Jaeger, and Schmidt lived for their genetic findings. Why would any of them put up with Bolantano stealing their most innovative invention?

Bolantano pointed to the pack of Lucky Strikes. Andreas nodded. The major lit one up and coughed, but continued to puff away. "I quit smoking eight months ago." He finally put the cigarette out in the overflowing, tin ashtray. "Frederik Richtor and I don't exactly see eye to eye. But I've got dirt on him. He destroyed all the sperm donations and replaced them with his own. You see, all three doctors wanted to father the babies. They were suppose take turns in spreading their seeds. Richtor is the only father. If Jaeger knew, well he'd probably kill him. After all, Jaeger always thought of this as his brain child."

"Richtor? Somehow, I'm not surprised. This is his convoluted way of making history. I still do not understand your new found friendship."

"Well, again, he is the father, but doesn't want the responsibility. I know he's curious. He mentioned the benefits of an uncontrolled environment and wants to see how they will interact with regular people. It's important to him to know how they make their way in the world without all of the privilege the others are given. As you know, the babies that I've stolen aren't part of anything. They will grow up to be regular people with regular problems."

"Regular? They will never be regular. And in an orphanage? That's another social and emotional can of worms," Andreas interrupted.

"It's normal compared to growing up in an elite circle. Listen, I'm not saying it's the perfect solution, but it is what he and I both want." Bolantano's voice cracked. His brown eyes lightened. Andreas saw a tear stream down his cheek. "General, what are these things for? What will they do for the world or *to* the world once they are grown? You must have your doubts. I pray that they are not here to start a war."

"You are one step away from being killed for treason. Don't turn this around. You don't know what they will do," Andreas warned. The truth was that Andreas questioned the goals of Operation Chrome more and more with each passing year. The first generation of babies were reaching adulthood.

"Treason? Come on. Don't threaten me. You know damn well that no one wants this out. I might be shot in my sleep or accidentally pushed off of a skyscraper, but no one is going to publically make an example of me. I will just disappear, same as you, once we've both outgrown our usefulness, or prove to be a threat. The only ones with any power are the beings, their creators, and the families who fund them."

The sweet, metallic smell of fear emanated off of Bolantano. He wiped his sweaty forehead with his hand. Andreas could see beads of sweat through the thinning strands of his graying hair. The man looked ill. Andreas asked, "Has someone threatened you?"

"No. Look, as far as I know, the only ones who know about the missing babies are me, Richtor, and now you. Add in one more person, whoever it was that you tipped you off about me, maybe four total. If we all keep our mouths shut, maybe we will die natural deaths."

"So, how many have you and Richtor given away to orphanages?"

"My original five, and then, once he knew about it, another eighteen."

"How many necklaces did you have made?"

"Twenty-four. I told myself at the time that I would stop once I was out of necklaces."

Andreas stared at the drop ceiling of his office. There were water stains in half of the panels, something he had been meaning to get fixed but never got around to. Bolantano had dropped a bomb onto his already guilty conscience. "Twenty-four, huh? Why twenty-four?"

Bolantano shrugged. "Because that's how many decent sized stones I could get out of the rock that I took from the space craft. The number has no particular significance."

Andreas stood up and loomed over his desk, his face close to Bolantano's, and said, "You should only have one necklace left. Are you almost finished?" Bolantano said nothing. "You really don't care that I know."

Bolantano looked him squarely in the eye. "No, I am not finished. And I won't be finished until I'm dead."

A challenge. Andreas didn't like it. He stood up, lit another cigarette and paced around the desk. Should he turn a blind eye to what the major was doing? Or should he report the man? A third choice gnawed at his gut, a choice he didn't want to even think about, yet say aloud. He paced a few times back and forth behind Bolantano's chair.

"So, Michael, tell me how they are doing," Andreas said.

Bolantano cracked his knuckles and then said, "The oldest one, and the first one that I took, is now twenty. He was in college, but recently dropped out to become a writer."

"A writer? A journalist?"

"No, a fiction novelist. Science fiction. He's an up-and-coming author. His name is Jay McCallister."

"And the others?"

"They are still too young to have really done anything. A few are in high school. The only common denominator is this-they are very intelligent. All of them have been placed in accelerated classes. None of them look like the A.B.s we once studied. They don't look like Richtor either. They must look like their mothers, the four women you had me take off of the street."

Andreas quit pacing and sat on his desk, looking at Bolantano in the chair. He remembered the first four women. They were butchered for eggs and then killed by the doctors. Not one of his finest moments. "But what about the babies who were placed within our circles?" The general already knew the answer. He kept tabs on the adopted babies.

"They have more common characteristics. Again, very intelligent. But they also are athletic, popular, and natural leaders. Some are in college right now. Five or six of them I believe. All Ivy League schools. All in secret societies. Their parents were legacies. Two of them have become classmates and don't even know they were from the same mother. But you know that. You know more. Do you think the A.B.s will come back?"

Andreas shrugged. He had no idea. He did know that the A.B.s were not the only race or species of extraterrestrial life that came down to earth for a visit. Intelligence from all over the world reported sightings of extraterrestrial beings with very different features than their A.B. friends.

"Michael, tell me, what do you think the point of all of this is?"

Bolantano laughed and threw his head back. "Power. That's what it has always been about. Too bad it's not about justice. As I just told you, I'm going to keep on stealing babies until I die. What are you going to do, Robert?"

The general pondered the question. What was he going to do? An idea stirred deep inside of his stomach. He needed to blurt it out. "Well, you will need more necklaces."

Bolantano's dark brown eyes brightened. He smiled and answered, "Yes, I will. I'll make more with the crystal that you will give me."

Bolantano had some balls on him, but he'd read Andreas correctly. "I saved a few chunks. Yes, Michael, I will give you more crystal."

Andreas put out his hand for a handshake and got a big hug instead.

Chapter Six

A cold, round shotgun barrel was jammed in the back of my head as a woman screamed at me in another language. I assumed the language was German. The barrel slid down to my back and then pushed at my vertebrae, she was motioning me to get off of the floor. I obeyed, and slowly rose to my feet. Still yelling, she dropped the rifle from the second story loft I was hiding in to the floor of the barn. Instantly, the young boy I met earlier picked it up and aimed it at me as I looked down the ladder. The woman descended and joined him on the main floor of the barn. I was cornered.

The boy handed off the gun to the woman. She waved the weapon and motioned for me to descend. I looked over my shoulder. There was a small open window behind me. The barn was only two stories. At worst, I might break a leg. *Too risky.* I wished I was home and divorced from Claude, living with Eric, instead of in this predicament.

I stepped down the first rung and wondered if the woman was going to shoot me. Claude's little helpers shot me and I didn't die. Was I immune to bullets? Guess I was about to find out.

Once I was on the ground, the woman commanded the boy to do something. He went to the far side of the barn, somewhere by the time capsule, and then brought back a spool of twine.

My options narrowed. I lunged for the gun. The woman squeezed the trigger. The sound was deafening. The bullet tore through my hand. Strangely, the pain that should have followed was absent. I looked at the wound. The hole was the size of a quarter. I watched the shell casing bounce and roll onto the dirt floor. I had no idea where the bullet went. Blood. There should have been much more. It was as if I had picked a scab or scratched a mosquito bite too hard. I should have been gushing. The woman and the boy stared at my hand, both amazed and afraid.

The quarter-sized hole was healing at a rapid pace. Only seconds later it was only the size of a dime. Was this why I survived the first attempt on my life? Memories of Jay flashed like a strobe light. Glenn mentioned he was shot a few times, but healed. Did I have the same genetic characteristics?

My wound was almost gone in what seemed like a few passing minutes. The boy and the woman dropped to their knees and waved their hands in their faces as if they were begging for mercy. They gave off an aroma of fermented fruit and ammonia. I knew that scent. Fear. Little did they know that I could never kill them. But I chose to ride their fear like a wave. It bought me some time.

"I need to go back home. English?" I asked.

The boy looked at the woman, both still in a bowing position knelt on the dirt floor. I tried to guess if this was his mother or sister. The woman looked so young. "A little. My uncle talk English. Home later," the boy said.

"Home. I want to go home. Do you know how to operate the capsule?" I asked, and then pointed to the other side of the barn.

"No. No touch. My uncle only," said the boy. He rambled something off in German.

Chapter Seven

Present Day
Las Vegas, Nevada

Eric O'Reilly slammed his cell phone on the dash of his Ford Edge.

"Fuck me!" he shouted after receiving a mysterious phone call. Twenty-four hours ago he was supposed to ride off into the sunset with the love of his life and live happily ever after. He wanted Maya to be his wife. They would have kids, dogs, and everything else that went with it. He wanted a wedding with his family, friends, and employees from his book store all there to celebrate.

I'm a coward, an idiot, a failure! Why did I let her out of my sight? he said to himself in the driver's seat of his car. This was all on him. If he had only told her how he felt before she married Claude, none of this would have happened. He blamed himself for all of it. If anything happened to her, if she was dead, he wasn't sure if he could take it.

Eric despised Claude the first time they had met. Claude was good-looking, sophisticated, charming, and charismatic. All of the things that Eric was not. He thought that Claude had made Maya happy. He was green with envy, but all he ever wanted was for her to be happy. There was one enormous problem. Claude was a bottom-feeder who would take all that he could, and then leave once she figured him out. Eric knew their marriage was doomed from the start.

Eric wished Claude was dead. That would solve all of their problems. It would have been so easy to drop hints to the police that Claude was behind Maya's disappearance. For all Eric knew, Claude staged the whole scene to work as an alibi.

Maya was beyond wealthy. Claude could have gotten millions for just signing the divorce papers. He would have walked away a wealthy and free man. Why would he risk such a sure thing?

Eric drove away from the police station for the second time within the last twenty-four hours, hoping the police had new information to go on. After the odd phone call, his hands shook and his heart raced. He parked in his nearby apartment complex and stayed in the car, trying to calm down. As he fiddled with the radio tuner, he slowly began to process the magnitude of the stranger's phone call. Maya was alive. Who was this 'friend'? Where was she?

An eerie overture played on one of the few AM stations that would come in on his car radio.

And now, Paula Linquist and the The Sixth Sense Radio Show, broadcasted from San Francisco.

Hmmm, Maya was just on that show. She had mentioned the hostess by name to Eric and told him that she was part of the new group of friends introduced by Jay McCallister.

For those of you who are tuning in for the first time, I wanted to pay the late and great Jay McCallister a tribute...

Paula, the host, talked about Jay's long list of accomplishments, T.A.H. Institute, and even Maya. The guest on Paula's show was Mercedes Garcia. Eric remembered her from a sitcom that he watched when he was a kid. Maya also mentioned her as one of her new friends. He saw the beautiful actress seated next to Maya during Jay's televised funeral.

Paula Linquist spent several minutes of air time talking about Jay and then effortlessly switched over to the T.A.H. Institute.

"Our board is lit up today. I know many of you have something to say about Jay's death. I am open to any and all conspiracy theories. Jay was killed by aliens, Maya killed Jay for the money, Jay was not dead, but really alive, Jay was frozen and wanted to wake up in a hundred years..."

And it went on and on. Eric could no longer hold back and made the call to the radio show.

"Hello, you have reached *The Sixth Sense Show*. This is Paula's producer, Joel. What would you like to say on air?" the man asked in a robotic fashion.

"My name is Eric O'Reilly. I'm a close friend of Maya's. Did you even know she is missing? These callers who are accusing her..."

"Sir, calm down. I'm patching you through immediately."

Seconds later, Eric was live. He questioned how safe it was to broadcast Maya's disappearance on a syndicated radio show. *Ah, fuck it! The more people who know, the more answers there may be. And the police would soon be releasing the information to the press anyway.*

"Hi Paula. Maya spoke very highly of you. I know that she trusted you even though your friendship was new..."

Paula immediately interrupted him and said, "Excuse me, Sir. *Spoke, trusted, was?* Why are you using the past tense? It's like you are saying she is..."

Eric interrupted her back. "Gone. She's gone. And I don't know if she's ever coming back."

"Hold on. Who is this? What do you mean she's gone?"

"I mean she was kidnapped last night. She might even be dead. Let me back up. I picked her up at the private airfield outside of Vegas shortly after Jay's funeral. Her marriage, well it was not going well. But you may know that."

"Yes, Eric. Go on," said Paula.

"I begged her not to stop at home, but she had to have some of her things. That was supposed to be her last stop. She and I..." There was a pause. Eric wiped away his tears.

"Eric, are you with me? Please go on."

"She didn't know if her husband was home. There were no cars in the driveway. She told me to wait in the car. She said I would only aggravate the situation. Oh God!" Eric broke down and cried. Moments later he said, "I need to tell you this. I need to tell all of your listeners this." He continued telling Paula in detail what had happened. Once he was finished, he said, "The house was trashed. Her husband was tied up. I have no idea who would want to... A man just called me. He told me she wasn't dead. She was found and she was okay, but I don't know who or what to believe."

Eric was immediately interrupted by a commercial break.

Eric could hear the commercial jingle and an ad for wrinkle cream in the background. "Eric," Paula said, "listen to me. You need to talk to my producer who is also my brother, Joel. I didn't mean to cut you short, but I think I know who called you. We are live with an eight second delay. I'm cutting the last part of what you said. It could put Maya at risk."

Eric heard the sound of buttons being pushed and then was transferred to Joel. His blood began to boil. He was still in his car. A quick glimpse in the mirror showed his face even redder than his reddish brown hair.

"Eric, this is…"

"Listen up Joel or whoever the fuck you are. Maya isn't some celebrity I'm clinging on to. She's the love of my life and I will do whatever it takes to find her, even if that means starring on every fucking talk show in the world. If I have to get the entire population looking for her, I will! I want some answers now. Who the fuck called me? You and Paula know something that I don't. I am sick of the cloak and dagger routine. For all I know, you and your sister are the ones who took her. You claim to be her friends, well I'm her best friend and I will not stop until I find out what happened. Either tell me where you think she is or I'm calling up every radio station that I can find."

"Eric, Paula has got to finish the show. It's got another hour. Please, stay calm. She's sliding me a note right now. She and Mercedes are live. The note says that Glenn Lucasek has her. You know who he is? He and Jay ran T.A.H. and now he and Maya will run T.A.H. He is also her lawyer. Maya is probably there. The institute is somewhere in the Ruby Mountains. Paula didn't want to discuss the location on the air. Right now she is telling her listeners that you got disconnected."

"Glenn Lucasek from *Alien Theories*? Maya used to watch that show. She mentioned that she met him through Jay. He kidnapped her? Why? Does he want the institute all to himself?" Eric asked.

"No. Listen, even if he did want the institute all to himself, it's not set up that way. Someone on the board would have to co-chair it with him. The board would have to approve the co-chair. The rules and bylaws of the institute make it impossible for one person to completely take over. But none of that matters right now. If you could just hang on for a few hours, Paula and Mercedes will take you to the institute. You can meet Glenn yourself, face to face. Maybe he will admit to making the call."

"Joel, how do you know that Glenn won't make me disappear as well?"

"Ah, I can see why Maya and you are friends. Paranoid is the smart way to be these days. Glenn has a plane that we all use. They will pick you up in Vegas, right? Why don't you take snapshots of the plane, huh? Let me think, oh, send the pictures to someone who you trust in case you disappear. Take a pic of Paula and Mercedes too. I know we are strangers, but you've got to trust us. We aren't the bad guys in any of this. And I don't think that Glenn is either. There has to be much more to the story. We didn't know she was missing until your call. Please, you've got to believe me, we all need to find her. We are all in this together."

Once pacified, Eric got out of his car and went inside his apartment. He grabbed the only two weapons he owned, a stun-gun and switchblade. He then quickly called his parents and told them that Maya was in trouble.

He arrived at the air field within an hour and a half, snapping picture after picture as he waited. Another two hours went by and the Gulfstream landed. The door opened and someone from the nearby hangar rolled out a set of stairs towards the plane. Paula Linquist and Mercedes Garcia stepped out. They must have come straight from the show. Mercedes hadn't aged a day since her hit sitcom of over a decade ago. Her hair was thick, black, and long and her face was still smooth and regal. He only recognized Paula from the Google images he searched on his phone. She was much younger than Mercedes. Eric guessed her around his age, late twenties or early thirties. She was African-American with flawless skin, high cheekbones, and large dark eyes. She wore her long hair in a fancy braided up-do. He walked up to the plane.

"Ladies, I'm snapping lots of pictures," Eric said as he snapped one of them walking down the stairs of the plane.

"No problem. I respect the safety precautions. I can't imagine what you are going through right now. You must be Eric. I am Paula and this Mercedes. Sorry for the wait. We briefly talked to Glenn, and yes, he was the one who called you. He is deeply sorry for scaring you. He would pick you up himself, but doesn't want to leave the institute right now in case of..." Paula's voice trailed off.

Eric immediately sensed something wrong. "Paula, what is it? Is she alive? Please tell me she is."

Paula looked like she was about to cry. Eric's heart sank to the center of the earth. Both women touched his arms and guided him onto the plane. Paula answered, "Yes, she is alive. But Glenn wants to show you what is going on. He needs to explain it to us. Did you get enough photos? Do you feel comfortable enough to climb aboard?"

Eric nodded dejectedly. *Maya is alive.* He should have been filled with joy, but instead wanted to throw up. It was obvious that both of these women were hiding something.

Once aboard the plane, he took a seat in a leather chair that faced the matching leather recliners the women sat in. A coffee table screwed into the floor was in between them. With everything going on, Eric still couldn't help but notice the opulence of the plane. It looked more like someone's stylish, gigantic living room than a jet cabin. He had never flown business class, let alone in a private jet.

Paula got up and went into the cock pit. She whispered something to the captain that made Eric nervous. She returned to their conversation area within the plane and plopped down next to Mercedes. "Eric, I know you don't trust us. But we don't quite trust you either. Before we go, there is something I need to do. Now I'm not always one hundred percent right, but my batting average is pretty good."

"Huh? Not sure what you are…"

"I read people. I'm a medium and reading people is one of my talents," Paula said and then lunged at him and held both of his arms. "Please stay still for just a minute."

What is this? Were these two beautiful women going to pin me down and kill me? He didn't fight back, but inched his fingers to the side pocket of his khakis where he kept his knife. While Paula held his arms, her eyes were closed. She hummed a tune that turned into a chant. Eric had his fingers inside of his pocket and slowly felt around for the handle of the switchblade. But something, maybe an aura, something he couldn't explain drew him closer to her as if she was some kind of magnet. He let go of the handle and submitted to whatever the hell she was doing. Several minutes later, she stopped.

Paula opened her eyes. She huffed and puffed as if she had just ran a marathon. "You love Maya. You've always loved her, since the moment you saw her. She walked into a library? You saw her take a book?"

Paula just read his soul. Eric took a deep breath. "Not a library, but a bookstore."

"Ah, it makes more sense. But you kept quiet until after she married. Mercedes, tell the pilot he passed my little character quiz."

"I passed?"

"You more than passed. It's crystal clear that you love her with every nerve, every fiber, every cell of your body. You would jump off a cliff for her if she needed you to."

"He's on a plane with a couple of strangers, Paula. You don't have to read his heart and mind to figure that one out," Mercedes said, and then smiled. "Eric, we are going to bring her back where she belongs."

The plane ascended into the sky.

Chapter Eight

Seconds felt like hours as I stood in the barn, frozen, and stared at the boy and woman who submissively knelt before me. If I understood the boy correctly, I would have to wait for the uncle to come home. And when was that? Tonight? Next week? Next year? Did he even live here or did he come over to visit and work on his time machine? Panic set in.

"What time is uncle coming?" I asked in a loud tone, as if talking louder would make the boy understand my English. He did understand something. I could see the recognition in his eyes. The woman looked lost. The rifle laid on the ground and I grabbed it for extra security. The boy and the woman put their hands over their heads.

"Soon," the boy answered. His voice was muffled. "In, uh," he said, and then held up three fingers.

"Three hours?" I asked and he nodded. "It's okay. I'm not going to shoot you. What are your names?" I held the gun upward and motioned for them to get off of the floor.

"Me, Heinrich. She, Gretchen," he said, and then slowly rose from the ground. The woman stood up as well.

"Is Gretchen your mother?"

Heinrich looked confused. "Nein. Schwester."

I was guessing, but I asked, "Sister?" He nodded. "I am Maya. Where are the controls for the time machine?" I pointed across the barn to where the capsule was somewhat hidden.

Heinrich led me over to the capsule and Gretchen followed. I kept both hands on the rifle as we slowly walked across the barn. Henirich moved one of the barrels that kept the time capsule out of full view. I could see a round piece of wood underneath the barrel, almost like a door. Heinrich pointed to the cord. I bent over, still holding on to the gun tightly, and pulled the cord. Underneath the makeshift cover was a large hole with a metal spiral staircase descending into blackness. I wasn't about to go down there alone.

The boy shot me a look of terror, as if I wasn't supposed to see this. His crystal blue eyes welled with tears. "My uncle! My uncle! Must wait!" he yelled.

I needed to use his hysteria to my advantage and hopefully get the hell out of wherever I was. He and his sister were both on their knees, bowing. I had them in the palm of my hand. Against my good nature, I said, "You first, Heinrich." I motioned with the rifle for him to go down the mysterious black hole. He started to cry and I felt a twinge of guilt. He looked at Gretchen and she nodded. His cry turned into a wail. "I said down, now."

Heinrich slowly stepped down the rickety staircase into the blackness. I heard a commotion and then saw a dim glow of light. The hole bottomed out only ten or twelve feet from the surface. I clutched the gun and stepped down the staircase. Heinrich turned on a lamp. I saw what looked like some kind of generator next to the stairs, and then a long control panel against the wall that must have run at least eight feet. *Oh shit*, I thought. There were at least fifty buttons. How was I ever going to get this thing running? In the middle of the room was the centrifuge. It wasn't anywhere near the size of Glenn's centrifuge at T.A.H., but must have worked because I was here.

The boy stood by the dashboard and rambled off something in in his native tongue, mixing in a few English words for my benefit, words such as "uncle" and "machine" and "danger". His uncle must have brainwashed him and Gretchen well. Despite the boy's warnings, I held tight to my rifle and flipped on any button within my grasp.

The noise that the whole system made was earsplitting. Smoke came out of the centrifuge. The dirt floor began to vibrate.

"Nein! Nein!" the boy shrieked.

Heinrich had me in quite a pickle. If I broke the machine, then I'd... I'd... well I would have to learn how to speak German. I didn't even want to think of the consequence. I still had the gun, and I still called the shots, but I couldn't think of what to do until the uncle came home. Maybe use the boy as a hostage or just point the gun in the uncle's face, and then they would send me back to where I belonged. I just needed to be patient.

"Okay, up," I said and motioned the boy to go back up the stairs.

Heinrich diligently obeyed. I didn't turn off the lights on purpose. Once Heinrich reached the top I was halfway up the spiral stairs only five or six feet away from the round opening and then the hole was covered.

"Heinrich! Gretchen! Open the cover!"

Nothing. I was trapped. Using the shotgun, I shot at the opening. The first shot I missed. I heard something being dragged above me. I shot again, this time I hit something. One more shot-nothing. I was now the one being held hostage.

Chapter Nine

1970
Broom Lake, Nevada

Major Michael Bolantano left General Andreas's office. Andreas was under the impression that the two of them had come to an understanding. *Have I lost my fucking mind?* He intended to punish Bolantanno for stealing babies, but somehow flipped a full one hundred eighty degrees.

After hearing Bolantano's story, he sided with him and wanted to help. Was this just another excuse not to retire? Or could it be more? A chance at redemption? Was God giving him a calling? The idea appealed to him, stealing the very babies that he enabled to be created. *They will have to push me out the fucking door kicking and screaming.*

What other options did Andreas have? Living alone in a house as a retiree and pretending to be a regular civilian sounded like a prison sentence. A high-paying job in the defense contracting industry didn't sound like his cup of tea. He needed to have a purpose. He had once been a hero, but now he was an old man who everyone wanted to go away. He longed to be a hero once more.

Andreas could get his absolution by going rogue. He could join the talk show circuit or even write a tell-all book. All of that would be public. Whistle blowers were always ruined. They were the stereotypical liars with an axe to grind, or the mental patients with misguided beliefs, or the lonely hearts begging for attention. The government made sure that they retracted their stories, backed down from publicity, or died very mysterious deaths. Not much would be accomplished. Secrecy was the safer, more productive choice.

As crazy as it was, Andreas felt invigorated, as if anything could happen. Maybe Kate would see him as a changed man and give him another chance. That was borderline ridiculous, but he dared to dream. Not retiring was a relief. Lamphrey would be pissed, as would so many other officers who wanted a bump up. They would just have to wait until a mandatory retirement age was put on the books.

As a four star general in charge of Broom Lake, Andreas had the ear of some of the most powerful people in the world. He was privy to the highest level of top secret information in the country, and he was the one who briefed the President, the Joint Chiefs of Staff, and America's leading business tycoons on the country's top secret files. He was the one leading expert who allied officials from all over the world would call when there was an extraterrestrial question.

Always loyal to his country, Andreas kept sensitive information to himself for decades. Ten years ago, he decided to document it in a journal. He didn't know why he wanted to write everything down, take pictures, and at times, tape meetings without other people knowing they were being recorded. His photos, journal, and tapes were kept in a locker at the airport in Las Vegas. He had a key, but now needed someone to give it to. Maybe he had always known he'd betray his government. He was covering his ass in case… in case of what? He knew what. He didn't want to think that he was so disposable.

Andreas knew that America and her allies talked about forming a global system of government. They were in the early stages. Presidents came and went. Most of them were someone's puppet. The elite families of the world were the real government, the real banks, and the real militia. They called for globalization. The Cold War was slowing up the process. It was 1970 and the first world countries were divided into two realms of thought. Cultures and traditions were no longer important. You were either a capitalist or a communist, nothing in between.

Andreas didn't play politics, in fact he never even voted, claiming that he wanted to be neutral in all elections. His neutrality granted him much respect within Washington. After talking to Bolantano, everything changed. He had the clarity of a prophet. The respect he earned over the decades could now be cashed in for something of a higher purpose. No, retirement would definitely have to wait. He was in the perfect position to rip Operation Chrome apart.

One day the Cold War would end. There would no longer be an "us against them" mentality, just a whole world that wanted to be in the United Nations, trade their products, and make money. Andreas could see disgruntled groups of people who would never get their fair share of the pie. He guessed these groups would refuse to give up their religion. They might shake things up from time to time, but would be no match for the rest of the world, who eagerly shed all forms of nationalism. The world would eventually operate as one. New World Order was the term some of the elite began to use behind closed doors.

Despite being in the thick of top secret information, Andreas's standing was not enough to gain him access into the world of the elite. This tiny group of people ran the world. Occasionally they left their fingerprints on a war or uprising, calling in favors to keep their mistakes out of the press. Andreas had cleaned up a mess or two over the years for a few of the families. That was to be expected. Power had always rested in the world's most wealthy. These families could make or break an economy with a phone call. They could also make those who got in their way vanish.

This nucleus of the elite had been planning for a globalized world for centuries. It was as if this plan was a religion and the elite were the fanatics who worshipped it with all of their heart. The Jews waited for Jesus to come, and Christians waited for Jesus to return. The Muslims waited for the Mehti. The world's elite were also waiting for someone or something to happen before everything clicked into place. Were they waiting for the aliens?

Andreas personally arranged to have forty of these families adopt babies from his operation. Some families received two. Did these babies have something to do with whatever they were waiting for?

The adoptive parents always wanted to know about the babies' parents, especially their DNA. Andreas would show them pictures of the aliens and the women, but never pictures of the fathers. He recently learned the only father was Richtor. The adoptive parents believed he was holding back, and he was, just not about paternity.

Occasionally the parents would insist on meeting the Nazi doctors. That was always a risk. All three of the doctors were as cold as the Tundra and as talkative as a mute.

Andreas frequently wondered about the babies. They could end up in a mental hospital. They were not human and no one was allowed to let them know. They were alone.

Stealing government babies was a passive way of committing suicide. If he got caught… Andreas shuddered at the thought. He was an old man whose time was about to run out. There was no turning back.

A week had gone by since he and Bolantano talked. Andreas spun around in his chair and noticed an envelope on the floor, inches from the door of his office. It must have been slipped under the door. He opened the small envelope and took out a half sheet of yellow-lined paper. "Flo's,

7pm" was all that it said. It had to be from Bolantano. Flo's was a bar that was technically called Ebb and Flo. It was located twenty miles away. Andreas finished some paperwork, changed into civilian clothes, and then headed for the bar.

Andreas arrived at 6:35pm. Despite being early, he saw Bolantano already there, tucked away in a booth in the far corner. There was a pitcher of beer on the table. He wore a wool sweater and jeans, looking younger than he was. Engrossed in the dinner menu, he jumped when Andreas plopped down across from him in the burgundy leather seat.

"Ah." Bolantano whispered. "You snuck up on me."

"Yeah, I'm early too. So, what looks good on the menu?" Andreas asked as he helped himself to a beer.

"I think I'll get the bacon cheeseburger," Bolantano said and handed Andreas the menu.

Without opening it up, Andreas said, "I think I'll just get the same thing." Looking around the room to see if anyone was interested in their gathering, Andreas finally felt comfortable enough to ask, "So, how does all of this work?"

"You mean how do we kidnap a baby?" Bolantano had a smirk on his face that irritated Andreas. "Sorry, that was meant to be a joke. Trying to lighten up the mood a little. As you know, there's a lot to it. And I don't want you to get your hands too dirty, I realize your involvement is more than I could ever…"

"Stop it. Skip the preamble. Michael, you need to call me Robert, especially in public. I don't want my position compromised. And let's communicate with straight talk. Now how do you want me to help?"

A young, pretty waitress approached. Bolantano interrupted her as she was about to ask what they wanted to order. "Bacon cheeseburger and my friend will do the same." He handed her the menu.

The second the waitress walked away, Andreas lit up a cigarette, waiting for Bolantano to give him some instructions.

"You handle the paperwork. You and the JCS. Newcastle, right?"

"Yes, Newcastle. Blanchard retired last year. He's more interested in the Cold War than our baby project. So, really it's just me. I have his signature stamp. All he really wants is a copy of the paperwork, which I send him once a month. He visited Broom Lake last year. No plans of coming back. The Russians take up most of his day."

"Well then, I think we could really speed up production."

"Hell yeah. So, what did you have in mind?"

"Well, you have always arranged the adoptions. Maybe you could arrange an *adoption*."

Andreas grinned. "You mean arrange some fake adoptions? That could easily work if you or Richtor make the drop. I could have one of you in charge of delivery. But then the other two doctors also get involved in the deliveries from time to time."

"We could keep them out of the loop. If they have to be involved, make up a fake family name. No one knows every elite family."

Andreas put out his cigarette and poured himself another beer. Scratching his chin, he said, "I don't even know who they all are. I'm just going by requests that are given to me by the JCS. He usually will call or sometimes will send me a letter with the adoptive parents' information. But I think what you're proposing is doable. It would take a long time before anyone asked any questions. You think Richtor will stab us in the back?"

"Not today. He knows I'd tell the entire base, the JCS, even the president if I had to that he's tampered with the experiment. The doctors would have him killed. But that's today. Is this worth the risk? You could take the easy road and go retire."

"That's not my style. Today the risk is worth it. Today I'm a crazy son-of-a-bitch who has lost his mind. But that's today," Andreas said as he finished off the beer. "Oh, I almost forgot." Andreas handed him a large shopping bag. "More crystal. This should get you a few more dozen necklaces."

Bolantano took the bag and smiled. "Robert, there is something else. Because of your clearance and connections, could you get us some Intel on the older babies? The ones we freed along with the ones who were placed. I want to…"

"You want to know if this was worth it. I get it. Listen, with the exception of the London baby, I don't know where to look for the ones you stole."

"I do. Or at least, I know where they started."

"Then yes."

The waitress came by and set down their mammoth burgers and fries. Both men instantly became silent until she left their table.

"So, Michael, how many are ready to go?"

"We've got six toddlers who just turned two and four more who will be ready within the next year."

The men temporarily quit talking and ate their burgers, both of them scanning the bar for anyone who might be a threat.

"Robert, if you could make up some paperwork for a black boy. After that, Richtor and I will walk you through it. Our next orphanage is in Algiers. I want to make the delivery."

The next day, Andreas spent the entire morning in his office scanning newspapers, books, and whatever else he could find on prominent black families within the inner circle. He found an incredibly wealthy couple with vast interests in the oil industry living in Morocco. *Congrats, you are now the proud parents of a designer baby boy you never requested* as he signed the phony documents. All someone would have to do is check. But he never checked. He doubted Newcastle would. He made a copy of the papers for the Joint Chiefs of Staff and reminded himself that he had been running Operation Chrome for two decades. He would not get caught.

Andreas went into the hangar and then descended into the laboratory, which looked more like a baby hospital. He remembered when the space was used as a cage. Now it smelled like dirty diapers and baby powder. The doctors hired an additional staff of six assistants, who were glorified nursemaids with exceptional security clearance.

With his fake papers in hand, Andreas approached Doctor Karl Jaeger and Doctor Frederik Richtor. He had no idea where Doctor Hans Schmidt was, nor cared. They were free to go when and where they pleased. Andreas had eased off detailing their whereabouts a few years ago. The last two presidents had them loaned out to a few top medical universities for their expertise in certain top secret operations.

Andreas and the doctors had an established routine that took place before adopting the babies. As usual, Andreas motioned for Jaeger and Richtor to join him in the elevator where they would ride up to the original laboratory. As usual, they rode in silence. Once they were in the old lab, currently used as an office space, Andreas got down to business.

Andreas showed them the phony adoption papers he created, and then had them sign off on the release. Their job had always been to prepare a care package for the new parents, along with testing the baby one last time. Blood, various tissue, and hair samples were taken and filed in a vault, as were a set of the adoption papers.

Loose ends worried him. Frederik Richtor was unpredictable. It was showtime. All he had to fool was Jaeger.

"Doctors, I have authorization to grant the Atika family a new baby boy. A black baby boy. You have one ready, yes?" Andreas asked.

"Yes, General. Never heard of them. What's their family business?" Doctor Jaeger asked.

"I believe they are in oil, but don't quote me."

As usual, Jaeger nodded and seemed uninterested.

"Bolantano will transport next week," Andreas added. Again, both doctors seemed bored. Jaeger looked like he wanted to say something. "Doctor? Is something wrong?"

"Quite the contrary, General. I wanted to tell you about my latest breakthrough. It will be the next biggest thing. You still smoke?" Andreas nodded. "Then you will be my guinea pig very soon when I save your life as you once saved mine."

"I beg your pardon?" Andreas asked.

"When your lungs give out, when cancer spreads to an inoperable level, I will make you a new pair. Or maybe it will be your heart. Whichever. I think I can take a cancerous, defective organ in the human body and clone it without the defect. I can use the new organ as a replacement, thus saving one's life. I just need more subjects. I have a couple medical schools who are helping me find desperate people."

Andreas knew the doctors considered their hybrid babies almost perfect. Operation Chrome was about production instead of discovery. He knew the doctors had applied what the A.B.s had shown them. This knowledge led them to new discoveries. All of this was top secret and meant only for the lucky few who conveniently were sick at the right time of their study. Andreas only assumed that the inner circle was on board. They probably had Jaeger cloning their organ tissue for the future. That was someone else's operation.

Jaeger was bragging about his newest discovery. The engineered organs were also meant to be gift. It was his way of expressing gratitude for saving his life and bringing him to America. Jaeger never showed emotion, but he shared other top secret projects that he and the Germans were involved in.

Andreas was almost touched by the strange offer. "Doctor, you know me. I'm an old fashioned guy. When my number is up, then it's up. Besides, I don't have anything to live for."

"General, look around. You created this. Once a tiny air base, it is now a top secret organization that will change the world faster than any silly space program. Genetics are the future and the key to progress. This is an empire and you are our emperor."

"Doctor Jaeger, I think you are laying it on a bit thick, but I appreciate your lung offer. For now, I will focus on Operation Chrome. Just have the boy ready for transport."

Jaeger nodded and Andreas left. This wasn't the first time the doctor had blew a bunch of smoke up his ass. Andreas was old and his job had an expiration date. Change was scary for all who were involved.

A week later Bolantano came into the makeshift gym while Andreas was working out. The room inside of the warehouse headquarters was originally meant to be an office. As he benched a few hundred pounds, Bolantano silently worked on a leg press. Andreas worked out every morning. Sometimes other officers would join him. Eventually Bolantano broke the ice and started talking about baseball. He nonchalantly left a pocket Bible on one of the benches and left.

Once in private quarters, Andreas opened up the Bible. A half sheet of paper dropped out.

Jay McCallister, 20, born 1950, white
1440 South Camden Drive
Los Angeles

Andreas knew what to do. Bolantano wanted an update on the young man's life. He was the first of a long list of stolen babies to check on. He had every right to be curious. Was this worth it? Before heading to Los Angeles, he looked through some of his old files, hoping to kill two birds with one stone. There was another twenty year old boy who lived in Beverly Hills. Maybe, with some luck, he and his family were still there.

Chapter Ten

I was trapped in a cellar by an eight-year old, or however old he was. That little bastard, Heinrich, outsmarted me. Just to think a few minutes prior, I had him and his sister, Gretchen, right where I needed them. Now I was in a dungeon, alone in the dark, without any bullets. I had nothing to negotiate. All I had was the hope of the boy's uncle coming home and getting me back to T.A.H. I held all of the cards and then lost them, underestimating a little boy and his sister. My guard slipped for just a second, damn!

I was a rat in the cage of a very smart captor. Light. I needed light. I fiddled around over by where the boy was, and eventually found the lamp, switching it back on as if it was my only hope in avoiding a mental breakdown. I told myself to breathe. Count to ten. Again and again. Finally my anxiety subsided.

Minutes later, I had calmed myself down to a rational state. Maybe this little prison cell wasn't a bad thing. If I could only figure out how all of the controls worked, then I could get back home in Eric's arms and reinvent myself all over again. Had Jay landed here when he traveled? How did he get back? He probably knew all of the mechanics of a time capsule. Glenn should have given me a crash course on how the machine worked. I had to teach myself. The room was still too dark to see anything. There had to be more than the one light.

I soon found an overhead bulb and the panel of controls. They looked like a bunch of gadgets that were once thrown in the garbage. The panel looked beyond amateurish, but then whoever made this didn't have the luxury of ordering a custom made dashboard for a time capsule. I had no idea what year it was, but I knew I was in the past, not in the future.

The centrifuge was at the opposite end of the cellar. I turned on some switches and the centrifuge began to spin. The ground shook and the sound was louder than the roar of engines at a monster truck rally. I pulled down on one of the levers. The vibration in the ground increased. I pulled it the other way and it decreased. The centrifuge at T.A.H. was loud despite the sound proofing, so I could only guess that the faster it spun, the louder it got, and the better it worked. I was making progress. Before Uncle What's-His-Name came home, I hoped to be back in the Ruby Mountains.

In the middle of the homemade dashboard was a large circle with a piece of construction paper glued onto its surface. The circle was divided up like slices of pie and colored brightly with markers. Did Heinrich do this? It had a kiddy look about it. At closer glance, it was some kind of label. On one side of the circle it read "A.D." and the other side read "B.C." Nothing else was labeled, just color coded. I assumed this might have been some kind of time dial.

"Halt! Halt!" screamed Gretchen who just opened the cellar door. She must not have liked the noise I was generating. I kept on hitting buttons and levers on dashboard, making the barn sound like a construction site. Heinrich came down the cellar ladder like a fireman down a pole.

"You will break!" Heinrich yelled. Or did he mean brake? I guess it didn't matter. I knew I was metaphorically cutting off my nose to spite my face. The boy turned every lit knob and lever the other direction. Despite my new predicament, I was beginning to understand the mechanisms of the machine. The rudimentary look of the equipment still had a certain pattern.

"Gretchen called Uncle Josef. He is coming now. Please, no fight. We go up to the house and wait. You will go home. Uncle speaks English and you like him," Heinrich said in broken English.

At this point, I would have liked Hitler if he'd help me get back home. I looked at the boy in the dim lighting of the cellar and wondered how he fit into all of this. He sure seemed to know his way around the dash.

Heinrich must have seen suspicion in my eyes. "We are sorry," he said and pointed at the ladder.

Maybe I should wait for Uncle Josef. I didn't think I had any other options. I climbed the ladder before the boy. He would not lock me in a second time. I followed him and Gretchen back to the farm house.

The house was set back far from the dirt road. The unkempt front lawn was filled with tall grass and weeds. As we got closer to the house, I noticed the white paint was cracked and peeling. Wood was rotting. The black roof sagged on one side and some of the windows were cracked. This was not a home. This was a hideout. I climbed a few stairs to the wooden door and entered.

The inside of the house wasn't any nicer than the outside. The wood flooring buckled in several spots throughout the first floor of the home. On one side of the foyer was a room with lots of books and an old blue velvet couch. The other side had a beat-up coffee table surrounded by a fancy loveseat and two winged-back chairs. A transistor radio sat on a small table in the corner. I didn't see a television. This narrowed down the time era I was in.

I followed Heinrich and Gretchen to the kitchen in the back of the house. Gretchen pulled out a rickety wooden chair and nodded. I sat down while she grabbed some pots and pans, quickly heating something up that came from the ice box. Several minutes of silence went by, and then Gretchen placed a plate of sausage and sauerkraut in front of me. It smelled delicious. For the first time since I had landed in this strange time and place, I realized how hungry I was and devoured every morsel. I drank two steins full of beer and felt somewhat lightheaded. Not good. I needed to be on full alert.

When I was finished, I brought my dishes to the sink and Gretchen instantly took them from me. Heinrich shook his head.

"Come." The boy led me into the room with all of the books. I sat in the old, blue velvet couch that Heinrich pointed to. "Wait here." He walked out of the room, leaving me alone.

I looked at the book selection in the dark oak built-in bookcases. All of them were bound with hardback book covers. Most of the titles looked like they were written in German, but some appeared to be written in French and Italian. One was even written in English, *Origin of Species* by Charles Darwin. I instantly recognized the title. Since Uncle Josef wasn't home, I needed something to do. Flipping through the famous evolution book might kill some time. As I approached the bookcase, two other books caught my eye. Both had the same title and author, *Mein Kampf* by Adolf Hitler. I learned about the book back in history class before I dropped out of school. Hitler wrote it back in the 1920's. *Mein Kampf* meant 'my struggle.' Both titles had the same cover. I pulled them both out of the bookcase. A third soft-covered book fell onto the floor. I put the soft-covered book to the side.

As I held both volumes of *Mein Kampf*, I remembered my world history teacher lecturing the class on Hitler. While in jail, Hitler dictated the book to his secretary, Rudolph Hess. The book outlined Hitler's planned takeover of Germany. Hitler also laid a foundation towards his hatred of Jews and Communism, claiming that they were the real enemy. He wrote about Germany's Aryan ancestry and the need for a National Socialist party, emphasizing the German's superiority in every way. He stressed that the masses needed to take down the parliamentary system. My time era narrowed even more.

I opened the first book or Band I of *Mein Kampf.* Everything was in German. There was a date, 1933, the same year Hitler became the Chancellor of Germany. This must have been a second edition. I remembered my teacher telling us that this book was equivalent to a best seller back in the 1920s. I flipped through the pages, all in German, and then set the book down.

I picked up the soft-covered book. It looked more like a journal than a book. The cover was blank. The first page read *Zweites Buch* which I assumed to be the title. Below the title was a loopy signature that was hard to read. After squinting, I figured out that the first name was Adolf, but wasn't certain of the last name. Could this be Hitler's signature? The pages within the book were not bound like *Mein Kampf.* They seemed to be loosely glued into the book's soft spine.

I flipped through a few pages, all in German, and almost put it back on the shelf. But this book was different. It was typed, but looked more like a manuscript rather than a published book. I continued to peruse the pages. In the middle of the book was a section of pages that contained handwritten mathematical equations. I tried to remember math. Trigonometry was as high as I went in high school. These equations were too advanced for me to understand. I flipped a few more pages and saw a diagram of what looked like the capsule I had exited from Heinrich's and Gretchen's barn. There were several pages of hand drawn maps. More pages were filled with some kind of code. Before I could flip to the next page, I heard the engine of a car.

"Uncle!" Heinrich yelled.

I looked out the window and saw an old, black car drive through the weeds. The car looked like the kind of car that would be used in a parade, long body, round headlights and huge chrome grill. It was an antique to me, probably not to the driver. The car stopped and a man who I presumed to be Uncle Josef stepped out and briskly walked to the door. I didn't want him to think I was snooping. I took the books and jammed them back on the shelf. Heinrich opened the door and greeted the man with a big hug. The man seemed uncomfortable with the boy's affection. He put his briefcase down and looked in both rooms that were adjacent to the foyer.

Uncle Josef's glacial blue eyes almost glowed behind his wire framed glasses. He quickly focused in on me like a laser beam. Ignoring the boy, he stepped into the library area. I got off of the velvet couch and extended my hand.

"Hello, I am Maya Smock. I came from your time machine in the barn. Heinrich found me. I would like to get back home." I said these words with as much bravado as I could muster, hoping he might fear me as well. I held out my hand to be formal in my introduction.

The uncle never shook my hand and I eventually dropped it back to my side. I didn't know what to make of him. He looked to be somewhere in his thirties with thinning blonde hair. He was tall and pasty with sharp facial features. The gray suit he wore made me wonder if he held a regular job nearby. Was I close to a city? Gretchen entered the room and rattled something off in German and then he replied. I did not know what was said, only that it had to be about me.

"Hello, Miss Smock. I am Doctor Josef Handel. Well, well, you found my time machine. Please do not be scared. I will get you home. But you have to understand something first. I have been working on that machine since I was a boy, not too much older than Heinrich. You being here, well, it's a moment of a lifetime. Please humor me and tell me more about yourself and where you came from."

"On one condition," I said. "You tell me where I am."

The doctor laughed in what seemed to be a forced laugh as if he was trying to be charming. I didn't trust him.

"Of course, Miss Smock. You probably figured out that you are in Germany. You are outside of Munich in the country. You came to visit in the most perilous time. It's April of 1944 and we are at war with much of the world. Heinrich and Gretchen are my nephew and niece. They are staying here, away from the city because of the war. They are not really farmers, but learning. This farm was abandoned. The animals were close to death. We even lost some of them, but the other animals are doing fine. Heinrich and Gretchen are my only family. They were my brother's children. He recently died in the war. His wife also died."

They were orphans just like I was. I looked at their faces once again.

"I do not live here, but come by quite often. Now it's your turn. You obviously are not Aryan. Where are from? What race are you?" The doctor smiled. He had thin lips and hideous, crooked yellow teeth.

I wanted to tell him more than anything that he would lose the war and his leader was a monster, but I had no idea who he was. Going by the autographed book, he might have been someone of importance. Chills ran up my spine. I knew that race was everything to Germans.

"Doctor, I was raised in an orphanage and then a series of foster homes. I never met my real parents and do not know my race. I come from the future, 2017 to be exact. We can actually find out our race by taking a DNA sample of our skin cells. A laboratory will analyze it and give you a breakdown of your ancestry. I have not gotten one, but plan to if I ever go home. In my country and time era, there is no master race, at least among mankind. The world is very diverse. In America people of all races and religions live side by side, work side by side, and even marry and have babies, further diluting any kind of specific ancestry."

The doctor looked through me again, causing my skin to crawl. Women's intuition told me to run. This man was evil, just like my husband. Unlike Claude, he wasn't motivated by greed. I didn't know what motivated him at this point. Science? Maybe. Unless there were time machines all over the Munich area, this man was my only hope in getting back home.

"Miss Smock, I started building that machine almost two decades ago. Over the years I've tinkered with it, made some adjustments, nothing. I have tried it out. Gretchen and Heinrich have tried. We all just get very dizzy. You are the second traveler that I've had in the last month. The first one was a man I never even saw. Heinrich saw him. An older man with long, gray ponytail. At first I did not believe him, but there were signs that the machine was used."

Jay. This is where he went. My heart leaped.

"And now you. Either I did something different, which I doubt, or you and this man are much more sophisticated than a human. Or maybe it's the farm. I took my machine and all of its parts from Munich, and then set them up here about three months ago. Maybe this farm is a portal. I don't know. Maybe it's some kind of combination." He looked at me. My eyes fell to the ground. He stated, "But as far as the master race goes, you and the man before you are clearly superior to us all."

"I'm no one special. But tell me this. How did this other visitor get back?"

The doctor smiled. "I am sure you would love to know how. He was very familiar with time machines. Perhaps he built one himself back wherever he came from. But you, you're not as knowledgeable. I'd be a fool not to benefit from that."

"So, you will hold me hostage? Beware, Doctor. I have powers that you are not equipped to deal with."

"I know you do. For instance, your skin is bullet proof."

Damn, Gretchen must have told him that when she rattled off a bunch of garble in German.

The doctor continued, "You see, Miss Smock, there is a master race. Don't tell the *Fuehrer*, but this race is not German or Aryan or Teutonic or whatever you call them back in the states. This race comes from Atlantis and they have everything to do with the future. This race has descendants. Maybe you are one of their descendants."

This doctor had no idea about my genetics and I wasn't about to confirm what he suspected. "Doctor, I am from Las Vegas, Nevada. That's in the western part of the United States. I am an author, and am quite ordinary. I am going through a divorce. Just lost my brother. But I have every reason to go home. Please, the love of my life is waiting for me. Please, doctor, send me back to where I came from. I aced my history class back in high school. I hate to break it to you, but Germany loses this one. You might want to make other plans."

"Maybe we will lose, but I am too close to the *Fuehrer* to give up. He has me working on things, top secret things. Maybe you can tell us where we went wrong."

This is where I needed to play dumb. Changing history for the worse was not part of the deal. "What is meant to be is meant to be. But as you probably know, Hitler was not in the right frame of mind. His decisions were not rational and the United States' involvement didn't help things go your way."

Josef looked through me once again and nodded. Maybe he didn't want to know the specific details or maybe he worried that I'd give him false information, whatever the reason, he dropped this line of questioning. "Miss Smock, I'll make you a deal you can't refuse. Let me take a few hair and skin samples from you. Come with me tonight and meet some of my friends. Afterwards, I promise to send you back to where you came from."

The doctor was right about one thing, it was a deal I couldn't refuse. I nodded.

Chapter Eleven

Present Day
Las Vegas, Nevada

The sun had been up for a few hours and Claude finally finished reading Maya's sequel on her computer. He almost forgot about Sam and Allie. They had called several hours ago. Supposedly, everything had gone according to plan. He made a fresh pot of coffee as they pulled into the driveway.

Claude couldn't believe that Maya was dead. She was so much more than a brilliant author. Her novels were clearly written for other reasons. Now he would never know. He'd assumed she was having an affair with Jay McCallister, but now he wasn't as sure. Maybe the books, the alien foundation, all of it somehow involved the work performed at the T.A.H. Institute.

Sam and Allie walked into the living room with exhausted and regretful expressions on their faces. They did not sleep since the night before. Sam had always acted like Claude's puppy, following him around, doing whatever was asked, including murder. Now Sam was involved in two murders. By the look on his face, he wasn't happy. Allie was all talk. Killing was not something that she pulled off effortlessly. Both of them were angry. Claude was losing control.

"Can I get you two a drink?" Claude asked as he walked to the bar. Neither of them answered. "Would you like some food instead?"

"A drink would be fine. Give me something with orange juice," Sam said as he plunked down on the couch.

"I'll have the same," Allie said as she sat next to him. There was something odd about both of their body language. They seemed emotionally closer. Was that because they murdered someone together, or was something else going on?

Claude brushed aside the twinge of jealousy and made the cocktails. He needed to hear every detail of what went down. "Okay then. So, please let me know how it all went. Did she see your faces?"

"Are you fucking serious?" Allie said in annoyance. "What difference does that make? She's dead." She looked older and colder. Her bright blue eyes were dulled. For a split second she reminded him of his mother.

"No, Claude. We wore masks the whole time. Did you know her boy Eric was on the radio? Just a few hours ago. We were on the way home and *The Sixth Sense* came on. I don't know the exact time he called. The show was taped in advance. But he was blabbering on about Maya's disappearance."

"Yes, he probably called in last night. He was let go much earlier than me. Maya was once on that show. The host is one of Jay McCallister's friends," Claude said. "She is syndicated on hundreds of radio stations at all hours of the day in every city in the country. Millions of people must have heard him. What'd he say?"

"Great. Fucking great, Claude. You might as well have had him put out an APB on us. I don't even think the police are looking for Maya. But now the whole fucking country is. You should have heard him. He was on a mission to find her. The host was totally on his side. He described our masks, her car, and you all tied up."

"This could be a good thing. They could find the body faster," Claude said.

"And throw our asses in jail faster. And sentence us to lethal injection faster. Sam and I did a lot of talking. We are not happy with your terms. We want one-third of her billion dollars. A third each. That's a fucking deal. We aren't even counting what T.A.H. is worth. Figure it out soon, Claude, or I'm going to the police. I need that money to get the fuck out of here and never worry about money ever again," Allie said in a low, numb voice.

Claude looked at her stone face. Where was the love? If she ever loved him, it was apparent she didn't anymore. Maybe she was with Sam. She was a gold-digging slut anyway. "I thought you wanted to be famous. What happened to that dream? With your fortune, you could buy yourself a career. Maybe invest in some plastic surgery. You're going to need it soon enough being thirty-five and all." Claude announced her age for Sam's benefit, not his. He doubted his little brother knew what he was getting himself into.

"I no longer dream of being famous. I just want to be free, out of jail. And rich. You know what, baby, I earned it. Every last cent. So did Sam. So figure out how you're going to pay me and I'll be out of your hair forever. By the way, she looked like a doll when Sam shot her in the head. A beautiful doll with huge brown eyes and long dark hair. She was so young and beautiful. She took it all like a lamb going into a slaughter house. How could you, Claude? I know I talked about it, even encouraged you and helped plan the idea, but all of this is wrong. You would have been so rich if you just divorced her. I can't believe I loved you enough to kill." Allie sucked down her tequila sunrise and motioned for Claude to make her another. "And if anything happens to me, I've got protection. I got pictures. So, don't even think about it."

Claude believed the bitch. So, this was it. Her morals were too high for murder, but the payout was another story. That's how it was with Allie. She wanted it all, then got pissed that she had get her hands a little dirty. Sam, on the other hand, would lay his life down for him. If Claude had any love or feelings for anyone, it was for Sam. All his half-brother ever wanted was to be loved. Sam didn't do this for the money. He did it for Claude. That bitch was putting ideas into his head about right and wrong. He didn't want a lecture. He already knew this was wrong, but it was all too late. All any of them could do was take the money and run.

Claude took a deep breath. "Allie, I understand you have buyer's remorse. I think we all do. But what's done is done. We all conspired to kill her. Suck it up. Guilt won't last forever. Now focus. Do you think someone will find the body? Remember the faster she is found, the faster you get your money and can go your separate way. Are you even sure she is dead?"

"Did you not hear me? Sam shot her in the head!" Allie sucked down the rest of her drink. Her hands shook in rage after she pounded the drink on the coffee table.

Sam looked at Claude and shook his head. They could read each other's minds. Jay McCallister didn't go down that easy.

"Claude, we shot her in the head and dumped her in a lake. If she's not dead, then she is not human. The smell. I'll never forget it. Like metal. Although there's no amount that was worth all of this, you are getting off cheap. Sooner or later we'll all burn in hell. That institute alone has to be worth a billion, maybe more. We want more, Claude. We want an even split of her assets," Allie said. She continued to repeat her new terms with a slur as the alcohol took effect.

Claude should have known she was going to be a total pain in the ass. For a split second he thought of strangling her right there in his living room, but quickly suppressed the urge. "Allie, she was my wife. I should have just divorced her. I will give you each a third, but you know damn well I can't do anything until she is pronounced dead and we are all cleared. That's going to take some time. I will give you each ten thousand right now, but that's all I can spare without looking too suspicious. The cops naturally suspect me. With a little luck, the cops will think this is related to Jay's death…"

"And it is," interrupted Sam.

"I mean, maybe they will think Jay's enemies are now hers. He had all but declared war on the government, accusing them of all kinds of things. The T.A.H. Institute believes that aliens are about to take over the world. It's all so crazy. Soon we will have plenty of money to blow, maybe even put towards a good cause." Claude was getting tired and wanted them to leave.

Sam fiddled with his phone and then said, "How much are in the accounts? Maybe we can just disappear now. Take what we can and start a new life." He slurped down the remains of his third tequila sunrise.

"Sam, why are you so paranoid? We came this far. What is so damn important on that phone?" Allie huddled over Sam's I-Phone.

"Look!" Sam yelled. "Maya is trending on Twitter!" Sam pointed to the number of retweets. "It's impossible! These people are claiming to have seen her. Look at these thousands of tweets. This has to be bullshit conspiracy theory!"

Maya Smock, new billionaire found in Ruby Mts.
Maya Smock emerges out of lake in Ruby Mts.
Maya Smock leaves gas station in helicopter.

"And you shot her in the head, left her for dead? You fucking idiots. You should have drowned her as well," Claude said. "I can't fucking believe this."

Allie cackled. "So, we fucked up because we shot her in the head but didn't' drown her? She can't resurrect herself. What are you crazy?"

Again Claude and Sam looked at each other. A long silence passed. Everyone was ready for another drink.

Chapter Twelve

Present Day
Nevada

The Gulfstream deftly landed in between the two mountains with little snow in the middle of nowhere. Eric knew he couldn't have been far from Las Vegas. The flight had been less than an hour. He politely chatted with Paula and Mercedes while they were up in the air. It didn't take too long to figure out that they too loved her. Maya certainly had that effect on people.

"So, Claude is not involved in any of this?" asked Mercedes as they waited for the plane to open after landing.

"Again, according to what I saw, I'd have to say no. But according to how I feel, I'd have to say yes. I wish I could be more certain. I will never trust the guy. Maybe it's jealousy, but he doesn't strike me as a person who is above killing his wife. And now with her publicized inheritance, oh, I am scared for her."

The door opened and a set of stairs were rolled to the door. All Eric could see was a hangar about thirty yards away, and a mountain range. His heart raced. Again he wondered if this was it. "Uh, where are we?"

Paula laughed. "In the Ruby Mountains. I can't be more exact, but you probably know that we are close to Vegas. Come. You are about to jump down the rabbit hole."

Eric laughed nervously. "I'm at the T.A.H. Institute, right?" Both women nodded. "So, where is the building?"

Both women chuckled as they all descended the air-stairs of the plane.

The weather was chilly. Eric wished he brought a coat. The night had bled into a new day as the sun peaked out colors of pink and orange from the largest mountain's summit. He squinted as he studied the mountain. "Is that a road? The top of the mountain is flat, as if someone deliberately flattened it out. Wait, the institute is inside?"

Seconds later, Eric saw some kind of vehicle appear out of nowhere and wind down the mountain.

Mercedes smiled at him. "That's our ride. And yes, this is the *They Are Here Institute*. I am very proud to be part of this place. It's been part of my life since I met Jay. He and Glenn have done wonders with it. Well now it belongs to Maya or at least part of it is hers. It's about as top secret as top secret can get. The government isn't even sure what goes on inside. Glenn has broadcast quite a few shows from here, but he is careful not to divulge the exact location. You cannot tell anyone the specifics about this place. Most know about its existence, but aren't sure where it is. Very few people get in and even fewer have complete access once inside. This place might have something to do with Jay's death. And who knows, it might have something to do with Maya's disappearance."

Eric watched the SUV idle towards them. "I always thought the show was just Hollywood stuff. You know, Glenn performed his alien views on a movie set somewhere in Los Angeles."

"Sometimes it's filmed in L.A. Sometimes here. It's not fiction. All of it's real. Ah, our chariot awaits," Paula said as she motioned for everyone to walk up to the SUV.

An Asian man somewhere in his thirties or forties was at the wheel. He stopped and got out of the car, opened the doors, and introduced himself. "I'm Doctor Wu. Just call me Chuck. Glenn sent me down. Mercedes and Paula, you both look beautiful as always. You are?"

"Eric."

Chuck nodded and shook Eric's hand. Pleasantries were exchanged between the Asian driver and the ladies as they spiraled up the mountain. Around halfway up, the car looked as if it was going to crash into the jagged, rocky side. A door opened and they drove straight in. Eric had just stepped out of the vehicle and there was Chuck, standing in front of him with an iPad.

"Eric, you are a visitor today. We don't mean to be intrusive, but you need to place your hand on the screen. I will make an I.D. for you in just a few minutes," said Chuck.

Eric looked at Paula and Mercedes for guidance. They rolled their eyes and shrugged. Something about their mannerisms gave Eric the impression that they were not friends with the Asian driver.

Paula took the screen away. "Chuck, do we really need to…"

"Yes, we do. It's T.A.H. policy and Glenn insists," said Chuck.

Eric was under the impression that Chuck was much more than a doctor. Paula immediately backed down. "Go ahead, Eric. It's just a finger and palm print that we keep on file."

Eric didn't like the invasion of privacy but took his hand and pressed it down on the screen. "Well, if it gets me closer to Maya, then I guess I'll do what I have to do." A detailed picture of his hand came up. The file automatically saved. Within less than a minute, a young woman came out from a large reception counter with an I.D. She said nothing and handed it to Chuck. He gave her a look and then she walked away.

Chuck took the I.D. and clipped it on Eric's shirt. "This is as invasive as we will get. Some of us have to get retina scans as well. Consider yourself lucky."

Real lucky, thought Eric. "Now do I get to see Maya?"

Chuck shrugged. "Well, now you get to see Glenn. He's in one of our...uh...chambers." Chuck looked at Paula with alarm. It was obvious that he didn't want to disclose too much information.

Eric was increasingly losing his patience. "Listen, I'm tired of all of this bullshit. You took Maya and did something to her."

Mercedes put her hand on his shoulder. "Eric, Glenn will give you some answers. But know this-we did not take Maya. None of us know for sure who took her. It was Glenn who found her, and Glenn who saved her. You need to talk to him." Mercedes walked off and motioned for Eric and Paula to follow.

Corridor, double doors, security scan, more corridors, more double doors, and more security scans. Finally, the retina scan came. Both Paula and Mercedes passed, but an alarm set off as Eric went through the doors behind them. Glenn appeared from the other side, toggled some switches, and then allowed Eric to enter the stark round room with some kind of machine set in the middle. A door that blended in perfectly with the white wall was partially opened. Eric could see panels of computers along with an even larger machine that looked like something out of NASA. Glenn looked more like a kind old grandfather in his gingham shirt and jeans instead of the head of an alien foundation.

Glenn looked at Eric with his pale blue eyes and said, "Hello, Eric. You must be confused, and very tired." He then led them through the white doors into the adjacent room. On the far side of room, perpendicular to the computers, joysticks, and keyboards was a long table with several metal chairs. A coffee station and small refrigerator were set up on one side. "This is our control area, our break room, anything really. The coffee is brewing. Would you like some? Maybe a soda?"

"No. I want some answers. Where is Maya? What the hell is that thing?" Eric pointed at the huge metal cylinder that sat opposite the controls about a half of story lower than the room's floor in a sub-basement. It quietly hummed.

Glenn set out four fresh coffee cups next to the pot. He looked into Eric's brown eyes and said, "Well, I'll start with the easy question first. That machine down below is a centrifuge. We use it to power the time capsule in the other room that you just walked through or the round room. This room controls the centrifuge, the capsule, all of it. Jay, Chuck, and I have been working on this for years. We finally figured out that time travel is possible, at least possible for a few. What I mean by a few is…well, not you, not me. Jay was capable. Maya is capable. Now the hard question, where is Maya? Well, that's a question I wish to God, if there is a God, that I knew the answer to. I don't know, Son."

Eric's heart sank. He tried to process what Glenn had just told him.

Paula picked up his hand and said, "Listen, there is a God and He is watching out for her. She's coming back. I can feel it."

"Paula, please. The man doesn't need any of your psychic pep talks right now, he needs reality. Listen, Eric. I screwed up. She got in that capsule because of me. I practically shamed her into it. The only thing that she asked was that I call you, which I did, but I screwed that up too. I don't know where she is and I don't know when she is."

"So, what are you trying to say? She's somewhere in time?" Eric asked.

"That's exactly what I'm trying to say. She is stuck in the fourth dimension. We just recently found out that we could travel in time, but do not have any of the specifics down. Here, let me show you something."

Glenn poured all of them a cup of black coffee and briefly told them what happened to Maya. "I believe Claude was behind this and so does Maya. A week ago Jay got through to the other side. He broke the barrier and traveled through time. Since they were related…"

"What? Jay and Maya are related? How?" Eric interrupted.

The little break room area fell silent. "I guess the cat's out of the bag," Paula said. "You see, they are brother and sister, probably half-brother, half-sister."

Mercedes could see the strained look on Eric's face, as if he couldn't believe any of this. "In the nut shell, they both have a gene that you and I don't have. Maybe even more than a gene, but we are still studying and comparing their chromosomes to human chromosomes. The gene we identified gives them certain advantages."

"A nonhuman gene? You mean Maya is not human?" Eric asked. His young face froze to stone.

"Let me show you instead of telling you." Glenn fired up one of the dozen or so computer screens. With a couple of clicks, he found the footage of Maya inside of the time capsule and played it. Within a few minutes, she disappeared. The video picked up the loud banging sound of the centrifuge and the whistling sound of the spinning capsule. Once the capsule seemed empty, the machine slowed down. Another few minutes went by until the machine was perfectly still. Glenn appeared on the film and opened the door to record what was inside. Nothing. Not even a trace of her clothes. He then played the footage of Jay's disappearance inside of the time capsule. He, too, disappeared.

"But Jay came back, right? He had to come back. He died in his pool," Eric said.

"Yes, this was filmed a week before he was killed. He didn't drown, Eric. I don't care what the police claim. Jay traveled in time and then came back. I sat here and waited an hour. The machine kicked on by itself. The capsule spun and then stopped. Jay was back with a full account of a barn he visited. I didn't call you right away because I thought Maya would be back. It's been close to twenty-four hours now. I'm scared."

"Then get inside and go find her. All of this is your fault," Eric said.

Glenn showed Eric another video. This one showed Glenn in the capsule. Less than a minute later Eric could see vomit splashing inside of the time capsule.

"Okay, Glenn. Let me go. Please, let me find her and bring her home," Eric begged. "She could be in a lot of trouble."

Paula sipped her coffee and looked at him with pity. "Eric, you don't understand. We, meaning you, me, Glenn, and Mercedes are not genetically capable of traveling. We don't have the right gene or genes. The reason Jay and Maya can disappear and float through time travel is because of their DNA. And then there are other problems. You see, we don't even know where this time capsule goes to. It could be the future or the past. It could be different for each trip. When Jay went, he didn't know where he was. He guessed Europe, maybe sixty years ago or so."

"How do you know that I can't travel? I want to try. Please, let me try."

Glenn shrugged. "Okay, I'll let you try, but you're going to be sick as a dog once we're done."

Glenn strapped Eric in the time capsule, turned on the centrifuge along with several controls. The machine turned sideways and spun, faster and faster with each revolution.

"That's enough!" yelled Mercedes.

Glenn quickly shut everything down. Eric got out of the machine, covered in vomit, and sat on the floor. His face was green.

Chuck and Glenn left him alone while they wiped down the time capsule. Once finished, they both helped Eric to his feet. Still dizzy, he wobbled to the sink.

"Are you alright?" Glenn asked. Eric shook his head. "You'll be alright in an hour or so. You've got a hard head, Son. I respect that. Now you know for sure that it's impossible."

Chuck handed him a clean sweatshirt from the institute's gift shop. "Welcome to T.A.H. It's a rite of passage we've all been through. It was only a week ago that we figured out that Jay could travel. And now Maya. Again, they are quite different than we are."

Eric washed his face, switched shirts, and then chugged down a half of bottle of water. Turning to Chuck, Eric said, "They have the genes, right? Or gene or whatever it is in their DNA that allows them to disappear."

Chuck looked at Glenn and smiled. "Go on," Chuck said. He nodded in a way that suggested he knew what Eric was going to say.

"Didn't you have Jay's body is frozen? Couldn't you take a sample of his skin and figure out the part of his DNA that makes him different?" Eric asked.

Glenn nodded. "Yes, we know which chromosome it is located on. We know more or less where it is on the DNA strand."

"And don't forget the book. We have the code, which would make it easier to look for on each DNA strand and..." Chuck said, and then stopped talking, as if deep in thought.

Paula looked at Mercedes with a raised eyebrow and then said, "Back up. What in the world are you getting at? What does any of this have to do with the price of gold? I'm completely lost."

Eric answered, "Well, I'm certainly not a geneticist, but what if Chuck or one of your other doctors could isolate the gene that allows Jay and Maya to time travel, duplicate it by cloning it and then, somehow insert the gene into me? Is this even possible? Am I being way too optimistic? You could show me how to work the time capsule. Anyway, maybe I could find her. I could bring her back."

Mercedes took his arm and then said, "And you could die. Getting the right gene in your body isn't like taking a pill. It is gene enhancement and gene therapy we're talking about. It's very new. What you are suggesting has never been done. To alter an adult's genes, well, it's much more complicated than designing a baby from scratch."

Ignoring Mercedes's warning, Glenn turned to Chuck and said, "Wouldn't we have to take something out before putting something in?"

"Glenn, you hired me because I am a physicist not a geneticist," Chuck said.

"Yes, but you have become invaluable to our genetic study as well. You and Doctor Blacksmith. I thought you both have been experimenting with a gene drive?"

"Yes, with animals. We've had a lot of success. Still, the location of where to insert the gene… I don't know. Maya told us where to find the gene in her first novel, but we have no idea where to insert it. Eric is on to something. I can at least match the gene's location with samples from Jay. He is perfectly preserved in the freezer… We could copy the gene…Eric, you're a genius!"

Something about the way Chuck said it, made Eric think he was being insincere, using the idea for something more.

Glenn asked, "But where do we insert it? What do we take out of Eric? We just can't guess. That could be deadly."

Chuck nodded. "Junk DNA is always a good place to consider. Maybe we get lucky. If Eric wants to volunteer, then why not let him?"

Paula got up from her chair and stood only inches away from Chuck. "Listen, you all have figured out something extremely important. Maybe the most important piece of information the world has ever seen. You know that hybrids have a certain gene that allows them to time travel. You know this gene is from another species of another planet. What makes you think for one minute that Eric's body will accept the gene? Eric, you're a young man. Your body could reject this gene for a million reasons. Your body could reject the gene editing. This is nothing but an idea. There is no proof, no study, nothing to suggest that this might work. You could die."

"I am willing to die. You all claim that Maya isn't a human being, but she is to me. It doesn't matter what you want to classify her as, a hybrid, an alien, or an advanced being. Maya was born here, planet Earth, and not some planet from outer space. This is where she belongs. If it's the only way that we can get her back, then I'm willing to chance it," Eric said. "So please, get some samples off of Jay. Then clone it and use me as a guinea pig. I'm begging you. All of this is my fault. If only I wasn't such a coward. If I told her how I felt, she never would have gotten involved with Claude and maybe, just maybe things would have been different."

"Well then, I think we have a plan. Mercedes and Paula, you both worry way too much. I will get the novel and double check it with the sequence we have in the lab. Once I am finished, Chuck will isolate the gene's DNA code from one of Jay's cells. We'll try to replicate it and then we will try to insert it into all of Eric's cells with a drive. This is going to take a while, days for sure, maybe even weeks. Maya could even show up before we risk Eric's life. If this works," Glenn paused, "there will be no limits to using this technology. Besides time travel, we can wipe out disease, prolong life, just about anything is possible."

"We can also destroy life without detonating a bomb or firing a shot," Paula said. "Eric, I'm begging you, please. This is not what Maya would have wanted."

"None of it matters. I need to at least try. Please understand."

Mercedes looked at Eric with sympathy and then whispered in his ear, "I understand perfectly. You must understand that Maya's interest is not a driving factor for this experiment." She looked over at Chuck and shot him a look that would freeze water. She then turned to Eric and said, "Be careful is all."

Chapter Thirteen

1970
Los Angeles, California

General Andreas was on a mission to gain information about two twenty-year-old men. The first young man was adopted by the incredibly wealthy Lansatti family. They lived in Beverly Hills when they adopted the hybrid. With a little bit of luck, they'd still be living there. The boy was one of the first babies created underneath the hangar at Broom Lake. A long list of the most elite families in the world wanted him. It was decided among a tiny group of United States leaders that the Lansatti family would be the first family to adopt.

The other man Andreas planned on visiting was the baby who Michael had stolen two decades ago. This baby had cost him Kate. She was both framed and blamed for the theft. This baby was also adopted, but not by a powerful family. He was adopted from an orphanage in Los Angeles by a middle-class family named McCallister. They had no idea about the baby's origins and probably assumed he came from a very young, poor, and confused single mother. Both of the boys grew up only miles away from each other and lived entirely different lives.

Andreas took a few personal days and drove up to Los Angeles. Although he rarely took off from work, everyone was expecting him to retire so no one thought it out of the ordinary. He was still careful not to leave a paper trail. After checking into a Hollywood motel under a false name, he drove around the city as well as Beverly Hills to get a sense of the neighborhoods of both of the grown hybrids.

The Lansatti boy lived in one of the most beautiful homes in Beverly Hills. Andreas easily found his estate. It was one of the biggest homes in the opulent suburb. The compound was deep within the hills, surrounded by tall, thick walls and high iron gates. Andreas couldn't get inside, but was able to see the massive Tudor home through the iron bars of the gates.

The adopted baby was named Leonardo, and assumed to live behind those gates. His family made it rich off of energy-coal, oil, nuclear, anything that worked. They had been experimenting with solar and wind energy as well, claiming it would someday save the planet. Bruno Lansatti, the boy's uncle, had just passed away. Andreas assumed all of the family members would be in town for the funeral.

Andreas's trip was originally planned for the next week, but after hearing about Bruno Lansatti, he moved the date up, hoping to see the whole family together at once. Bruno and his brother, Angelo, were born in America around the turn of the nineteenth century. They had wealthy parents, but turned their inheritance into a billion dollar industry in only a matter of decades. Bruno was seventy-five and died of a heart attack. Rumors about his sexuality circulated for decades. He never married nor had children. Those who knew him best assumed he was closest to his vice president. Both men had lived together for over a decade. Bruno left a will, but Andreas didn't know who got what.

Andreas circled the street several times before deciding it was not a good idea to park. The neighborhood was much too exclusive. Each house had to have some kind of security. He settled on one of the major streets in the hills and pulled onto the shoulder. He had a map out in case a nosy cop stopped to offer assistance. He sat and watched luxury cars enter and exit the connecting residential streets, wondering if Leonardo was in one of those cars.

Leonardo was now twenty years old and attended Harvard. He was studying business and law. Andreas assumed he would be groomed and trained for a high position within his father's and uncle's company like the other children in his family. He was the youngest of three and the only one who was adopted. With his blonde hair, pasty, white skin, and blue eyes, he stood out from the other Lansatti children. The family had come from the southern part of Italy where everyone had black hair and olive skin with dark eyes. Andreas's Intel reported that Leo's older brother and sister adored him. His parents were in their late forties when they adopted him. Their natural children were already in high school. The age gap didn't seem to matter. The family came off as a tight-knit group who spent lots of time together.

A limousine pulled out from one of the streets onto the main road. It was Friday around noon. Andreas thought about the funeral. He assumed Bruno would be buried on a Saturday or Sunday. But what about the wake? It could be today or even tonight.

Another limousine soon pulled onto the street, going the same direction as the previous one. On nothing more than a hunch, Andreas followed. Within thirty minutes he was somewhere in Los Angeles. The limousines were obviously going to the same place. A third limousine was spotted several cars back from his position on the road. He assumed they were going to a funeral home, and as the first two limousines turned right into Harrington's Funeral Parlor, he smiled with satisfaction.

By the door of the funeral home were five big men, all dressed in black suits. Andreas immediately thought of former military who turned private security. There was no way he was getting in. He quietly parked in the adjacent lot of a strip mall. A few minutes went by and people finally got out of the limousines. He recognized most of them from his file. The second he saw Leonardo, his heart stopped. The man looked like Richtor and the white prostitute Andreas's men had taken off the street. He was average height and weight with fair coloring. His blonde hair was thinning. Andreas predicted he would start to recede before the age of thirty. The boy was not handsome, however his family name probably got him plenty of women.

The immediate family walked into the funeral home. Soon, the wake would open. Andreas didn't dare test the waters by pretending to be a guest. He was a well-known general in certain circles and his presence at this funeral would have been a complete bust.

Andreas sat in the parking lot for another couple of hours before a Chinese man came out of the dry cleaners and told him to move. Claiming to be lost, he promised to pull away within the next ten minutes. This seemed to pacify the man as he went back into his shop.

With his timeline cut short, Andreas started the car. He recognized several of the guests from Leonardo's file, yet did not know any of them personally, or professionally. That soon changed. Just as Andreas put his car in reverse, another limousine pulled up to the door. He recognized the diplomatic plates right away. Four men stepped out of the car. Two of them he knew, the sitting Secretary of State and Newcastle, the new Joint Chief of Staff. *Interesting,* he thought. *What do they have to do with renewable energy?* Andreas hoped they would not be at the funeral. He had planned on attending.

Andreas pulled into a gas station a few stop lights down the road from the funeral home. The day was still early, only mid-afternoon. The other adopted boy, Jay McCallister, lived close to the funeral home. But that was all the information that he had on the young man. The secret file that Bolantano gave him had little information. McCallister's parents had died a few years ago in a car accident. The details of the crash were unknown. Bolantano had hand-written question marks all over the file. *He thinks they were murdered,* thought Andreas. *That would mean there was a leak.* Andreas didn't want to think about it. He just started this little rebellion. Maybe it was just that, an accident.

The most recent information that Bolantano had on the McCallister boy was that he dropped out of UCLA to pursue a career in writing. Andreas did a little investigating on his own and found the man's name attached to science fiction novels. Of all of the genres the boy could write about, he chose science fiction. *Maybe that was irony*, Andreas thought, *or maybe inevitability.* Andreas brought two of McCallister's novels with him on his trip, waiting for a chance to read them.

As Andreas thumbed through Jay's first novel, *We Are Not Alone*, he studied the professional picture of Jay inside of the jacket. He looked nothing like Leonardo. His hair was medium brown and his eyes looked to be brown or hazel. If Richtor was the father, then who was this man's mother? He thought back to the beginnings of their experiment. There were four prostitutes, one white, one black, one Hispanic, and one Native American. Was Jay part Hispanic? With a white father and an alien, his mother could have been any one of them. He looked white, but his coloring was very different than Leonardo's coloring. It was hard to believe they were brothers.

Andreas took out his map and then headed towards Jay McCallister's home. He drove deep into the city and passed a book store he would not have normally noticed. An entire window display of Jay's newest novel, *The Rise and Fall of a Starman*, was lit up. Andreas pulled in his rental car and parked. He entered the bookstore and quickly found a whole table dedicated to both of Jay's novels. A clerk approached.

"May I help you, Sir?" the young man asked.

"Yes. What do you think of this new author, McCallister?"

The clerk smiled and replied, "I'm a big fan. Everyone who works here is a big fan. He comes in fairly often for signings. His next signing is tomorrow. That's why we have the window display. He's a local and he's also going to be the next big thing. It's just a matter of time until these two books become movies. He's a great guy. Hard to believe how young he is. He's got a hot wife too! I think they just got married. If you like sci-fi, this is your guy."

"What are they about?"

"The first one is about a race of aliens who are using us as their slaves. The government knows about it and helps them control the masses. The second book is about a super-race of both humans and aliens who save the planet from another race of aliens. They sound silly, but once you get scratch beneath the surface they raise a lot of questions about how much the government knows about aliens and yet refuses to tell us. He's almost like a prophet of what is to come."

Andreas had to grin. If only the man knew the prophecy had already come true. These books should have been sitting in the nonfiction section of the store. "What time is he here tomorrow? I got his books in the car already. I want them signed."

"He should be here before noon. Can I help you with something else?"

"No and much appreciated."

Andreas got back in his car. This trip was proving to be well worth while. A signing. He would get to meet him and maybe even his wife. Andreas knew that he would have to tell Bolantano the Intel was old. Maybe Jay's address was old too.

Andreas drove another twenty-five minutes into a posh neighborhood, per Los Angeles's standards. He turned down a few residential roads and found Jay's address. He lived in a small, but pretty, green ranch home with a wrap-a-around porch and flowers everywhere. Yes, he was definitely married. A twenty-year-old man was not about to plant that many flowers in his front yard. There were two newer cars in the driveway. Both Jay and his new wife were home. *Now what?* thought Andreas. *Do I just knock on the door and tell him that he was created in a lab?* He parked a few homes down the block to collect his thoughts. *I know, I'll claim to be with a newspaper or maybe even magazine. UFO Today, that's it!*

Andreas straightened his tie, combed his hair, and then tucked a small pad of paper and pen in the breast pocket of his suit coat. He drove the car to the front of the house and parked. He walked up to the porch and knocked. It wasn't too late, not quite the dinner hour. A man opened the door, a man whom Andreas instantly recognized to be Jay McCallister.

"Hello, Mr. McCallister. I am Donald D'Angelo of *UFO Today*."

"Do you have identification?"

Shit. His plan was going downhill. *Play it cool.* "I.D.?" Andreas checked his pockets and pretended to look. "I must have left my wallet at the hotel. Oh please. I just want a minute of your time. Well, maybe ten minutes or so. Just a quick interview for our new magazine. I hate to bother you at home, but I couldn't wait until your book signing tomorrow. I am such a fan of your latest novel, *The Rise and Fall of a Star Man*. I just gave it a five star review in our magazine and, please, I'm new at this. I'm a retired cop, second career. Just a few questions."

"So, you're from Nevada?" Jay asked.

Damn. He saw the license plates of his Oldsmobile. "Yes, but I live here now. Need to get my plates changed."

Jay's eyes narrowed. "Well, I suppose. The weather is nice. Maybe we can sit on the couch over there," Jay said as he pointed to a wicker couch on the porch. He looked paranoid and uncertain. *The boy is smart,* thought Andreas. *But he is more ambitious.*

"Okay, then I won't take up too much time. You write about a government conspiracy as if the government and aliens are in on taking over the world. Your style is captivating. Do you believe that it's possible?"

Jay looked straight into Robert's dark brown eyes and, without blinking, said, "Yes. Very possible, if not altogether true."

"Why?"

"Self-preservation. Better to be on the side of the winner than the loser. Sometimes evil prevails. A race of beings who know more than we do are obviously superior. Listen, Don, that is your name, right?" Andreas nodded. "I don't mind talking to you, but you're not a reporter. And I doubt your name is Don."

Stunned, Andreas asked, "What gave me away? I thought we were having a nice interview?"

"You look military, maybe CIA. I am guessing that you work at one of the many bases in Nevada. Oh, and then there is no *UFO Today* magazine."

"And here I thought I was so clever. So, if you know that I am lying to you, why are we still talking?"

"Mr. Military, can I call you that?" Andreas nodded. "You and your kind of people have been following me around since my first book. I know that I am on to something. My stories are pinching a nerve with you. I am not afraid. If you wanted me dead, I'd be dead. You all want to see what I'll do next, what I'll write about next. You wonder if it's me, or am I in some way communicating with them." Jay looked up to the sky which was starting to darken.

"You're right. I'm military. But I'm not here in a military capacity. That's why I can't tell you my name. You're a smart guy. I'll try to level with you, but the truth is I could get court martialed for being here."

"Why" Jay asked. "Are you here to kill me?"

The man didn't even blink, as if this was almost routine. Andreas was speechless. A moment went by and Andreas opted to come clean. "Alright Jay, I've got nothing to lose at this point in my life. I'm old and washed-up. Before I retire, I have some business to clean up. I have gone rogue. You say that you're being followed? That's us, me and my colleague. Let's just say that I am a fan of yours. Maybe your biggest fan. Hell, I just started your first novel, but I get the theme. I live the theme. A clerk at the book store you hang out at told me about the stories. Where you get your ideas is not what I am interested in..."

"Because you already know?" Jay interrupted.

Andreas nodded. "Yeah, I know. You're not crazy, Jay. In fact, you're a genius for seeing through all of the crap and having the guts to write about it."

"Then tell me who you are."

"I can't. At least not today."

"Then who am I? I don't have anyone in my life who can answer that question. You see, I lost my adoptive parents a few years back when I was just a boy. Can't seem to find any information about my real parents. I'm alone in this world. My wife, she's making dinner right now, she doesn't love me. She doesn't know me. Hell, I don't know me. If you can't give me answers, can you give me hints?"

Andreas crossed his leg and took out a cigarette, offering Jay one. Both of the men lit up. A few minutes passed, and then Andreas dropped the proverbial bomb. "Jay, do you believe aliens and humans can mate? Can there be a super-race of beings, the best of both of us?"

"So, what are you saying? Is that who I am? An extraterrestrial hybrid? Are my books more than coincidence?" Jay asked. Andreas could see his eyes well up with tears. He paused. "Was I engineered in some way?" Andreas nodded. "You know, I've wondered about this my whole life. I just assumed I was insane. It's why I dropped out of school. It's as if someone or something is whispering these stories in my ear. I can almost feel my left ear buzz. Then I am compelled to write. The buzzing and the ideas come to me in waves. It's not like I am hearing voices, but almost like I am uploading information. When I drink, the buzzing stops."

"Like some kind of telepathy?" Andreas asked.

"Yes, like I am being channeled through automatic writing. I am not alone. I have read about others who are being used like a radio."

"Have you ever been sick?"

Jay shook his head.

"Suicidal?"

Again, Jay shook his head.

"Lonely? Sad?"

Jay shrugged.

"I am so sorry. But you're not alone. There are others like you. You must know that on some level. There was a green crystal…"

"A green crystal rock? I know it. Moldavite. I got rid of it when I was a boy. Cracked it in half and then it bonded back together again. It scared the shit out of me. I tossed it into the ocean. There are others who have this same rock? Is that supposed to identify us? Mark us in some way? Do I have brothers and sisters out there?"

Andreas nodded. He put his hand on Jay's shoulder and said, "Yes, you do. And the crystal does identify you. I can't give you all of the answers quite yet, but please believe me when I say that you are one of the lucky ones. I guess that's why I tracked you down, to tell you that. I wasn't sure how to go about it, so I lied. I am so sorry. You can call me Mister Military from now on. Soon I will be Mister Retired Military. And if it's okay with you, I'd like to check in with you from time to time." Andreas stood up and held out his hand.

"Wait, I have so many questions. Why are you doing this? What is your real name? How do you know so much about me? Where are my brothers and sisters?"

"I'll tell you more with each visit. And you can bet that I'll be at that signing tomorrow."

Chapter Fourteen

1944
Germany

I nodded after Josef promised to get me back to the present. Or maybe it wasn't the present. Maybe 2017 was actually the past, and like Josef, I lived in the past. Time was no longer a tangible concept, but rather a vague description of an era. I just wanted my life back. Josef would take some samples from me, introduce me to his friends, and then I would supposedly be on my way. He said he was a doctor. I had him figured for some kind of scientist.

"I am very hungry, Miss Smock. Excuse me." Josef dismissively left me standing in the doorway of the tiny library and walked off into the kitchen.

I smelled the sausage and sauerkraut Gretchen had served me an hour or so ago. I didn't know what to make of Josef. All I knew was that he was my only hope of getting back.

I went back to the same book, *Zweites Buch*, and continued thumbing through the pages. Whoever penned this manuscript had to also be a scientist, or have access to scientists. My first guess would be Hitler, but then this book wasn't mentioned in history class. The written part of the book was typed in German and looked like it was copied. There were very few words I could make out. The pages that held the drawings piqued my interest.

As I flipped through more pages, a hand drawn map of part of the world showed a dotted line that ran to and from Germany and Antarctica. There were two routes drawn. I didn't know the starting point, but assumed it to be northern Germany. One route was through the English Channel and another route went around the British Isles. Assuming Hitler wrote this notebook, I guessed this was about his famous Antarctica expedition. Or was this Plan B, after he lost the war? Did this even happen yet? 1944, April. My history dates were jumbled. The only thing I was sure of was the importance of this manuscript.

Thumbing through some more pages and more notes, I saw the number two hundred eleven written in by the upper portion of Antarctica. I wondered if this was his base. The next page looked like another map, possibly a constellation map. *Oh Jay*, I almost said aloud. *Wish you were around to teach me these kinds of things.* I was about a third of the way through the soft covered book when Josef crept up on me. I almost screamed when I saw him quietly staring at me as he stood in the doorway. I slammed the book shut, looking guiltier than a cat that ate a canary.

"We are leaving now."

I put the book back on the shelf and followed Josef to his big, black car that reminded me of something straight out of a gangster movie. The car jostled down the dirt road, and then bounced over the cobble stone roads. I estimated twenty minutes had elapsed since leaving the farm. Eventually, the road smoothed out, and then he spoke.

"That book you were reading, it's from the *Fuehrer*. It was supposed to be published and will be published someday, win or lose the war. He wrote it after *Mein Kampf*. He talks about *Lebensraum* or living space. It's one of the reasons that Hitler wants to rule the world. Those maps you were looking at are about Germany's secret base called 211. You ever hear of it?"

I answered him truthfully. "Yes, I heard something about a Nazi fortress in Antarctica. Some people believe that Hitler found aliens and space ships there, but most think it's pure conspiracy theory."

"What do you believe?" Josef asked. I shrugged. "Don't be so sure it's a theory. That book you were reading is very special to me. Only a handful of people have a copy. Do you read or speak German?"

I shook my head. When Josef mentioned a handful of people, I thought back to what Jay believed-an inner circle of elites who ran everything. Maybe even the war. Cautiously, I asked, "So, you are a close friend of the *Fuehrer*?" Josef nodded. "Are you building the time machine for him?"

Josef looked at me with disappointment. "No, not at all. I am building, or shall I say built, the machine for them." He looked at the ceiling of the car which had to have meant the sky. "You see, I cannot use the machine. Gretchen and Heinrich cannot use the machine. Even the Great *Fuehrer* himself cannot use the machine. We all tried. As you have proven, it's not the machine that is defective, it's us. We cannot travel in time. At least not in that capsule. The beings who guided me in the right direction didn't consider my human limitations. You must not be fully human. You are one of them."

"How did they show you how to build it?"

"I met one of them when I was very young, in a forest not too far from the farm. His craft crashed and it caused quite a commotion within the village. I was already interested in anything to do with science. He touched me and I knew. It was like telepathy. He gave me a... how do you say, oh yes, inspiration. The basic material math was given to me through brain waves. That was the last thing he said to me."

Inspiration. Jay had mentioned that word before. A spirit breathing an idea into you. Kind of like the two books I wrote.

"Did he die?" I asked. Josef didn't answer. I commented, "Humans have thought about travelling in time for centuries. It's always been a fantasy, like something one would write in a novel..."

Josef seemed agitated before he interrupted me. "These beings looked nothing like you. How...Why...Who made you?"

"God made me. He made everything."

"God, bah! He didn't make the time capsule, I did. And here you are."

"So, you have met aliens before?" I asked.

Josef nodded. "Yes, the one who touched me. Later in my life, I saw some dead ones. We found a flying machine in the mountains of *Berchtesgaden*. Inside of it were four bodies. The *Fuehrer* had them preserved for research purposes."

"What about the ship?" I asked, fascinated.

Again, Josef refused to answer my question so I immediately stopped talking.

We drove in silence for several miles. I estimated that an hour had passed since we left the farm. The silence became almost comfortable. I concentrated on my surroundings. From no traffic and driving through the middle of nowhere, we drove into small villages with traffic signs in a short amount of time. The sun dropped. I had no idea what time it was. Josef told me it was April. The temperature was mild and the trees were green. The day seemed long.

The villages soon faded away. The new landscape consisted of dense, thick forests, mountains and valleys. The ominous scenery reminded me of the forest within the Ruby Mountains. Claude had his lackeys shoot me and then leave me for dead in a lake. I could have been fish food or a snack for a wild animal.

I had no proof it was him, just lots of intuition and circumstantial evidence. If I ever returned home, he would pay dearly for what he did. I thought of something slow and painful, torture. Maybe I would Google ISIS for ideas. I thought of clamps and needles and then his penis. Nah, I needed to be more creative, more poetic about the end of his existence. But he would pay.

The sun had almost disappeared, leaving just enough light for me to see the rest of our mysterious route. Josef put on his headlights. The stark isolation of the mountains caused my heart to race. This could be the end of me. I began to sweat despite the cool air in the car. It wasn't the usual kind of sweat that one smells in a gym locker room. I emitted an odor that smelled like an array of metals and rotten hardboiled eggs. It was the smell of fear. Josef smelled it too. He looked over at me and grinned wolfishly.

"We are almost there."

"Almost where?" I asked as I looked into the wilderness of forests and mountains.

"How do you say…the bird's nest?"

"Huh? You are taking me to a bird's nest?"

Josef smirked and shook his head. "The *Fuehrer*'s home. Bormann had it built for him for his fiftieth birthday a few years ago. I made the call and our group wants to meet you. They know nothing about you, just that you are a person of interest."

We drove through a brick tunnel as the road began to incline. "And then you'll take me back to the machine and send me back home," I said meekly.

Josef nodded and looked into my eyes. I had no reason to doubt him, but then again he was a Nazi who was a friend of Hitler's. I was screwed. Then it dawned on me. I blurted, "Eagle's Nest! That's where we are!"

Josef smiled. I could see the home sitting high on top of the mountain. It was casting off a ton of light. I expected to drive up to the front door, but Josef stayed at the foot of the mountain and casually drove around to the other side. The sun was long gone and the car's headlights were weak. My sweat poured out again as the car slowed. We stopped in front of an arched entrance that looked like another tunnel. I got out of the car with Josef. The air was chilly, but my face was slick with sweat. He waved at me to follow him inside. Cautiously, I stepped into the tunnel. I looked up, nothing but carved stone. He led me to the end, into a circular room with a dome-like stone ceiling. There were two elevator doors.

The doors opened. Two military men with guns stood in the elevator and motioned us in. The elevator car was enormous. At least fifty people could get inside. The upper half of the walls were polished brass with Venetian mirrors. The lower half of the elevator was upholstered in green leather with benches on three sides. Josef sat down.

As we ascended up to the estate, Josef looked up at me and said, "We are going four hundred and seven feet up, but then I am sure you are not impressed. You travel through time. He is here. He will want to meet you."

He is Hitler, I assumed, also known as the devil. I didn't answer him and silently prayed to God. I had recently become sort of religious and vowed to learn more about God once I had the chance. I knew He was the only being who could save me, and I wished I knew Him better.

Then another thought hijacked my brain. It was the same kind of feeling that I got when writing my novels. Maybe this visit was an opportunity. Maybe I was meant to come here and do what needs to be done. Maybe I was supposed to save the world from additional grief. I continued to pray. *God, grant me the bravery and the conviction to kill Hitler if it is Thy will.*

The elevator doors opened. Josef got off of the green leather bench and motioned me to follow him. The two guards remained standing outside of the elevator. We were instantly greeted by an older man and young woman, both dressed in servants' uniforms. The woman took my coat but looked at me with surprise. The man glared at me with disapproval as they both walked away. Then I remembered that I didn't blend well with this crowd of lily white Germans. I was some kind of minority mixture that I hadn't bothered to get checked. Throw in some alien genes, and I was in a class by myself now that Jay was gone. My brown skin, black hair, and dark eyes were not welcome much less tolerated.

Josef sensed their prejudice. He leaned down and whispered in my ear, "They have no idea who you are and what you are capable of. Ignore their ignorance."

I whispered, "Easy for you to say, with your blue eyes and blonde hair. Tell me now. Am I going to get gassed in the shower tonight?"

Josef looked at me with surprise. "How do you…Never mind. And please, keep your mouth shut about the outcome of this war. The *Fuehrer* hates to hear anything negative. You don't want to see him angry."

Our conversation was interrupted again as a short, squat, man with dark hair approached us as we stood in the hallway. He wore a military jacket with all kinds of regalia. I instantly assumed him to be a man of importance. Josef saluted and then nudged me to do the same. I obeyed. The man looked at me with disdain, and then rambled off something in German to Josef. I was clearly an outsider to this conversation and imagined they spoke about me.

"Maya, this is Martin Bormann. He is Hitler's private secretary and the one who built the house. He doesn't understand how you managed to walk out of my time machine without being Aryan," Josef said. I almost saw a sneer as he looked at Martin and assumed that Josef did not like the man.

"A woman, a non-white woman came out of your time machine?" Bormann said in English with a thick

German accent. He obviously doubted I was capable of this miracle. Part of me agreed with him. All of this was too fantastic and mystical to be true. Bormann continued, "Well, Maya, we need to get some samples now, before our *Vril* meeting begins."

Josef said, "Allow me."

I looked at Josef with a raised eyebrow. "But aren't you a physicist?"

"I am a scientist who knows a thing or two about physics and engineering, but genetics is actually my field of expertise. I have been studying both sciences since I was a boy. I can take some samples and show these important men you are exactly who you say you are."

Martin shook his head. "No, I will have Wolfgang and Hans do it. We will keep this lab unbiased. Yes, Miss Maya?"

What was I supposed to do? Object? I might be immune to bullets, but had no idea about gas. I submissively nodded and followed Martin Bormann into a small room down the hallway. The room had a wooden desk, bookcases, filing cabinets, chairs, and a small couch. Bormann sat behind the desk and ruffled through a few drawers, pulling out a pair of scissors, a needle, and a small, wooden stick. A few minutes went by. Two men who looked like Josef came into the room, grabbed the medical equipment that Bormann set out, and started to poke and prod me. My hair, skin inside of my mouth, and blood were taken. Pictures of me were snapped. I was treated like a rare animal in a zoo.

"This will be quick and painless. We are almost done. These doctors will have this analyzed as soon as possible. We will know if you are telling us the truth," Bormann said. "If you are who you say you are."

"Am who I say I am? The only thing that I said is my name, Maya Smock. I came out of this man's time capsule. His nephew found me and now I am forced to come here..."

"Enough!" shouted Bormann.

I was worried. Did they think I was a fraud? Did they think Josef was a liar? Bormann slapped my face. The two other doctors took my samples and left the room. Would I ever get back home? Was I stuck here forever as their test subject prisoner? Would I be killed? An odd metallic, egg smell poured out of my armpits and forehead. The smell filled the room.

"Come." Bormann led Josef and me out of the room, down the same hallway, and into a large banquet room. The tall ceilings had wood beams. A large fireplace blazed, and several chairs were set up in a circle. There must have been at least forty people in the room, all white. Most of them had blonde or white hair. Their eyes were a full spectrum of blue.

"You will meet some of our friends. We all belong to the *Vril* Society. Tonight, you are our guest of honor," said Bormann in his thick German accent as we stood in the entryway. "Excuse me for now." He walked into the room towards a group of men who were smoking pipes and cigars by the fireplace.

My eyes darted around the room's walls, scanning the people who showed up at this impromptu meeting. I couldn't help but notice the women, all young and gorgeous. I wondered if they were the men's wives, girlfriends, or just plain prostitutes. Most of the men were middle-aged and dressed like Bormann.

My eyes continued to soak it all in. Bormann quickly wormed his way into the group of men who stood in front of the fireplace. One man I recognized instantly. My heart stopped. This man wasn't especially tall, but had the presence of a giant. His blue eyes were alive, dancing with evil. Hitler. Speechless, I stood like a statue, hoping that I would not blink. Those blue eyes met my brown eyes and the putrid smell of my sweat returned. Hitler was angry. He whispered something to Bormann who quickly marched across the banquet room in our direction.

"He doesn't believe you traveled from the future. You are not Aryan. Go to him and explain now. I will get the test results as soon as I can. Be careful with your words. He is a man with little patience for fraud. And you better hope there is something extraordinary in your blood and tissue samples."

Chapter Fifteen

Present Day
Ruby Mountains, Nevada

Eric was determined to do anything for Maya, even allowing his body to be used in a brand new experiment. No one could change his mind. He was well aware of the consequences involved. Doctor Wu seemed especially giddy about his offer. But Chuck's ulterior motives didn't matter to him as long as they could get his body to accept time travel. He knew that it somehow involved turning into tiny particles and then, once landed, having the body put itself back together.

Chuck wasted no time, and instantly picked up the phone. "Doctor Blacksmith, I am sending you a young man who needs a DNA analysis. His name is Eric. We need to compare his DNA to Jay's DNA, looking for a particular sequence that you have been studying. Do we have Maya's DNA too? That might also be helpful.... Great. Get her sequenced as well. We also have her novel. Maybe we can somehow inject the exact sequence into Eric. It's a theory that he is willing to test. He'll be up in a few minutes." Chuck hung up the phone. "Eric, Doctor Blacksmith is ready for you. Your plan is brilliant. I just hope it works."

Mercedes and Paula began a chorus of protests, concerned that Eric was about to commit scientific suicide.

"None of us know enough about this! Please, there has got to be another way," yelled Paula. "Playing God has a price."

"Eric, she might just be stuck. Jay knew how to operate a time machine which is how he got back. Glenn never even taught her how this thing works. Maya just might be playing around with buttons right now, figuring out what to do, wherever she has landed. It has only been two days. Please, sleep on this before you…"

"Ladies, I know you mean well. And although I hardly know you, you have made it completely obvious that you love her. Well, I love her too. Glenn, please take me to the laboratory. I'm doing this. My mind is made up."

Without hesitation, Glenn grabbed Eric's arm and led him through a maze of corridors, and then a set of stairs to the laboratory. After the fourth turn, Eric was completely lost. He couldn't find his way out of the mountain if he had left a trail of bread crumbs. The enormity of the place set in. This was the NASA of scientific alien research, his only hope. The laboratory was huge. Rolling chairs, long tables and microscopes were everywhere. An older woman with a beautiful, softly lined face approached him from the far corner of the room. She had been sitting at a long table with at least six computer screens.

"Eric?" He nodded as she approached. "Doctor Blacksmith. Glenn, nice to see you." She extended her hand to Eric which he shook.

The woman wore a lab coat, jeans, and sneakers. Her dark hair with strands of gray was tightly swept up in a bun. There was an aura of warmth, unlike the Asian doctor in the round room.

"I'll be back in an hour or so. Let me leave you two alone. Eric, what you are doing is unprecedented as well as heroic. We are all in debt to you here at T.A.H.," Glenn said somberly before he left the laboratory.

"Well, well, well. Heroic? You suddenly became the most important man here at the institute. You'll have to fill me in on the details. I know virtually nothing about what's going on. Now sit down over here and tell me why I am comparing DNA sequences of you, Jay, Maya, and the hidden code in her novel." The doctor led Eric to a bank of chairs that sat in front of a wall and motioned for him to sit down. She moved to a nearby cabinet and rooted around. "Roll up your sleeve, please." The doctor tapped his arm looking for veins. "Ah, here they are." She held a rubber tie, gloves, and a new needle.

Eric followed her directions. She swabbed his arm, tied the rubber strip, and slowly massaged one of his veins on his forearm. "Well, Eric, why does Chuck want me to do all of this work?" She plunged the needle into the vein and drew a vial of blood.

"Well, he said something about giving me the gene that allows Maya and Jay to time travel in that machine. Doctor, wait, I am not sure what any of that is."

The doctor bandaged the tiny hole in Eric's arm and put the vile in a stand on the counter. "That gene, huh? It might be more than one gene that we are talking about. And then certain genes can regulate other genes in turning on or off certain traits. You know, like a switch."

"No, I don't know. All of this is over my head. Are you a good doctor?" Eric asked.

"I'm considered the best, the bloody best, not to be a braggart. Every doctor who works here is the best. We were picked because of our accomplishments. Jay recruited me many years ago."

Noticing her accent, Eric asked, "Are you English?" She nodded. "I like your accent. That's a good sign, right? You say that you are the best and I like your accent. Well then, I have nothing to worry about," Eric said.

Doctor Blacksmith smiled. "Eric, there's a lot to this. It sounds simple. First, I isolate the gene or even genes that make Jay and Maya eligible for time travel. As you were probably shown from the footage, they disintegrate while in that capsule. The speed of the centrifuge has to be just right. Air that is heavy in oxygen is filtered in. The capsule has to be at the right angle, the right speed. And there's more, but that is Chuck's area of expertise. What you are asking is that I clone this gene or genes, and then insert it into you. Your idea is possible. Maybe you have heard of this process. It's called gene enhancement. That's kind of like designer babies." Eric nodded with the familiar reference.

The doctor got up from the chair and unlocked a steel cabinet that looked more like a safe. She showed him a gadget. "This is a gene gun. I would probably use this to shoot the gene inside of your body. I invented this little gadget. Not bad, aye?"

Eric nodded.

"It's the most advanced gene gun on the planet. There are other ways to get the gene inside every one of your cells. We could use what we call a Crisper. It's an acronym, C.R.I.S.P.R. It's only been done on bugs and animals though. I would take your DNA sequence apart and patch in the extraterrestrial gene. Either way, we play Russian roulette with your life."

"Why so many doubts?" asked Eric. He not only liked this woman, but trusted her as well. "I have every confidence…"

"I don't have every confidence," the doctor interrupted. "A human genome has around nineteen thousand genes, maybe thousands more. To shuffle the genetic deck, adding in a gene, taking out a gene, well, it could mutate you or disable you, and even kill you. In theory, it's all possible. I have no experience with this. No one has."

"Well I don't know anything about genetic enhancement or Crisper, just try your best and get that time capsule working for me," Eric said.

"Let's say we do figure it out. I have a team of researchers that work for me here, at T.A.H. How would we know the time capsule will take you to the exact spot as it took Maya? Chuck is one of the best physicists in the world and he has no clue to where the machine takes the traveler. In fact, he just figured out it even worked a week or two ago, before Jay was killed."

"Why do you think he was murdered? Because he travelled through time?" Eric asked.

"Very well could be. He was the most honest, kind, intelligent, generous chap in the world. But he knew things that he wasn't supposed to. I guess we all know things that are above our social status. Jay was famous and had little privacy. He publicly criticized the United States and so many other super powers. He opened up the biggest alien research institute in the world without any help from the government. We really don't know who or why he was killed, just that it was not an accident. Now enough about Jay. We need to focus on you. Eric, there are all kinds of things that could go wrong with this experiment."

"I know. But I love her. I always loved her. She was only a kid when I met her. A wounded kid with emotional scars that flashed brighter than a neon sign. I caught her stealing a book from my bookstore," Eric said as he rolled his sleeve back down to his wrist.

"And then what happened?"

"I hired her." He smiled. "It was the only way I could think of keeping her around. With each passing day, I loved her more and more. Years went by and she went from a dysfunctional teen to a young, beautiful woman. She is my best friend, my one true soul mate. Doctor, I messed it all up. I sat on my feelings and she married her agent. But now we have a chance. I got to try, Doc." The doctor looked into his brown eyes and they both felt a connection. "You are her last chance, my last chance."

"Get up. Once I analyze all of the DNA, I'll have a better idea of what to insert and delete. Obviously, there is no changing your mind. Actions certainly do speak louder than words. But I am somewhat of a romantic. Never found someone to love as much as you love Maya. I guess my career has always come first, just like my father."

"Well, your father must have found someone at some point. He has you," Eric said.

"Had. He died some time ago. He loved my mother, but their love was complicated. His life was about his career. It wasn't much of a life. In the end, he was full of regret, depressed, and tried to make everything right. Kind of like you, Eric. For the record, you're a bloody idiot. Give me a few days, maybe weeks, and then we can proceed."

Glenn walked out of the lab and back into the main lobby of the institute. Chuck, Paula, and Mercedes were there, cornering him into answering a list of questions.

"Does Doctor Blacksmith think any of this is possible?" Chuck asked.

"Is he actually going through with this?" Mercedes asked.

Paula wiped away a tear. "Does he realize that he may die? Or end up disfigured or brain dead or, I don't know. In fact, none of you know! You're playing with this man's life the same way you played with Maya's. Glenn, I'm so mad at you right now. You never even taught her how to work the time machine. This is all your fault."

Glenn took the verbal blows for several minutes before speaking. "I was in a hurry with Maya. I worried the machine would only work in a full moon Sagittarius constellation. I might have been wrong about the star alignment."

Paula's mouth dropped. "And if you were right about that, then we won't see her until next December? Or the next full moon? Or, as usual, you are guessing? Playing with people's lives on a hunch?"

"Alright, Paula, you got me. I don't know, I don't know anything. The chance was there and I took it. To hell with the consequences. The greatest scientific breakthrough, the greatest truth in the universe was at my fingertips, and I caved. Right and wrong were not considered in any of my decisions. I'm so sorry. We are going to get her back, so calm down."

"Glenn was not alone in this. I was his prime instigator. Don't just blame him, much of this is my fault," Chuck said. "I know you ladies have never liked me. But time machines are not a new invention. I found evidence of them when I was boy back in China. You don't understand the magnitude of this breakthrough."

"Enough." yelled Mercedes. "Alright, what's done is done. But what about Eric? What's going to happen to him?"

Glenn answered, "We don't know yet. Doctor Blacksmith is getting his blood and some other DNA samples. We will compare them to Jay's. I also have some samples of Maya's that Jay collected when she stayed at his home only weeks ago. And we have the novel. But I don't know if any of this will work."

"So, you are about to mutate Eric, another innocent bystander. When are you going to learn? This is all guess work. You can't do this." Paula said.

Glenn looked gravely into her eyes. "You're right. We need more information."

"But…" Chuck protested.

"But nothing. We can't just slaughter him on a hunch."

Mercedes looked at the floor and then screamed, "Wait, There's another novel, a sequel to her first. Could she have embedded more information?"

"Her husband has that computer. We could send someone to break in, get it back… she just finished the new novel. If anything, we'll give that SOB husband of hers some money. He won't understand what we want it for," Glenn said, his blue eyes dancing.

Mercedes, Chuck and Paula looked dumbfounded. Glenn further explained, "Her sequel has got to be the key to all of this. Once we get a hold of it, we can get her back. Maybe we can even get revenge in the process."

Paula gave Glenn a sharp look. "If you don't have a real plan to get her back, then I'm pulling the plug on this institute. Don't push me, Glenn. I am on the board, and will use every second of the airwaves to talk about what is going on here. Do we understand each other?"

Glenn understood perfectly well. This wasn't the first battle he had with Paula, and probably would not be the last. For now, he promised to get the book back.

Chapter Sixteen

Present Day
Las Vegas, Nevada

Claude turned on the television and flipped through every news channel. Nothing. Either Sam's Twitter feed was fake news, or they were ahead of all the other media. An hour went by. Claude found the story on the local Las Vegas news.

Could it be true? Was Maya alive? Claude was strangely relieved. "So, you two fucked the whole thing up. Well, on the bright side, I guess I'm off the hook for murder, or shall I say we are all off the hook for murder…I hope you are telling me the truth about the masks."

"I don't understand. She was shot in the head. Her limp body sunk in the lake. We stayed there for an hour to make sure," Allie said. She pushed her drink aside and poured herself a straight orange juice.

Claude thought about Jay McCallister. He and Sam shot Jay three times. They had to drown him to finish the job. "When you put her in the lake, did you hold her head down? Make sure she drowned in the water?"

Sam shook his head. "What are you saying? She is like Jay? What species are they?"

If they only knew what I knew, thought Claude. He kept his theories to himself. "Well, Allie, looks like you can kiss your precious money goodbye." The color from Allie's reddened face drained, leaving her as white as a ghost. "But I'll tell you what, as long as Maya didn't see you, you're in the clear. Once I am divorced, I will quietly give you and Sam five million dollars each. Not bad for a day's work. This was a mistake, a big mistake. Consider this screw-up a gift. And Allie, I never want to see you again. I will have Sam deliver your money when the time comes. Both of you need to leave. Go home, back to Los Angeles. Here's a few thousand." Claude took out his wallet and handed Sam the cash. "I need to be alone."

Without any threats, protests, or theatrics, both Sam and Allie left the house in Sam's car. Claude promised to call his half-brother later. What were the odds that Jay and Maya both would be immune to bullets? They had to be related in some way. But how? Was Jay her father? Her uncle? Maybe even brother? The affair that Claude had been so sure of seemed to be too simplistic of an answer to Maya's and Jay's relationship.

His eyelids felt like they were holding up anvils. He needed to rest. Before he laid down, he made sure the house was locked and drew the blinds. Paranoia set in. He worried that Allie and Sam would come back, furious, wanting his head on a platter for all that they had been through. When satisfied that both of them were truly gone, he laid down and continued watching the news for any new information. The story was gaining popularity. Maya's attempted murder and current disappearance was talked about on a few channels.

How was he going to play this? Would she accuse him? Where was she now? Dozens of scenarios flashed through Claude's head as he lay in bed, watching the news. His exhaustion surpassed his troubles, sending him into a coma-like sleep. Several hours passed when he awakened to a nonstop ringing doorbell. His phone was dead. After putting it in the charger, he noticed that he had forty-six messages and eighty-one emails since he last checked in the morning.

The media wanted answers. Claude grabbed the computer and went straight to the T.A.H. Institute's website. He was betting that Maya was there. She was seen flying away in a helicopter. It had to be Glenn Lucasek who rescued her. Claude dialed the number to the T.A.H. Institute. To no surprise, he was answered with a standard business recording.

"You have reached the T.A.H. Institute. Press one for visiting hours. Press two for research. Press three for *Alien Theories'* producers…"

Claude pressed the number three on his keypad. Another maze of phone options came up for him to navigate through. Finally, he had the option of leaving a message.

Shit, what do I say? "Hi, this is Claude Kazinsky, Maya's husband. I think she is there. I have her laptop which might be of interest to your genetic code department…" The machine cut off the rest of his message. *Not a bad bluff. Let the games begin.* Who was helping her? Was it Glenn and T.A.H.? It had to be.

Claude had no idea what he was doing, but he needed to talk to her, to feel her out, to know if his ass was in the clear. He no longer wanted her dead, just to know everything was going to be alright. He had been wrong on so many things. If anger and jealousy had not gotten in the way, if he valued what he had, if, if, if.

Jay and Maya both knew something that most of the world didn't. They also transcended the laws of humanity. Who, or what, was immune to bullets? Had he not seen it with Jay, or heard it from Sam and Allie, he would dismiss it all as pure fiction. Something was going on, something big. Was his wife an alien? Was T.A.H. a legitimate institute? He had assumed Glenn's TV show, Jay's eccentricities, the institute, all of it as being pure bullshit. But a voice inside of his head kept on saying-*Maya was shot dead and thrown into a lake, but resurrected herself. You don't have a fucking clue.*

Were Sam and Allie thinking the same thing? Sam had to be. He shot Jay McCallister and nothing happened. They had to hold him under water until he could no longer move. Both of them dismissed it all as being a fluke. *The bullets were bad, their aim was off, he moved in the nick of time....* Sam and Claude made up their own logic to explain it all. But Sam didn't take that extra step with Maya, and who would?

Claude went on his computer, straight to the T.A.H. Institute's website, determined to get answers. An email might go farther than a phone call. Before he could copy the email address, the phone rang. Claude grabbed it.

A male voice said, "Claude Kazinsky?"

"Yes."

"This is Glenn Lucasek. I am returning your call. For the record, I am well aware of what you've been up to. Maya is alive and well, so your attempt to end her life was in vain. You will be prosecuted to the full..."

Blah, blah, blah. He called back within fifteen minutes. He must be worried about her sequel. "Let me talk to her. I know about the novels. They're part of a special DNA code. An alien DNA code."

The pause in the conversation was encouragement to continue Claude's bluff. "She's part alien, isn't she?"

Claude waited for a reaction, but the silence said it all. "Glenn, go ahead and have me prosecuted. I want to speak to Maya one last time before I'm incarcerated."

Again silence. "Didn't Eric go to the media? A radio friend of yours, right? I, too, can use the media. I was so hoping to be on your show. I guess I'll just have to open up my front door and tell the media that is camped outside on my front driveway all about Maya the alien."

"Claude, she doesn't want to ever speak to you. You tried to have her killed."

"Prove it."

"Too busy right now, but when..."

Claude was feeling more confident about his hunch. "Busy? Doing what? Making more monsters with your alien DNA code? Does the U.S. government know about this? Is your institute approved by the A.M.A., F.D.A., W.H.O., and the other likely regulators? You think they would approve of what you are doing in your secret laboratory?"

"What the hell do you want, Claude? You want to spout conspiracies all over the tabloids, be my guest. You wouldn't be the first, and probably not the last. You're the one who tried to kill your wife…"

"Me?" Claude interrupted. "Or maybe you're the one. She now owns half of your empire. Talk about motive, you have more to gain than I do. Don't threaten me, old man."

"Do what you gotta do." Glenn Lucasek hung up.

Chapter Seventeen

1970
Los Angeles, California

Andreas left Jay McCallister's house in a hurry. He said too much, but oddly, didn't regret it. Andreas wondered if all of the babies felt like Jay, different and alone. Was there something in them that worked like an extraterrestrial receiver? Could they all communicate with aliens from outer space? Or were other aliens already here, guiding them telepathically?

The general could only guess that Jay's novels must have been an attempt to document what was going on inside of his head. He wished he could take the man with him and have him observed, but that would be too much to ask.

The day slipped away much too fast. Andreas went back to his hotel room, watched some television, and arose at five o'clock the next morning. He went for a run around Hollywood Boulevard, and then turned onto Vine, taking in the sights. Five o'clock in the morning was an interesting mix. Drunks and druggies shared the streets with the workforce. As he ran, he thought mostly of Kate. He wanted so badly to tell her all about Jay. For now, he'd have to settle for Bolantano.

After three miles, he turned around and ran back to the hotel. He felt a set of eyes on him and kept looking back. No one. The paranoia made him jittery. A homeless man blocked the sidewalk, begging for money. The man smelled like garbage. Was he some kind of tail? He ran around the vagrant, and again looked back. The man stood in the same spot, now focusing on a man who was dressed for office work and about to get into his car. He vomited some water along the sidewalk as he ran. The conversation with Jay McCallister was taking its toll on his mental state. The hotel was only another mile away. His jog became a sprint at Olympic speed.

Once back at the hotel, Andreas showered and dressed for Bruno Lansatti's burial. There was a bank of pay phones in the small lobby. He made sure that he had a few handfuls of change, and then called Major Michael Bolantano. It was now almost six o'clock, still much too early to call, but he assumed that Bolantano, like most military, was an early riser.

"Yes," Bolantano answered on the first ring. He sounded wide awake.

"It's me," Andreas said, purposely leaving out his name. That same paranoid feeling returned. He felt someone was watching him. Looking around the small lobby, there was only him and the hotel clerk. Maybe it wasn't someone's eyes. Maybe it was someone's ears. Andreas and Bolantano had discussed the possibility of their phones being bugged. Bolantano even mentioned that he was constantly taking his phone apart and checking for plants. One could never be too careful.

"Our first subject will be at a funeral today. The wake was heavily guarded, retired military or CIA. I recognized a few, which I will tell you about later. The deceased had no heirs. Please see if our guy benefits from his death."

"Alright. What about the second person?"

"The second man I made contact with."

"Oh?" Bolantano asked. Andreas could hear the alarm in his voice.

"I gave no details, but the man is aware of something. He knows he is unique in some way, despite having little or no information…" He paused. Andreas wasn't sure if he was clear, but would talk to the major once back at the air base. "It's not fair. No one ever told him…" Andreas paused again. Bolantano seemed to be holding back. "Hello? Are you there? Are you alone?"

"Yes, yes, please, go on."

Something was definitely wrong. Andreas continued anyway, feeling as if this might be his last opportunity to relay this information. Andreas wiped the sweat off of his forehead, undid his tie and unbuttoned his shirt. Breathing heavily, he continued, "He claims his career is not by choice, but by force." Andreas assumed that Bolantano knew he was talking about Jay's writing career.

"Do you think that was wise? What if he goes public? You just about confirmed his suspicions."

"Well, he already is public. He's more afraid of *them* than we need to be of him going public." Andreas could hear Bolantano's breathing. "What's wrong? You sound very worried."

"Well, yes, it wasn't exactly wise to see him, but maybe something good will come of it. Listen, I realize I might sound a little off, but there is something that I found out through my Intel that you need to know. I'm really glad you called. I wasn't sure how to get in touch. I don't know how to tell you this…"

There was a long pause. Was this some kind of reprimand? Did he ruin their operation already? "Spill it. What did I do wrong?"

"No, Sir, it's a personal matter. A very dear friend of yours, the same friend that connected you with me, is not doing well. She is at Saint A's in the same city in which she lives."

"Kate!" *Shit.* He was supposed to avoid names, but it was too late now. "Is she alright? What happened?"

"Sir, I don't know any of the details. She went in the ER yesterday morning. There is a direct commercial flight this afternoon."

"Book it."

"Alright. Finish up your business and call me from the main airport around noon. I'll give you details."

Bolantano hung up. Andreas stared at the ground for what seemed like eternity.

Total trepidation caused Andreas to sit down and catch his breath. Was Kate sick? Did she hurt herself? Or even worse, did someone put her in the hospital? Was this his fault?

Andreas went back up to the hotel room to take a moment for himself. He found two tiny bottles of vodka in the room and mixed them with his complimentary orange juice. The booze made him feel less anxious. He didn't have to be at the airport for hours. Kate was probably fine. He was here now. Might as well finish what he started before flying off to London. So much for trying not to leave a paper trail.

As Andreas drove to the cemetery, he assumed no one would be there. It was the perfect time to stake out the place without drawing too much attention. He had no idea where Bruno Lansatti's grave would be. He drove around and quickly figured it out. There was a freshly dug grave next to an enormous tombstone and statue of the Virgin Mary. Despite the man's gay lifestyle, he and his family were devout Catholics who put on a show about being religious. The file Bolantano had built on the family was filled with annual hefty donations to the Vatican.

Andreas slowed down his car and pulled to the side, watching the empty area. While waiting, his mind drifted back to Kate. He talked himself into believing this was all routine. He'd fly to London and she'd be out of the hospital in a few days. He would take her up on that rain check she offered, and then they would tour London together, picking up where they had left off.

Andreas saw Jay's *Rise of a Starman* novel on the passenger seat. Needing some kind of distraction, he picked it up and began to read. Another thirty minutes went by. Jay McCallister was one hell of an author, but the book was much more than reading entertainment. Andreas had only finished two chapters and could already see that the book wasn't fiction. Jay somehow knew what the government tried so hard to hide. There were too many similarities between the Advanced Beings Andreas had once caged and the characters in the novel. Only twenty pages into it and Andreas believed the young man. Some other force was guiding his pen and making him write this story. Some being or force wanted the world to know that Advanced Beings were real. Did all of the babies in Andreas's lab feel like Jay? Were they programmed to know where their ancestors came from?

Andreas put the novel down after seeing a truck park near the freshly dug up grave. Two workers quickly set up several of dozen chairs in neat rows in front of the grave. The weather was beautiful, around seventy degrees and sunny. The smell of pollen and freshly cut grass irritated Andreas's nose. He had been used to sand and rock. Spring's foliage made him wheeze.

Minutes later a hearse and two limousines pulled alongside the curb. There he was, Leonardo Lansatti. He and his immediate family had arrived. Soon everyone else would as well. No one seemed to notice Andreas parked a few hundred feet away, but the same paranoid feeling from morning had returned, making his eyes feel as if they bulged out of his face.

Andreas wanted to grab his camera, but that would have attracted attention. He might have already blown his cover. His Nevada license plates could be run by the police. Although the information would register as military plates without details. That would have been enough for the Lansatti family or any of their guests to question. He was leaving a trail of breadcrumbs straight back to his base. Stupid mistake. Other cars began to pile in, making him blend.

The logical side of Andreas's brain urged him to leave. But it was too late. If he left now, he would really look suspicious. He wondered if he should get out of his car and join the crowd. There had to have been at least sixty people there with more to come. He was dressed for the occasion.

Andreas's heart thumped so hard he thought he might have a heart attack. The crowd began to seat themselves. He chose the back row. Looking around, he recognized a few leaders in industry, some members of the Council of Foreign Relations, and one sheikh from Saudi Arabia. The sheikh had received one of Andreas's designer babies last year. This was a very dangerous group for him to show his face. All he needed was one person to recognize him, and major questions would be raised. Andreas looked around.

A cardinal arrived. Traditional passages about death and eternal life were read. He asked everyone to pray for Leonardo who would now take the helm of the family business. "…This young man, just a junior in college, will now have an empire to run, will now be responsible for thousands of jobs, let us pray…"

So, he does inherit it all.

"Let us pray for Bruno's family, who loved him and will miss him. May he be with our Father…" the cardinal droned on. Bruno's lover did not get the attention a widow would have. He sat in the second row as if he wasn't part of the family. Andreas was only half paying attention, still scanning the guests in fear of getting caught. But then the cardinal said, "We believe, we are sons of Lam." Almost everyone repeated this phrase. Andreas wasn't exactly a religious man, but he had been to enough funerals to know that this was not the gold standard of prayers in honoring the dead. *Did he say Lam or Lamb? Who was Lam?* He would have to check into that later on. Glancing around, he still scanned the crowd for someone who knew him.

The cardinal signaled Leonardo, his father, and his siblings to approach the casket. They slowly lowered it into the grave, throwing flowers and shoveling dirt on top of it. Andreas stopped paying attention to the burial ritual and looked behind him, still on high alert. His heart almost jumped out of his chest. Jay McCallister stood in the very back with other late comers. What the hell was he doing there? Their eyes locked. Andreas's face froze. Time had slowed down to a dream state.

Several minutes later, after the Lansatti family announced that everyone was invited back to their home for brunch, the crowd got out of their seats to socialize. McCallister gave him a smug look and motioned that they take a walk away crowd. They walked toward a giant oak tree by Jay's car. Jay leaned on the trunk and sneered.

"Hello again, Mister Military," Jay said. "Cigarette?" He took out a Marlboro and lit it, offering it to Andreas. He readily snatched it up and inhaled.

"I'd prefer a drink, or two, or three, or five. Don't you have a book signing today?"

"Yes, in an hour, so I don't have much time. I had you followed last night after you left. My wife actually. She lagged behind until you parked at your hotel. I got to the hotel around four-thirty or so this morning. Almost missed you. If I had slept just a little bit longer…You are one early riser. And quite the speedy one for such an old timer."

Andreas couldn't believe the man's audacity. "Cut the crap, Jay. I realize I deserve this. If you were sincere with me last night…"

"I was," Jay interrupted.

"Then I left you in a worse state than you already were. Maybe I should have never have paid you a visit. But I wanted to see. I was curious."

"Did you know me as a baby? Are you my dad?"

Andreas had to smile. "No. I'm definitely not your dad. But the truth is I did know you as a baby. You were the first of many more to come. The greenish rock marks you and your kind. You see, that rock is not from this world. It's from another planet. I'm not sure which one. We believe it powered a spacecraft."

"We? Who are you, Mister Military? What were you doing with a spacecraft twenty years ago? What does that have to do with an experiment with babies?"

Andreas looked around the cemetery. People were still socializing with the Lansatti family and the cardinal. Leonardo was looking in their direction. The same paranoid fear returned. He looked straight at Jay. "Listen, kid, quit following me. Go to your book signing. I have a feeling you're gonna be the next Ray Bradbury of the sci-fi world. I promise you I will answer all of your questions, maybe even give you a tour of your birthplace, but not here and not now. Do you understand me? People are watching us. Very powerful people. And I need to leave." Andreas started walking away.

"But when?" Jay called out as Andreas walked away. "I need some kind of time frame or I'll…"

Andreas did not take kindly to threats. He turned around and marched a few steps toward the tree where Jay still stood. "Or you'll what? You'll kill me? I'm an old man, already dead in so many ways. But you're young. Don't ruin your life. One day I'll tell you about the sacrifices that were made for you to be free of it all. You better get to that book signing."

Andreas turned around and walked to his car, ignoring Jay as he continued to call out. Hopefully no one caught wind of their conversation. He should have gone straight to the airport and just sat at the gate and waited. Bolantano would not approve of this little scene that Leonardo might have witnessed. Should he have a similar conversation with Leonardo as well? That boy also had a right to know where he came from, but then again, he might already know. His adoptive parents could have told him or will now tell him. He, too, must feel the same way-different.

Andreas pulled into LAX around eleven o'clock in the morning. He worried about his car. Hopefully Bolantano would somehow retrieve it in the next few days. He found a bar located around the international flights and waited until it was noon, the time Bolantano said to call. His nerves were shot, but still felt the need to continue scanning his general location. After a few martinis, he began to relax. He got Jay's novel out of his travel bag and began reading. After another fifty pages, Andreas noticed a theme of dominance and control starting to emerge. Jay's imagination was filled with paranoid claims of alien domination and human extinction. He looked at the clock above the bar's cash register. Time to make the call.

As previously discussed, Bolantano took care of all of the transportation. The call was brief with Andreas leaving out the details of Bruno Lansatti's burial. He slept for most of his ten hour flight, dreaming of the aliens in Jay's novel. They seemed to merge with the ones he once studied in an underground cage. Kate was also in that cage, screaming.

The captain's announcement abruptly awoke him out of his slumber. He would be landing in less than thirty minutes. The sky was a drab gray, but it was early morning per London time. He would rent a car and drive to Saint A's. He wasn't sure what the A stood for.

"Excuse me, Miss," Andreas said to the young, pretty stewardess. "Are you from London?" She nodded. "Where is Saint A's hospital?"

"Aye, you mean Saint Andrew?" Andreas shrugged. "That's the only one I can think of. Family member sick?" Andreas nodded. The girl continued. "Once you are out of Heathrow, follow the signs. It's in the middle of the city. I hope everything is alright."

"I do too." Andreas nervously read a few more pages of Jay's book before landing. He read about the aliens exterminating any and all humans who got in their way or were too old or sick to be of any use. The story line became chilling. The more he read, the more he thought about World War II and Hitler. Jay's work paralleled the concentration camps and the Jewish prisoners.

An hour after the plane landed, Andreas was in the Saint Andrew Hospital parking lot in his compact rental car. Would Kate be alright? Would she even want to see him? Was he somehow responsible? He gave himself a pep talk, got out of the car and walked into the main entrance. He lied, telling the hotel clerk that he was Kate Osbourne's brother. In return, he learned she was in the ICU, Room 204A.

Andreas took the nearest stairwell. Once reaching the second floor, he saw Lori in the waiting room and knew he was in the right place. The young woman looked up at him with puffy, hazel eyes, Kate's eyes, obviously sleep-deprived and red from crying.

"Lori, do you remember me?"

"Of course, Robert Andreas. My mother's ex-fiancée." She stood up and gave him a hug. "I am in shock. How did you know…"

"I have my sources. Came as soon as I could. What happened?" Andreas asked as he sat next to her on a chair.

Lori looked around the room nervously. Her eyes bulged and her lips twitched. "Well, the official story is heart attack. She has high blood pressure. She has been taking medication for the last few years. I found her on the kitchen floor when I came home from the orphanage two days ago, Friday night. She had to have open heart surgery. It doesn't look good. I'm waiting for the doctor. Come on. I want her to see you."

Lori took Andreas's hand and led him to her room. Feeling somewhat reluctant, he said, "I don't want to upset her or disturb her or …"

"She's probably sleeping. You came all of this way. Maybe seeing you will help."

Kate was the only patient in the two bed room. She was hooked up to two machines with several wires and tubes. She looked old, frail, and helpless. The machines blipped a certain rhythm that synced with her breathing. He didn't want to cry, not here, not now, but the tears gently streamed down his face. He had stuffed his feelings for her for years. Their happily ever after had slipped away again, leaving him empty.

Andreas approached the bed and knelt down, taking Kate's wrinkled, small hand, careful not to loosen the attached taped-on tube. "Kate, if I was a religious man, I would say a prayer. You know, I think I'll say one anyway. God, please, God, if you are out there, if you exist, don't let her go. Not like this, not now. I love her…" His words turned into a moment of hysteria. Tears gushed out and he began to blubber like a little boy.

Kate's hazel eyes opened. She squeezed Andreas's hand and faintly smiled. "Take care of her," she said. "She's yours."

"Take care of who? Lori? You got it. But we will do that together, when you're out of here. I'm not fooling around anymore. I will put in for my retirement immediately, as soon as you are home. To hell with

Michael's little project. I'm not spending another day without you. I let you get away once before…" The blip on the heart monitor hummed a high note without a break and the green line flattened out. Doctors, nurses, and orderlies rushed in, motioning for the general and Lori to leave.

Twenty minutes of silence went by in the waiting room. One of the doctors came out with his clipboard. "We did everything that we could. I'm so sorry. She's gone."

Chapter Eighteen

1944
The Eagle's Nest, Germany

My mind went blank. Hitler thought I was a fraud. Bormann and two men left the banquet room, supposedly to finish testing my blood. I had no idea what they were looking for. And now I would probably be gassed, or used as a test subject for Doctor Mengele, or some other monster. I knew that I was immune to bullets so at least they couldn't shoot me.

Josef was saying something, but his voice was drowned out by my thoughts. And then I could no longer think. A faint ringing sound that was randomly interrupted by static stung my ears. Something was going on inside of my head. Instead of being petrified, I felt sedated, almost as if I was in a trance.

There were eight other women at this meeting, all gathered at a table in the corner of the room. Six of the eight women were flaxen. The other two women were technically brunette, but their brown hair had plenty of gold highlights. All of them were young, tall, and thin. All looked like they walked out of a 1940 Vogue magazine. Each had really long, shiny hair that was swept up into a ponytail. I felt sorry for them. They must have been there for the men to use at their whim.

There was something more to them than their beauty. Looking at them made me calmer. The most beautiful woman of the group, a blonde with high cheekbones and giant blue eyes, looked straight at me. The ringing in my ear got louder. Was she trying to communicate? My ears were burning. I cupped my hands around them. What was she trying to say?

"Maya," Josef said. His voice sounded a mile away despite him standing next to me. "Maya." He touched my shoulder and gently shook it. "Maya." His voice became clear and the ringing stopped; the dream-like state ended. "We're about to start. Are you alright?" I nodded. He looked at me with skepticism. "Is there something you are not telling me?"

"Listen, Josef, I just want to get back to 2017. For some reason, Glenn's machine dumped me here, in World War II Germany…"

Josef interrupted, "Glenn? Is he your master?"

The magnitude of the situation took its toll. "Master? No, women of the future don't have masters. Women are equal to men. You probably have no idea what I am talking about. Look, I took your tests and fulfilled my end of the bargain. I want to go home before you have me gassed for not being Aryan. I never said that I was Aryan…"

Again, Josef interrupted, "Get a hold of yourself, please. If you don't, you surely will get gassed. Your voice is much too loud. Others can hear and you've already attracted a great deal of attention. Please, bear with me a little longer. I will make good on our arrangement."

I wiped the tears from the corners of my eyes and took a few moments to collect myself. The group of women were staring at me, but no one else seemed to notice my moment of weakness. I was obviously part of their conversation. Maybe I wouldn't be gassed, but used as some kind of sex slave. I thought of my last set of foster parents and became angry. I'd rather be gassed than forced into pleasuring these monsters.

"Josef, you want me to join the little harem you got over there? You know, get your men off when they are in the mood..."

Josef looked confused, and then tightly grabbed my arm. Although he spoke English, I was using too many idioms for him to keep up with. He had an idea of what I said and then answered, "Whatever you think is going on, you're wrong. Those women are not what you think. The striking blonde who keeps staring at you, that's Maria Orsic. She is the leader of the women and the leader of this meeting. She looks young, but she is close to fifty years old. All of the women are much older than they look."

"Then what are they? Witches?" I asked.

"What? No. They are mediums. Advanced beings from outer space have chosen them to act as translators. Maria has given us more information than the rest of them put together, but they have talent. They might feel threatened that you are here."

Mediums, like Paula? "My ears were ringing so loudly. Was that them? What do they want from me?"

The men in the banquet hall began rearranging the chairs the tables. The hall was quickly transformed into a circle of a few dozen chairs. In the middle of the circle were eight chairs and a table.

"They're setting up. You'll see what they do and I'll explain later," Josef said.

Maria Orsic sat down in one of the chairs that were set in the middle of the circle. Her seven female followers ignored the other chairs and sat on the floor around her like a kindergarten class would sit around their teacher. Josef and I took a seat in the outer circle as did everyone else in the room. Someone turned off the lights, leaving only the soft glow from the dozens of candle flames that were placed all over the banquet hall. The room was instantly transformed from a dinner meeting area to a candlelight theatre. Maria Orsic owned the stage.

Now that I was only feet away from the group of women, I could see the fine, delicate features on their beautiful faces. Their ponytails looked more like strands of silk. Their porcelain skin glowed. I couldn't believe they were decades older than me.

The room was as quiet as a cemetery. Maria soon broke the silence by saying something in German.

Josef leaned over and whispered in my ear, "She said 'good evening.' I will try to translate for you."

Hitler sat on the opposite side of the circle. He was glaring at Josef and me. He must have figured out that I didn't speak German. This was just another reminder to the *Fuehrer* how I did not belong. Maybe this was an opportunity. If I could kill him, then my trip would not be in vain. I would do the world a favor. If only it was the beginning of the war and not the end of it. Still, I would save lives. He was said to be charismatic, but I didn't see an ounce of charm. All I could see was pride, ego, and insanity. He was chaos.

There was an exceptionally long and awkward moment of silence. I looked over at Josef and shrugged. Maria began to hum. After a minute passed, her followers hummed along with her, all in unison of the same note.

Josef leaned in and whispered in my ear, "It takes a while, several minutes, maybe longer. She usually says something in Akkadian. It was the language of the Babylonians. Sometimes Maria takes the tablet and draws Sumerian script. She's not a fake. With her lack of education, there's no way she'd know any of these languages. We've got two professors to your right."

I looked over. The two men were the ones who took my blood earlier. "Did they review my blood work?"

Josef nodded. "Yes. I don't know their results. They are very good geneticists. We work together. But I am better. I guess I have a conflict of interest in your test results. Anyway, those same doctors can translate the ancient languages that she speaks. Sometimes they are not needed. Sometimes Maria knows what was said to her. Other times she can't remember. She seems to go into a trance. She's the key to much of our technology."

I looked around the room and saw others whispering while they waited for Maria to stop humming and make contact. The hum turned into some kind of chant. I couldn't understand the sounds that came out of their mouths. Feeling secure enough to talk, I whispered back to Josef. "Did Maria help you with your time machine?"

"She helped me decode a few messages. These aliens, or advanced beings, as I prefer to call them, have somehow adopted us Germans to share their secrets. This only gives Hitler more credence to his theory on Aryan superiority. He believes that we are their descendants."

"But you are not so sure?" I asked rhetorically. After sizing Josef up the entire day, I decided to label him a monster, just like the rest of them, but he had a rational side. I was under the impression that he didn't believe every idea that Hitler was selling. The women were still humming and chanting. I approximated at least ten minutes had gone by. "If Germans come from these advanced beings, then where do the advanced beings come from?"

Josef looked around to make sure no one was listening to us and whispered, "Maria has made it very clear that these beings are from the star of Aldebaran. It's sixty-four light years away. You know about the constellation Taurus?" I nodded, wishing I knew more about astronomy, wishing Jay was around to teach me. Josef continued. "Aldebaran is the eye of the bull in the constellation. They had a queen many thousands of years ago who travelled here and helped our civilization. Queen Isias. Sound familiar?"

I shrugged. All I could think of was ISIS, the terrorist group. But he wouldn't know who they were.

"Queen Isias sounds like Isis. Doesn't it?"

"Yes, it does. Like the Egyptians and the pyramids. So, it's not a coincidence?"

Josef replied, "Exactly. She and her minions settled in the Middle East and gradually made their way to Thule or the northern part of Europe. Thule is where the Germanic tribes came from. Maria even said that these aliens ruled Atlantis."

"I thought the Annunaki ruled the Middle East and Atlantis. Some have called them the Nephilim. Enoch wrote about them. They were the fallen angels." I looked around the room. Maria and her followers stopped chanting and continued to hum. Others were whispering. I was under the impression this was the norm on how their meetings started.

"Very good, Maya. But the Annunaki come from Nibiru, not Aldebaran. They are a different race, an inferior race."

"So, there is a hierarchy of alien races? Some extraterrestrials are considered superior to others?"

"Yes. Some have achieved more than others. We are only the sum of our ancestor's achievements." Josef paused. His poker face made him hard to read. Did I hit a nerve talking about another race of aliens? He watched Maria for a moment and then leaned in and whispered, "You are probably wondering what Vril is."

"I am. Why did you all name your society the Vril Society? Is that another name for these Advanced Beings?" I asked.

"Yes, no, maybe." Josef smiled. It was the only warmth he had given me since I met him inside of his farmhouse. "We call our society the Vril Society because of a novel. The aliens were called Vril-ya. You ever hear of *The Coming Race*?" I shook my head. "It's a science fiction novel written by a man named Lytton, but it's really much more. It describes the Vril-ya people who lived within the Earth. They could create energy with their minds, either for good or evil. Vril refers to their energy. It gives credibility to the hollow earth theory. Anyway, the story is believed to be a thinly veiled truth that introduces us to the aliens who are here."

A lightning bolt shot through my brain. Jay and I weren't the only ones writing novels about aliens who set up camp on planet Earth. I wondered if this Lytton was another one of my relatives. These aliens wanted everyone to know about them, but in small doses. They had been using us to act as their historians while disguising it as fiction. Was all the world really a stage for these things? Were we nothing but puppets? What were they using the Germans for during World War II? What are they using us for now?

Josef looked at my face, but misread my thoughts. "You probably think all of this is insane. Hitler has a secret society based on a novel. But that's only a small part of it. Because of Maria, the novel, and several other factors, we have an advantage of air power the world has never seen. And what we have in the works... It will change the way wars are fought."

"When did this society begin?" I asked.

"This society has been around for over twenty years. Maria has been here the whole time, channeling the aliens, allowing us all to communicate. So please, take this little history lesson back with you to 2017. Win or lose, this society, these aliens, all of it are not going away. I see your doubts," Josef said with a look of caution. "You came out of a time machine from the future. This must look very primitive to you. A female alien communicator and a science fiction novelist give a political genius the foundation to wage a world war. But we built so much more than our army, than our weapons. All of it comes from these advanced beings."

He had no idea what I was thinking. How long were these Advanced Beings using us? I kept quiet about my true feelings and encouraged Josef to talk. All of a sudden the humming and the chanting stopped. All whispered conversations, tapping, shifting and loud breathing stopped. The silence was unnerving. Josef raised his eyebrows and gave me a look. Maria was about to speak. Every blue eye in the Eagle's Nest was focused on her. My brown eyes wandered. I was more curious about the facial expressions of Hitler and his generals. They didn't look at Maria with lust, but with awe. She was their goddess, perhaps even their messiah.

Maria began babbling short phonetic sounds. I couldn't repeat anything that she said and assumed it was Akkadian. The language was so different than English or even European languages which I didn't speak, but had heard before.

The professors were the only ones writing every word that came out of Maria's mouth on their writing tablets. Their intensity suggested that their lives depended on what she said.

While Maria babbled on, her underlings hummed softly. Was this for effect? I wanted to believe this was real. The Nazi's ties with aliens would somehow legitimize all of the conspiracy talk that came from Jay, Glenn, Paula, and Mercedes. But this had a staged feel to it.

Every few minutes that went by, Maria would say something in Akkadian or Aramaic or whatever ancient language to the woman with the darkest hair. The woman was called Sigrun and she seemed to be the second highest in the chain of command. Like Maria, she was stunning. Sigrun announced something to all of us in German. Maria's voice changed. The language she now spoke was still unrecognizable, but different than the first language. Her blue eyes were not a soft, pale blue anymore, but a bright, almost neon royal blue and occasionally rolled back into her head, showing nothing but white eyeballs.

Her new voice was deep. It was a man's voice and I had heard it before. Where did I know it from? Several more minutes went by with her speaking in a new language. I think she was describing a time machine, Glenn's machine. There was no logical explanation how I knew that. Sigrun was scribbling on a drawing pad. I had a sick sense that she was drawing the time capsule in the round room at T.A.H.

Maria's eyes continued to glow royal blue and roll back. Her voice became sharp. I felt anger, but not necessarily from her. Whatever had possessed her body was very upset. She stood up and yelled sounds as if she was reciting an alphabet. She turned around in the circle for everyone to see her, and then violently spun like an out-of-control ballerina. Our eyes met. She stopped as if she was never in motion and stood in front of me.

"Maya Smock. We are here," Maria said in her male voice. "Your will is in vain."

The hair on the back of my neck sprung up, leaving me in a flight or fight frame of mind. My will? What exactly was she talking about? Before I could even guess, Maria lunged at me, swinging her long, skinny arm towards my left eye. I ducked, and then pushed her as hard as I could, sending her to the ground by her minions. She lay motionless. Sigrun kneeled to the floor and stroked her cheek while chanting in some ancient language.

The calm little journey of alien communication turned into a three-ring circus. Hitler glared at me and screamed orders to his men. Pure instinct, minus all common sense, took over. A man behind me had a pistol strapped on his chest. I reached inside his military jacket and grabbed it. The man looked at me with confusion.

Hitler was across the room, irate, still barking and growling like a pissed off Rottweiler. I stepped closer in between the chaos of the crowd. I was going to die regardless. Might as well die for a noble cause instead of dying as one of his many casualties. I pointed the pistol once I had a clear view. I squeezed the trigger. It was over.

Chapter Nineteen

Present Day
Ruby Mountains, Nevada

Glenn was infuriated. How dare that piece of shit husband of Maya's threaten him, blackmail him. He was nothing but a sociopath. His anger would have to wait. He needed that novel. Paula and Mercedes were right. He couldn't use Eric as another rat in an experiment. All Doctor Blacksmith had was a theory. Maybe the novel would offer more.

Glenn thought back to the last time they tried to genetically alter a human being. What they had done to the man was illegal, immoral, unethical, and inhumane. Chuck bought a sixty-one year old man from a Chinese prison with T.A.H.'s money. The man cost five thousand dollars. The goal was to use him as their rat in an experiment that was designed to reverse aging. The man was promised a get-out-of-jail free card after the experiment was over. It was an easy sell-freedom, youth, and a chance at a new life in America. The purchased prisoner was more than enthusiastic.

Chuck had left out most of the details. The man was not told that he was the first human ever to be altered with their genetic findings. Although their theory of turning back the clock by gene editing seemed promising, it was practiced on animals with only limited success. Doctor Blacksmith wanted to try out her procedure on a fresh cadaver. Chuck offered her the real thing.

Doctor Blacksmith inserted cloned embryo stem cells in their prisoner's DNA with her gene gun. She believed these cells were associated with aging. She extracted some of his genes as well, completely altering all of the DNA within the man's body. Everyone involved in the experiment was excited to see if she discovered the fountain of youth, even immortality.

The sixty-one year old man became younger in every area-muscle mass, I.Q. points, reflexes, endurance, as well as tighter skin, disappearing age spots, and more hair. He reversed his aging process at warp speed. In less than a week, he appeared to be in his twenties. But the experiment would not stop reversing the man's age. In another three days, the man transformed into a pre-pubescent child. Another week went by and he was an embryo.

No one knew how to keep the man alive. In a panic, Glenn dumped the embryo inside of an aquarium filled with salt water while Lori frantically tried to put the aging genes she extracted back inside of the man's DNA. All of it was too late. The nameless sixty-one year old man was nothing more than a tiny mass of dead cells. Everyone, especially Glenn, felt responsible. After the deadly experiment, they made a pact about sticking with animals until theories became proven facts. Extraterrestrial DNA was never even an option in their experiments. They were chartering unknown territory and everyone knew it.

Maybe Maya's novel had new information, DNA locations, encoded procedures, anything that would raise the odds of Eric's survival. Doctor Blacksmith would only be able to guess at this moment that the time travel sequence involved Hitler's number, the number eight. Everyone knew that she would never kill another human being based on a guess. Chuck would, but he was the physicist, not the geneticist. Glenn needed her expertise. If she was going to alter Eric for the time capsule, she needed that book.

Once Glenn was off the phone with Claude Kazinsky, he went up to the lab to talk with Lori. Chuck was there with her, comparing slides.

"Lori, I wanted to talk with you. Glad Chuck is also here. Got some good news, but also got some bad news."

Both doctors looked up from their microscopes, oblivious to what Glenn just said. Lori was the first to speak. "Yes, of course. We were looking at Maya's and Jay's genes. They both have the H gene in the same location. They both seem to have other genes, human, but rare and in different spots of the sequence. I'm not sure if that has anything to do with time travel. When you look at Eric's genes, he has junk DNA in the same area. Maybe we could resequence…"

"Lori, you've done so much amazing work already. I can't believe you even found the time travel gene. But I don't want to guess any more than you do. I think I know a way to know for certain. Maya wrote a second novel. It's not published yet. It might give us the rest of the information that we need," Glenn said.

Lori seemed annoyed. "Okay, then where's the book?"

"Well, that's the bad news. The book is on the hard drive of her computer. And her computer is with her husband, Claude."

Glenn told them both how Maya thought it was Claude who tried to kill her. He also shared his threats on talking with the media.

"We'll get that son-of-a-bitch. I'll bring Devon. He and I will get that computer. Claude will be too scared to talk to anyone. We'll rough him up first, and then…"

Lori looked at Chuck with pity. "This isn't China. We can't go roughing people up. The whole thing could backfire, and then we'd be up, front, and center in a media buzz. It's already a miracle that they haven't found this place with Jay's death and now Maya's rescue. You said that Claude has the media outside of his door. How are we going to break-in without getting noticed? Let's be smart about this. He already insinuated that he'd flip the script and try and blame you, Glenn, for killing her. Well, she's missing in time right now. Hard to prove that you didn't kill her. She was seen flying off in a helicopter that could easily be traced here."

Glenn pointed to the microscopes and Lori nodded. He took a peek at the slides they were comparing. "I'm not a scientist, just a lawyer-turned-TV host. You two have taught me everything that I know in terms of DNA, inertia, centrifuges, well, all of it. Despite our initial failure…"

"Initial? You blind-sided me into killing that poor man!" Lori snapped. It was clear to all of them that she still resented them for getting her involved.

"Yes, and I take full responsibility, but now you and Chuck know so much more. Chuck, she's right about Claude. We can't operate that way. You both have the DNA of two extraterrestrial hybrids, maybe guessing would be more like almost knowing. Maybe you could…"

"Glenn and Chuck, listen for just a minute, I am not putting another human in danger. That poor man. I think about how he died. It was so gruesome. I can't do it. You want me to kill Eric, then I quit. You know what, I think I'll join Claude at his media press conference as well. You want to break both of my legs, Chuck?"

"So, what do you want me to do? Bring Claude into the fold?" Glenn asked.

"He's a gold-digger. Throw some money at him and make him go away," Chuck said with a knowing look meant only for Glenn. Glenn nodded back.

"He'll probably copy everything on that hard drive, if he hasn't already," Lori added.

"Yes, but the book was going to be published anyway. The average person won't understand the code, let alone know how it applies to time travel and genetics. He's bluffing on all of it. Glenn, Lori is right. Call the fucker up and pay him off. We'll eventually get even." Chuck looked at Glenn again. Claude would not be getting a dime. The appeasing conversation was meant to calm Lori down.

Glenn nodded. "I'll send Mercedes and Paula, maybe even Eric, if he's up for it. We've got some time to kill."

"No, no. I want to handle this. And I promise not to hurt the man," Chuck said. "I'll bring Devon from security. We'll get what you need."

Glenn looked down at the floor. Devon ran T.A.H. like the Mafia originally ran Las Vegas. He had a way of keeping off any and all trespassers through unconventional means. He knew exactly what Chuck had in mind and chose to turn a blind's eye. All that mattered at this point was getting Maya's sequel.

Chapter Twenty

Present Day
Las Vegas, Nevada

Claude Kazinsky had all of the confirmation he needed after speaking with Glenn. The man's voice cracked after Claude made several accusations. He wasn't the most skilled liar, but he was pretty damned good at omitting information. Maya had him worried. If she was alive, what'd she know? Did she see Sam and Allie? There were too many unknown variables for his comfort level, but one thing was certain. Glenn would be calling back with a lucrative offer in exchange for the novel.

Claude turned Maya's laptop on and inserted a memory stick, copying every file that she had saved. There weren't many documents because the computer was new. He wondered if she bought it, or if Jay McCallister bought it for her. It was much too high-tech.

Once Claude was finished copying her files, he looked out of the window. A small crowd had formed, waiting for his statement regarding his estranged wife. He turned his phone back on. Forty-one messages since he last spoke with Glenn. It had only been a couple of hours. He briefly listened to the messages, deleting the ones who were left by reporters. Allie left a new one. Delete. It was another blackmail threat about him giving her money. She turned out to be a real greedy bitch. He failed to see the irony of the blackmailer getting blackmailed. The last message was from Glenn, sooner than Claude had expected.

The message said, "I want that laptop. How much do you think is fair?" Click. Claude admired Glenn's directness. He had no idea what the book was worth to the egg-heads over at T.A.H., but it was really important. Maya's sequel needed another read.

Claude's ability to speed read had served him well as literary agent, but this time, he needed to slow down and look outside of the story for clues that made the book so valuable. The code with DNA proteins that appeared in the first novel continued in the second novel. He only could guess that the code was some genetic strand. The geeks at T.A.H. were splicing and cloning and who the hell knew what else. The book must have been part of an experiment. What struck Claude as odd was the epilogue. It didn't sit right the first time he read it. Now it glared at him, challenging him to figure out what was written.

The writing style was completely different from the rest of the book. The sentence structure was short throughout the ten pages. The adjectives were simple and repeated themselves. Maya wrote the first book and the second book in first person, but the epilogue was written in third person. Claude read it a third time. The content served its purpose by wrapping up the story and tying up loose ends, but he didn't believe Maya wrote it. The epilogue seemed to have a dual meaning.

Maya would not have been the first author to write a fictional story that was meant to be an outer layer of something more. Maybe the coding was only part of it. Maybe the actual story was meant to be a thin veil of truth. That would of course mean that aliens were real and the government knew about it for a long time, two conspiracies with legs. Claude continued to read. Maybe Maya would make him a believer.

He looked at each sentence and paragraph with scrutiny. No more DNA proteins. The epilogue did have a code. It was clear that Maya encoded the name Lansatti throughout the last ten pages. After reading it a fourth time, it was even clearer that the wording was not a coincidence. The short sentences all started with "L". The second and third words all started with "A" and "N". And then the rest of the sentence would read with words that started with "S", "A", "T", "T", and "I". Every sentence had eight words that started with the letters of the Lansatti name.

Claude heard of the Lansatti family. He Googled them for more information. The family was old money, first in Italy and then America. A few of the family members had ties with Mussolini during World War II. Although it was a large family, Claude would have to guess that Leonardo Lansatti might be one of the members or the member that Maya referred to throughout her epilogue. Why him? Claude had no idea.

Leonardo had never been involved in any scandals. He was still married to the same woman who he met decades ago. They adopted two boys from Romania after seeing the boys suffer in a decrepit orphanage. The boys had grown and had children of their own. Leonardo lived an opulent, but quiet life of a billionaire.

Leonardo ran VYA Energy, one of the biggest energy companies in the world. His career expanded into politics, first as a California congressman, and then as Secretary of Energy under the last administration. He currently was helping the United Nations with some kind of energy bank for mankind. *Saint Leonardo*, thought Claude as he read the man's biography. The only thing missing was his Nobel Prize. What the hell did he have to do with aliens, T.A.H. and Maya? Was she zeroing in on another family member?

Claude read the last chapter and made a bold decision. The ending closed off the story, yet left an opening for a third book of Maya's *The Master Race* series. With a click of a mouse and the press of a button, the epilogue was gone. If Maya was alive, she would notice. Soon he would find out the truth.

Claude's phone continued to chirp and his doorbell started to buzz. The mini-crowd of reporters was getting restless. Claude had an idea. He returned Glenn's call. "Glenn, I want to talk some business. But before we make a deal, I have other business to take care of. Please feel free to listen in."

Claude could hear his heavy breathing, obviously upset and wanting this negotiation to be over. The second floor of the Spanish style mansion had a large game room with double French doors that led out to a balcony. Underneath the balcony were at least two dozen reporters and cameramen who waited for Claude's statement. Claude opened up the doors to the balcony and looked down at them as if he was a king. All eyes and camera lenses turned up towards him.

With the theatric flare of a Shakespearean actor, Claude said, "Hello, Media. I'd like to make a blanket statement." He held his iPhone in one hand and could hear Glenn's protests coming out of the receiver. "Maya is still alive. She is at her newly inherited *They Are Here Foundation*, studying something top secret."

Glenn was pleading in the phone. "Claude, we don't need the attention. Name your price. Just stop, please."

Claude lowered his voice into the phone and softly said, "I want half of a billion dollars sent to me in an offshore account or I will tell all of my so-called crackpot conspiracy theories to the press."

"I don't have that kind of disposable money…"

Claude interrupted him. "Then you better find it fast. You have forty-eight hours. I will call in twenty-four hours with more information." Click.

He didn't know if he loved the money or the game, but both had their perks.

The reporters all asked questions at once, causing Claude to hold up his arms. "I don't know what is going on at the foundation, but I was once thought to be a suspect in my wife's disappearance. Now it's become apparent that I was not involved. Based on her new inheritance as well as being named as Jay McCallister's successor, I believe she was taken by our own United States government. But something must have gone wrong. It's been recently reported that she is indeed alive. That is all I have for now. Once more proof and evidence come to light, I will call a press conference. Now please get off of my property."

Chapter Twenty-One

1970
London, England

Kate was dead. Movements and words were seen and heard in slow motion, but everything else moved at warped speed. Andreas felt more like a spectator as he watched his life play out over the next few days.

Andreas stayed for the funeral and helped Lori with all of the arrangements. He met Kate's friends and colleagues along with her dead husband's friends and colleagues. Again, he was reminded of the life she had created after Broom Lake. When all of the formalities were over, she was buried next to her husband with a cross on her tombstone. Andreas wished it was his grave that she was buried next to. He dreamt of the hospital making a mistake, of him and Kate living in her flat, and then of him dying first and avoiding the pain of loss. Karma had a way of giving others exactly what they deserved.

The cross on Kate's tombstone symbolized her deep faith. Apparently, she had found God after Broom Lake. Was this her husband's influence? Her born-again Christianity didn't seem to fit with her life of experience. It was another layer to her that he had not seen. Maybe he never knew her at all. Now his window of opportunity was permanently shut. At least he told her that he loved her.

Andreas made arrangements to go back home, trying to focus on something else. His work with Bolantano could also be over. He might have screwed it all up before barely getting started. Before packing, Lori talked him into staying for another day. How could he say no? She had just lost her mother. Her father's grave was also fresh.

Andreas barely knew Kate's daughter, but sensed she was frightened. She even inferred that Kate's heart attack was intentional. Heart attacks were known within military circles of being easily induced. Air embolisms, potassium chloride, and calcium gluconate were just some of the more common ways to kill someone without causing suspicion. But why? Kate's top secret work happened decades ago, or did Hanover Auto have her working on something for the military? Maybe her death was related his visit. He wondered how much about Kate's past Lori knew about.

It was a beautiful spring afternoon in London. The fog had finally lifted from the city, yet still failed to lift from Andreas's mind. Lori wanted him to pick her up at Kate's house, now her house. He arrived at noon and offered to take her out for lunch.

"I can't eat a thing," Lori said. "How about a drink? Getting bloody plastered is just what I need. There's a pub right up the road. Let's walk."

Lori wore a wool sweater and jeans and carried a large tote. Her dark hair was swept up in a bun. She looked so much like Kate. Sticking out of her tote were the brown and manila edges of envelopes and folders. He assumed she had something to show him. As they walked down the sidewalk, Lori would frequently stop and turn her head. Her beautiful hazel eyes bulged with fear.

"You're obviously scared. You looked scared back at the hospital. I thought you were trying to tell me something. Are you in some kind of trouble? Was your mother in some kind of trouble? You can tell me anything. I know that I'm not your father…" Andreas said.

Lori abruptly cut him off. "Actually, Robert, you are my father. I have the paperwork right here to prove it."

She patted her tote bag. "As soon we have the opportunity to sit down, I'll explain."

"What?" Andreas stopped walking and leaned on streetlight pole to steady himself. He breathed heavily and then lit a cigarette.

"Do you think one of those is going to help you right now?" Lori asked. She put her hand on Andreas's shoulder. "You're probably doing some math in your head. You think that I'm eighteen. That's what my mother told you. How could you be my father when you hadn't seen my mom in twenty years? I'll help you with that one. She lied. I'm really twenty years old, twenty-one in December. She wasn't ready to tell you. When you two broke up, for lack of a better term, she left the U.S. pregnant. She was over forty and I was her only chance at motherhood. She thought that I was worth the social ramifications of her time and was fully prepared to be branded a whore. Then my stepfather came along. He didn't care that she was pregnant with someone else's baby. He fell in love with her and nothing else mattered. He was that kind of man-ahead of his time, never caring much for the judgment of others. He loved her, hell, he bloody worshipped her. You know, climb the highest mountain. My mom loved him, but never as much as he loved her. He was a wonderful father in case you are wondering. And she didn't tell me about you until that baby with the weird crystal rock showed up in my orphanage. So, I'm trying to process this new information as well. Please, let's walk."

Andreas put out his cigarette and kept pace with her brisk walk. "I'm forever in your stepfather's debt. Please, I had no idea. She never told me." Lori continued scrutinizing her surroundings while they walked. "How did they meet?"

"Neighbors. And spare yourself the guilt trip. I am well aware that you had no idea. I am well aware of many things. You used her as a scapegoat when your little operation had a setback. She said that one of the engineers she worked with set her up by planting baby supplies in her desk. He was jealous of her in so many ways. You believed it all. You fired her, and then broke her heart. The pub is just another block ahead."

Lori wasn't letting Andreas off the hook. He couldn't believe that Kate would have told her the details about Operation Chrome. What else did she know? But the more she talked, the more he liked her. She reminded him of Kate, smart as hell and tough as nails. She was her mother's daughter alright.

Andreas began to hope that they might have a relationship, maybe a friendship. She was his last chance of being anyone's father. His two other daughters hated him and he knew it was all of his fault. He had knack for pushing away the people who were most important in his life. Kate left him a gift. Maybe this time things would be different. He was going to give this everything he had. He hadn't realized it, but tears were streaming down his face as they walked. He hated men who cried. He wished the tears would stop. Lori was still too busy being on the look-out to notice. She glanced at his face.

"Buggers! Get a hold of yourself. Now is not the time for this. Please, I am begging you. We don't need to draw attention."

Andreas discreetly blotted his face with his sleeve and walked even faster. Lori was at the pace of a slow jog. "Is someone following us?"

"Yes. Behind us there's one who just ducked off into that alley. Then there are two up ahead who seem to be waiting. See those two men at the intersection? One is sitting on the bench and one is standing by the trash, talking on his radio. They haven't moved for several minutes since I spotted them. They don't appear to be friends, something is off."

Andreas saw two of the three men Lori described. They were young, white, and blended in with the rest of the neighborhood. She was spot on. Their attempt at looking casual was phony. "You keep watching them and I'll cover the rest of the proximity. Turn. We'll see if they are really interested in us."

Lori and Andreas turned the corner before the major intersection. There was a dress shop they passed with another entrance as they turned the corner. They ducked inside and hurried to the front window of the store. Both of the men Lori was watching were gone.

"Good eye. They're tailing us alright. Hope the third man bowed out." Andreas looked at the racks of dresses. "You in the mood for a new dress?"

Lori smiled. "Not today. I guess we'll wait it out."

The elderly shop clerk approached them and asked if they needed help.

"Actually yes, is there a way out of this store without using one of the two exits?" Andreas asked.

The woman looked out the front window. "Cops?" Andreas shrugged.

"Yes, there is a way. But it's only for paying customers."

Andreas understood the woman perfectly. Having Lori change her clothes was a good idea anyway. Within minutes, Lori changed into a khaki skirt and floral shirt. She picked out a jean jacket as well to take the place of the sweater. Andreas bought a black leather jacket and ditched his windbreaker. It wasn't much of a disguise, but might buy them some time.

After the purchase, Andreas and Lori were taken up a flight of stairs from the backroom of the store. The clerk led them up to the second floor of building.

"This floor is all apartments," the clerk said and then waved them off, locking the door once they were apart from her store.

Andreas and Lori walked down a long hallway of brass-numbered doors to the staircase of the main entrance of the building. It was a grand staircase with white spindles and a curved bannister. Andreas could see a bank of mailboxes on the first floor along with a doorman who sat behind a tall ornate desk. A three story window took up the foyer-entrance of the apartments. It gave them a strategic view of the corner that they had just turned.

Andreas sat on the top step of the second floor landing, and lit a cigarette. He offered Lori one and she declined. "Good. Glad you don't smoke. These things will kill you."

"And so will those men outside," Lori said as she pointed out the giant window.

Andreas nodded. "Hope this place is locked. The third man finally surfaced. Looks like we lost them for now. Did you know you were being watched?"

She nodded. "I had a feeling. The pub is just up the next block. Bollocks, I really wanted a drink. Great place. Very charming. You would have loved it. English crests and armor all over the place. A real gem for tourists and the perfect place to talk."

"I'll get there someday. Or shall I say, you'll take me there someday. But this place is as good as any to talk. So talk, before those three stooges start checking the local businesses and figure out where we are."

Lori sat down on the step next to Andreas. "Alright, then." She fished out one of the folders from her tote bag. "Here's the first part. My birth certificate. I was born at the end of 1950. My stepdad's name is on the birth certificate, but he had type A blood as did my mom. I have B. What type do you have?"

Andreas observed the document. "I have B as well. Lori, I believe you. I know I can never make up for lost time…"

"You want a relationship. Great, so do I. Even though I hardly know you, I believe that I can trust you. But there is more, so much more. So here goes. I am sure that Mom was murdered. Her heart attack was not a natural heart attack. Here, it's an x-ray of her heart." Lori handed Andreas a stack of photos. "It's one year old. There's some plaque, but the doctor said it was basically healthy. She took high blood pressure medication. Now look at this picture. I took this Friday from the hospital." Lori handed Andreas a Polaroid photo of Kate in her hospital bed. "Look at her arm. See the pinhole marking in it? As if someone stuck her with a needle? I noticed it at the house. Once the ambulance got her to the hospital, I thought it best to take a picture of her arm. The doctors dismissed the whole thing, claiming the pin hole was from the IV that the nurses gave her."

Andreas noticed the large red mark immediately. "Oh no. But who would want to kill her? She worked for a car manufacturer, right? She was an engineer who married a professor. Doesn't make any sense, unless it's from her time spent at Broom Lake. I visited you a month ago. Is it because of me?"

"You? Why would a visit from a U.S. general who was her former fiancé cause suspicion?" Lori asked. Andreas sensed some sarcasm. "I'm sorry. Maybe your visit had something to do with it. Didn't you both used to work with aliens and UFOs?" Lori looked deep into Andreas's eyes. She was judging his reaction.

A door slammed, causing both of them to jolt from their seated positions on the floor. Down the hall a woman had just closed one of the doors. Andreas smiled at the woman as she headed towards them. He stood up to let her pass. Once she was out of the building, he asked, "Your mother told you that?"

"She did, but I figured it out before her confession. You see, I was always a curious kid. I loved puzzles and secret codes, all of it. Mother was like the ultimate enigma. I spied on her for years, up until the day she died. It wasn't until your visit that she finally leveled with me. And to answer your question, I believe her death was mainly related to her position at Hanover Auto. She might have started designing cars and engines, but she soon graduated to using alternative forms of energy in some of their more specialized vehicles. Did you know there was a landing a few years back, here in Great Britain? A landing like in Roswell." Andreas shrugged. "Anyway, someone at Hanover had to have known about the work she did with you along with the Nazi scientists." Lori let him thumb through the remainder of the photos.

Andreas studied them closely. The aliens in the photos had a darker colored skin that looked rough and bumpy. In one photo Andreas could see the being's teeth. They were large and pointy, like a predator's. None of them had any hair. They looked like an odd combination of humans and reptiles. The space ship in the picture was not disc-shaped, but shaped like a cigar or a long cylinder with pointed ends. He smiled. "These beings, or as we used to call them…"

"Advanced Beings," Lori interrupted.

He smiled. "Yes. They are not the same ones your mother and I studied. This spacecraft is different."

"That's what Mom said. What do you think all of this means?"

"I don't know. Maybe we are being invaded? I think you're right about your mom. Someone killed her. She knew more than I know, more than the Nazis who I work with. She was a liability to someone. My airbase must have a leak. Two races of aliens and two different kinds of spacecraft just don't coincidentally fall in one person's lap."

"Robert, our friends are back. They just came out of the drugstore across the street."

Chapter Twenty-Two

1944
The Eagle's Nest, Germany

I did it! I fucking did it! I killed Hitler and changed history forever! The pistol, still warm, felt comfortable in my hand as I watched Hitler topple to the ground like a house of cards. His top cronies clustered around him. Were they trying to revive him or was it all pretend? Maybe their loyalty only existed in the history books. I watched with a sense of triumph.

Josef rushed over to me as the room erupted into pandemonium. His icy blue eyes were filled with terror. "Do you understand what you just did? We're both dead. You stupid, stupid..." His mouth moved, but I couldn't hear his voice.

I couldn't hear anyone's voice. The room was thick with an eerie silence. I felt an omnipotent presence take over and instinctually knew that this force had hijacked the room. Then I felt a pull, as if a giant vacuum had been unleashed. I looked around the room. Everyone except me had slowed down to a frozen state, all looking like mannequins in some kind of midstream pose.

The banquet room looked more like a three dimensional still photo. I ran over to Hitler, squeezing in between the two immoveable statues who were bent over his lifeless body. He laid on the floor in a small puddle of blood. His body was still warm. Then the floor shook violently as if an earthquake had erupted. Nobody's position changed except mine. I was thrown to the middle of the circle, next to Maria who was also laying on the ground. I then remembered that I had pushed her after she tried to attack me. What the hell was going on?

Whatever force took over the moment, had finally turned the volume back on. I heard voices of the people inside of the room, but their words sounded like garble. I thought of Maria's performance. It wasn't the kind of garble she was uttering. Seconds later, the room filled with jerky, odd movements. The monsters were waking up? No. They were moving backward as if a cosmic rewind was in play. Soon Hitler was off of the floor, standing up and screaming.

My body involuntarily moved back to the chest holster of the soldier I had taken the gun from. Some unexplained force compelled me to put the gun back. I kept moving backward to the point where I pushed Maria away after she attacked me while conducting her alien séance. The garble everyone was spouting stopped. German language filled the room. I was back to where I started. Some almighty force had pushed the reset button on me. I was helpless. Either the universe did not want Hitler dead or the universe did not want me to get killed. The former option made more sense.

Was I the only one in the room who knew what had just happened? Hitler still looked as if he wanted to kill me. Martin Bormann rushed up to him out of nowhere with a stack of papers in his hand. He, Hitler, and a few other men who Josef had called professors had a brief conversation. My ears were ringing. They were talking about me. I was clearly being vetted. Should I go for the pistol again? Maybe now the time is right. I could shoot all of them. Hitler wasn't the only demonic creature in the room.

I looked at the soldier I had just taken the gun from. He seemed disoriented. Before I could make my move, someone tapped me on the shoulder.

Maria was no longer on the floor, but standing with Josef. Both of them approached me. Josef whispered, "She saw what you did. She said you tried to kill the *Fuehrer*. You kill him, you kill us. You also kill your chance at going home." He ushered Maria and I to a cozy bar in the corner of the room away from potential eavesdroppers.

I couldn't figure out how Maria knew what I attempted. She, like the rest of the room, was motionless. I felt dizzy. Maria's and Josef's faces became blurry. My knees buckled and I tumbled towards the floor. Both Maria and Josef pulled me back up. "Let me make us all a drink. We all could use one." Josef ducked behind the small bar and poured three amber-colored drinks in cut crystal glasses.

"Is she going to hit me?" I asked. Maria's demeanor had changed since she attacked me while in the circle. She was now very solemn. If everything had reversed, then how would Maria know what I tried to do? Did Hitler know I tried to kill him?

As we drank our liquor, some of the soldiers walked up to Maria wanting to talk to her about her performance. Without fear, she waved them off. I couldn't understand what exactly was said, but she was in complete control. She said a few things to Josef. He then explained that she didn't speak English, but he would translate. I couldn't help but wonder how this woman spoke Babylonian, Hebrew, Akkadian, Sumerian, and who the hell knew what else, but not English. As he spoke, I guzzled my drink. I think it was whiskey.

"Are you out of your mind?" Josef whispered, and then looked around the room. I shrugged.

I debated on whether I should run or try to talk my way out of this. Hitler was clearly alive so no harm was done. Choosing my words carefully, I asked, "Did you see me kill the *Fuehrer*? How? Why is he over there, alive and talking with his henchmen?"

"Watch your tone," Josef warned. "Maria saw you. That is why she lunged at you when she was in the circle. She wanted to stop you."

"But you didn't see me kill Hitler?" Josef shook his head. "Since I'm still alive, no one else but Maria saw me kill him either. Correct?"

He nodded, and then translated my words back to Maria. She appeared to be angry, and then quickly responded to my brilliant defense. She then looked me square in the eye and pointed her finger at the oblivious soldier I took the pistol from. Josef repeated the whole story. I now understood the respect Maria warranted among the crowd.

"Josef, ask her if her associates over there also saw me," I said. Maria grabbed my chin and turned it to her face and stared. I heard her voice calling me a liar, but her mouth didn't move. I looked at Josef. Did he hear her?

Josef shook his head. "Maria is trying to communicate with you through brain waves."

"I think she just called me a liar," I said. Maria nodded. With her other hand, she tapped my head. Josef nodded as if to encourage me to try to talk to this woman without words. Things kept getting weirder.

Okay then. Let's say that I did try to kill Hitler. Why isn't he dead and why doesn't he seem to have any recollection of the event? I thought as I looked into her beautiful pale blue eyes.

Josef refilled all of our drinks. The booze stopped me from shaking and calmed my nerves. All of this was impossible. Yet here I was, knowing full well I wasn't dreaming. Now I was talking with a woman through brainwaves.

You are stuck in a paradox, Maria said without talking.

"Paradox? Josef, I think she told me I'm stuck in a paradox. What is that?"

"It's a contradiction, an inconsistency, an impossibility, an absurdity," Josef said.

I whispered, "Like being able to time travel. Maria being able to see the future. Me attempting to kill…" Josef nodded. "Can you or she explain any of this?"

You are the real thing. You are the future, the reason why they come, Maria thought as she grabbed my chin and looked deeply in my eyes.

"She says I am the real thing," I said to Josef.

"Yes, she believes you are a hybrid, part extraterrestrial and part human. She is not sure of your race."

"Neither am I. I might be part Mexican, part American Indian, maybe even black…"

Josef interrupted me and began speaking German. He and Maria talked over me for a minute, then he switched languages.

"Maya, neither of us care about your race here on earth. We are more interested in the alien side of your ancestry. There are several extraterrestrial races who have landed here. She doesn't know if you are an ally or foe. I told her that you didn't come here to kill Hitler, but rather you were forced to be here by me. I took you here as my trophy, to prove that my time machine works. Your reason for being here matters. You see, when you tried to kill Hitler, you proved that you are trapped inside of a predestination paradox. Time travel has rules. You cannot change the future. We are all predestined to live our lives a certain way, which will have a certain outcome. If you keep on trying to kill Hitler, sooner or later your attempts will serve to his predestination, not yours. He is protected from outside interference. Those who want to kill him can't."

"Wait, someone besides me tried this?" I asked, dumbfounded. "Other time travelers have come here to kill him?"

"Others from this era have tried and failed." Josef rattled something off to Maria and she responded. "But I will ask Maria about other time travelers." There was another lull while the two of them whispered in German. "Very good, Maya. Actually, you are correct. Other time travelers have tried. And like you, they have failed. Don't try it again. You will fail. She knows he will lose this war and has even told him. It's the one piece of advice he refuses to hear."

This time I took Maria's hand and placed it on my chin. She smiled. I thought as deeply as I could. *Are you going to tell Hitler what I tried to do?*

No. She shook her head.

Josef watched us communicate as if this was nothing out of the ordinary. His beady blue eyes occasionally scanned the room for eavesdroppers. He then said, "Maria finds you much too fascinating. She wants you to speak tonight. All of us do. She wants you to sit in the circle and tell us about yourself, bits and pieces of the future, obviously leaving out how Germany loses. But we want to know anything and everything about the future." Maria said something in German and Josef laughed. "She says that she is jealous. For the first time in many years she is no longer the most interesting person in the room."

"You want me to speak inside of that circle? What? So, I would be the guest speaker at this lunatic convention. What then? Hitler kills me? This is crazy," I said. Maria grabbed my chin again and I pushed her hand away. "I am done with all of this. Please, Josef, can we go now? I've fulfilled my end of the bargain we struck. Now it's time you fulfill your end. I just want to go home, to the present time."

Hitler and two of his top brass were approaching the bar. It looked like I wasn't going home quite yet. He barked out something in German to Josef and Maria. Both of them nodded.

Maria took my chin in her hand again and looked at me with pity. *You have no choice. Come. I will sit with you for a while.* The exquisite woman led me inside of the circle. Everyone resumed their seats. I was now the star of this little soiree. I took a seat next to Maria. Her group of women sat on the ground facing both of us. I had no idea where to start. All of women's ponytails bobbed as they began chanting. My nerves instantly calmed down to a dreamy state. Fear left my body. If Hitler had the universe's protection, then maybe I did as well.

I had to rely on faith, but then what was faith? Who or what do I have it in? If I was to place it with the aliens who were at some level orchestrating this insane meeting, then which alien race should I believe in? The only being who I wanted to trust was God. I silently said a prayer to Him while Maria and her ladies performed their spiritual preamble for the second time this night. I prayed for bravery, for home, for Eric, and even for an opportunity to change the past despite the paradoxes that Josef warned me about. I prayed to the point my mouth was moving and my eyes were closed. I opened them, surprised to see a room full of Nazis staring at me.

Maria spoke once again in that same male voice she did earlier, the voice I had heard once before. This time the voice spoke English. Was that for my benefit? Where in the world did I know it from? And then it came to me-Paula! She was speaking with the same voice on the last night I stayed at Jay's house. The next day Jay was drowned. It was the voice of Lam. Jay had told me about the spirit at his pool.

Lam was some kind of being that used talented mediums to communicate. He was famously summoned up by Aleister Crowley, and then several mediums since. Some believed he was a demon, or even Lucifer in spirit. But everyone in this room saw Lam as an extraterrestrial force. Crowley's drawing of Lam resembled what most people believed gray aliens to look like. Lam came to Paula and now Maria, both times in my presence. What did he or it want from me? Whatever Lam was, he made the hair on my arms and neck stand up.

"Why are you here?" Maria said in the deep, haunting male voice.

I paused, took a few deep breaths, and then mustered up the bravery to answer. "Lam? I heard you once before through another medium in another era. I don't know why I am here."

Hitler motioned Josef over to him and his top brass. I think Josef was translating what was being said. With Lam's voice, Maria asked me question after question about my life, my job, my love life, all of it. I answered. Eric, Claude, the novel, the institute, holding back nothing. I even told them about how I might have been part of a genetic experiment that enabled me to travel back in time. Tears dripped from my eyes as I told them all that I just wanted to go home.

Still using Lam's voice, Maria said something in German while looking straight at Hitler. Whatever was said, I saw a flicker of fear in those cold, blue eyes of his. Maria then turned to me and said in English, "Tell the *Fuehrer* who wins the war."

"I…I am not political…" I said, my voice cracking. I prayed in silence for my life.

"Tell him!" she yelled in that deep, male voice which made me shudder.

I felt nauseous. I prayed again. I was ready. Armed with truth, I said, "Well, I speak English, not German, and I come from the United States, not the Third Reich. We are not and never been a colony of Germany. With all due respect, you lose. The history books reported that you and your new bride, Ava Braun, kill yourselves right before your inevitable defeat."

I was still alive. No one shot me dead. Hitler screamed at his generals. Veins popped out of his forehead. He looked at me, yelled something in German, and then motioned as if he wanted me to keep talking. I had to toss him a bone, but what could I say? Then it all came to me.

"America and the Soviets were the big winners after the war, but according to many conspiracy theories, you got away." I paused and let Josef finish that translation. "You killed your double, and then took off to Argentina and began the Fourth Reich which still lives on today."

"How do I lose?" Hitler said. He struggled with the English sentence.

I silently prayed again. I didn't want to tell him that he was fighting too many powerful enemies on too many fronts. I didn't want to tell him about Normandy or Russia's winters or the codes that we broke. I didn't want to tell him that his racism had cost a heavy price in terms of Jewish scientists who created the bomb.

Hitler rambled something off in German. Soldiers lunged at me as I sat in the circle. I kicked, squirmed, and scratched, but I was no match for six or seven men. Someone slapped my head and my consciousness faded to black.

Chapter Twenty-Three

Present Day
Nevada

Glenn Lucasek did not strike Claude as an avid science fiction reader. His life's work was based on the real deal. But Maya was writing for reasons beyond entertainment. Was truth of extraterrestrials also hidden in between the lines of Jay's novels? One day, Claude planned on reading all of McCallister's work. But that day would have to wait. He was too busy gathering up the tidbits from both of Maya's novels that supported his hunch about DNA code.

Claude still had some unanswered questions. How would Maya know anything about genetics? She had a G.E.D. from high school and worked as a book store clerk. The complicated coding aspect of DNA ladder strands was not easy reading material. If Maya was with Glenn, then why couldn't she just tell him about the new code she embedded into her novel?

Claude second-guessed himself about the dollar amount he asked for. Half of a billion dollars might have been a ton of money, but it was much less than half of what Maya was now worth. He wanted his fair share, once they were divorced. He saw the money as part pay-off, part divorce settlement. Glenn was Maya's lawyer, and could easily make this all happen while looking legitimate.

The next day the media had cleared away, leaving Claude some freedom in leaving his home. Before making his errands, Claude set up an offshore account. Once he had his routing number, he needed to give himself some leverage in case Glenn planned on double crossing him.

Claude made two copies of Maya's unedited sequel on two memory sticks. One stick he addressed to Sam and the other stick he addressed to his literary agency in Los Angeles. He dropped off the two packages at the post office.

Claude's next stop was his local bank. He sent one thousand dollars to his new offshore account. Once home, he checked online. It worked. He dialed Glenn's number at the T.A.H. Institute. Glenn didn't pick up, but Claude left a message with instructions just the same.

"And if the money isn't in the account by tomorrow, I am calling a press conference and educating the media about DNA sequences that are found in both of Maya's novels." All Claude had to do was wait.

An hour later Glenn called him back. "By the end of tomorrow's business day, you'll have your money. But I need Maya's computer. I will send one of my employees to Las Vegas. Name the place." They agreed to meet at Claude's bank.

After Glenn's call, Claude felt somewhat relaxed. He had over twenty-fours to wait before his life changed forever. He called Sam who didn't pick up, leaving a message about a package. He was as vague as possible. This would make it up to his baby brother. Once he had his money, Claude would toss Sam a large chunk to enjoy.

Claude was feeling especially magnanimous. If Glenn didn't try to screw him over, he would forward the memory stick with the epilogue to T.A.H. without any further requests. Claude was almost rich.

Feeling celebratory, Claude checked his wallet. Six hundred bucks. He deserved a night on the town. First, he would go gambling, and if he had anything left, maybe get a room and hooker to end the evening. He showered and shaved for his night out.

As Claude cruised the strip, he pulled into the Luxor's parking valet. He spied a blue Chrysler sedan behind him. A valet approached the door. He changed his mind. Claude had been to the Luxor too many times. He waved the man off, wanting to try a hotel he hadn't been to. He drove out of the valet area and turned back onto the strip. The same Chrysler was still behind him. Was he being followed? He deliberately drove by the strip. The blue car was gone. Since he was low on gas and out of cigarettes, he pulled into a Seven Eleven store. He gassed up, and then went inside. When he walked back to his car an Asian man and a white man were sitting on his hood. *What the fuck?*

"Hi, Claude. I need that novel. Is it in your house? Your car?" the Asian asked with a poker face.

"Get the fuck off of my car before I get the cashier to call the police."

The white man laughed. He was really tall, at least six and a half feet and built like tank. "The police. Weren't you just questioned for killing your wife? You wanted her dead, right? To inherit all of that new money of hers," he said with an Australian accent. "We're not fucking around, Mate."

"Neither am I. Glenn promised me money. Call it a divorce settlement or pay-off, whatever. Until tomorrow when he wires me my money…" The Asian kicked his leg out from under him and in a split second pushed him up against the passenger side door. Claude's arm was pinned behind his back and he could hardly breathe. These were not TV people from Glenn's show.

"Like my friend said, we're not fucking around. Here's the new deal, asshole-you give us Maya's computer and we let you live," said the Asian man as he squeezed Claude's arm. One false move and it would break. "Open the back seat and get in."

Claude's mind instantly jumped to the memory sticks he mailed. He still held a card. The epilogue of the novel had to mean something. He slowly slid in his backseat. The Aussie slid next to him. Claude couldn't help but notice his legs. They were as thick as tree trunks.

The Asian man hopped in the driver's seat and pulled away from the Seven-Eleven. Claude's car was a push-start. His key fob was in his pants. If he could just throw the fob out of the window. The car would eventually have to stop. He nonchalantly inched his left hand towards his pants pocket.

The Aussie took his fingers and pressed them back. Something snapped.

"Ah! That fucking hurts! Ow!" Claude howled.

The Asian screamed back. "Quit fucking around! Give my friend the key fob!"

Claude complied. The Aussie tossed it up front to the driver, and then took a plastic tie out of his pocket and cuffed Claude's hands. He then took out an iPad and pressed a few buttons.

"Here. I have something for you to watch," the Aussie said.

Claude's heart raced. He no longer felt his broken finger. His knuckles were swelling up to the size of a golf ball. With trepidation, he pressed the play arrow. The video showed a bound and gagged couple with black and blue faces riding in the back seat of a car. His jaw dropped. Allie and Sam! He almost didn't recognize them.

"Like I said, we ain't fucking around. You want to play, we'll hurt them even more. I know your address. We are heading back to your house," the Aussie said as he put away the iPad.

"Are you going to kill them?" Claude asked. Although he didn't want Allie to die, if she had to be sacrificed, he could still sleep at night. These men didn't know that. Sam, on the other hand, already suffered enough for his greed. His baby brother was the closest relationship he had ever had.

The car turned onto another busy street. The Asian man said, "Maybe. It depends on you. I know you don't give a shit about the girl. She used to be your girl. She's fucking your brother now. We've also got your mother. That prison she's holed up in has got lots of guards with big mouths. But we're working on your dad. Can't find him. Something tells me it's a waste of time. I understand he's a scumbag. Like father, like son."

Sam and Allie. That's all Claude could hear. He had a feeling they bonded after their attempt on Maya's life. Oddly, he wasn't even jealous, just worried. If Sam or Allie started telling their captors about Jay and then Maya, a new dilemma would pop up and he wasn't prepared to deal with it. "My house is another five minutes or so. Exit on the Henderson exit. I'm a few streets away from the exit."

"I know where your fucking house is. Quite the media circus you've had going," said the Asian.

"They're gone. I got rid of them after my deal. Really wish they were still there to save me about now."

The Aussie laughed. "I'm sure you do, Claude. So, Maya's laptop is there?" Claude nodded. Within minutes, they pulled into the driveway of Claude's Spanish-style mansion. *What a beautiful house I had. A beautiful life, a beautiful wife, everything, and I fucked it all up. Maybe there's still a way out.*

The Aussie pushed Claude out of the car and onto the front porch. Claude dialed in the security code and unlocked the door. He thought of pressing the panic button which was hidden on the keypad of the alarm. *They got Sam...* For now, Claude would have to concede to these goons.

"Where is it?" asked the Asian.

"It's in the backyard. The outdoor fireplace in the woodpile."

The Aussie went straight back to the French doors that led to the patio. He threw out all of the wood from the opening next to the pizza oven in the brick fireplace. There it was-the Alien laptop. "Turn it on. I want to see the document." Claude complied. "You didn't change anything, did you?" Claude shook his head. The Aussie smacked him in the jaw. "You sure, Mate?" He nodded.

Both the Asian and the Aussie seemed to be satisfied. Claude just wanted them to leave, but they seemed to linger.

The Asian smiled mechanically at Claude, and then said, "You're going for a ride."

"The hell I am…" Before Claude could finish his sentence, the Aussie head-butted him. He crumpled to the floor.

Claude awoke in a windowless room, lying on a cement floor, facing a stark white wall. His eyes squinted up at the glaring florescent lights. His hands were still cuffed in the plastic tie and now his feet were also cuffed. He heard voices. As he turned to face the other direction, he saw a few roll chairs, a long table pushed against a wall with several computers on it along with his two captors, the Asian man and the Aussie man. He tried to speak but his throat was swollen and dry. All he could remember was the head-butt and had no idea how much time had lapsed.

The two men looked right at him, disinterested, and turned back to face the computer. Claude could see on the screen that they had downloaded Maya's novel onto their computers. They were deep in thought. Both men were taking notes as they read with lightning speed. The novel was definitely some kind of code.

Several minutes passed. The Asian man finally got up, went to the mini-fridge in the room, and got a bottle of water. He gave it to Claude, and then made a call from the phone in the room. "He's awake. Alright." He hung up. The Asian man then helped Claude to his feet and pushed him towards the door. "We're going for a walk."

Claude walked through corridor after corridor, turning in what seemed to be a very large box, still clueless as to where he was and what would happen to him. Had he thought for one second that the TV host Glenn Lucasek could resort to murder, he would have never made a deal. He always prided himself on being good at reading people. This time his senses backfired. The man acted one way on television and another when pushed for money. After walking through some kind of dark, cavernous laboratory, the Asian finally stopped by a set of metal double doors. He pressed his eye up to a camera and the doors opened. "Claude, as soon as we are done with the novel, you will go home. There is food, water, and a toilet in here. I'll check on you later." The Asian pushed him into the room and closed the doors.

A dim light from the ceiling was on. Claude looked at his new jail cell, which was similar to one he just left. In the corner of the room on two air mattresses were two sleeping bodies. Claude approached. One of the bodies flinched and sat up.

"Claude?"

Oh fuck, thought Claude. "Sam, I can explain everything."

Chapter Twenty-Four

1970
London, England

Andreas's head was about to explode. Lori had just told him enough information to rip the ground out from under him. He had known that Roswell was not the only UFO crash in the world. Intelligence reported that Argentina and Brazil had each had a similar crash. He was unaware of any crashes in Great Britain.

Andreas had suspected that other races of aliens existed. He had only seen the A.B.s at Broom Lake. Doctor Jaeger brought with him a preserved head of the same race inside of a jar, proving that Germany had also made extraterrestrial contact. Rumors circulated from other high-ranking officials. A race that resembled a reptile had been spotted in both Europe and the U.S.S.R. His own daughter had the pictures to prove their existence. Kate was somehow in involved. Andreas wondered what she worked on at Hanover Auto. These A.B.s were slowly making their presence known.

Andreas barely knew Lori. This elaborate conspiracy might be some kind of payback initiated by Kate before her death. Yet here they were inside of a building hiding from three very real men. Andreas had seen a very real gun jutting out of one of men's jacket. This was no set-up. Lori had to be right. Kate was murdered and Lori might be next.

Andreas was not surprised that Kate landed once again in the epicenter of top-secret Advanced Being intelligence. She had outstanding credentials. Discretion was definitely one of them. She also had a reputation for excellence in the field of alternative energy as well as a top-secret resume that involved reverse engineering in regards to extraterrestrial aircraft. But how would Hanover Auto know any of this? Alien landings were something not used in former job descriptions. Operation Chrome was filled with leaks. Someone must have fed Hanover Auto Intel about Kate. He wondered who it was.

All of Andreas's questions would have to wait. Their three friends were back. Andreas saw them through the giant picture window of the main lobby. They met up across the street. After they had some sort of discussion, two of the men went around to the side of the building. Andreas guessed they would be entering the clothes store soon. The other one was trying to get in a locked bank of doors at the front of the building. Soon he would find a way in.

"Grab your stuff. We've got to get out of here now," Andreas said to Lori as they both stood up from the stair's landing.

Lori shoved her file of pictures into her tote bag and followed Andreas down the hall. "So, what's the plan?" she whispered.

"Well, to get out of here without getting shot. Sorry, that's all I got right now." Andreas turned his head, looking for an escape. "Hey, over there is a stairwell. I believe two of them are on the other side of the building. We might get lucky."

Both of them flew down the concrete stairs to the bottom floor. Andreas swung open the exit door. They were now outside on the side of the building, exposed.

"Now what? Buy some guns and maybe a car?" Lori said. There was a tone of sarcasm in her voice.

Andreas saw a double-decker bus lumbering down the adjacent street. "C'mon! Run! The bus is slowing down. That must be a stop across the street." They darted into oncoming traffic. Horns blew and tires screeched. The bus saw them running and waited. Andreas handed the driver a ten pound note and waved off the changed. They both could see the three men running towards the noise, using radios to communicate.

"Well, that was real smooth, bloody smooth! Bollocks!" Lori snapped as the bus took off from the stop.

"Thank me later," Andreas said. "Keep your head low. They are looking at this bus right now."

The bus drove down a few more streets before slowing down. Andreas was pretty confident they had lost all three men.

"Lori, do you need anything of real importance from the house?" She shook her head and patted her tote bag. "How about hanging out with me for the rest of the afternoon? My hotel isn't too far. We can take a cab the rest of the way." Lori nodded.

A few stops later, they exited the bus and hopped into a cab. Another fifteen minutes elapsed and they were inside of Andreas's hotel room. He called for room service and ordered them both a few pints of beer and some sandwiches.

As they waited for the food, Andreas asked, "So, you think your mother was murdered?" Lori nodded. "Do you want to go to the police? I'll take you there." She shook her head firmly. "I completely understand," Andreas said. "Those three goons looked like cops, or even British Intelligence. You seem to know an awful lot about your mom's work. The Kate that I knew was never a threat. She wasn't one to reveal top-secret information. Why would someone want to kill her?"

Lori went straight to the mini-bar and took out two mini-bottles of rum. "You interested?" Andreas nodded and reached for it. She sat at the small table in the corner of the room. He joined her. She opened her bottle and held it up as if to toast. "Well, that was a near kerfuffle. Cheers," she said. They clanked their mini-bottles. She guzzled hers down in one gulp. Andreas got up from the table to get her another one. "Thanks, Dad."

"You don't have to call me that. We both don't know each other well enough. Robert is fine for now."

Lori smiled and then said, "Okay then, Robert. But you need to know something. I have a few friends, none of whom I could ever talk about aliens with. I was the closest to my mum, and now she's gone. I was also close to my father, but Mum was my rock. She vouched for you despite all of your short-comings. You are all I have so if you fuck me over, then I'm dead. If I don't trust you and go it alone I'm also dead. So, I've got nothing to lose at this point. I know I already laid on quite a heap of shit, but there's more."

Lori downed another mini-bottle of rum and motioned for more. "Judging by your stuffed tote bag, I assumed you had much more to share. Sorry, no more rum. Vodka okay?" Andreas asked.

There was a knock at the door. Both Andreas and Lori nearly jumped to the ceiling.

"Room service," called out a male voice from behind the door.

Andreas smiled and opened his wallet. He looked through the peephole first, and then ushered the young man inside of the room. He wheeled in a cart of food and beer. Andreas paid him and he left. He set the food and drinks on the table.

Lori was more interested in the mini-vodka bottle and pint of ale. "If ever there was a time when I needed to get pissed...Robert, the story begins around the time my mother married my father, Jacob. I am not trying to offend you, but he raised me so he will get to keep that title."

"No offense taken. Please, go on."

"My father was a religious man, a Christian. He and Mum married in a little, Protestant church on the edge of the city. They dragged me there as a kid, but then I eventually got my way and they quit making me go. At first, my mum played along, going through the motions in order to make my father happy. But then she got the bug, the religious bug. After he died, she became different, maybe unbalanced. She gave him a Christian funeral, and then buried him with a Christian headstone."

Andreas noticed that Kate had been buried the same way. This must have been her explicit instructions. Lori was giving him the idea that she was not part of Kate's born-again behavior. "Unbalanced? Your mother was the most level-headed person I ever knew. How did her religion get in the way of her job?"

"I don't know for sure if that was it. I'm trying to figure it all out. Everything has happened so fast," Lori said. The alcohol had calmed her down. She looked relaxed. "Mum seemed very cheeky about her job over the last few months. I attributed it all to losing her husband. I assumed he left her some money and the job was starting to get to her. Maybe retirement was on her mind."

"Did he leave her a lot of money?" Andreas asked. He wasn't sure how it was relevant to anything, just curious about her husband who he saw as a rival.

"Uh, well yes, I mean she wasn't rich, but was comfortable. She didn't have to ever work. My father made enough as a professor. But the Kate that we both knew loved science, engineering, mechanics. Soon after I was born, Hanover Auto made her an incredible offer. I don't know if she applied for the job or they recruited her, but she took the position and moved up the ranks very quickly. As you might already know, they are much more than an auto-maker. She was in charge of dozens of engineers." Lori paused and took a few bites out of her club sandwich.

Andreas was confused. "Alright, but what does that have to do with religion? She was not religious back in the States."

"Well, as her belief system changed, so did her entire personality. Towards the end of her life, she almost had a death wish. A real in-your-face careless attitude about what other people thought. That's probably why she called you when I found that crystal in the basket of one of our babies. Please don't get me wrong. I loved her so much. I'm not insinuating…"

"I know. So, her change was a change for the better or a change for the worse?" Andreas asked, and then took the last bite of his sandwich.

"Maybe it was a change for the better in God's eyes, if there is a God. But not in Hanover's eyes. She told me she was in charge of studying spaceships, both here and in the States. Somehow her faith saw these things that are coming to Earth as a threat. She stole all of those pictures. I am not sure what she was planning on doing with them. Maybe the media? I don't know. She told me this a few months ago. She believed the Reptilians were much more than extraterrestrial. She called them demonic. She even told her colleagues that they were doing work for the devil. She was about to quit. The president of the company wrote her up for causing a disturbance. He started a smear campaign about how she was losing her mind. Two weeks ago she did quit. No pension, no retirement package of any kind. And she didn't care."

"So, you think Hanover killed her?" Andreas asked.

Lori looked scared. "I really don't know. It could have been them, but it also could have gone even higher." She stopped eating her lunch, pushing the plate away.

Andreas was assuming the worst. How many more countries were in the know besides the U.S., Germany, Brazil, Argentina, and now the United Kingdom? Which race of aliens was friendly and which one hostile? Was there an intergalactic war going on? Was earth a prize for the victor? Or maybe he had it all wrong. Maybe they were here to observe. Why did they even care about this planet? So many questions that Andreas had were beyond his comprehension.

He wondered if anyone knew what Bolantano had been doing with the babies. Was he on anyone's radar? This top-secret world of Advanced Beings had become a chess game that he wasn't smart enough to play. "Lori, does anyone know I'm your father?"

She shook her head. "I just found out, and Mum never told anyone except me."

"Have you seen those men before? The three who followed us?"

She nodded. "They were at the hospital, and then I saw them lurking around the house. That's why I grabbed all of these files. Then you came over. They want something. Maybe they were the ones who killed Mum."

"Did Kate or you tell anyone else about the baby from the orphanage?" Lori shook her head. "What about the people who work there? Did they tell anyone? I mean the crystal is very weird."

"That I couldn't tell you. But when I told Mum, she was very upset. That's when she started coming clean. That's when she wrote you."

"Lori, give me a minute. I have some connections. I am a five star general. Let me make some calls. Maybe I can find out who is tailing you."

Andreas walked over to the bed and dialed the phone. "Michael, glad you picked up. I need you to run a check for me. By the way, Kate died…Thanks. I almost missed it… supposedly, her heart gave out. But her daughter suspects foul play. She is with me now. We are both a little bit shaken… Three white males, all under forty, were following us. They've been watching the house for at least a few days. See what you can find out with Scotland Yard... Okay then... I'll be here, waiting for your call." Andreas hung up the phone. "Lori, maybe you can come back to the U.S. with me. I'm about to retire. Well, let me take that back. The truth is, Michael, the man I just called, and I, are working on something very important. As soon as I can find someone else to continue our work, I will retire. One day I will fill you in on everything, but not today. As of the moment, you might be safer with me, but that could change. What Michael and I are doing might not be considered legal."

Lori laughed.

"It must run in the family. I'm betting you don't always play by the rules. Anyway, I'll pay for your school. The U.S. has so many great schools. You can live with me in between school breaks..."

"Can I help you and Michael?" Lori interrupted. "Whatever the bloody hell the two of you are up to, I couldn't be more gobsmacked than I am at this moment."

"You don't even know what we are doing," Andreas answered. She reminded him so much of Kate. "One day. First, we need to get you out of this mess."

"And second?" Lori had a glint in her eye and a half of smile on her face.

"I suppose you might want to study genetics. I need more doctors who specialize in that field."

"Well I have completed two years at the university where my father once worked. I took all general education classes. I suppose they will transfer over to America."

Andreas took the trays of food and put them outside of the door. "I like that idea. You in America, taking classes. But you will need to keep your mouth shut, lay low in school, and then I might use you. Is there anything left at Kate's home?"

"Well, there are lots of things that I want to keep as remembrances, but the files, pictures, and the crystal are all that I need right now." Lori handed him her tote bag. Her hazel eyes looked inside of her tote and nodded as if to give Andreas her permission to rifle through it.

He dumped everything onto the table. Photos of Reptilians, space craft, more crystal, and then the baby found in Lori's orphanage were carefully examined. Copies of letters between Hanover employees were also in the file, all related to the Advanced Beings.

"Wow. This must be a lot for you to swallow. Before your mother opened up to you, did you believe?"

"I don't know what to believe in anymore. But beings who are more intelligent, more powerful, and more advanced are waiting for something."

The phone rang. "Michael? Wait, let me put you on speaker. I want Lori to hear whatever you have to say." Andreas pushed a few buttons until they both could hear his voice coming out of the phone's speaker.

"Lori?" Bolantano asked.

"Yes."

"I knew your mom well. She was brilliant, charming, and very beautiful. So, so sorry," Bolantano said.

"Thank you. Have you found anything out from your contacts?" Lori's voice quivered as she spoke. Her mother just died and she had no time to grieve.

"As a matter of fact, I do know someone who works for Scotland Yard. Your mother made a lot of waves before she died. She was fired…"

"No she wasn't! She quit," Lori said defensively.

"Maybe that's what she told you, but the corporation claims she was fired. She didn't leave quietly. I guess she made all kinds of threats about going to the press. She believed the world needed to know about some of their secret projects. Once she left, the president of Hanover made a few calls. One of them had to be MI5."

"Who is that?" Lori asked.

"They are higher-ranking police. They can carry guns, have more power and can get more information. They are like the American FBI, if you ever heard of them. The bottom line is this-the folks at Hanover were very worried that your mother would breach their top-secret security. The investigation started because they thought she had leaked out some classified information."

Andreas gave Lori a worried look. "Michael, to whom? Lori? Is that why she is being followed? Is she in danger?"

"That I don't know, but she's definitely on their radar. Your house is no longer safe. Can you leave for a while and have someone pack everything up and sell it for you?" Bolantano asked. "My source claims that you made a spectacle of yourself at the hospital-shouting murder, conspiracy, cover-up..."

"Very good, Michael. Your source is right, but I was upset."

"No, perfectly understandable. I wouldn't be a bit surprised if you are right about everything. But for now, there is no proof. My source is my source because he is in the same line of work that I am, that Robert is. We all work on similar top-secret projects."

"Michael, it's okay. She knows all about it. Kate told her everything. Even left pictures."

"So, she did leak out information. Lori, you might be in grave danger," Bolantano said.

"I know that, Michael. Lori is my daughter. When Kate left, she was pregnant. I threw her out of Broom Lake when she was pregnant! Oh God."

"God will forgive you. I want to meet your daughter."

"You will. She is coming home with me."

Lori then added, "Michael, I plan on getting a degree in genetics very soon. You and the general will need me."

There was a long pause on the phone.

"I didn't tell her, Michael. Kate did before she died."

"I owe you a congratulations, General. You ol'dawg, you! Kate left you quite an inheritance. Yes, bring her back, get her educated, and then we will see what we can use her for."

Chapter Twenty-Five

1944
The Eagle's Nest, Germany

I woke up in a dingy room that was dimly lit by a stained-glass lamp. The lamp sat on a dresser, and casted shades of yellow and orange on the walls and floor. It didn't belong in the room. I doubted the dresser or bed belonged in the room either.

My hands were tethered to the brass headboard, one hand per each post. The decorative rods that held the two main brass pieces of the headboard together had prevented me from sliding my hands together and untying myself. But I guess that was the point.

I looked at my feet. They were bound together. A couple of pillows had me sitting upright. I was cold. The mattress was filthy with dirt, semen, piss, blood, and plain old rot. My nose twitched and eyes teared. The wooden floor was equally filthy and stained. The foul smell could have also been coming from the floor. It made me think of death and decay. As a few minutes passed, I almost got used to it. I had to forget about my discomfort and think. Think or die.

Josef had been lying to me from the beginning. Did he know where I was? Was he part of my imprisonment? Was I still at the Eagle's Nest? The last thing I remembered was Hitler's henchmen knocking me out in the banquet hall.

The rope that bound my feet was tight, but my feet were small. I pointed my toes like a ballerina, and then flexed my foot-point, flex, point, flex. This alternating movement didn't do much at first, but calmed me down. Gradually, the rope loosened. My big toe dug in between the rope coils. A moment later my feet were free.

This small victory gave me hope for the next step-freeing my hands. I swung my legs over my head and cupped them around my right tied-up hand. My feet felt the knot at the back side of the headboard. I swung my legs to the other side with the same result. My legs were too short to fiddle with it. Despair spread over me like the plague. I was trapped like an animal and would have to accept my fate. I would eventually die here, but first have to live through torture, rape, and neglect. *Oh God, if you are out there, I need your help!*

Breathe deep, I told myself repetitively. I swung my legs to the side of the bed, making me think of a lady equestrian riding side saddle. Sugar-coating my current predicament helped me concentrate. One of my legs touched the floor. I ran my foot along the base of the headboard, feeling bolts and screws that ran up the brass rod. One of the screws was somewhat loose. My toes fidgeted with the nut. I heard a tiny sound of metal dropping to the floor. Clink. My big toe pushed the heavy bolt out of the hole of the bedframe. Clink. My foot patted down every centimeter of floor that it could reach until it found the bolt. With all of my toes, I clasped the bolt and then transferred it into my tied up right hand.

My fingers frantically sawed the rope down in seconds. The rope was cut and my hand was free. With my newly freed hand, I easily untied my second hand. I rose from the disgusting mattress and walked over to the sole window within the room. The sun had set, but the white caps on the mountains and the full moon enabled me to see outdoors. I had to be at the Eagle's Nest, probably an empty bedroom. I tried to open the window, but it was nailed shut. The door was locked. I contemplated smashing the window and jumping at least twenty-five feet down to the ground and making a run for it. There was a click-the sound of the door lock. My heart sank. All of the work for nothing. I was never going to make it out of here alive.

The door creaked as it opened. Three men wearing Nazi regalia walked in. I instantly recognized the first one, Martin Bormann. The other two looked familiar. I assumed I had seen them at the banquet. At a closer look, one soldier was the one whose gun I nabbed to kill Hitler. The two soldiers looked at me like a piece of red meat. They talked to each other in German as if I wasn't in the room.

Martin Bormann looked at me and said, "Forty-five minutes. You were knocked out for forty-one minutes, awoke, and then freed yourself in four minutes. A record. Our last experiment took the subject four hours and seven minutes."

"Well, if this is a test, then I guess I passed. Please get Josef, and we can get out of your way."

"Shut-up!" Bormann yelled. He and the other two soldiers had another German-speaking conversation. The soldiers looked at me hungrily.

Was I about to get raped?

My mind flashed back to my last foster father, and his friend. The thought of their touch caused bile to rise up my esophagus. They forced me to be their slave, the toys they used, the clothes they made me wear, the words they made me say... That was probably a day at the beach to what these whacked out Nazis were going to do.

The nightmare of my past played out as the two blue-eyed wolves bared their teeth at me. Bormann was giving them permission. He patted both of them on their shoulders, and then left the room. Should I have been grateful? Were two rapists better than three?

The man who I took the gun from earlier did not remember a thing. Maybe he still had his gun. Hell, if I could get a hold of it again, then maybe he could die with me. Maybe all of us in this sick torture chamber could die. This nightmare would be over.

I heard the locks on the door click. That must have been Bormann. The two soldiers began to circle. They were tall, well over six foot. The one with the gun still had it on him. I could see the shoulder holster underneath his jacket. The two men giggled as they came closer.

"*Schone Dame,*" said the one man with gun. "*Schone Dame.*"

The other man unfastened his belt, and then kicked off his shoes. I jumped on the bed as he lunged at me. Both men were clearly enjoying the chase, like hunters about to kill an animal in a cage. I had one card left to play and it better be an ace or game over.

Looking at the man with the gun, I gave him the best come-hither look that I could muster up. I then winked. More German conversation went on between the two of them. I assumed they worked out a new agreement as to whom would screw me first. The other man immediately kicked off his shoes and then unzipped his pants. I jumped off the bed and rubbed my hand on his penis. As he smiled while enjoying my touch, I slid my other hand under his coat. I had it. I had his gun.

Without wasting a nanosecond, I pulled the trigger. Blood splattered all over me as he fell onto the bed. Quickly, I turned to the other man and fired. More blood gushed out as he dropped to the floor. The filthy bed and floor got a new coat of filth. Both men were dead.

The door frantically started clicking. Maria was the first one who came through the door. Her hands were up high. "Maya!" Four soldiers with their weapons drawn were right behind her, all shouting something in German. I dropped the gun and kicked it over to Maria. Martin Bormann and then Hitler came inside of the room. All eyes were on the two dead soldiers, one on the floor and one on the bed, both limp in their pools of blood.

What in the world...? I assumed Bormann and maybe some more guards were outside of the door, but Hitler and Maria as well? Was it common for all of them to listen to a woman about to get raped? More German conversations erupted within the room. They sounded frantic, almost scared which scared me more. I assumed they were brainstorming together on all of the ways they would torture me and then kill me. As I watched the macabre scene of pandemonium, I felt more like a spectator and less like the center of attention.

I looked at Maria. She held my gaze while Bormann talked at her. Her blue eyes were hypnotic. Earlier in the night, she spoke to me telepathically. Would she try to talk to me now? My ears rang.

Hold on, my dear Maya. I know who you are. These men just need some convincing.

Maria was communicating to me loud and clear. But she didn't realize that these men were beyond convincing. They refused to see logic of any kind. My eyes wandered over to the other soldiers in the room. They all had guns that were still pointed at me.

I looked at Hitler. He was staring at me the way one would stare at a freak in a circus. I did not see any hatred in his eyes, which surprised me. I had just blown away two of his soldiers. No, he was looking at me in both amazement and disgust. I heard my name, and then Josef's name from Bormann as he still barked at Maria. Out of the corner of my eye, I saw Hitler's prying eyes.

"*Schweigen!*" Hitler yelled. The room went from chaos to silence. He pointed to the dead bodies and then looked directly at me. "You are not human, but extraterrestrial."

My eyes went straight towards the soldier next to him. He was no longer pointing a gun at me, but held the gun by his side.

I heard a voice. *It won't work.*

My ears burned. It was Maria' voice. I cupped my hand over my ears and looked over at Maria. She wouldn't look at me and continued looking at Bormann as he spoke. Did she say that aloud or telepathically to me? With all of the concentration I could gather, I thought the words *'Why not? I am young and have a wonderful life back home. If I am going to die, then why not take out a few more Nazis?'*

Nothing. Maybe she couldn't hear me. A moment passed.

Have patience. Have faith. Josef is being questioned right now and you will need him.

Bormann finished his monologue aimed at Maria and gave her a moment to talk. She began to ramble off some German, but I could also understand.

She didn't murder anyone. You know that was self-defense. Think, Martin, think. She freed herself in record time, she killed two big men...

Oh no, I thought. Was she going to tell him that I killed Hitler in a parallel universe? Sweat dripped down my face and the metallic odor came back.

...And Josef said she was bulletproof.

Bormann cut her off and yelled something at the soldier standing closest to Hitler. He then looked at Hitler for approval. The *Fuehrer* nodded. The soldier pointed his gun at my foot and pulled the trigger twice. One foot was hit and then the other.

"Ow!" I sank to the bed, grabbing both of my feet. "You mother fuckers!" I pushed the dead body off the bed so that I didn't have to look at his dead blue eyes. The soldier pistol-whipped both of my feet. There was some blood, but the pain was crippling. Seconds later, the bleeding stopped and the pain dissipated. My feet felt much hotter than the rest of my body. The holes that were caused by the bullets had gotten smaller. One foot pushed out the bullet lodged inside. With exception of Maria, all eyes were on me as my feet magically healed themselves. Maria had fallen into a trance.

A few more minutes elapsed and my feet looked like they did before they were shot. Hitler approached and sat on the edge of the bed, away from the wet, bloody stains that belonged to the dead men. Placing both of my feet on his lap, he looked at them with skepticism. His cold, clammy skin touching my warm feet sickened me. My first instinct was to kick his ice cold face in and make a run for it, but that would be suicide. Maybe it didn't matter anymore.

I looked at Maria for guidance, but she was too involved with the spiritual world to witness the warped scene of Hitler feeling up my feet as we sat on a bed of blood and filth. Maria was humming to herself and occasionally speaking some archaic language. Had she lost her mind? This wasn't the time to channel an alien. I wish she would snap out of it and speak to me. I needed to live another day.

Hitler motioned to Martin and the other soldiers to look at my feet. One by one, they took up a dry spot on the bed and felt my feet, all looking mesmerized as if in their own trance. By the time the last soldier sat down, Maria turned from the doorway and glared at me.

Aloud, she said, "Jay McCallister."

Chapter Twenty-Six

Present Day
Ruby Mountains, Nevada

Glenn sat at the reception desk of the main entrance and watched the security camera. Chuck and Devon, the institute's head of security, manhandled Claude down the corridor. They were taking him to the same room as two other security guards had taken Allie and Sam only hours earlier. The guilt hadn't set in. Maybe it would never surface. Glenn had always believed the end justifies the means. Getting Maya back was the highest priority.

Glenn should have been worried about the current felonies he and Chuck had raked up. As of today, he was guilty of kidnapping, false imprisonment, and maybe even manslaughter. Doctor Blacksmith would not approve. He needed to be careful that she didn't get a whiff of what was going on. He also needed to keep Paula and Mercedes in the dark. Eric was different. Although Glenn wasn't going to tell Eric that Claude and his gang were locked in a room, he had a feeling that the young man would enjoy seeing all three of them suffer. It was all in the name of getting Maya back.

Chuck had made several copies of Maya's manuscript and passed them out to a small list of approved doctors, board members, and security. Glenn had loaded the copy onto his iPad. He especially wanted Doctor Blackwell's input on any potential coding within the new novel. As he walked up to the laboratory, he wondered if the doctor had made new strides in altering Eric's genetic makeup.

Glenn assumed that Claude had read the novel. The man certainly had formed some new conspiracy theories, many of which were true. Claude, his brother, and his old girlfriend would be dealt with later.

Hopefully, the novel would give Doctor Blacksmith enough information to send Eric through time. She identified the gene and had started to clone it. All the doctor needed was the correct location on where to insert it within Eric's DNA strand. One false move, and who knew what could happen.

Glenn approached the double doors and looked into the retina scan for security. The doors opened. The second set of doors he used his keycard to open. Doctor Blacksmith was preoccupied with a microscope.

"Doctor?" he asked.

Lori almost jumped from her stool. "Oh, you've startled me. Good news. I am getting closer. As I've already told you, it's surprisingly easy to clone. This gene is so different than all of our genes. It seems to have tachyon properties. I've never seen anything like it." She spoke to him while she switched slides and looked back into the microscope. She was not about to lose a second of work to conversation.

Glenn raised an eyebrow. "Tachyons? I thought there was no such thing. Tachyon particles are just a theory."

"Well, it's a little more than a theory. But I am dealing with dead cells of both Maya and Jay. Some of the tiny parts within the cells are still moving. They move so fast that I barely noticed them under my strongest microscope. I can't imagine how fast they would be if they were live cells."

"Faster than the speed of light?" Glenn asked.

"Well, Chuck would be much more qualified to measure its speed. I'm thinking this must have something to do with time travel."

"Excellent. Then I will get Chuck more involved."

Lori replied, "Wonderful. Once I have enough cloned genes, maybe another couple of days, I will be able to insert them into a segment of Eric's DNA strand. I am still unsure of the location."

"Where are the genes that you are cloning?" Glenn asked.

"Over there, in those test tubes and petri dishes." Doctor Blacksmith pointed to the middle of the lab.

"Ah. Very interesting. You mentioned his junk DNA might be safe for the gene editing."

Lori walked over to another telescope and said, "Yes, but where? That is the question."

Glenn touched her shoulder as she hunched over another microscope. "I think I might be able to help you with that. In fact, that is why I am here. The novel," Glenn said as he handed Doctor Blacksmith a flash-drive. "This might save you some time. I plan on reading it as soon as possible. A few others are also reading it. You really think this will work?" The doctor shrugged. "Has anything close to this ever been tried on humans?"

"Well no, not for time travel. These procedures and new technologies are mainly used for modifying plants. If humans are being tested, the trials are top secret. No one has published a word about it. Ethics are in question. Although there are a lot of whispers about using gene therapy for treating Alzheimer's Disease. No one is using extraterrestrial genes. We are the first, true pioneers in the field of time travel. I'm worried. Wish I had some practice beforehand."

"Don't worry. Just read. I'm sure Maya left us with a trail of breadcrumbs on how all of this works. I'll leave you be." Glenn exited the laboratory.

He had a few ideas of his own that would not involve Doctor Blacksmith, Mercedes, or Paula. Eric was going back and getting Maya, with or without morality getting in the way.

Glenn walked downstairs towards the centrifuge. Chuck was usually in the backroom, monitoring the machinery. As expected, Chuck was there, reading Maya's novel on his laptop. He looked up at Glenn and smiled.

"So far, this is a great read. I'm about fifty pages in. She left us some clues. There is a definite code. Our little extortionist is locked up safely with his brother and ex-girlfriend," Chuck said. "With Doctor Blacksmith's genetic technique along with me fine-tuning the centrifuge, I think we'll get Eric through the worm hole. Just hope he lands in the same place as Maya did."

"I saw them all in the holding room. Devon's taking care of them. I need to sit down and read too. Chuck, how well are you versed in genetics?"

"Doctor Blacksmith is your expert. She is one of the leading geneticists of the world," Chuck answered with a smirk. The two men stared at each other for a moment. "But I'm self-taught. Been around labs my whole life. All of the sciences cross paths at some point. I consider myself a self-proclaimed geneticist and can step in when needed."

Both men understood each other. Glenn smiled and then said, "That's why I hired you. You've always been brilliant, but I most admire your ability to play any position for the team."

"Glenn, let's drop the sports analogy. You know I will do whatever it takes. We are on the brink of changing the world. You think a speed bump is going to slow any of us down? For the record, I think Blacksmith feels the same way. You give her too much credit in the decency department."

"Not this time. We are about to change the world, aren't we?" Glenn said as he ran his hand through his thick, gray hair. He wanted to see time travel happen during his lifetime, but there were doubts. "Chuck, I can't help but worry that the world might not be willing to be changed. Do we even have a right to change it? This kind of knowledge can erase the past that we know, setting off chaos the world has never seen."

"If we don't discover this, someone else will. Then they will control its usage. You know, China wants to use it as a weapon. Don't worry about everyone going back to change their future. There are many theories that state the universe is protected. In reality, we know very little about what's on the other side of that wormhole. Jay proved to us that we weren't dreaming. Maya will open the door to even more. Since we are getting so philosophical, have you ever wondered why these A.B.'s gave us such ambiguous directions on how to time travel back in time, ahead of time, throughout the universe to various planets? Everything we know has been given to us in bits and pieces. Only those who know what to look for-"

"*Those* is the key word. Yes, we are not alone in solving this ultimate riddle. Other foundations and governments know about Advanced Beings and their hybrids. We know there are other races from other planets who have made contact. What do you suppose they want?" Glenn asked.

"Maybe it's some kind of evolution. There could also be an intergalactic war going on with this planet being one of the spoils. Earth could have some resource that they need. I've been searching for those answers all of my life. You know that's why I am here. The Chinese government was never going to share all of its data with me, or any doctor. You gave me the chance to do the kind of work I always dreamed of." Chuck looked back at his laptop. "I've got more pages to read. When we are all done, we need to have a little book club."

Glenn laughed. "You, me, Doctor Blacksmith, Mercedes, Paula, and even Devon can discuss the fine literary techniques Maya used in encoding DNA." He then waved and left the room. He sensed that Chuck was determined to finish the novel and then help get Eric into another era.

Over the years, Glenn relied on Chuck more and more. Mercedes and Paula resented it. They saw the middle-aged Chinese doctor as an ambitious outsider. Both women questioned his loyalty on numerous occasions. T.A.H. had had its fair share of leaks, both before and after Doctor Chuck Wu came to work for the institute. Glenn couldn't help but agree that he could be aloof and suspicious. However, Chuck's contributions to T.A.H.'s research showed a great deal of progress. If Chuck was giving others information, he must have also been getting it. The Chinese physicist would never be fully trusted, but he was much too valuable to let go. Mercedes and Paula never saw it that way, but Jay did. Sometimes there had to be a compromise.

Glenn walked into the institute's library with his iPad. Eric was asleep on the leather couch with an iPad left on the floor. *Sleep*, Glenn thought. *You'll need all of the rest that you can get.*

Mercedes and Paula were also in the library. They shared a long table. Mercedes had her manuscript printed out. She sat with a highlighter and notebook, taking copious notes as she read. Paula had her feet up on an empty chair using her laptop to read the manuscript. Both women looked up and nodded, making it clear they were too busy for conversation.

On the opposite side of the library there was a leather-wing chair set away from the tables in a cozy nook. Glenn sat down and propped his feet up on the matching ottoman. Genetics was not his forte, but he knew much more than the average citizen. While everyone seemed to be searching the novel for DNA sequences, he chose to concentrate on the story. He remembered that Maya's first novel wasn't exactly fiction. She had a clever way of masking the truth behind the characters and plot.

The Master Plan picked up where the first novel left off. Reptoids had taken over the Grays on the planet next to the Zeta II Reticuli star. But some of the Grays managed to escape to planet Earth. The Reptoids followed them to the planet and declared war. Being no match for them, they soon became the Reptoids' slaves. Most of the Earthlings were unaware of the Reptoids. An inner circle of humans soon befriended them. The Reptoids formed a partnership, ensuring the small group of humans a right to rule the planet once a one world government was formed. The only languages that would be used in the global edicts were German and English. Glenn put the book down for a minute to think. *German and English. Was this a World War II reference?*

Glenn was about half way into the novel. He read about the expansion of the Incorporated Nations. This Earthly group wanted embassies in every major city on the planet. They controlled all security, education, and property while emitting constant propaganda on how the planet was in danger. An unlikely extraterrestrial hero emerged. Together with the Grays, he and his army toppled the Reptoids and the Incorporated Nations, never once claiming to colonize Earth.

Glenn enjoyed the book, but thought the ending was very abrupt. There were several loose ends left for the reader to think about. He thought that Maya intentionally left it that way so that she could write a third book. *Shit! Was there going to be even more code to go through? Or maybe this wasn't her final draft. Maybe she and the editor planned on touching up the ending.* Glenn's mind raced. Sheer exhaustion caused his eyes to droop. He soon fell deep asleep.

Glenn dreamt of scaly monsters, test tubes, and flying discs that flew over the institute. He dreamt of Maya, alone and scared, in a filthy room with a blood-stained mattress. He dreamt of Jay, dead, preserved in his cryogenics chamber. Jay's eyes twitched and then opened.

Glenn missed Jay. He had been so preoccupied with the institute and time travel to grieve for his best friend and partner. This was supposed to be his and Jay's moment. Chuck was a lousy replacement for their life long research. He had always admired Chuck, but trust was another thing. Jay could be trusted with everything, including his life.

Jay, Glenn said in his dream. He approached the chamber and touched the cool glass. Jay's eyes were staring directly into his, and then his mouth began to move. *Jay!* Glenn could not hear him outside of his glass chamber. He was saying something. Jay then used his finger and wrote on the inside of the chamber the word "Maya". The letters were inverted. Jay then wrote "trouble". *Where is she, Jay?* Jay wrote 'Germany, World War II'. His eyes closed and his hands went limp.

"Wait, Jay! No! Come back!"

Glenn woke to the female screams of Mercedes and Paula. Mercedes hands were on his shoulders.

"You had a dream. I had to shake you. You were screaming Jay's name!" Mercedes said.

"How long was I asleep?"

Paula looked at the clock on the wall and said, "About four and half hours. You saw Jay in a dream?"

"Crazy, really. Jay was alive in that frozen chamber. He told me Maya was in trouble. She was in Germany, World War II."

Paula's brown eyes darkened. "Was it a dream or an omen?"

Chapter Twenty-Seven

The late 1970's
America

Andreas convinced Lori Osbourne to leave London, and her life, behind. He would help her start fresh in Nevada. She was too scared to refuse. Andreas used this fear to tighten his grip. Old age had made him wiser. She was a gift that he did not deserve and he wasn't about to let go.

Andreas rented her a house in Las Vegas and enrolled her at Stanford University for the following fall. She had the credentials to go wherever she wanted. Her brains along with her beauty were from Kate.

Kate's death hit him hard once back at the airbase. He envied Jacob Osbourne. He got to marry Kate and raise Lori. Regret was always the elephant in the room when it came to Lori. But she never made him feel guilty. She only showed him love and gratitude. They were a family.

The only one at Broom Lake who knew about his long-lost daughter was Bolantano. Andreas kept it that way. He had given Bolantano permission to include Lori in some of their business. The genetic end of creating the hybrids fascinated her. The methodology wasn't mentioned in any of her college textbooks. The Nazi doctors' research was decades ahead of the world. After graduating from Stanford, she attended medical school at the University of Southern California and specialized in gene therapy. The years rolled by. Lori made a name for herself in the field of genetics, staying close with her father.

By 1978, Bolantano had run out of crystal a second time. Lori donated some huge chunks that Kate had stolen so long ago when working at Broom Lake. Time had run out for Andreas. He was pushing eighty-years old. General William Lamphrey had given up waiting for Andreas to retire. He was once his protégé, but became bitter as the years rolled on. He accepted a lucrative job with a huge defense contractor. Lamphrey became more like the Nazi doctors and less like the hero he had been in World War II and Korea. He wished Andreas well when he left. "Hope you live forever," Lamphrey said. He mentioned his plans on running for public office and Andreas promised to vote for him. That was lie. Andreas never voted and if he did, it wouldn't be for Lamphrey. The man was heartless. He would throw away or burn the babies who developed deformities, diseases, and disabling conditions.

General Lamphrey wasn't the only one who wanted Andreas to leave the base. Andreas's higher-ups were pushing him out. They couldn't force him to retire, but there were already questions about his health and memory circulating. Anyone who only half knew him could see that he fit as a fiddle and sharp as a tack. His competency was still questioned.

As Operation Chrome evolved into a manufacturing plant, the doctors grew more sloppy, emboldened, and careless. No one seemed to notice missing babies. Andreas didn't even have to cook the books with phony adoptions. There were too many babies to count. The staff of airmen and airwomen were not trained to be nurse maids, yet because of their top-secret clearance, they were the only ones allowed in to take care of the giant nursery.

Doctor Hans Schmidt passed away from a short battle with cancer. The two remaining Nazis, Richtor and Jaeger, hired another doctor from Argentina, Doctor Rodrigo Herrara. He didn't look South American. He looked German and had an amazing resume.

Doctor Herrara was both brilliant and brutal. He made Schimdt look like a saint. He gave Operation Chrome a new product, hybrid organs. He thought the preserved organs might be valuable to someone who needed a transplant. A whole new wing was dug up underground to accommodate this new top secret business of organ donations. The idea gave them even more funding to play with. Doctor Herrara proved to be the most sadistic of the Nazi doctors. He used some of the infants for experiments. Like Lamphrey, he also threw the defective babies in the garbage. The babies were seen by many at the airbase as scientific advancements instead of human beings.

Bolantano and Andreas had seriously talked about burning the base down, but a new nursery factory would pop up in its place. Too many military generals and high-ranking politicians knew about Broom Lake. They wanted to see Operation Chrome continue under any and all circumstances.

Andreas's work grew more and more important with each year. He was saving lives. One day it might matter on a different level. Andreas knew he would never see all of the fruits of his labor, but Lori might. She was what kept him going. Bolantano was prepared to take his place very soon. Andreas would fall on the sword if everything turned to shit.

Lori Osbourne, who became Doctor Lori Osbourne, knew more about genetics than the doctors in med school. Andreas had slid her volumes of the research conducted at Broom Lake. It was one more act of treason to add to Andreas's growing list of crimes. He wanted his daughter to stand on his shoulders and do something that would change the world.

Doctor Richtor knew Andreas was taking files and copying them, but never said anything. He wanted something out of it. He once said, "General, I want to make sure that whoever you are giving this to will credit me in

217 • The Sequel

his or her research." Years later, Lori made good on that promise. She called one of her methods for isolating a gene the Richtor method.

Years went by until Lori discovered something else. She told her father and Bolantano that all of the hybrids' blood had a negative Rhesus factor. They didn't know what she was talking about.

"Well, most humans hold an inherited protein found on their red blood cells. Some humans don't have this protein, but it's very rare. It's the Rh negative factor. There are many theories attached to people with this rarity in their blood," she said. She went on about the cloning problems. She then told him how many scholars and scientists believed that the Rh negative factor was linked to the blood of 'gods' during ancient times. It was one of the biggest stumbling blocks in evolution theory. She wondered if humans were already hybrids of some kind, modified thousands of years ago.

***

One hundred and forty-two babies were stolen out of Broom Lake. Only a handful of them were adults. A larger percentage were in school. The largest percentage of the babies were under five years old. Andreas, Bolantano, and Lori grew bolder with each year. If Doctor Richtor hadn't covered for them, the number would be much smaller and they would probably be dead. They owed a great deal to the man. But he wasn't helping them out of the goodness of heart.

Andreas and Bolantano had to keep him in the loop. He wanted to know about their lives. Richtor believed that one's intelligence, health, and success were tied to his or her DNA. He theorized that the stolen babies would somehow find their own paths to greatness by using any opportunity that came along. So far, he was proven wrong.

Environment seemed to play a more important role. One thing was certain-Operation Chrome had no intention of slowing down. A few more doctors and assistants were brought in to continue the program.

Andreas, Bolantano, and Doctor Lori Osbourne compiled separate dossiers on every baby that was created inside of Broom Lake. The adult babies held the most interest. The ones adopted out to rich and powerful families seemed to have similar lives. Starting with Leonardo Lansatti, the first of his kind, the babies raised by the elite took advantage of all of their opportunities. None of them were arrested or diagnosed with an illness, mental disorder or addiction. In fact, they seemed perfect.

The stolen babies were a different story. There were already two suicides among the uncontrolled group. Some were diagnosed with depression and some had major problems with drugs and alcohol. The financial success of each one varied. Many of the babies grew up to be anti-social. Some had been arrested for petty crimes. None of them were felons, at least not yet. All of them were still young, but a few were on their second marriage.

Jay McCallister stood head and shoulders above all of them. Andreas had promised the up-and-coming author that he would visit again. Time was running out. It was time to make good on that promise before it was too late.

Andreas would have flown into Los Angeles himself, but his eyes had gone bad. He stopped flying planes years ago. He still had his driver's license. Bolantano flew him into a private airport outside of Los Angeles, and then he rented a car. Jay still lived in the area, but his address was different.

Andreas drove out of the city and into Hidden Hills. He wasn't familiar with suburb, but could see it was a very affluent area. He knew Jay had become quite prolific, but did not know he had become so wealthy. Andreas had read that his work was considered prophetic in some circles.

Hollywood was paying close attention. His *Bent Time* series was rumored to become a movie series.

Andreas pulled up to a wrought-iron gate, and then rolled down the window and pushed the intercom button. It was around dinner time and he hoped that he was not interrupting.

"Yes," said a female voice with a Spanish accent.

"I am here to see Jay."

"And your name?" asked the woman.

"Tell him I am an old friend who once visited him years ago at his old house in Los Angeles."

There was a long pause before the gates opened. Andreas slowly entered the estate. Flowers and fountains took over the front lawn. The landscaping looked professional. The large white portico gave an elegant look to the understated brick Georgian. The house was big, not mansion big, but big, especially for L.A. standards. Andreas was very impressed. From the exterior of Jay's home, he seemed not to be having too many problems. Life was good at the McCallister residence. He hoped Jay was happy.

Before Andreas walked up to the doorway and attempted the short set of stairs, the woman who answered the intercom had come outside to help. She looked Mexican and was short, thin, frail, and almost as old as he was. She wore a gray and white maid's uniform. He didn't think he needed the help and almost resented it. He still didn't see himself as old.

With her thick accent, she mumbled, "Follow me."

The general followed her down a long hallway which ended in the family room. The back wall of the house was all windows. He could see Jay sitting by the pool with a young, beautiful woman, enjoying a cocktail. Andreas allowed himself a moment of pride like a father would have for a son who had done well. He hoped that all of the stolen babies were doing well or would do well as time passed.

The maid opened up one of the many sets of French doors that led out to the patio and motioned for Andreas to follow.

Jay's head turned. "Well, my mysterious friend. I haven't seen you in what, almost a decade? Thought you forgot about me. This is my new wife, Stephanie."

Andreas could hear the slur behind a few of his words. He guessed Jay to be a drink or two away from completely shit-faced.

Andreas shook hands with both Jay and the bikini-clad blonde. She looked like a model. She was definitely more attractive than his first wife.

"Stephanie was Miss March, 1975," Jay said.

Andreas nodded. He'd be sure to get a copy of that particular issue. The woman smiled, revealing perfect white teeth.

"Steph, if you don't mind, this gentleman and I have some unfinished business. Go help Juanita with dinner."

"Sir, didn't catch your name?" she said as she stood up.

Jay cut her off. "You need to give us some privacy." Stephanie did not go back in the house with the maid. She went to the far side of the pool and began swimming laps. "She'll go inside in a few minutes. Sorry, she's curious. Besides, the swim will sober her up. We've been out here for a few hours now, just drinking."

Andreas smiled and nodded. "Congratulations on everything. I had heard you were a big success, but not like this. Wow! This place is gorgeous. And your new wife is stunning. Sorry it didn't work out with…"

"It doesn't matter. After our first meeting, I almost thought I had imagined you. That you weren't real and I was losing my mind. But then I did a little digging. Jeez,

I'm hungry. The booze just hit me. I hope Juanita whips something up fast."

"Please eat. I have come a long way and at my age, this might be the last time I can ever come. I'm obviously old, but I am being forced into retirement and who knows, I might even meet with a mysterious accident or unforeseen health problem if you know what I mean. I am not being melodramatic or paranoid." Jay nodded and looked concerned. "My name is Robert and I have much to tell you. As you already know, you are different. I told you that the first time we met. According to the plan, you weren't supposed to end up here. A rich, privileged family was supposed to raise you and give you the kinds of opportunities that's so few of us have. And just look at you. With no one's help, you've made it to the top anyway on your terms, not theirs!"

Juanita came out of the house with a big ceramic bowl full of chips and a smaller bowl of salsa. She set three plates on the table. Jay looked over at his new wife and shook his head at Juanita. She took one of the plates away.

"She eats inside," Jay said. Juanita nodded and went back in the house.

Andreas's bubble of how great Jay's life had turned out began to deflate. Evidently, Jay did not trust the gorgeous Stephanie, but that was a good thing.

The men snacked on the chips. Jay guzzled down a few glasses of water. He talked a little about his best-selling novels, and then moved onto his first wife. Apparently, she was whore. Andreas thought Jay sounded like a bitter old man who had yet to turn thirty. How many wives would he have by the time he was Andreas's age? Juanita returned with a platter of tacos and beans. Andreas looked at the delicious food and became hungry. Both men scarfed down the platter. Stephanie had gone inside and ate alone while watching television. Andreas saw her through the window, but couldn't hear the TV volume.

As if reading his mind, Jay said, "Good sound proof windows, General Andreas."

"Yes, they are truly sound-proof. Wait! How did you know my last name?"

"How do you think? I'm rich. I bought the information. You're practically a ghost. My guy had never seen anything like it."

Somewhat surprised, Andreas asked, "Okay, then tell me about myself and I'll tell you if you got your money's worth."

"You're an air force general. World War II hero. You run a base in Nevada. I'll admit that I didn't get an exact location, just somewhere close to Las Vegas. You are in charge of a top secret operation that makes super weapons based on alien technology. You are close to figuring out time travel. Your base along with NASA have secretly sent astronauts to other planets."

Andreas laughed. He was light years away on the truth. "I'm impressed, but they are all rumors. Makes for a great novel. Maybe you could write about it. Seriously, the only truth that you got out of your guy is the alien technology. But we aren't using it for weapons. We are using it to make hybrids. Humans mixed with aliens."

"So, an alien mates with a human?"

Jay seemed to have sobered up quite a bit after the dinner. Andreas decided to spoon feed him his ancestry. "Well, you are way off. These special beings are created within a lab. The lab is in my base, and my base is in Nevada. He got that part right as well. As I alluded to before, the first time we met, you are one of the first of these hybrids."

Jay dropped his glass of water on the concrete patio. Juanita was back with a broom. Andreas helped by picking up the larger pieces. As they cleaned, Jay meandered over to the bar and poured himself a large glass of tequila, and then lit up a cigarette. *Damn!* thought Andreas. He needed Jay sober.

"Want one?" Jay asked.

Andreas nodded. "Alright. Just one. Please, Jay, I need your mind clear. I need you to remember everything that I tell you. There's more. I'm pushing eighty years old. If I'm lucky, I'll die soon of natural causes."

Andreas told him the abridged version of the danger he personally faced, the death of Kate, and the danger Jay could be in if he wasn't careful. "Jay, you are not alone. We took a lot of babies from the base and dumped them off at orphanages around the world."

Jay sucked down the tequila and to Andreas's dismay, poured himself another one. "So, if we are here, then they are here. What do they want?" His slur was back. Jay had gone from half-way sober to drunk.

"Ironically, you write about them. You told me that they may be influencing your novels." He nodded. Andreas's heart turned heavy. "Jay, have you been in direct contact with any aliens?" It all of a sudden occurred to Andreas that these Advanced Beings might have been communicating to the hybrids.

"Just when I write. Something takes over. I almost don't remember writing anything. It's like I'm forced into recording someone else's story. I've been told that's part of automatic writing. The only time my mind is clear from these stories is when I drink. Are we all like this?"

"You are one of the oldest. But we've lost two of your kind to suicide. If only I talked to them, let them know they are not completely human. Please know that you are not crazy, just cursed. Could these Advanced Beings be using you as a kind of historian? Or maybe your novels are really some kind of truth that is read between the lines. As we talked about before, my partner and I leave each baby that we steal with a green-yellow crystal. We hoped it would be a sign or symbol, something to connect with each other. The base has no plans for stopping the manufacture of babies. There will be more like you, more that we can hopefully place in orphanages. Your kind was meant for something else."

"What kind of alien do I come from?" Jay said meekly. He continued to guzzle down the tequila. In some respects, Andreas couldn't blame him.

"I have no idea what they are called. This race crashed their craft in Roswell, New Mexico. There are more than race, though. Maybe the other races are doing the same thing, making hybrids. I'm glad I came here and I hope I gave you some kind of peace of mind. What you are doing is so much more important than writing a book. You are changing the world. Keep it up."

Chapter Twenty-Eight

1944
The Eagle's Nest, Germany

"Jay McCallister?" I asked Maria Orsic in disbelief.

She looked at me with alarm. Her thoughts burned through my head. *Something isn't right. I am not familiar with this feeling.* No one seemed to notice our telepathic conversation. All of the attention in the room was directed towards my feet, which were almost fully healed. German whispers from trembling mouths were too preoccupied to notice.

Maria, if you can hear my thoughts, Jay McCallister hasn't been born yet. He was created inside of a lab. He told me that I was also created from a lab. He recently died and left me his legacy. Time travel is part of it. If he is somehow communicating to you, please do not shut him out.

Maria looked at me with her giant blue eyes and wiped away a tear. *All he said was that Eric is coming to save you.*

My brown eyes teared up as she said it. Eric was even more doomed than I. He would surely die. Was he an idiot? He had a chance at meeting someone new, maybe that new girl at his bookstore. He hired her as my replacement after my writing career took off. I wanted him to have a life and be happy. I wanted him to forget about me.

Hitler started screaming as everyone was gaping at my feet. Two soldiers dragged the two dead bodies out of the room and returned with cleaning supplies. I was escorted out as they scrubbed the floor and the bed.

Two men took me to a nearby bathroom, and then stripped me and threw me in the tub. As they flung my pants on the floor, the coins and bills that Glenn had given me fell out of the pocket. The coins clanked down to the tiled flooring. The two soldiers scooped them up and examined them. I knew they were minted in more recent times. Both men rambled off some more comments in German. One of them took the paper money and coins and left. I only guessed they went to show Hitler.

As soon as the soldier was finished bathing me, another soldier gave me a white, shapeless dress to put on. It looked part nightgown, part hospital gown. One of the soldiers reached inside of his pocket and pulled out a syringe. In less than a second he stabbed me in the neck. My knees wobbled as I collapsed to the floor. The last thing I remembered was someone lifting me up.

I woke up in a dentist chair with my feet strapped in stirrups and my hands strapped to the arms of the chair. My gown was hiked up to my waist. I had no underwear and was fully exposed. Was I raped? My crotch pulsed in pain. I was definitely violated, but I suspected some kind of medical procedure was performed. I saw a small puddle of blood on the seat of my chair. Did I heal, like my gunshot wounds?

The room was different than the room they used to bathe me. They could have moved me to a new location. I had no idea how long I had been knocked out. This room appeared to be some kind of crude examining room. The walls were white, the floor was off-white, and the cabinets were yellow-white. The only color in the room were the pink tiled counter tops by the sink.

Whoever bound me to the chair was either careless or wanted to leave me an escape. Maybe this was another test. I easily wriggled my way out of the straps and tried to stand up. Dizziness consumed me. I fell back in the chair. The drug they had used had not worn off. My mouth felt like cotton. I got up again and threw myself at the sink. I drank from the faucet like a dog drinking from a hose. The cold water tasted like rust, but quenched my thirst.

Clutching the walls, I made my way to the door. It was a locked steel door. Another dead end. I looked up at the very high ceilings. On one wall there was a bank of windows. I imagined they were used as some kind of observatory for captors to watch their prey. I couldn't see anyone, but instinctively knew I was being watched. I wished they would just kill me. I was too tired to fight them. They won. I was no match, even with some of my Advanced Being properties. Maybe I could travel through time and magically heal from a gunshot, but that was not enough to get me out of this mess. It were, however, the only reasons why I was still alive. For the time being, I fascinated these little monsters.

I sat back down and waited for someone to come in and torture me some more. Then I remembered Maria. She said aloud 'Jay McCallister' and then said to me through telepathy that Eric was coming. I wanted to cling to that ray of hope, but knew it was a waste of time. I hoped and even prayed that Eric would not come. There was nothing exceptional about him to hold their interest.

A long time had passed, maybe an hour or more, and I had grown tired. I rested my eyes and tried not to fall asleep. Soon I heard keys jangling and locks clicking.

Josef appeared. "Maya, are you alright?"

I laughed at the absurdity of it all. He was the reason I was here in the first place. If he had just let me go back in his little time machine. My laughter turned into a high-pitched hyena sounding cackle. I never heard the sound come out of me before. The laughter had an edgy shrill. I was losing it and made no attempt to get it together.

Kill me! I'm going to laugh my ass off as you try. Tears rolled down my cheeks and my side ached. I had trouble catching my breath.

"Enough." Josef screamed.

His anger only made me laugh harder. He hit my face so hard I thought one of my teeth was going to fly out, but it didn't. My tongue played with it as it rocked back and forth inside of my mouth.

"They want me to show you something," Josef said.

My laughter began to trail off. "They? The same 'they' who knocked me out and examined me? Was I raped? Did they take out my ovaries? I heal so damn fast, there are no scars." I looked into Josef's icy blue eyes and saw pure trepidation.

"I took some eggs and some other samples. Listen, I didn't mean for any of this to happen. I thought, I just thought...you came out of my time machine and I knew you were special. I wanted them to see that it worked. I had no idea..."

I spit at him and then said, "If this is your idea of an apology, it's not going to cut it. Not now, not in the future, not ever. You are every bit as wicked as they are. Don't even try to play the misunderstood doctor or whatever the fuck you are. How dare you..."

Josef interrupted me. "Shut up!" He looked up by the row of windows, reminding me that we might not be alone. "You can reprimand me later, but I have to show you something. And it was only me."

"Huh? Only you?"

"I was the one who examined you. Under the *Fuehrer's* orders of course, but he wanted the samples. He wanted your DNA. I don't know why, but can only guess he might want to breed you one day. You are rare, maybe one of a kind. Let's go."

My eyes scanned the long, dark hallway as we walked out of the examining room. My fight and flight instincts were back. I was checking my surroundings for a possible escape. Maybe Josef was as well. He didn't seem to be in the so-called Nazi in-crowd. He came off as more of an employee who did what he was told.

"So, where are we?" I asked as he led me into a huge chamber.

"We are in the basement of Eagle's Nest. Now we are going to wait."

"Wait for…" I stopped mid-sentence. Josef gave me a frightened look that chilled me to the core. He was having a hard time keeping it together.

Josef led me to the one wall that had a light switch panel on it. There were several switches. He pressed a few of them. A bank of lights illuminated the room. I could see the basement. It was dingy, concrete, and vacant with exception of two dead bodies in the far corner. This basement was the archetypal setting for all kinds of atrocities. I wished there was a chair. My knees couldn't support me for much longer. The meds made it almost impossible to stand.

"Over there, are they the ones who I killed?" I asked as I lifted up my arm in the direction of the two bodies. The uniforms looked familiar, but I couldn't get a good look at their faces.

He nodded. I stumbled and Josef quickly caught me. He said, "Listen to me. We haven't got much time until… you were given morphine. Please, try to stand. You'll look weak if you don't. Your strength is the only thing keeping you and me alive."

I nodded. There was the sound of a motor in the distance. A long crack in the wall ran from the floor to the ceiling. As the motor sound grew closer, I watched the crack. Something about it wasn't right. The floor started to rattle.

"Is that an elevator shaft?" I asked. Josef nodded. He was also staring at the crack. "Is that some kind of hidden door?" He nodded again.

The crack, which was really a seam, opened up. A slab of concrete pushed out, and then to the side like a barn door. I could now see the track for the top of the door that was affixed to the ceiling. The elevator opening was now obvious. I had to admire the design of the very well hidden door.

The elevator car was large enough to put a truck inside. Bormann and three armed soldiers walked out. They were dressed in different Nazi regalia. How many days had I been drugged? One? Two? Three? It couldn't have been more than three days. Was time the same in 1944 Germany as it was in 2017 Nevada? My curiosities had to be put on hold. Bormann and his henchmen were not alone.

Two huge animals slithered out behind the group of men. I felt faint, but remembered what Josef said. With every ounce of strength I stood my ground. I had never seen this species in my life. They had a large head that looked almost human with exception of a small snout and flattened skull. I speculated they might be some kind of chimera of humans and crocodiles. Their brownish-green skin looked more like leather with jagged bumps that ran down their backs. As they slithered, they looked snakelike, but I could see their limbs were tucked to the sides of their long, shapeless body. They both had a ridged tail that was a few feet long. They had to be some kind of reptile.

Both of these reptile beings appeared to be searching for something. One of them was looking at the dead bodies in the corner. Soon both of them were on top of the bodies, ripping the dead men's clothing off with their short, leathery limbs and tearing into the flesh with their razor sharp teeth. I could see a double row of pointy fangs chewing up the dead flesh. I lost my balance and stumbled to the floor.

Josef knelt down and whispered in my ear. "You want to end up like them? You want to be their next meal? Get up and try not to shake and stutter." He gracefully lifted me up. I continued to watch these things rip off limbs and then gnaw on them as if they were eating corn-on-the-cob. My hands shook and my nerves were shot. Josef squeezed my hand tight and gave me a stern look. I couldn't help but shudder.

What terrified me most were the reptiles' eyes. They were a yellowish-green, the same color as my and Josef's crystals. Their eyes were ice cold, yet filled with intelligence. Several minutes later, the reptilian beings had devoured the dead bodies, leaving nothing but bones and remnants of their uniforms. They even lapped up the blood on the floor as if licking their plates clean. Once finished, they slithered over to where we all stood.

I was the main attraction. The reptilians weren't staring at me, but staring inside of me. One of them began to slither around Josef and me while sticking out its doubly pointed tongue. Josef sensed that I was about to fall. He put his arm around me as a brace. I was afraid to look at him for the kind gesture. These beings seemed to be taking in every move that we made, like a computer analyzing every byte of data.

The reptile who circled us had lifted itself up. Its limbs were now away from its sides. It looked more human as it stood upright. The other reptile also stood up. Both of them were absent of genitalia. Were these things asexual? They were at least a foot taller than I was and towered Josef by several inches. Both of them loomed over us.

Bormann said something in German. One of the things answered back. Its voice was not deep or high-pitched. Again, I struggled with assigning a pronoun to these reptile-like beings. The voice could have belonged to a computer. It was undistinctive, but crystal clear. I heard every phonic sound in every syllable. There was an edge to its voice that projected an inherent evil. These reptiles spoke German? I trembled in fear. Josef's hand stiffened as it held me up by my waist.

"Josef, here," said Bormann as he handed him a file, choosing to speak English. "Explain this."

Josef's face twitched and hands shook. He opened the folder and read something in German. The reptilians nodded. He then said to me, "Your DNA sequences do not match their DNA sequences. Although your DNA is similar to human DNA, it doesn't exactly match either. You have a few genes that I have never seen before."

One of the reptilians nodded, and then took the file from Josef's hand. The reptile had six fingers on each of its hands. Its hands were dexterous and human-like, but with shorter and thicker fingers without nails. The fingers were partially webbed with crackled skin that covered each of the joints.

The reptilian who did all of the talking looked at me with its cold, yellow-green eyes and said, "You come from America."

My heart rate accelerated. I needed to sit down. Josef's firm hand dug into my side as if he knew how I was feeling. I pushed myself even harder to stand. My voice cracked as I answered. "Yes, I am from the United States."

"Do you know who made you?"

The question was dehumanizing, but asked in a scientific demeanor. My feelings were never once taken into account. I was their captive, their guinea pig, their subject for experiment. I was an object to be poked and prodded at their whim. Nobody was particularly interested in my life in 2017 or how I got here in the first place. The only thing that seemed to matter was my genetic makeup.

I shook my head and with surprise, I answered, "I have no idea who my maker was, but God is my Creator."

He seemed uninterested in my religious declaration. Instead, he stated, "We might know who your extraterrestrial parent was. You come from a line of Advanced Beings who excel at genetic modification. If we are correct, then you are quite a surprise. Your ancestors are practically extinct."

Bormann's face turned white as a ghost. His expression was a mix of worry and insanity. "Is this race that is practically extinct a friend or foe to you, to us?" Bormann asked in a mumbled English tongue. He sounded like a little boy.

"Time will tell if she comes from a friend or foe. Through her, this nearly extinct race wants to survive. But then we all want to survive," said the reptilian in its monotone voice. He almost sounded like a recording from a language lesson. Its thick, scaly tail wagged. It looked at Bormann with its bright, intelligent eyes and said, "You will lose this war. Your *Fuehrer* made too many mistakes. But we will proceed anyway."

The other reptile looked at me and said, "Zykedo, you might be wrong about her sequence. Her race is not practically extinct. There are some who live. They are slaves. I think whoever made her wanted to create a new species with humanity. Maya is an interesting name. Who named you?"

"Well, I really don't know. I was placed in an orphanage when I was just a baby. I am assuming the nuns who ran the orphanage named me. Since you know my name, can I ask what your name is? Your friend is Zykedo?"

"He is Zykedo. I am Hensa."

"So, you both are males?" I asked.

Hensa replied, "Not exactly. Our race is called Reptilian. We are both male and female, but we refer to ourselves in the masculine pronouns. Now Maya, back to you. When you say you were brought up in an orphanage, do you have any idea who saved you?"

"Saved? Living in an orphanage and then being tossed around a string of foster homes is hardly considered saved or rescued." I didn't like the tone that came out of my mouth. I sounded indignant, maybe even disrespectful.

Hensa smiled and flashed a double row of his jagged teeth. I cringed in fear. "Sorry. That came out wrong. I had a rough childhood, I ran away when I was in high school."

"Ah, but you became a successful writer, yes?"

How did he know that? Bormann? Did I mention that when I was in the circle with Maria? I nodded.

Hensa continued. "Maya, you are a hybrid who writes science fiction. Don't you understand? You were not only saved, but chosen. You think your life was hopeless, but it's so much better than what was planned out for you. You were bred to be someone else's puppet. Here you are. Back to the beginning of your beginning. The ultimate causal loop. If you pay close attention to Zykedo and me, you might return home with some revolutionary new advances."

I just heard the word *home*. "You will send me home?"

Zykedo and Hensa looked at each other, flashed their dingy white fangs, and curled their mouths upward. It was either an encouraging smile or I'd be their next dinner.

Zykedo said, "Yes, we will help you get back, but there are conditions."

Bormann's face fell. He looked as if this was the first he'd heard of me going home. I could feel Josef's fingers dig into my waist. I could tell he was both happy and surprised.

I nodded and smiled at them. Conditions. Whatever they were, I had no choice, and we all knew it, even if it was my soul. I had allied myself with Hitler's alien advisors or whoever they were to the war.

As if reading my mind, Hensa said, "We don't work for Hitler. He works for us. Come. We have much to show you."

Chapter Twenty-Nine

Present Day
Ruby Mountains, Nevada

"You saw Jay?" Mercedes asked. "Where? How?" She and Paula hovered over Glenn in T.A.H.'s library.

"Please, I just woke up. Let me think. Yes, I was definitely dreaming. What wild dreams I was having. I usually never dream. Aliens, spaceships, Jay. I just finished Maya's book. It gave me plenty to visualize."

Paula rolled her eyes impatiently. "But what about Jay?"

"Well, he was in the preservation room."

Mercedes raised a perfectly tweezed eyebrow. With barely any sleep, she looked twenty years younger than her real age. Her clothes still managed to look fresh and pressed and her black hair looked as if she just left the beauty shop. She was still just as glamorous as when she graced TV screens decades ago. "You mean the freezer with those Advanced Beings? Oh, how morbid. You should have had him buried. But go on. You said that Maya was in 1944 Germany. Jay always believed he was created by Nazis. Is this your subconscious? Or do you think Jay actually talked to you in a dream?"

Glenn scratched his head. "Well, if I could get a word in edge-wise with you two, maybe it was both. I honestly don't know. I have this horrible feeling that it's true. She's back in World War II."

Unlike Mercedes, Paula looked like death warmed over. She had bags under her young dark eyes. They looked red and puffy as if she had been crying. The stress of losing

Jay and now Maya was taking its toll. She had always been the most sensitive of their little group. Her eyes briefly flashed anger. "I think you're right. And it wasn't just a dream, it was Jay. Damn it! I should have thought of this before."

Glenn wasn't sure where she was going. Her face looked animated. "You're not thinking of…"

"Yes, I am. A séance."

Glenn ran both of his hands through his gray hair and sneered. "Where? In the freezer where we keep him and the Advanced Beings?" She smiled and shrugged her shoulders, making him angry. "Are you nuts? We almost lost you last time, right before Jay died. Lam took over and you lost complete control. You could have died. No, I won't allow it! We've lost way too much over the last month. Oh my, I just remembered it will be Christmas soon. No, please, I can't handle losing any more of us. We got a real chance with Maya's sequel to get her back. Lori will have more direction on what to do with Eric. Please, give it chance."

Paula was about to interrupt, but Mercedes held up her hands and motioned for her to sit down. She then said, "Paula, he's right. At least for now. That book might be the key. Ironic, isn't? I mean she writes a book that has a DNA code for a gene that allows you to time travel, and then needs someone to time travel and bring her home. Almost like she planned it that way. I know, I am over thinking this."

Glenn shook his head. "A closed loop. A form of predestination. How many more like her are out there? And Jay found her. Another form of predestination. But then what do I know? I'm just a lawyer turned TV show host."

Mercedes smiled at him. Her teeth still gleamed like the TV star she once was. He had always held a torch for her, but never acted upon it. She flipped her long, black hair and said, "You are much more than that. Always were. By the way, what did you think of the book? Something about it was odd. I wasn't thrilled with the ending. It left too many holes."

Glenn looked over at Eric who was still sleeping soundly on the couch of the library and then whispered, "Personally, I didn't read it for the code. Chuck and Lori are doing that. I read it for the story. Like the first novel, it was obviously another allegory."

"Yes, but with no master race. No one particularly wins," Paula added.

"Exactly. Maybe that's what she is trying to say, or warn us about. We've got a new villain, the reptoid, in the story. Chuck mentioned a race called Reptilian Advanced Beings back in China. Maya has never seen any of these beings, yet she told the tale as if she personally knew them. How could she have known?"

Paula laughed. "She also knew plenty about genetics, yet dropped out of high school. Don't you get it? She's just the messenger. Just like Jay was. I thought the book was more of a warning, or even a doomsday prophecy. She did such a great job crafting the story and then gave a weak explanation at the end. Much seemed to be missing. Lots of loose ends. It was weird. Seemed as if someone else wrote that last chapter."

Eric lifted up his head. His reddish hair was a mess. "Are you talking about the book? She didn't write the last page. Claude must have added that page and erased the rest of it. He's hiding something. Oh, I'm starved. How long was I out?"

"You've been sleeping for about twenty hours. Young man, you will be glad you got the rest. But you're right about the book. Mercedes and Paula, can you get someone to feed him?" They nodded. "Listen, whatever Maya did or didn't do in that last chapter, I'm going to see what Lori thinks. If she can piece the code together, we can get Eric to bring her back. Paula, promise me you won't do anything stupid?"

Paula nodded, but Glenn wasn't too convinced. When her mind was made up, that was it. He didn't have the time to shadow her. After leaving the library, he went up to the lab to talk to Doctor Blacksmith. She was deep asleep, sitting on a stool with her torso and head slumped on the cold steel countertop of the lab cabinets. Her arms hung off the table. She looked so uncomfortable. Her iPad and a spiral notebook sat in front of her face.

Doctor Lori Blacksmith had been an acquaintance of Jay's before T.A.H. had been constructed. Since Maya's disappearance, she hadn't left the institute. Glenn wondered where she lived. He wondered about her family. He knew so little about her.

The doctor's notebook was right in front of Glenn. He couldn't help but peek. Glenn watched her eyes and pushed the notebook closer to him. Her notes might as well have been written in another language. He didn't quite understand what she had found. However, he could see the questions she wrote at the bottom of the notebook.

The ending is wrong. The sequence can't end there. Huh? What happened to the rest of the code?

So, Lori also thinks the ending fell flat, Glenn thought. Glenn thumbed through a few more pages and saw Lori's hazel eyes glaring at him.

"What are you doing?" she curtly asked.

"Oh, you're awake. I didn't mean to snoop. I was just really curious to what you found in the book." Glenn hoped he didn't have a guilty look on his face.

"I just couldn't keep my eyes open. The book is amazing. I can't believe Maya wrote this. She basically encoded a DNA map on where the isolated time travel gene should go. It's as if she wanted humans to be able to travel. But there's a problem." Kate picked up her notebook, stretched her arms, and yawned. "Excuse me. I am still exhausted. Without getting into too much detail, the last part of the strand is left off. I'm not sure which chromosome it falls on. Without it being complete, there are three maybe four possibilities on where it should be placed without worrying about any real damage to our poor guinea pig, Eric. It's still too risky. Big chance for error."

Glenn expected her hesitation. She didn't have the stomach for things when they went south. "What other options do we have? Maya is in real trouble. If we can't go looking for her, she will die. I had a dream, Doctor. I don't think it was just a dream. Jay spoke to me and said that she was in trouble. She's in World War II Germany and needs our help."

"Sorry, but losing her or losing her and Eric are our current options. And I'd rather lose one instead of two people. It was irresponsible of you and Chuck to stuff her in that capsule in the first place. You both never even thought of showing her how to work the bloody thing!"

Bloody. Glenn had noticed her English slang before. She nor Jay never mentioned the British Isles. Her resume put her in the U.S. for decades.

Lori continued to lecture him on his lack of ethics. "You and Chuck have always put your ambitions first and to hell with everyone else! I don't know how much longer I can work here. Jay was the only reason I stuck around. I am not doing another thing unless I know the exact location."

"I understand. You're still angry about the Chinese prisoner. But must I remind you that Jay also wanted to see if reverse aging was possible. And it was. None of us were completely innocent. Great discovery sometimes requires great sacrifice. I hope we can pick back up to where we started. Maybe stick with animals. Back to the problem at hand. I agree with you that part of the book is missing. I might be able to…"

"What? Put a gun to her husband's head? Her publisher's head?"

"No, nothing that distasteful," Glenn lied. She had no idea that Claude, Sam, and Allie were locked up a few dozen feet beneath her. "Give me another day. Just another day. I will try to kindly persuade those who might know something. By persuade, I mean bribe." The doctor nodded. "Good. Thanks. I won't disappoint. Please look at Jay's genes. You might narrow it down that way. Maybe you will figure it out yourself."

"That's a decent idea. I am personally out of ideas."

Glenn nodded and abruptly left. He knew examining Jay's DNA would take longer than a day and he needed her expertise. Chuck was nowhere in her league when it came to genetic splicing. No one was. If he had to get ugly, he would. They came too far.

The doctor said there were three or four possibilities on where to place the time travel gene into Eric's DNA strand. This gave him an idea. He called Chuck and Devon for a private meeting. They met by the centrifuge.

"Doctor Blacksmith believes that Maya's ending was changed or even deleted. That seems to be a growing consensus around here. I think Claude knows exactly what's happened. This is his ace he's been sitting on," Glenn said.

Devon cracked his knuckles and scratched his face. He hadn't shaved in a few days. "Maybe that's why the fucker has a smirk on his face. The three of them are locked up and cuffed. He's not even flinching. What do you want me to do? We could water board him for starters, and then maybe move into toe removal…"

Glenn's stomach soured. He hated making these kinds of decisions alone. But without Jay, it was his call. "I've got a better idea. Bring all three of them here, into the round room." Devon nodded and left the room. Once he was gone Glenn said, "Chuck, get some photos of Lori's notes, but without her knowing. Try to pick her brain. How will we place the gene into Eric's system? Will it automatically know where to attach itself?"

"Doctor Blacksmith told me she would use a virus to get it placed within the correct part of the strand. She believed a gene gun would probably be more effective and quicker than an injection. I'll find a way to get her notes. See you very soon."

A few hours went by and Glenn had everything he needed. Claude, Allie and Sam were cuffed and gagged, sitting on the floor of the centrifuge room. Chuck had photos of Lori's notes and understood her plan. Jay's time travel gene had been isolated and cloned thousands of times. The rest was guess work-a 1 in 3 or 4 chance of getting this right.

Glenn and Chuck were done waiting. Both men wanted to know the secret to human time travel. Chuck would have done anything to get to this moment. Glenn wanted Maya to come home, but was also salivating for success. This discovery cast a spell on the two men.

Glenn and Chuck looked at each other and then at Devon. "Ungag Claude. We need to have a chat."

Devon took out the wadded up rag from Claude's mouth and then loomed over him with a glock in his hand. Devon's height and body builder frame made Claude seem small. As the big man pushed him against wall, Claude seemed unruffled.

Yes, Claude knew something alright, thought Glenn. Devon was one of most scary men around and Claude was still unflappable.

Devon could have took down twenty Claudes all armed with weapons. The former marine and Eragon Defense mercenary had been at T.A.H. for five years. He had met Jay at a book signing. He asked Jay for a few minutes of his time, and then quickly revealed he had fought off a small unit of Advanced Beings in Afghanistan. He and his squad were never the same. Jay hired him on the spot as head of T.A.H.'s security. He, in turn, handpicked thirty men to keep the hidden mountain fortress secure. He was both brawn and nerd-a whiz at computers. Glenn wished he hired someone like Devon to watch over Jay at his Tiburon home.

Now that Claude was ungagged, he still had nothing to say. The smug look on his handsome face reminded Glenn of a spoiled movie star who was stewing over an insignificant line in a movie. He acted annoyed when he should have pissed his pants.

Glenn wanted to smash Claude's face in, but stuffed his anger deep down, and then calmly said, "When do you plan on telling us about the ending of the sequel?"

"What? You don't like it? Everyone's a fucking critic." Devon punched him in the gut. "You don't play fair, Glenn. I gave you everything you asked for. What did I get? A trip to hell with my brother and ex? We had a deal. I hope you fry for kidnapping. Unless you want to uphold what was promised, I really have nothing to say. Kill me for all I care."

Devon took out a stun gun from a leather case attached to his waist. He zapped Claude in the neck. His body shook as he sunk to the floor. A few minutes went by until he became coherent. Allie and Sam moved closer to each other against the wall as they watched in fear.

"Claude," Glenn said, "we're not screwing around. What did you delete?"

Again, Devon zapped him in the lower stomach, and then looked at Claude's crotch area and smiled.

"Fuck you! Fuck you all!" screamed Claude. He didn't appear to be scared, just angry.

"I realize that you are smart enough to know how desperate we are to get the end of Maya's novel. Last chance, Claude," Glenn said.

Devon zapped Claude's crotch as he laid on the floor. He howled in pain as he shook. Still nothing. Claude was one tough nut to crack. Maybe this was it.

"Okay then. We are on to Plan B," Glenn said, and then exchanged a knowing look with Chuck.

The prisoners were pushed into the adjoining room. Chuck dragged Allie by the hair and strapped her into a heavy wooden chair. He calmly opened a large briefcase and took out the prototype of a new gene gun that Doctor Blacksmith had designed. He looked at Allie and smiled.

"Do you think we really are the first to try this?" asked Glenn, immune to the hysterical sobs coming from the wooden chair. "Think about it. All of these genetic companies that have cropped up, advertising that they will figure out your ancestry or your health and aging process...I mean, could it be possible that these companies are a front? I believe they exist to collect DNA samples from an old military operation or perhaps even the world."

Chuck loaded up the gene gun with a vial of cloned time travel genes. "It's more than possible. You are probably right on the money. If Maya were here, she might even send in a sample of her DNA to get some answers about her race. She was curious about her ancestry and with good reason. Can you imagine what they'd find...very dangerous world we live in. But we can't dwell on what others might know. We need to carry on as if we were the first." Chuck tapped the gene gun and sealed up the tiny chamber. "I think we are ready. Just think of the limitless possibilities."

Glenn looked around. Devon was transfixed on what Chuck was about to do. Allie squirmed and sobbed in the wooden chair as Sam watched, tied up and completely helpless. Claude sat next to him and silently watched.

There was a dark feeling in the room as if the devil was there himself, directing the scene. Glenn's stomach turned. This wasn't right.

"Yes, Chuck, this does have limitless possibilities, but it also has consequences. Maybe I'm old, but I'm getting very nervous. You know, at the end of Jay's life he wondered if any of this was worth it. He even thought that God might exist because we all get a feeling of what's right and what's wrong."

"Sorry old man, we're not turning back. Here we go." Chuck turned on the gun and started shooting the gene into Allie. He shot into her arms, legs, stomach, neck, head, butt, hips, almost everywhere. Her blood drizzled all over the floor. The gag did not contain her shrieks. "Glenn, please turn on the centrifuge."

Glenn walked into the back room and hit the switch. He knew Chuck had recalibrated it at a higher speed in preparation for this moment. In the corner was an iPad, probably Chuck's. Glenn walked over to it and turned it on. The last chapter of Maya's novel lit up the screen. Chuck had highlighted a few of the sentences. Glenn walked over to the screen.

'We are not alone. They are here. We can pretend to live in harmony, but will always be their slaves. We can fight to keep what is ours, but we risk extinction.'

"What the hell was she talking about," said Glenn aloud to no one. The hero in Maya's novel chose peace. But peace through enslavement? *What did Maya mean in her book?*

Glenn didn't have the time to analyze Maya's novel. At this moment, all that mattered was the ending. If Claude wanted to play games, then he would pay. Taking a deep breath and pushing guilt out of his mind, he returned to the round room. Allie had thin trails of blood all over her body. Her tears had stopped, but she held the gaze of a traumatized victim. Sam's red eyes were filled with terror. Claude still held onto his poker face.

"Where's Chuck?" Glenn asked Devon.

"He'll be back in a flash. He took a sample from the girl to see if the sequence had changed."

Minutes of silence went by. Claude had started to lose his cool. His handsome face had a green cast to it. "What the fuck are you doing to her?"

No one answered. Sam started crying again. Glenn wondered if there could be another way. It's either her or Maya...He was about to achieve the biggest scientific advancement the world had ever seen.

Chuck walked back in, smiling. He said, "It took. Her body accepted the new gene. We are good to go." Chuck nodded at Devon. He picked Allie up like a rag doll and stuffed her in the time capsule, clamping her arms and legs down. Before closing the door and sealing her in, he ungagged her. The door shut. Despite the ultra-thick glass, everyone could hear her screams.

"Maybe we should wait and see what Lori comes up with. She is studying the genetic placement of Jay's DNA sequence. That might give us a more exact location..."

"We've gone this far. There's no turning back." Chuck dashed into the computer room and pressed the button. The capsule began to spin. Vomit splattered onto the glass as they all watched. Would she disappear like Maya? Minutes went by and Allie still screamed as the capsule spun. Something was wrong.

"Stop this. It's not working." Glenn stepped away from the capsule and headed towards the bank of computers in the next room.

Chuck held his shoulder. "No. Give it another minute. Please."

But Allie never made it through another minute. Blood splattered against the glass tube's walls. Her screams ceased. Claude screamed in horror as her head ripped off of her neck and banged around inside of the tube like a tennis shoe inside of a dryer.

Chuck ran to the centrifuge and shut it down. He then turned off the capsule. Once it stopped moving, blood dripped from the interior glass. Everyone could see the headless body of a blood soaked woman. Her head lay sideways on the floor.

"I'm sorry, Glenn. But look at the bright side. We narrowed it down to two, maybe three possibilities on where to insert the gene. Maybe Sam could be our next volunteer."

Claude was a greenish white, looking almost like a zombie. He stuttered out some jumbled words, and then finally got audible words to come out of his mouth. "Holy fuck, fuck, shit, you just fucking killed…You're fucking crazy! You're worse than Frankenstein! Fuck! Okay, please, please. At least let my brother go. I might have something that you need."

Chapter Thirty

Late 1980's
Nevada

Andreas celebrated a few more birthdays while running Broom Lake Air Base until things began to change. Operation Chrome had taken on a new division in genetically engineered organs. Doctor Rodrigo Herrara was an expert in duplicating various organs. The program was a huge success. The base was making more money than some of the Fortune 500 companies. The sale of organs led to more donations. Broom Lake was virtually untouchable. Government oversight was all but nil.

Now that Andreas's little air base was a cash cow, he knew his reign would soon end. With each passing year, his power to oversee the base was limited. The enormity of the base's success combined with Andreas's age made their little underground baby snatching operation even more pressing. Andreas and Bolantano had grown more and more reckless. They both recruited Lori from time to time. Andreas did not want her involved, but she insisted. She looked up to him. He was saving the hybrids from their fate. Their luck was running on fumes.

Andreas had hoped he was not ruining her life by getting her involved. Lori had quite a future ahead of her in gene therapy and gene modification. She had taken a position in a Los Angeles hospital as a research doctor. Andreas drove up to the city a few times a month to see her. He also checked on some of the babies who were planted within the area. He and Bolantano took advantage of the multiple orphanages within the city.

The job was the perfect fit for Lori. She already came to the table knowing more than everyone on her team of doctors. However, Andreas warned her not to divulge too much. That would draw attention. Richtor gave permission to spoon feed some of his findings into the scientific world. He claimed that his discoveries had the ability to save lives. Andreas never knew if it was ego or he really had an idyllic side to him that he kept private. Whatever the real reason, it must have hurt him to keep all of these advancements a secret.

When Andreas did stay with Lori, she would tell him about her job and how corporate America had already warped their advancements. She saw some of her work being exploited for profit. Andreas was so proud of her, yet he wished she had more than a career and a sketchy past of helping him steal babies. He was so old. The Grim Reaper was just around the corner. He hoped Lori would meet someone special and have a family. She was so beautiful, like her mother. She could have had anyone, but never showed interest in dating. Was she gay? That would have been fine too. He didn't want her to be lonely.

Months before his eighty-seventh birthday, Andreas was politely told he needed to resign. He didn't fight it. His mind was still sharp, but not as sharp as it had once been. He was putting Bolantano and even Lori in jeopardy. It was time. He wrote a formal letter of resignation and even recommended Bolantano to take the lead. Bolantano was now in his mid-sixties. To Andreas's surprise, the top brass gave Bolantano the nod. Everyone else who once dreamed of getting the job had given up and moved on years ago.

Bolantano became General Bolantano, Commander of Broom Lake Air Base. It was a long overdue promotion, and seemed too good to be true. Andreas knew that Bolantano was one of the few people in the world who knew how to run a baby hybrid factory. The brass must have known that too.

As Andreas put his belongings in a box, Bolantano stopped by. "General Andreas, what a long, strange trip it's been. Now pack up your shit and get the hell out of my office!" They both laughed wildly. There was a long pause. "I can't do this without you. It's not over. We're not over. Not as long as I'm here."

"Michael, you're like my son, you are my family. I will always help you in anyway. You gave me something I had lost after the war. You gave me a purpose. You helped me get my soul back. I never said this before, and I should have, I love you." Andreas walked around his desk and hugged the new general.

"I couldn't have done this without you, Robert. Plain and simple. You are the fuel that has kept us in business. Although we had some other key actors. Richtor. Who knew he would come in handy? But what we did here, we did it for the world. They are our hope. When the time comes, they will side with us and all of humanity."

Andreas looked away and wiped a tear off of his cheek. "Don't be a stranger. I got myself an apartment right off of the strip. It's got a pool, a workout area, and some tennis courts. I'm right by the Desert Inn. I guess I'll try some golf. I plan on visiting Lori even more. I'm sure she'll just love that." He smiled. "Goodbye, Michael."

"You can't go now. The men are setting up a little party for you. We even got a cake."

"Maybe some other time. I'm too emotional. They can't see me crying like a baby. Let me slip out and I'll be back to visit."

Bolantano nodded and helped him carry his boxes to the car. He drove off in his Buick as a private citizen, leaving the only life and family he knew.

A year of retirement had passed. It wasn't as bad as Andreas had thought. He learned how to golf and play tennis. He enjoyed the pool several times a week and even had his eye on a lovely older lady who lived on the floor above him. He planned on asking her to dinner, but kept chickening out.

Andreas drove to Los Angeles frequently and kept track of the adult babies who had remained within the city limits. He even made a baby drop for Bolantano. The newborn was a beautiful Mexican girl who was left at the Saint Catherine's Orphanage in San Diego. He still loved being part of the game.

Lori took on a different role in their little counter-Chrome Operation. She took tissue samples of all of the babies and isolated a few genes she believed to be extraterrestrial. Her next step was to figure out the traits the genes were responsible for.

While she went to work, Andreas would check up on Jay McCallister. The young man impressed him. He had his fair share of problems, especially with alcohol and women, but he was a force that surpassed the writing world. His conspiracy theories were spot on. He was attracting attention from all angles. Maybe too much attention.

Bolantano ran the base with the same ease as Andreas did. No one was asking questions and all suspicions were kept at bay. Too many years had elapsed, and too many babies had been stolen without notice.

One sunny summer afternoon, Andreas should not have had a care in the world as he sat out by the pool. Today was different and he didn't know why.

He loved sitting in the sun. The Vegas temperature was ninety-five degrees, yet the dry heat made it bearable. He brought out a couple of beers and a pack of cigarettes and tried to relax. He picked a lounge chair next to a clean, plastic table and settled into a comfortable position. The pool was empty and eerily quiet. He had a difficult time concentrating on the newspaper. Was Lori alright? Did Bolantano need him to run another errand? His eyes eventually drooped, and then he finally drifted off into a nap.

Someone's hand shook Andreas's shoulder. He jolted out of his lounge chair. "Oh my, you scared me! Doctor Jaeger? What a pleasant surprise! Please sit down. Let me get you a chair." Andreas pushed a nearby chair next to his lounge chair.

Jaeger was well into his seventies, but he didn't look it. His blonde hair had thinned and turned white, but that was the only part of him that matched his advanced years. His ageless face never smiled. Andreas thought that might be the secret to having no wrinkles. He sat down in the chair, yet still looked uncomfortable. "Hello, General. Retirement suits you."

"Bullshit! But thanks anyway. You tracked me down. So, tell me, Doctor, what do I owe for the pleasure of your company?"

"In the interest of time, General, I'll skip the small talk."

Andreas smiled. "Doctor, you always did skip the small talk. And I am very interested in time. My time is about to run out. Do you want to talk in my apartment?"

"No. Here is fine. By the way, you might want to check your phone. I believe someone bugged it last week."

Bugged? "Doctor, you have my full attention. Please continue." Andreas's eyes scanned the area. He no longer felt safe.

"First things first. I want to get the elephant out of the room. I know. I have known for decades. I caught Richtor helping you sneak out a baby and he confessed. Frankly, I kept my mouth shut because I liked the idea of two groups of infants, one controlled, one uncontrolled. Your mission and Intel only enhanced our newer babies with better genetic modifications and add-ins. But now Richtor is dead. So we haven't got much time."

"Dead? How? When?" Andreas stood up from his lounge chair and lit a cigarette.

"He supposedly shot a bullet into his head while alone in a hotel room. He was in Toronto. General Bolantano couldn't make the drop, so Richtor volunteered."

"And the baby? Did it make it to the orphanage?"

"Actually, this was a legitimate drop. The baby girl went to a pharmaceutical giant. The drop was successful. Something went wrong. His cover was blown. I am not sure how. Things will be changing very soon, and not for the better. We can't fight them. It's time to abort and hide. But this might be of use. I understand you have an egghead for a daughter, a doctor and a scientist who has been using our work to advance herself."

Andreas was horrified. Was Lori's cover blown as well?

Jaeger looked at Andreas's face and continued talking. "I don't know her name. I just know bits and pieces. Actually, I don't even know her field of interest. I'm assuming its genetics. She would know people who could use this. I am not here to make trouble. Here. Keep this somewhere safe." He then handed him a large manila envelope.

"I don't understand. I saw Michael last week."

"General, much has happened in week. Part of our operation has split off on its own. Doctor Herrara, do you remember him? Anyway, he has taken his cloned organs and set up a lab in Utah. It's a new and enormous base. Plenty of room to move Operation Chrome to. I fear it won't be long until our base will be compromised or even cut-off. General, I know you never trusted me. I was a patriot by German standards, a true insider with the *Fuehrer.*"

"That's why I recruited you all those years ago. You proved invaluable to the U.S. government."

"Yes. I've lied to you. You probably know that. Remember the head that I brought over here, the one of an A.B.?" Andreas nodded and lit a Lucky Strike. Jaeger continued his story. "I found it, but it was already dead. There were thousands of them, dead. At least, I assumed they were dead. The Nazis found them in Poland, France, Germany, Russia, even Antarctica. I had a few of their corpses to study. They were the same race as the A.B.s you found at Roswell. After seeing the Roswell A.B.s come to life and then leave us, well, I thought that maybe the others weren't actually dead, just sleeping or waiting for a spacecraft to bring them home."

"What did you do with all of those bodies?" the general asked as he scanned the pool for unwanted company.

"Some of the bodies were passed around for research. Hitler believed they were Atlanteans. He believed that Aryans were the descendants of the Atlanteans."

Andreas was getting annoyed. "You said there were thousands of bodies. What did Hitler do with them all?"

Doctor Jaeger looked uncomfortable. He looked around the pool, making sure they were alone. "There was another race, the Reptilians. They look like human lizards. Anyway, they were especially interested in the dead bodies. They took them all."

Andreas thought back to Kate's photos from Hanover Auto. She also was worried about this Reptilian race. "Why? Where did they take the bodies?"

"I don't know. Richtor and Schmidt didn't know either. All I really know is that the Reptilians are very dangerous. They taught me a great deal about genetics. Hitler allied himself with them during the war, but there was a fallout."

Andreas fanned himself with the envelope that Jaeger had just given him. "So, what are you trying to say? We aligned our hybrid program with a race that is supposed to be dead?" Andreas stood up from his chair and faced the doctor. "Are the Reptilians planning on taking over this planet?"

The German doctor shrugged. "They certainly want to. But the timing isn't right. The Atlanteans have other plans for this planet. They showed us even more than the Reptilians did. They gave us step by step instructions on how to make hybrids of themselves mixed with humans. I think they want to save us as well as themselves. These Reptilians are pure evil. You thought Hitler was Satan, well who do you think he got so many of his ideas from? Our time has run out. I don't know who else to give this to. I have kept it to myself for all of these years. No one in the U.S. to my knowledge has figured it out. Germans know about it. I know about it. You won't understand it. To summarize, it's a series of equations mixed with genetic markers that enable one to travel time. That's how the A.B.s move around the universe. Our hybrids will naturally be able to do it. One day human beings will be able to as well. There are some other equations that will help a physicist with a machine. I also have maps in this envelope, maps that Hitler was interested in. Maybe you or someone could look into it. Hide this in a good place. Again, check for bugs."

"Is that it?"

Doctor Jaeger looked like he was in a hurry. "Yes, that's it. I am not going back to Broom Lake. You might want to change your address as well."

The doctor disappeared into the adjacent parking lot. Andreas took the envelope back up to his apartment. He scanned the property from the pool and parking lot to the balconies above his unit. He saw a truck pull into a parking space with a familiar face getting out the driver's door. The man was a neighbor. Everywhere else was quiet. Was he being followed?

Andreas thought of Kate. Her death was suspicious, and now Richtor supposedly blew his brains out. Was he next? Where they cleaning house in regards to Operation Chrome? Out with the old and in with the new? One of their most important doctors was just transferred to Utah. All Andreas knew for sure was that Jaeger was scared. He needed to call Bolantano.

Once Andreas entered his home, he drew the blinds and locked the door. Taking the cordless phones from both the bedroom and the kitchen, he opened them up and easily found the bugs. He had checked his phones before, but had grown complacent. *When was the last time? A week? A month?* He couldn't remember. Was Lori in danger?

Andreas flushed the two bugs down the toilet and looked around for more. It appeared his phones were the only devices that were compromised. He sat down at the kitchen with the envelope and dialed Lori's number. No answer, just the machine.

"It's me. We really need to talk. I had a visit from an old friend. Check your phone like I taught you before calling me back. And I love you." Andreas rarely told his daughter he loved her, another mistake he acknowledged. At least he managed to say it a few times throughout the years. The words only would stress the importance of the call.

The next call he made was to Bolantano. Again, no one picked up. He didn't leave a message though. Bolantano might have been spooked. He just lost Richtor under sketchy circumstances. Andreas took a peek inside of the envelope. There were handwritten pages of math equations and DNA sequences. As Jaeger had told him, the papers were nothing but gibberish to him. He fished out a roll of duct tape from his junk drawer in the kitchen and walked around the apartment. He wanted to find the perfect hiding spot. *The toilet*, he thought. He lifted the lid and set the porcelain on the floor. He was about to tape the envelope to the inside of the lid, but changed his mind. He knew they, whoever 'they' happened to be, would find it. He walked around the apartment some more, eyeing up the air-conditioning vent. Nope, another popular spot.

Andreas then walked into the kitchen and looked in the garbage. There was a think piece of brown cardboard from a delivery. He pulled it out of the garbage and then yanked out his junk drawer. The cardboard was big enough to cut down and cover the bottom part of the drawer. He dumped the drawer out and turned it upside down. After taping the envelope to the bottom of the drawer, he then cut down the cardboard and covered the envelope. It looked enough like plywood. Happy with his hiding spot, he assembled the drawer back into the bank of cabinets.

Andreas lit a smoke and then burned the cardboard clippings in the ashtray. After his cigarette break, he dumped his butts and ashes in the garbage and anxiously stared at the phone, hoping Lori or Bolantano would call. She normally had Saturdays off. Maybe she had to work. Or maybe she had a date. He wanted her to meet someone and be happy.

It was late afternoon and he still hadn't gone for his daily walk. Andreas used to run every day. By his eighty-fourth birthday, arthritis had gotten too painful to run. Walking had taken its place. He made it a point of walking three miles a day. He put on his tennis shoes, grabbed a water, and then headed out.

Andreas usually walked the Vegas strip. He enjoyed watching the new hotels being built and the vacationers going in and out of the casinos. Today, he changed his usual routine and walked the perimeter of the apartment complex. Nothing seemed to be out of place. It was dinner time. The parking lot was busy. It was Saturday night and many of his neighbors were dressed up. He assumed they were going out to a nice dinner and maybe even a show. He wasn't sure how many miles he walked, but felt more comfortable and secure.

Once back inside, he heated up a TV dinner. He took it to the coffee table and turned on the news. Every major news channel was broadcasting the same story. "What the hell?" Andreas said aloud. "Broom Lake?" He turned up the volume and got out of his chair to get closer to the TV screen. His head spun as he listened to the news story. "No fucking…" A black-gloved hand had covered his mouth. He struggled to free himself from someone's choke hold. There was another person who soon had him pinned onto the floor. The last thing Andreas saw was a pillow smash into his face.

Chapter Thirty-One

Late 1980's
America

Lori woke up much too early. It was Sunday, and she didn't have to work. She should have snoozed until the late morning, but she wasn't used to sleeping in someone else's bed. Leaning over, she looked at Belinda. She looked like an angel, so beautiful, with her platinum blonde hair cut into a stylish bob. Her hair was natural as was everything about her.

Lori had been seeing Doctor Belinda Murphy for over a month. They had known each other for two years. Both women were doctors who specialized in genetics at the Smythe Hospital in L.A. For Lori, there was an attraction from the beginning. She was not ready to come to terms with being gay. She had tried to date men, even slept with a few to appease her sexual curiosity, but men were not for her. There was a natural attraction towards women, but she never acted on it. Rejection scared her more than the aliens that she studied. Trolling lesbian bars and putting ads in the newspaper seemed desperate and even dangerous. Somehow Belinda fell in her lap. She could see right through Lori.

Belinda took it slow by first asking her to lunch. A year's worth of lunches soon moved to after-work drinks. On a night where both women were tipsy and inhibitions were down, Belinda kissed her. They were inseparable ever since.

Both women worked in genetics, but Doctor Belinda Murphy was most interested in the chemical reactions that took place in somatic gene therapy. She was exceptional in locating genes on DNA strands. She then analyzed the reactions that took place once copies of the good genes were inserted into the plants that they were studying. She hoped to one day cure genetic disorders in human beings. Lori admired her ambition.

Belinda's findings were considered revolutionary by most doctors within the field of genetic break-throughs. Lori never mentioned that most of Belinda's research was discovered decades ago in the underground lab of her father's air base. However, Lori liked Belinda's methodology better. She had a way of simplifying things in both work and their personal lives.

Lori daydreamed about sharing DNA samples from Operation Chrome with Belinda. She had a huge box filled with studies taken from Broom Lake as well as top secret information her mother had snatched before her death. Belinda would be amazed, adding new insight to it all. They would dominate the field of genetics together. But her dream was far into the future.

Lori was pushing forty years old. She was uncertain of where this love affair would lead. Belinda could be her biggest ally as well as her biggest enemy when it came to studying the DNA of anything. In fact, Belinda's competiveness and ambition left Lori questioning if her new girlfriend could ever be trusted.

When Lori's father gave her all of his files, he never mentioned one way of the other if she had his permission to read them. Like Pandora and her box, Lori couldn't keep them sealed up forever. She read about the stolen babies so many times that she practically had their lives memorized.

A couple of the hybrids lived in the area. One of the babies was in her early twenties. She had joined some religion that sounded more like a cult. Andreas had lost touch with her whereabouts. The other baby, Jay

McCallister, was also pushing forty. He was Lori's favorite author.

Jay McCallister's DNA might have something to do with his writing. Lori knew her father had made contact with him. Times and dates of their meetings were in the file. She never talked to him about it, but sensed he liked the author a lot, maybe too much.

Jay McCallister's career seemed to know no limits. Every book he pumped out was a best seller. He had grown very critical of the government, claiming cover-ups and misinformation regarding anything that had to do with Advanced Beings.

The famous author lived thirty-five minutes away in Hidden Hills. Against better judgment, Lori drove past his home a few times. She had to see him in person. She even spent a day following him around town as he shopped and ran errands. He had kind mannerisms and intelligent eyes. While Lori stalked him in the mall parking lot, he looked up and caught her glance. He smiled and she smiled back. It was a mild flirtation that he was prepared to act upon. Lori was a beautiful woman and Jay was in between wives. As he approached her in the crowded food court, she decided meeting him was a bad idea and ran out to the parking lot. That was the last time she followed him around.

Lori wondered what her father would think of her stupidity. She further wondered what he would think of her once she told him she was gay. They had too many secrets. She believed that he wouldn't have cared about any of it. All he ever wanted was for her to be happy.

As Lori thought about her father and watched Belinda sleep, she decided to get up and make some coffee. As the pot brewed, she grabbed a bowl of cereal and turned on the news. She sat at the breakfast table and flipped channels. The same repeating news story seemed to dominate the airwaves.

"An explosion that leveled Broom Lake Air Base has killed at least nine airmen and airwomen early this morning, including General Michael Bolantano, the base's chief-in-command. Twenty-seven more airmen, airwomen, and civilians are unaccounted for. Firemen are putting out the remainder of the fires, and clean-up crews are digging through rubble, hoping to save any possible survivors. Reports on this explosion are sketchy. Unconfirmed reports state that this devastation may be some kind of fatal mistake, an experiment that backfired. Broom Lake has always been a target for conspiracy theories due to whispers of the military's top-secret projects that have taken place..."

"This is bullshit!" Lori screamed. She reached for Belinda's phone and dialed her father's number. No one picked up.

Belinda ambled into the kitchen, still half asleep, with a confused look on her face. Her pale blue eyes looked worried.

Lori chose her words carefully. She wasn't ready to drag Belinda into her world. "I...I need to go see my dad. He might be in trouble. He's not answering the phone. I'll be back in the few days. Please cover for me at work."

Belinda nodded and kissed her mouth. Lori could feel the compassion. Did she look completely pathetic at the moment? The only thing Belinda really knew about Lori's father was his advanced age.

Lori raced out of Belinda's parking lot, caught the earliest flight that she could, and then rented a car. Within four hours, she pulled into her dad's apartment complex. She tried calling him multiple times. Still no answer. Something was very wrong.

God, don't take him from me. Not like my mother. Please, God.

It was the first prayer Lori had prayed in a while. Her mother found religion, but Lori had always doubted. Science took over as her god. Now she was not so sure about anything. Her stepfather died when she was young, and then her mother was murdered. As her mother would say, "It's not about the crap that we get in this life. It's about what is waiting for us in the next." Is that where her father was? In his next life? He was like her, not particularly sure either way. Like her father, she needed proof to believe in anything.

As Lori got out of the rental sedan, her stomach did backflips. Andreas had always called her back, but then she wasn't home. Since retirement, she always knew where he was, unless he was making a drop. All she had was hope.

Lori walked passed his car, the old Buick, as she neared the main entrance of the building. Her heart sank. All hope was sucked out of her. She felt empty. Slowly, she walked up a few stairs to his unit. It was late afternoon and the place was eerily quiet.

Lori fished her key out from her handbag and turned the lock. "Dad?" she said as she tiptoed inside the apartment. No answer. She remembered that he mentioned a lady friend. *Maybe they went out and played some slots. Maybe he was at the pool...Stop it!*

Lori's hands trembled as she jangled the keys back inside of her bag. She left the door open. Down the narrow hallway she could see his foot pointing upward towards the ceiling.

Oh God, not like this!

With all the courage she could gather, she proceeded to walk down the hall. Each step felt like an anvil was strapped onto her leg. As she turned the corner, she saw him unconscious. "Dad? Dad?"

Chapter Thirty-Two

1944
The Eagle's Nest, Germany

Zykedo and Hensa motioned Josef and me into the enormous elevator. Before the doors closed, Bormann and his guards tried to join us. Hensa flashed his double row of chompers and grunted. The message was clear.

Once the doors closed, I leaned against the rock-like wall. The elevator car reminded me of a cave. The drugs that were forced into me were still in effect. I needed the support. We descended into the earth for what seemed like eternity. Time changed its tempo to super slow motion. Were we going to Hell? I shuddered at the thought, but then Hell couldn't be any worse than my current predicament, or could it?

Whatever was going to happen, I refused to give up. If Maria's vision was correct, Eric was coming. I had to stay strong. Maybe he could somehow get us both out of here. I felt my veins pulse with adrenaline and I suddenly felt warm. The brain fog from the drugs was starting to lift.

As the elevator descended, it seemed to pick up more speed. It was going so fast that my feet barely stayed on the ground. It was as if we were no longer on a track, but free falling into the center of the earth. The Reptilians and Josef were silent.

Something about Josef's facial expression gave me the impression that he had not been here before. He looked at me and me at him. We both wanted off this ride. The speed abruptly came to a screeching halt, causing me to stumble into Zykedo. His skin felt cold and rough. He smelled like a terrarium from a pet store. Chills ran through my body.

Once we were at a complete stop, the doors of the elevator finally opened. My heart raced so fast that I thought it would spiral out of my body. The effects of the drugs that Josef gave me were completely gone. But what I saw before me, made me wonder if someone had slipped me something new.

The world in which we descended into was more like an LSD hallucination. Amazingly, there was light. I could see strands of the sun streaming through some kind of glassy, blurry ceiling. The makeshift sky was cloudless, but blue. More like an aqua blue rather than a baby blue. The brightness put a strain on my eyes. I could see movement in this sky which made me uncomfortable.

My eyes moved down to the terrain. The elevator car opened up to a shallow, muddy stream that flowed away from the car. Walls of earth were on each side of the stream, as if the puddle of running water was inside of a huge ditch. I thought that maybe a river once flowed in between the earth's walls and now the water level had drastically been reduced. This stream continued as far as the eye could see.

There were trees everywhere, all so different. Some had red leaves and white trunks. Others had purple leaves and mossy trunks. I had never seen trees like these. Several yards beyond the trees were giant hills, maybe mountains. There was something artificial looking about them. I felt like I was on movie set. This could not be real.

Hensa touched me with his fat, nailless fingers and gently pushed me forward. I stepped off of the elevator, straight into water without shoes, still wearing my patient nightgown. The stream was warm and shallow, probably a couple of feet deep. Something metallic and teal swam by my feet. I wasn't sure if it was a fish or some kind of extraterrestrial piranha.

"Ah!" I screamed.

No one else got off the elevator. Hensa and Zykedo snarled at each other. Was that a laugh or were they having an argument? Were they about to leave me here in this convoluted version of Oz? I guessed that they wanted a show. I kicked the water and more of the metallic teal things swam around me.

I screamed even louder and then ran to the dirt wall, scaling it onto the soft bank of the stream. The bank was sandy and littered with different kinds of leaves. Dozens of sparkly rocks were embedded into the bank. I plucked one out of the wet, heavy sand. It looked like some kind of gemstone. Something in the trees hissed at me and I heard some of the leaves rustle. I threw the rock at the nearest tree. "Oh no!" I screamed. Dozens of brightly colored snakes slithered out from the branches.

Hensa and Zykedo were loudly grunting. Their grunts had to be laughter. This psychedelic horror show was not in the least bit funny to me. Were these mutant snakes going to bite me? Was this how I would die? Was this where I would die?

Hensa and Zykedo motioned for Josef to get off the elevator car, and then they did the same. All of their feet were soaked as they stepped into the shallow stream. The Reptilians dropped to their bellies and slithered onto the land. They approached the snakes and hissed them away. It was obvious that they were the kings of this jungle.

A couple of prehistoric birds with emerald green feathers dove out of the trees, low enough for me to touch. "Is this a dream?"

Hensa laid on his belly and then arched his back. He nodded in my direction and said, "Did you ever hear someone say that the earth was hollow?" I nodded. It was a major conspiracy theory that was usually met with eye rolls and scoffs. "Then you already know that it's not a dream."

My eyes glazed over. Hollow earth? This couldn't be happening. "Did you give me a drug? I have to be in some kind of hallucination."

Zykedo slithered by my feet. "This is more than possible. And it's been possible for a few thousand years. Let us give you a short tour. We want you to understand us, all of us. We want you to write about this and prepare your people for what is to come. We have much ground to cover. Follow me."

I waited for Hensa and Zykedo to slither ahead of me. Josef's pale face was now as white as a blizzard. It was my turn to encourage him. I continued to foolishly believe that he and I would somehow escape and he would send me back home in his time machine.

As we walked through the colorful and tropical jungle, the light that streamed through the sky rippled like water. I speculated that the ocean must have been some kind of ceiling. Sunlight somehow filtered through and allowed life to flourish.

The trees, animals, and the plants looked like an amateur copy of a renowned masterpiece. I thought of the starving artist fairs that were held outside of the mall that I used to work at with Eric. I went to many of these fairs, but never bought anything. Some of the paintings were beautiful replicas of famous paintings from Da Vinci, Van Gogh, Cezanne, Renoir, Seurat, Dali, and Matisse. The artists' talents were obvious, yet none of them could hold a candle to the original. That was the Hollow Earth, an artificial replica of a masterpiece.

Everything was altered in some way as if the engineer wanted to put his stamp on this mutated world. It was almost as if whoever designed this land wanted to trump God in His creation. But this designer didn't trump anyone, much less God. Like the fake masterpieces at the mall, he or she was way off the mark. This was a childish funhouse in comparison to the world above. As I judged the outlandish animals and color clashing plants, I almost forgot that I, just like this warped creation, was engineered in an unnatural image.

Hensa did most of the talking. He had to have wanted something more from me than to write about his hollowed earth. These Advanced Beings were trying to pitch me, but I had no idea what they wanted to sell. They held all of the cards and I was at their mercy.

As I walked with Josef and the Reptilians, I looked up at a tropical tree with lime leaves and saw a monkey with blue eyes eating a bright orange banana. I looked at Josef. His eyes had an expression of caution in them. The more we walked, the less afraid I became.

"Did you and Zykedo create all of this? Are you the only ones who live here?" I asked. As we walked, the stream became wider, now resembling a river. The water had turned a pinkish hue. I could see a waterfall cascading from a mountain in the far distance.

"No, no. We, meaning our Reptilian race, sometimes called the Reptoid race, improved upon what was already here. Another race started the project after the Great Flood. Our ancestors took over few centuries later. To answer your other question, we are not the only species of Advanced Beings who live here. In total, our population is around five thousand beings, but we have thousands visitors. This hollowed earth attracts many Advanced Beings who use this place as a hotel, or maybe a rest area."

"Five thousand? There are that many other Advanced Beings here, inside of the earth? How? I mean, look at yourselves. Your race is not exactly inconspicuous."

Hensa flashed his double row of pointy teeth, which I interpreted as a smile. "Well, some of our visitors are sleeping. I guess hibernating is a better word. When we surface on the earth, we have ways of blending in. You might call it shape shifting. I might show you later on how it's done."

Josef's face had regained some color. Finally, he had enough nerve to ask, "Where are your ancestors from?"

Hensa looked at him with a sneer. His green eyes narrowed. "You were never told? Well, as one of Hitler's top scientists, you should have been briefed. Another one of our *Fuehrer*'s mistakes. Our Reptilian race comes from a small, but wealthy planet next to the constellation Draco. You can see Draco in the northern sky. We've been here before civilization, but only as visitors who were passing through. A few thousand years ago we decided to make our visits more permanent. We used slaves, both human and alien, to manually dig these underground tunnels, hollowing it out for habitation. We used genetic engineering to create plants and animals that could thrive down here. Through advanced physics, geothermal energy, some chemistry, natural resources, and a little help from the sun we managed to filter light through the inside of earth. We invented a natural and limitless fuel source for our little society. This power source is what impresses the handful of humans who know about us."

"The power is called Vril, isn't it? Like Hitler's secret society," I said and Hensa nodded. I could see the water fall more clearly as we walked. We were about a mile away from it. The streams of water were a kaleidoscope of pastels. Again, I was reminded that all of this was a cheap, gaudy knock-off of Earth. "Hensa, if the earth was already here before your race visited, then who created the earth?" Hensa didn't answer me. Either he didn't know or he didn't want to get into God.

We soon approached the waterfall and the landscape began to change. Crude roads appeared from the forest that led towards the waterfall. I had to be in the epicenter of something.

Hensa's silence prompted Zykedo to respond. "We don't know who created earth. Someone or some race that is or was superior to all of us must has created this planet as well as all of the universes. Some call Him God. We don't believe what we can't see or understand. Whatever started it all is now gone and it no longer matters. These planets are not built to last forever. You see, planets come and go. Wars and weapons, natural disasters, pollution, destruction. No planet is immune. By creating what we see above the earth's crust, we are preserving it in a way. Everything in this hollowed out earth is meant to protect us and act as a temporary environment for the continuation of our existence."

We walked on the other side of the cliff that the waterfall fell from. A small village of little houses and streets were in the distance. I could see a few Reptilians surrounding dozens of other Advanced Beings. This race looked completely different. They stood upright and walked like humans. Their skin was a chalky, dove grey. Their noses were triangular in shape, but didn't appear to have any nostrils. All of these short beings had large heads with no hair. They could not be any taller than I.

This new race was busy building a new building at the far end of the village. They carried large rocks from the mountain to the work site while a handful of Reptilians watched. It looked like this little village was expanding. One of the Advanced Beings put down a bundle of rocks on the ground and sat down. Within seconds, a Reptilian loomed over him and snarled something. I was still too far to hear. The Reptilian took a brick and smashed it into the sitting alien's head.

"Oh my! Did you just see that?" I yelled as we walked closer to the village. We were close enough for me to see the eyes of the Advanced Beings. They were blue, gray, and light green.

Hensa said, "Yes. We have no tolerance for slackers. We have a time line for new projects. It's about accomplishment. I know this a great deal to take in. As I might have mentioned, we are not the only species who live here and utilize the Vril power. There is peace, but with peace comes a pecking order among races."

"I don't understand. You live with other Advanced Beings, but your race is superior? You use the others as slaves? How long have they been here?" I asked. I thought about Hitler's concentration/work camps. This seemed to be the same concept, but I held my tongue.

Hensa stood next to me and pointed at the little town. "The builders you see are not slaves. They are known as the Grays. We conquered their planet centuries ago and brought various groups with us to our colonies within the universe. They have one purpose and that is to build."

"You said there were other races who live here," I said.

"Yes. One of the races might be remnants of your parents. They are what is left of the Altanteans. Most of them drowned in the Great Flood. Drowning is one of the few ways that one can kill an Atlantean."

"What are the other ways?" I asked.

Hensa flashed his pointy teeth and said, "Wouldn't you like to know. We saved them, the ones who were left here. We preserved them. They have been sleeping for years and we don't know when they will wake up. Please quit shaking. You are not in danger. There is no reason to be afraid."

There was more to the story. My instincts told me that the Reptilians and the Atlanteans were not on friendly terms. "Are there any other races of aliens who live here?"

"The Pleiadians. They are more like long-term visitors. They are here to observe, report, and enjoy the land. We Reptilians are in charge of the Hollow Earth, but it's a peaceful kind of rule. As you probably know, history has taught us that the most aggressive species on any planet always thrives. They do not face extinction because they fought for the right to exist. Long, long ago, we made a pact with the others."

"But not the Altanteans, the ones sleeping?" I asked for clarity, interrupting Hensa as he spoke.

Hensa sneered at me. "Let me finish, child. You can ask all of the questions that you want. You will write about us and the Hollow Earth. We hide nothing. You see, we are very proud of what we accomplished. It's something no one has done before."

"So, you want me to write about this Hollow Earth?" I asked, keeping the venom out of my words. "You have a pact? With whom?"

"Our ancestors were tired of war, but we needed to fight if we were to survive. We wanted peace without risking extinction. We designed a world in which we live together in harmony," Hensa said.

As he dictated the information, I wondered if he wanted me to write all of this down. "This world that you live in is harmonious? You, the Grays, the sleeping Atlanteans, and the visiting Pleiadians?" I asked for clarification. In truth, it didn't seem like peace would be too hard to achieve with sleepers, slaves, and visitors.

"Don't mock what you don't understand. You forget your own race, human, but then again you really don't qualify. Hitler is already part of our pact. We want more humans to join us. Earth is the only place that our peace seems to be working. None of us are from this planet and we have no sense of nationalism. It's like neutral territory."

The words 'pact' and 'peace' scared me. They seemed to go with New World Order. I asked, "You want all beings to share rule of the earth? Both inside and out?"

Hensa looked into Zykedo's fluorescent green eyes and answered, "We are waiting for some other things to fall into place. You see, we can indirectly affect the present by showing humans bits and pieces of our progress. But we have a long way to go until humans are ready to share their planet with us."

"Why align yourselves with Hitler? You know how to time travel. You know that he loses."

"He found us," Hensa replied. "Through mystics and occultists, he learned about our hollowed out earth. A group of Tibetan monks found us centuries ago. We co-exist without any issues. But Hitler is only using us, much like he uses Japan. He worships his Aryan heritage, and he believes that the Aryans were once Atlanteans."

"So, you are second best? He can't exactly join forces with a bunch of sleeping aliens, can he? You offer him knowledge, weapons, maybe even strategy that will help him win the war," I said.

Zykedo nodded. He seemed to approve of my analysis. He finally said, "He thinks that the Atlanteans are dead. Little does he know that we are taking care of them as they sleep. They are important to us, to everyone. They have more history of this amazing planet. Maybe they made the Aryans. We don't know for sure. All we really know is that they lived in peace before the Great Flood. We might not be Atlantean, but like Hitler, we want to know more about them."

I looked at both of the Reptilian's green eyes and was once again reminded of my pendant. In the village another Reptilian was beating a Gray with a mallet. *That's peace?* "Did Hitler give up on the Atlanteans? I thought he held séances for them. He must still have hope."

My questions and comments were not welcomed. Hensa hissed at me. I caught a glimpse of Josef's blue eyes pleading.

Zykedo replied, "Careful, Maya. Your voice is filled with disrespect. Hitler reveres our work, the Hollow Earth, and the future of this planet. We have great power and influence. Our progress supersedes all others within the universe."

"What about the monks who found you? They must be in awe of you," Josef said quietly.

"Oh, they are. We showed them our capital city. They call it Agartha," Zykedo said.

We were now standing only feet away from the village. My nerves were shattered. These quaint buildings had an old world look of charm, like a story book from centuries ago. However, I could feel an aura of evil, even smell it. At times I would catch a whiff of charred flesh drift by. Again, I thought of Hitler's concentration camps, but in disguise. I didn't want to get any closer. The village seemed more like a trap. The frightened look on Josef's face made me even more afraid. In an attempt to stall, I kept on talking. "Is Tibet your entry point to Earth?"

"Yes, deep within the Himalayan Mountains. But it's not the only one. We have a few. Like I said before, we come up from under every now and then to oversee what humans are doing." Zykedo said.

Zykedo stopped slithering on the moist ground and then stood up on his hind legs and stood on the other side of me. I was sandwiched in between these two Reptilians. Josef was a few steps behind me, amazed by the nearby construction at the end of the block. The Grays were almost finished completing the copper dome roof of a twenty story building at the end of the block. The feat would have taken humans weeks to complete. The crew of Grays had started it less than an hour ago and were close to finished.

Josef's hands were shaking, but he mustered up the courage to ask a question. "The South Pole is another entry, isn't it? Hitler once spoke about it."

Hensa nodded. "The Eagle's Nest is also a new entry that we just built a few years ago. Every entry we build has to get approved by our council."

I looked out at the village and wondered how many of these little towns were under the world's feet. "A council? So, you have a formal government?" I suddenly thought of Jay and his suspicions of the ruling class.

Hensa started walking and motioned for us to do the same. I really didn't want to meet any of the town's residents on the other side of the waterfall. He answered me. "Yes, we have a council. It's how we keep the peace. As long as we all live in peace, your world will not be threatened by us. We, someday, want humans to join our council. Earth has everything we need-food, the soil to grow more food, water, minerals, and even gold. But there are other reasons why we are here."

Zykedo interrupted. "In the past, we couldn't respect each other's cultures. All of us at one point or another were like Hitler, each thinking that our race was the superior one. We are trying something new. We thought that Hitler could eventually try something new as well."

I watched the Grays go back and forth from the mountain with bundles of rocks for their new structure. It didn't look like peace. It looked like bondage. Were the Grays on the council? Did they vote to work in bondage?

It was no longer important. I needed to get out of here. A terrible feeling of dread hung over my head like a black cloud.

"Maybe she's not the one," said Zykedo. He said it in English, obviously wanting me to hear.

Hensa looked at me and said, "She's the one alright. Fearless. Maya, you saw us eat two dead men and now you see what you think is slavery. I understand your lack of trust. But first, let us explain that those men were dead. That's what we eat, the dead. Just like bugs and vultures and many other species. Our aggression has been diminishing within each generation. Those beings who are building a new village over there are the great builders of the universe. We couldn't get anyone more talented than them."

"I don't understand any of this. You and the others are obviously much more intelligent than humans. Why do you hide? Why build an alternative world inside of the planet?"

Hensa replied, "As we speak, humans are creating nuclear weapons that have the power to destroy the entire planet. In truth, the progress of humankind is going in the wrong direction. Humans are on their way to becoming a threat to us and this planet. We like it here and want to keep it safe. We want to save you all from yourselves. Down here, we have laws. Earth can have what we have. Maya, I know you don't believe us, but all we really want from you is to write about us, write about this place. Do it in a novel first and then hint that it might be true. Spoon feed the masses. We want you to be our spokesman, a historian of sorts. Now please, let's come inside of the village and meet some of the others."

They wanted me to be their Josef Goebbels and write propaganda for them before taking over the world. Hesitantly, I walked onto the cobblestone sidewalk. This was another set-up. The Grays did not even look at us. My heart rate doubled. Josef was behind me. I looked back at him and mouthed the words 'we got to get out of here.' He ever-so-slightly nodded. Then an opportunity arose. The ground started to shake. All of us were tossed in mid-air, separated. The Hollow Earth was having a quake.

I looked up and saw one of the Grays' indigo eyes staring at me. I froze like a deer in headlights as the ground shook. He was trying to communicate like Maria Orsic. I focused and then heard '*You are not supposed to be here. He is coming to save you. Save yourself and then save us…*'

While the earth continued to shake, I yelled to Josef, "Run!"

Like bats out of hell, Josef and I raced back to the elevator and prayed that the door was still open.

Chapter Thirty-Three

Present Day
Ruby Mountains, Nevada

Glenn watched in disbelief as Chuck and Devon picked up Ally's body parts, and then dumped them into jumbo black garbage bags. They carried on the task with the same mentality as a college fraternity cleaning up after a wild party. He looked over at Claude and Sam, who were both bound and gagged next to each other on the floor. They quietly sobbed at the horror that was just witnessed. Claude had said he was ready to negotiate. Glenn hoped he was scared enough to quit playing games.

An overwhelming feeling of guilt weighed upon Glenn's shoulders. He had just allowed a woman to be blown to smithereens in the name of science. He was no better than the Nazis who conducted despicable experiments on the Jews. *Anything to get Maya back.* But it was more about the discovery than Maya.

Glenn also believed that Allie deserved to die. Her greed and poor choice of friends were what got her here in the first place. It was confession time and Claude needed to start talking.

"Claude, cut the tears. You never loved her, or Maya for that matter. In fact, I bet you used Allie as your pawn, a fall guy in case things went to shit. I'll bet she was part of your master plan to kill your wife. When we found Maya not too far away from here, she told us that you tried to have her killed. I'll bet your brother was also in on it. He's the next to go inside of the capsule. His body parts will be splattered and dumped into some garbage bags. No one will ever know how or where he disappeared to. Do you love him? Who cares. Lastly, it will be you. And then we won't need the book. The process of elimination will tell us what sequence works and which ones do not."

Sam's sobs turned into full blown hysteria. He did not have the stomach for any of this. Claude gave him a look that would stop a train in its tracks, but his hold on his little brother was slipping. Sam was done playing the loyal servant.

Sam started grunting and Glenn removed the gag. He had the same blue eyes as Claude. Sam said, "Allie and I tried to kill Maya for Claude. Claude and I also killed Jay."

Glenn dropped a pen he was holding. "What? Jay drowned in his pool...You drowned him? But, the government...They wanted him dead."

"If they wanted to kill Jay, we beat them to the punch. We tried to shoot him, but he wouldn't die. So yes, we drowned him. It was the only way that old timer would go down. I'm so sorry. Please have mercy on me. I promise to change. I don't want to do any of this anymore. Money was never the reason that I got involved. You see, there's nothing I wouldn't do for Claude. He practically raised me. I used to worship him. He's got some major issues. I see that now. There will never be enough money for Claude to ever be happy. Please, give him a chance to make this right." Sam's tears made it impossible to hear the rest of what he was saying. But the message was clear. Sam had just realized that his brother was a user and still begged for his mercy.

"But why would Claude and you want Jay dead? Did you even know him? He was a harmless, eccentric, generous, and kind old man. I don't understand," Glenn said as he looked at Claude who had a gag stuffed into his mouth.

"He was so jealous. He thought that Maya was going to leave him for Jay. They were having an affair. She adored the man. Had three shelves in her office that were devoted to Jay's novels and the movies that came from his work. Then she left for a week to hang out with him. He gave her his empire. Who wouldn't think the two of them had something going on? Was he right? Was Jay the love of Maya' life?" Sam asked Glenn.

Glenn knelt to the floor and looked Claude in the eyes. "You can talk now. I want to hear your side of the story." He yanked the gag out of his mouth.

Claude stared into Glenn's blue eyes and said, "Everything he said is true. You want to put me in that fucking blender, go ahead. But leave Sam be. In return, I'll give you what you want."

"Mister Kazinsky," Chuck said, "what exactly do you have that we would want?"

"Let me make one phone call."

Devon manhandled Claude into the adjoining office and dialed the number Claude had recited. It was his literary agency. Within fifteen minutes, they had the original manuscript downloaded from the flash drive that Claude had sent. Glenn quickly went to the end of the document and saw a substantially longer end chapter along with an epilogue that wasn't originally in the first manuscript.

Glenn dialed Doctor Blacksmith's extension. "Great news. My bribery idea worked. Like we all expected, there is much more to the book's ending. Take a look and work your magic. I'm forwarding you the document as we speak."

There were twenty more pages to read that were originally unaccounted for. Chuck, Devon, and Glenn moved Claude back to the time capsule room, and then sat down and started reading from their iPads. Chuck looked for code while Devon and Glenn read for clues within the story. Claude kept quiet while they read, but Sam was a complete mess. He sobbed off and on. After a while, no one paid attention.

About halfway through with the new pages, Glenn looked up at Claude. Claude was watching him read. "Yes? Do you know something?"

Claude answered, "The epilogue has the word Lansatti embedded in it several times. I believe it's a name. Go ahead, see if you can find it."

Glenn thumbed through the epilogue on his iPad screen. A few minutes passed and he sat down on the floor next to Claude. "Devon, set his hands free." Devon cut through the cable-tie cuff, and then Claude took the iPad and pointed out the code.

"See. Right here, on this page. First letter of every word spells Lansatti. It's here and here, here, and here, and here, and also here." Claude showed Glenn all of the book's locations where the word kept cropping up.

"I'll be damned. Here we are looking for DNA letters A.C.G.T., never even thinking there are more codes. Amazing," Glenn said. "The story has a different ending than the *edited* manuscript."

"I'll admit to making the changes and deletions. I was in a hurry and wasn't trying to shore up any holes that my quickie ending had created," Claude said.

"The story ends without a master race, but a takeover of an organization, kind of like a United Nations for various planets. I still think the ending is odd. Although there is no master race, the Atlantean race who was once believed to be extinct somehow reemerges into this planetary council. Lansatti, Atlantean, Atlantic, Atlantis... Hold on, let me get a pen and paper." Glenn dashed into the adjoining office of the time capsule room and quickly came back with a pen and paper. He scribbled down some letters and laughed. "Oh Maya, you are a clever one. Lansatti is an anagram of Atlantis."

Claude nodded. "Interesting. This has to be related to the Lansatti family. I Googled them. All extremely rich. Leonardo Lansatti runs the family business. It's become a multi-billion dollar energy corporation. He was recently in the news because his company is drilling for oil in Antarctica. His critics say his corporation is a monopoly and he has our government as well as several European governments in his pocket."

"Yes, yes. It wasn't that long ago that I remember Leonardo Lansatti getting elected by the General Assembly to the U.N. Security Council. This can't be a coincidence."

A buzzer inside of the room went off. Glenn set his iPad on the floor and looked up on the wall at the security camera. Lori was outside of the room. She was taking a retina scan to pass through the second set of doors. There was an ear to ear smile on her face. She passed through and opened the final door into the time capsule room.

As Lori entered, her joyous expression vanished. Her eyes went straight to Claude and Sam on the floor. "Ah! Are these the men you said you were going to pay off? Looks closer to kidnapping. One of you must be her husband."

Glenn was relieved that the splattered body parts and blood inside of the time capsule were wiped clean. He nervously eyed the two black garbage bags that were set by the door. They were filled with bits and pieces of Allie. Thankfully, the smell hadn't set in.

"I'm her husband. And I was never paid off. Your boy, Glenn, backed out in the worst way. Look over there," Claude said. He looked at the bags. Lori took a brief look inside and screamed.

"That was my girlfriend," Claude said.

That little fucker, thought Glenn. *How dare you squeal like a pig.* Lori went into a tirade.

"I can't believe this. I fucking quit. Oh, buggers. I am calling the fucking cops. Nothing but arseholes around here. You just murdered a woman. For what? To narrow down the sequence? That's sick, sick, sick! Maggots. Since Jay died, you have all turned this place into a concentration camp." Lori continued to scream, bitch, rant, and complain for several minutes.

Chuck was finished listening to her. "Are you done yet? We have an explanation for all of this. But first, hear me out. I know very little about gene editing. I barely know how to work your gene gun. If you quit, what will happen to Eric? He's going in that thing no matter who scrambles his DNA. I got a whole box of black garbage bags if that's how you want to play. Call it emotional blackmail, but I'm telling you we are so fucking close to unlocking the secrets to time travel that there is no way I am pulling the plug just because your conflicted. If I were you, I would not be going to the police. Your hands are just as dirty." Chuck's brown eyes did not have a shred of warmth in them.

A moment of silence had lingered on for too long. Glenn was the first to talk. "Lori, there's more. These *victims* are not all that innocent. They have some very bloody hands." Glenn calmly told Lori about Sam's confession of Jay's murder and Maya's attempted murder. "I know two wrongs don't make a right, but these are not good people. Put the self-righteousness aside just for a minute. Now you came here to tell us something and I suspect it was something good. What did you find out from the unedited novel?"

Sam sat on the floor and sobbed. He looked like a teenage boy who just lost his puppy. He might have turned into a decent human being had it not been for his dysfunctional environment.

"They murdered Jay and tried to murder Maya? Oh, dear God. Now I don't feel so bad for them. To answer your question, Glenn, Maya left us everything. There's no more guess work. Chuck is unfortunately correct. If I don't edit Eric's DNA, then both he and Maya do not stand a chance. Unlike everyone in this room, myself included, Eric is a good person. Maya is also a good person. Too bad Jay wasn't here. And Claude," Lori said, and then walked over him and spit in his face, "that's for Jay." She slapped him on the cheek. "That's for Maya." She walked over to Sam and slapped his face. "That's for being stupid. You might be going home in one piece. Claude, I do not know about you. Now someone please get both of these men out of here. We have a lot of work to be done."

Glenn looked at Devon. Within a few minutes, a couple security members from T.A.H. were outside of the door. Claude was cuffed with plastic ties again, and then he and his brother were escorted out of the time capsule room.

Glenn looked at Lori and said, "They're both murderers. You might find some future use for them."

"Not now..."

"Okay, Lori," Glenn added, "but we found something else. I don't think it has to do with the code. The word Lansatti appears over and over in the epilogue. I fiddled around with the letters. Ironically, it seems to be an anagram for Atlantis. What are the odds of that being a coincidence?"

Lori's face fell to the ground. She clearly knew something, but chose to shrug her shoulders in ignorance. Glenn knew so little about the doctor. She had always been Jay's friend, and. Jay avoided all questions about how that friendship originated. Lori was just as evasive. There was definitely no romance between them. Glenn had always suspected that Lori preferred women.

Lori's credentials were amazing. How would Jay know a brilliant geneticist? All Glenn really knew about her was an extensive list of accomplishments, a resume. She occasionally let a trace of a British accent slip during conversation. He assumed she had spent some time there, but she refused to acknowledge any of her past. She was so damn private. He doubted that he could get her talking, especially now when it was clear she had no trust for him and planned on leaving the institute.

"I brought the gene and the vector for Eric. We will use both the gene gun and a syringe. Have someone bring him here. We are ready." Lori walked over by the desk where the gene gun lay and began to take it apart. She went over to the sink and meticulously cleaned it.

Glenn radioed Devon to bring Eric down to the round room. A few minutes later Devon came into the capsule room with Eric. He looked well rested and ready to go into the capsule. Glenn wondered if he too would splatter all over the inside of the time machine.

Lori smiled at him and motioned for him to sit down on a stool by the desk. She reloaded the gene gun and then pulled out two syringes. "This is going to hurt a little. In the syringe as well as the gene gun is a solution that contains the gene that is responsible for time travel. It's one of the genes that make Maya and Jay special. Maya had it encoded in her first novel. We will send it to the junk part of your DNA in all of your cells with a vector. In your case, the vector I am using is bacteria. You can still back out if you want to. Glenn has not been completely honest with you and needs to tell you something before we get started."

Glenn sighed in anger. With his back against the wall, he told Eric about Claude, Sam, and the Allie. He also included their confessions and his own part in kidnapping them for the unedited novel and holding them captive inside of T.A.H. He could see Eric's eyes light up.

"Glenn, I like your style! I knew he was somehow involved! Hell no, I am not backing out. I would love nothing more than to kill that son-of-bitch Claude with my own two hands! But I think we should let Maya decide what to do with them when I bring her back," Eric said.

"I'm surprised at your enthusiasm. I thought you would be more reluctant in being the doctor's lab rat," Glenn said. "This gene therapy certainly didn't work on Allie."

"Because once again, Chuck was involved, and once again, used absolutely no caution," Lori said. "Okay, Eric. Here we go."

She shot him at least a hundred times all over his body with the gene gun. Blood trickled on the floor. She stuck him in the neck and the buttocks with the syringes. He took every new prod, poke, and puncture without a flinch. The man was determined to rescue his damsel in distress.

"Now we wait," said Lori.

Glenn couldn't help but noticing the extra steps that Lori had taken, versus the rushed job that Chuck performed on Allie. Another dead body was on his conscious. As they waited for the genes to insert themselves on the junk part of Eric's DNA strand, Glenn escorted Eric into the adjoining rooms that contained the control panel and centrifuge. Glenn showed him the speed that was set, the air flow button, the screen that showed the atoms separating, all of it. He quizzed Eric on how the control panel worked, and explained the possible other ways a control board could be set up. "I strongly believe that Maya is in Germany, circa World War II. The German centrifuge and control panel are not going to be as sophisticated as this one. Please be aware of the remedial differences you might face."

A few hours passed and Glenn quizzed Eric again. He passed with flying colors. Lori came into the room and took some blood and tissue samples from Eric. "I'm going back to the lab to see if everything went according to plan. Hopefully, we will be ready to proceed."

Eric looked around the room nervously and then asked, "Where did Paula and Mercedes wander off to? Devon came and got me. They said they would be here shortly. I want them to be here. I want their take on the unedited version of Maya's manuscript. I want their support. This isn't just about Maya, but about everything you, Doctor Wu, and Doctor Blacksmith have been working so hard for all of these years. You proved time travel works on certain people. Now you are about to prove that it works on all people once genetically modified. You have discovered the key to a whole new kind of transportation system."

Glenn smiled. "Eric, if this works, if you get Maya back, there will be statues of you both all over the world. You two will be heroes to every science geek who ever had a dream. You're right. This is even bigger than all of us here at T.A.H. You're also right about Mercedes and Paula. They need to be here. They've been part of this place for years. Devon, please page them here, into the round room. They will know where to go."

Lori was back, outside of the entrance and in view of the security camera. She held a case of test tubes with a smile on her face as she clumsily looked through the retina scanner. The doors opened. She announced to all in the room, "We are a go. I even compared Eric's new strand to Jay's and Maya's cells. Before we get you into that capsule, do you know how to work the controls?"

Eric nodded. "Guess Mercedes and Paula don't want to see me off." He looked somewhat disappointed, and then delicately stepped inside of the capsule. The inside wasn't perfectly clean. Bits of blood and debris were splashed in hard to reach crevices. The remains had belonged to the late Allie Calloway, Claude's former girlfriend. Chuck helped buckle him down and closed the door. Chuck then dashed off to the centrifuge. A loud rumbling sound filled the room. They were almost ready. A moment before Chuck was about to turn the capsule on, Glenn saw Mercedes through the security camera. He opened the door before she looked through the scanner.

The unflappable and perfectly poised Mercedes was wild-eyed and paper white. "Stop! Wait!"

Chuck moved his hand from the control panel and backtracked over to the centrifuge, killing the power.

"Devon, get security and a first responder in the freezer room now! Paula is not waking up! Please go and help her!" He abruptly flew out of the room and radioed other security members.

Mercedes streamed tears down her face, causing black waterfalls of smeared mascara and eye liner. "We held a séance, just the two of us. We channeled Jay. We were sure it was him, but then something happened. Somehow someone else, something else, took over. Maybe the same spirit as before, the day before Jay died. Anyway, Eric needs to hear this now!"

Glenn opened the door to the capsule and Mercedes approached. She hugged him through the nylon restraints. "Oh, Eric. I can't believe you are going to go through with this."

Eric held Mercedes hand. "The doc said I now have the time travel gene within me. She is taking good care of me. I can go find Maya. Please do not worry. Go and help Paula. I will be fine. Relish in this moment. T.A.H. is about to make history and change the world forever."

"Forget about history, Eric. If you are set on doing this, please listen. In the freezer, in that creepy container Jay was laid to rest, he spoke to us. I am sure it was him. He had so much to say, but something cut him off. Maya is in real danger. I know we were against you risking your life for all of this, but something bigger than you, Maya, this place, everything will soon happen. We need her back. Listen up. You will land in Germany, on a farm. Maya is not there anymore. Somehow, some way you need to get to Eagle's Nest. That's one of Hitler's Nazi hangouts. But she's not in Eagle's Nest, she's under it. I don't understand anymore, but you've got your work cut out for you if this capsule does its job. Do whatever it takes to get her back to the here and now."

Eric hugged her one last time and shut the door. Chuck clamped the door shut, turned on all of the cameras in the room, and made sure they were recording. The centrifuge rumbled. Without waiting for another distraction, Chuck hit the start button. The capsule began to spin.

Eric jostled around, but no one could see any vomit splash on the inside of the windows. A few minutes later he vanished into thin air, just like Maya, and Jay. They all succeeded in sending an ordinary man through time.

Chapter Thirty-Four

Late 1980's
America

Lori stepped over her father and tiptoed to the kitchen. She grabbed the largest knife that was in a block on the counter. With pure stealth, Lori covered each room within her father's tiny apartment. His dead body in the living room did not seem to affect her emotions. Once again, she found herself naturally go to survival mode as she checked for unwanted company.

The hallway, coat closet, living room, kitchen, powder room, and bedroom were empty. All that was left was the large walk-in closet. Her heart thumped louder than a stampede of buffalo. She kicked in the cheap bi-fold doors and flipped the light on. Swiftly, she moved racks of clothes to one side, checking for anyone who might be hiding. Nothing. Remembering she left the front door open, she quickly ran back and locked it.

She looked again at her dead father crumpled on the floor. No blood, wounds, or weapons were left behind. Could it be possible that he had a heart attack? *Hah, just like my mother*, Lori thought. Natural deaths did not run in the family. She then remembered that Broom Lake was leveled in an explosion. The coincidence was too great. Bolantano was also dead. The powers who secretly ran everything had cleaned house-out with the old guard and in with the new.

The house looked like it always did, unused and immaculate. Lori had all of her father's files in her apartment. His life savings was not invested in anything. He chose cash that sat in a security box. She had the key with her on her key chain. Was there anything else he kept that she didn't know about? If so, he would have hid it well. Andreas had always been good at hiding things, especially secrets. He withheld too much from her. Lori had her work cut out for the rest of the day.

Starting in the general's bedroom, she combed every nook and cranny. She found several packs of cigarettes hidden in the cut-out pages of books stacked within his nightstand. *Damn it! He told me he quit!* She always told him that his smoking would be the death of him. She was way off on that one.

The inside of the pillows and mattresses were checked. The vents, books, pockets of clothes, shoes, and cabinets were checked. Lori even ripped open the seams of the drapes and the bases of the lamps. The bedroom was clean. She checked the master bath with the kind of thoroughness of an FBI agent.

The mirrors and the drains of the shower and tub were disassembled. Lori moved on to taking apart Andreas's toiletries and shaking out his towels. There was nothing inside of the toilet base, but something was jammed within the hole of the toilet bowl. Lori took her hand and yanked out a piece of metal that barely was in view. *What the hell?* Without knowing much about surveillance, she assumed the metal gizmo had to be some kind of a bug. *Dad must have found these right before he died.*

Lori finished up in the master bath and then proceeded to the living room. With the same methodology and diligence, she checked the couch, the chair, the drapes, the vents, the coffee table, books, knick-knacks, and pictures. One of the three pictures he had framed were of her. The other one was of her mother and the last one was of Bolantano. She looked at the picture of herself. It was taken on the day she graduated medical school. The picture of her mother must have been taken before she was born during the happy times of their relationship. She looked just like her, hazel eyes, mass of dark hair, and delicate features. Bolantano's picture was different. It was a professional picture taken in uniform. She knew her father thought of him as a surrogate son. The three people he loved the most, two of them murdered. *Shit,* she thought. *Whoever killed my father now knows what I look like.*

Lori's little break lasted much too long. She needed to finish what she started then get the hell out. She was now a potential target. The cheap, beige carpet was pulled up, and the TV panels were unscrewed. Another metal gadget was found on the side of the TV. Andreas was being heavily monitored.

Lori combed through the kitchen cabinets, the appliances, refrigerator, and freezer. She emptied each drawer and turned them upside down on the counter, looking for something, anything that might be worth dying for. The bottom of one drawer was a brown cardboard color while the other drawer bottoms were made of murky gray material. The material was shiny and thick. She zeroed in on the cardboard drawer bottom.

The brown cardboard was perfectly cut to fit the bottom of the drawer. With a small paring knife, she carefully cut around the perimeter of the drawer. The cardboard popped right out. In the center of the drawer bottom was a large golden brown envelope. She gently removed the tape strips. *I knew it. Dear ol' Dad, what was so important to go through all of this?*

Lori opened the metal clasp of the unsealed envelope and took out a small stack of papers. In the corner of the first page was a "To: General, From: Doctor Karl Jaeger". Following the tag, there was a series of equations. Thumbing through more of the papers she saw small diagrams, maps and even DNA sequences. *What the hell?* She didn't have the time to study any of this. Stuffing the envelope inside of her jeans, she quickly and quietly left the apartment and headed for her rental car.

Did she really want to go home? Was she next on the Operation Chrome kill list? She was such a minor player. Richtor, Bolantano, and Andreas were the ones who stole the babies and then placed them with orphanages. Was Richtor still alive? Was Jaeger alive? Could someone have gotten lucky? She needed answers before walking into a possible hornet's nest at home.

Before returning the rental car, Lori went to her father's bank and cleaned out his security box. He had accumulated over six hundred thousand dollars throughout his life. *Thanks, Dad,* Lori thought. She needed the cash more than ever. She was officially on the lam until she could find out more.

Lori pulled up to a public phone at a gas station. With the growing popularity of cell phones, public phones were harder and harder to find. She made two phone calls, one to Belinda and one to her work. Both times she hit the answering machines and left the same message, telling them that she would be out of town for several weeks because of her father's illness. She was intentionally vague and didn't much care if she got fired. Once the dust settled, Belinda would get a better explanation about what was really going on. She owed her the truth.

Lori returned her rental car and then bought a used Oldsmobile sedan at a shady car lot on the outskirts of Las Vegas. With cash in hand, no one asked for identification. Lori put the car in a business name, Chrome, Inc. That was the best name she could come up with on the fly.

Lori headed back to California. Although she was afraid to go back to her apartment, her parents' files were all she had left of them. Was her house broken into? Were the files still there? She shuddered at the thought. Without those files, her parents died for nothing.

Lori was either a walking dead woman or the biggest asset the conspiracy world had even known. Her next move was crucial. If she was careful, she might live another day. One false move and she would not see her fortieth birthday.

As Lori drove her Oldsmobile, Los Angeles came up much too quickly. She was much too deep in thought to make her next move. It was dark and she needed to find a hotel room.

As she circled the city and its suburbs, the radio station covered the Broom Lake explosion. General Michael Bolantano was announced dead. The radio host reported that Bolantano ran Broom Lake. His body was charred from the explosion, but the investigators were able to identify him through his dental records. Another 'accident' she had to live through. Bolantano was family. Lori couldn't remember too many holidays without him. They would all gather at a restaurant and gorge themselves with food, exchange presents, and enjoy each other's company. He was like an uncle to her. He, her father, and she were like the Three Musketeers. Life with them was an adventure and a purpose. Now it was over. Was all of Operation Chrome dead? Or did it just change management and relocate?

Lori began to slow down as she drove through Hidden Hills. She remembered Jay McCallister didn't live to far from the intersection she stopped at. *Jay McCallister…* She scanned the next two busy intersections and found a hotel on the corner. She pulled into the parking lot. Using cash, she paid for a room. On the other side of the street were a McDonald's and a liquor store. She walked across and bought a value meal and a bottle of Seagram's. Armed with her essentials, she bunkered down in a tiny room for the night.

The burger and fries were quickly devoured and then came the after-dinner drink. She poured the Seagram's into the remaining part of her large 7-UP and drank the cocktail through a straw. The booze briefly offered some relaxation from the day of hell, but made her focus on all that was lost.

Lori's father was dead, probably murdered. He would have made it to ninety. He might have made it to one hundred. At least he died in the name of doing something right, something good, something that God would approve of. He wasn't a typical religious man, but he believed. His faith wasn't as clear cut as her mother's. Nothing that either of her parents experienced could ever be clear cut. Nothing could ever be black or white again.

Broom Lake had the perfect excuse to wipe out its staff. The base was known for their state of the art fighter planes. Everyone had assumed that was the secret the base was hiding from the public. There were explosives and nuclear weapons hidden underground in various tunnels. Lori still didn't know what happened to the German doctors. She fixed herself another drink and then turned on the TV, hoping for updates on the explosion.

After flipping through channels, she found a snippet of the names of the bodies found in Broom Lake. Doctor Jaeger's name didn't come up. Neither did Doctor Richtor's. Were they spared? Her father never trusted either of them. As Lori watched the news and drank more Seagram's, she wept.

Her entire family was gone. Her life as a geneticist was over. Her new relationship was on shaky grounds. There were limits on everything. Having Belinda put in jeopardy was more than she could ask at this early stage of their affair. Everything good that ever happened to her was poof, gone. Another drink, and in came the thoughts of ending it all right there in this room. If she had a gun, she probably would have pulled the trigger. At the moment, she was just too drunk to think of another way to do it.

The booze made Lori queasy. She rushed to the bathroom and vomited in the toilet. Hours later, she woke up on the cold tiled floor in the dark bathroom. She staggered to her feet and then looked in the mirror. She saw her mother's reflection staring back. What would her mother do in this situation? Her mother wouldn't have run, but her mother was dead. Lori felt another wave of nausea and bent over the toilet. A sugary liquid that hurt her throat came up through her esophagus. She immediately felt better. Her shirt was damp. She hadn't had any clothes to change into, so she just took a wet towel and patted herself down.

The sun was rising. It was the first day of a new kind of life she did not want to live. Suicide was still on her mind. She thought about Bolantano and all of his Bible talk. He was somewhere, maybe heaven, shaking his head and pointing his finger at her. No, she would not kill herself. Someone else would have to do it. She would not go down without a fight. She remembered the envelope she found hidden under a kitchen drawer in her father's apartment.

Lori unzipped her jeans. It had sank into the leg part of her pants, but remained dry after vomiting. She drank a full glass of water and sat down at the tiny table next to the bed. From what she could gather, it was some kind of mix of DNA sequences. The formulas looked like they were from an advanced physics class. She didn't understand the physics equations, but the DNA sequences had some logic.

Lori hypothesized that the sequences could come from the hybrid babies her father had stolen. They might have even been the strands of the babies' parents. Doctor Karl Jaeger was the one who gave the papers to her father. She would need to compare them with the slides she had kept in her apartment.

The last few pages of Doctor Jaeger's papers looked like some kind of a map. She recognized some of the longitude and latitude markings, but there was much more. It almost looked like a written diagram of a relationship between space and Earth. Again, this was out of her element. She needed an expert. Whatever this stack was, it got her father killed and she was prepared to guard it with her life. Jay McCallister was the only person in the world who she thought she might be able to trust, and he was a stranger who she never actually met.

A shower and some food put her in a much better frame of mind. She rinsed out her puke-stained shirt and then blew it dry before putting it back on. A fresh set of clothes was on the list of things to buy for the day. But first, she needed to see Jay. She had known where he lived for some time as she used to follow him around a couple of years back. He might have something to offer, advice, or even a plan. She knew her father had liked the man very much. Hopefully, Jay felt the same way. Maybe he would feel a sense of duty and help her out of respect of her father.

It was still much too early to go dropping in unannounced, but desperate times called for desperate measures. She was at the front gates of his mansion ringing the intercom before seven o'clock.

A woman's voice came on the intercom. "Who is this? Do you know what time it is?"

"Yes, I do. I'm sorry to come here so early, but I must see Mister McCallister. It's urgent. My father is dead. General Robert Andreas."

A minute or two must have passed and the gates opened. Jay sat out on the stoop of his Georgian mansion wearing pajamas and a white bathrobe.

Lori got out of her Oldsmobile. She was a little dizzy and still felt slightly drunk from the night before. She wore no make-up. Her dark, long hair was still wet from the shower, and her clothes probably smelled, despite her efforts to clean them. Shaking like a leaf, she said, "I'm sorry. I have nowhere else to go. He's dead, the base has been obliterated. Everyone he worked with is dead. In one fell swoop, everything is gone. I am terrified to go home."

"I saw the base on television and knew something was up. But I very much doubt that this the end of their little hybrid program. Too much is at stake. Please, come in. You're safe here. My fiancé will probably be jealous, but we won't involve her in any of this."

Lori understood what he was saying. He would rather have a fight than to tell her the truth. Like her, he had a problem with honesty in a relationship. They were stuck carrying a secret so deep, so big, and so incredible that both of them could die for it. The stakes were too high, even for love.

Lori couldn't help but notice the elegant home as she followed Jay out to the patio. They sat outside at an iron table next to the pool. She looked at him and cried.

"I'll get some coffee. Everything will work out. You know, your dad sat in the same spot that you are sitting in right now. I had a different wife the last time he was here. But that's the only thing that has changed." Jay said with a smile. He went back inside, returning with coffee. "My fiancé made some. Here, I brought sugar and cream." He reached into his robe pocket and put them on the table. "Sorry, that's all we have. Lisa and I drink it black."

"No, this is fine. And thanks. I truly appreciate everything that you are doing right now. But we both know that I am fucked. Maybe I should go. I don't want to bring any danger onto you."

Jay laughed. "I've been on Big Brother's radar forever. I catch a few tails following me now and then as I drive around town."

Lori didn't say anything, but she had followed him around in the past. Maybe he was referring to her. She smiled. Now was not the time for a confession.

"I'm your age, about six months younger. My mother was there when you were born as was my father. Michael, oh Michael, he was there when you were born. In fact, he is the one who set you free. He stole you from the base and put you in an orphanage. You were the first of many. Because of Michael, my father got involved, years later. Oh God, I hope they are in heaven looking after us."

"Did the general ever talk about me?" Jay asked.

"My father or Michael? Michael was also a general later on."

Jay scratched his chin. "Your father, of course."

"Yes, you were like a son to him. He tried to keep up with your life. You weren't the only baby he kept track of. There were a few more, but you were his favorite. You gave him a reason to keep on stealing the babies. He was so proud of you and everything that you accomplished. That's why I am here. I have nowhere else to go." Lori's tears would not stop running. Jay awkwardly gave her hug.

"I didn't know he felt that way. He came by every few years. If I had to place a number on it, maybe he visited me a total of seven or eight times. I wished he introduced me to my brothers and sisters. We are all part of some elaborate plan, some damn grand conspiracy. I'd imagine the ones who don't know anything are probably going a little stir crazy. I'm glad that your dad thought so highly of me, but believe me, I've got some issues."

Lori looked at him and raised an eyebrow. "I've got plenty of issues as well. My mum, I mean mom, also was murdered. It was made to look like an accident, but I know it wasn't."

"You're English, aren't you?"

Lori nodded.

Jay smiled. "I heard the mum. You are English yet you hide your accent, not very well I might add. It's alright. Your secret is safe with me. Yeah, you got issues alright. But you're not insane. I hear voices all of the time. I wonder if my siblings also hear voices. I was left with a crystal necklace."

"Yes, I know that crystal well. My mother took some from Broom Lake when she worked there as an engineer. She told me it was used as a battery for spacecraft."

Jay nodded and then said, "It had a life and a pulse of its own. The rock terrified me. I got rid of mine when I was a child. Recently, I met a woman at a book signing. She told me about her adopted sister who had a crystal. It sounded much like my past. She's dead and her sister thinks it was murder. Here I am, this rich sci-fi author. Most of the country thinks of me as a kook. When you are a nobody, they say you need help and want you put away in a hospital. When you are successful and famous, they say you are eccentric. It's all a bunch of crap. I try to put my beliefs into my work. They are here and deep down we all know that."

Lori drained her coffee and then said, "The eccentric author role works for you. Because you write fiction, no one really believes you. Just a handful of us who know the truth. Maybe your ancestors planned it that way. Something big is brewing. These Advanced Beings are waiting for something.

"There are still so many unanswered questions. I have files from both of my parents. They are stored at my apartment. I hid them, but I wasn't as good as hiding things as my dad was. These files, well, they offer some evidence that these beings exist. There are different species. Both the British and American governments are going out of their ways to hide this from the public. I am willing to bet they are not the only nations that know. I also have slides. These

Advanced Beings have different kinds of genes than humans. Some of their proteins are different than ours. I also have some slides of various tissue samples from you and the other babies."

"They exist, alright. Some of the stuff I write about is not coming from me. Something or someone has been trying to channel me for years. I don't like the feeling. It's like a powerlessness. I fight as hard as I can. To be honest, drinking alcohol and doing drugs make the voices go away. But some of what is channeled does end up on the pages of my novels. I'd delete it, but it's too compelling. It makes for a great story."

The truth was always more interesting that fiction. Lori asked, "What do you think they want from you?"

"I think they want me to write in some kind of code or formula. Like they are using me to get a message across to others like them. I don't know, it's probably crazy."

A chill went up Lori's spine. She reached inside of her purse and held onto the envelope. She had to trust him. He was all she had. Do or die. "Jay, I want you to look at this. I believe my father was killed because of it."

She handed him the envelope. Jay carefully studied the pages. "I recognize some of it, and maybe if I didn't drink all of the time, I'd recognize all of it. Lori, we have to get those other slides and files out of your apartment before it's too late."

Chapter Thirty-Five

Present Day
Ruby Mountains, Nevada

Eric screamed in horror as he watched his limbs and torso disappear. He could not hear a sound and yearned to be alive. There was no pain, just shock, as saw himself transform into tiny particles. Eventually he couldn't see anything, but knew he still existed. He felt as if he was in a zillion different pieces that floated in space. Would he survive once he landed? Instead of panicking, he chose to enjoy the weightless feeling. Pure peace. He almost forgot about Maya. *I need to save her. Please, God, let me live. Please let me take her back to where she belongs. How much longer will this trip last?*

Suddenly, Eric's vision returned. Seconds later, other body parts regenerated from specs in the air. He was whole. The nylon straps that bound him inside of Glenn's time machine were now leather. The windows of the capsule were different. He was sitting in a whole new capsule. Doctor Blacksmith was a genius. Her plan worked.

Eric unbuckled himself from the straps and then put weight on his feet. He then hit his hand on the capsule's glass wall. He pulled his hair, punched his gut, and gently stabbed himself with the prong of the buckle from the leather strap. He was alive and awake. This was not a dream. He felt as if nothing had just happened. He wasn't dizzy or sore or weak. In fact, he felt invigorated. Doctor Blacksmith and Doctor Wu succeeded in sending the first human through time. Eric's grin turned into manic laughter.

If T.A.H. got him this far, then rescuing Maya from the Nazis should be a snap.

Eric walked out of the capsule, which looked rudimentary in comparison to the capsule at T.A.H. He wondered how many other time machines were built. When was the first one completed? Was this the first one that worked?

Eric looked around the barn and through the windows. Mercedes was right. He was on a farm. He looked all over the barn for the controls and centrifuge of the time machine. Nothing. He needed a way back. Was this the reason why Maya was stuck? He was also stuck. Again, he looked out of the windows. There was a long dirt road that led to a shabby white house about a hundred yards away from the barn. All he could do was ask for help.

Eric walked up the dirt road and tried to think of what to say to whomever answered the door. *Hi, I just came out of your time machine.* That didn't sound too ridiculous. After all, they built it in hopes of having it work. *Hi, where the fuck is the centrifuge? And by the way, can you loan me a car so that I can drive up to the Eagle's Nest and rescue my girlfriend?* No, that was too abrasive. *Maya.* Yes, Eric would start with Maya. Somehow, she went from here to the Eagle's Nest. Someone must have taken her.

Eric stepped on the dilapidated front porch and knocked on the rickety door. He thought the house might even be abandoned. White paint was peeling and repairs were needed all over. He looked through the filthy window and saw a young woman step slowly to the door with a shotgun in her hand. A young boy around eight or nine tumbled down the stairs. Were these two people both squatters?

The inside of the house matched the outside of the house. This could not be a safe place to live. He understood the woman's precautions.

"Hello," Eric yelled. "I came through your machine. Do you know Maya?"

The boy whispered something to the woman and then slowly opened the door. The woman aimed the gun straight at Eric's torso.

"English?" Eric asked with his hands up in the air.

The boy answered, "Speak little English. My sister is learning. We are German. You are in the southern part of Germany. It's May of 1944 and we are at war with most of Europe and the United States. Do you speak German?"

"*Ich spreche ein wenig Deutsch*," Eric said, trying to think of his German classes from high school. He didn't remember too much. "But mostly English." Both the woman and the boy nodded, encouraged. Again, Mercedes was right. She said he would land in Germany during World War II. "I came here to bring Maya back home. You have no idea what I went through to make it here."

The boy translated what Eric said to the young woman. Her shotgun slightly lowered. She said something back in German. Eric recognized the word *maschine* or machine in English.

"Yes, *maschine*!" Eric said excitedly. He smiled at the woman in an effort to calm her down. In another era, she could have been a movie star or model. Her flaxen hair, pale blue eyes, and delicate features gave her an innocent beauty that belonged in an old European fairy tale. The boy who had called her his sister looked much like her.

"I am Heinrich and this is Gretchen. We want to help you. Our uncle took Maya to the *Kehlsteinhaus*. He has been gone for days. We are worried."

Eric assumed *Kehlsteinhaus* must have been Hitler's hangout also known as the Eagle's Nest. He was happy that the young boy was in a helpful mood. "I will go and get both Maya and your uncle, but first I have to know how to work your time machine."

Heinrich took his hand and led him back to the barn. Once inside, Heinrich moved one of the barrels that sat in front of the machine and dropped below the dirt floor. "Come. Everything is down here," he said as he descended down the ladder.

Eric obeyed the little boy. Once underground, he saw a remedial looking control board marked up with marker and colored paper. The knobs looked like they once belonged on kitchen cabinets. Behind the controls was the centrifuge. It was much smaller than the one at T.A.H. Eric began to panic. What if he could only travel to World War II Germany? What if this machine was not sophisticated enough to bring him back? He remembered that Jay had come here and then came back only weeks ago. It had to work.

Through a mix of English and German words, Heinrich explained how the time machine and the centrifuge were powered. Eric repeated the directions aloud at least a dozen times…Second black switch to the right, top row turns to the center marking, three switches on the side turn on the centrifuge, the dial needs to be turned onto the blue triangle, and the joystick needs to set on the "R" letter.

"You have five minutes to climb back up, strap yourself in, and then travel back to the future or everything will power down and you have to start all over. I can't travel. Neither can my sister or uncle. We saw an older man a few weeks back. He came here and then went home. Somehow he knew how to work the machine."

Eric imagined that Jay could operate any time machine. Mercedes and Paula told him much about Jay and T.A.H. Institute. The man was a genius. His prophetic writing was only a sliver of his capabilities. Once he had enough money to get the T.A.H. Institute going, he delved right into physics, genetics, astronomy, politics, and so much more. Jay had even contributed to building the time capsule.

Eric muttered the directions to himself a few more times and then said, "Well, I am not special like the man who you saw a few weeks ago or the woman who you just met. I am like you-human. A doctor had to go through a great deal of trouble to modify my genetic structure to come here. I could have died. I need to bring Maya back. Heinrich, you are way too young to understand this, but I love her. I always have. That's why I came here."

Both Eric and Heinrich climbed up the ladder and moved the barrel over the opening. As they walked back up the dirt road, Heinrich looked at him before reaching the front door and said, "I want you to bring her back. I need you to bring my uncle back."

"Do you love your uncle?" Eric asked.

"We lost our parents." Heinrich had tears welled up in the corners of his blue eyes. "Uncle Josef is not the warmest man. But takes care of Gretchen and me. If it wasn't for him, we'd be in orphanage. We have another car over there, in one of the out buildings. It was my parents." Heinrich pointed to the right of the barn. "Please come inside. We talk about how you will save your Maya and my uncle."

Eric didn't press the boy on his past. He assumed they were two of the many casualties of war. The young woman made him sit at the kitchen table and then served him bread, sausage, and coffee. Eric devoured it, not realizing how ravenous he was until he smelled the food. Once finished, he said, "*Danke.*" He asked in broken German if Gretchen would allow him to use their car.

Gretchen nodded and then conferred with Heinrich in German. Their conversation was much too advanced for Eric to interpret. Gretchen ran out of the room and came back with a Nazi officer uniform. She laid it over Eric's shoulders. It looked like it would fit.

"Eric, you wear this so that you can get inside. We wait in the car for you, Maya, and uncle. Our plan will work. My uncle calls it predestination paradox. You and Maya cannot change anything in the present just as we can't change the future. You both are destined to go back. I just hope uncle's time is not up. He believes that we lose this war. If anything happens to him…" Heinrich's eyes welled up again.

Eric didn't know what to do so he gave the little boy a hug. He quickly changed into the Nazi uniform. Gretchen waited in front of the house in a tan Volkswagen. It was a long car ride, well over an hour maybe two. Most of it was spent in silence as Eric looked out the window of the countryside and tiny villages as they drove by. He felt sick. This could very well be a suicide mission. All he could do was put his faith in a little boy who knew an awful lot about paradoxes.

"Is there a basement underneath the Eagle's Nest?" Eric said.

Heinrich and his sister spoke to each other in German and then he answered, "My uncle never spoke of basement, but he told me about rumors of an empty earth…"

"Empty earth? Wait, do you mean a hollowed earth? Like an underground civilization of Advanced Beings?" Eric asked.

The little boy nodded. Anxiety made Eric's hands shake and his feet tap. This was not good. Eric versus Hitler was overwhelming, but Eric versus aliens was absolutely no contest. *Mercedes, Paula, Jay, if you are around, guide me.*

Gretchen pulled the car off the road and into a field. She got out of the car and pointed upward to the Eagle's Nest, saying something in German.

Heinrich said, "There it is. We wait here. Go get them. And remember, fate is on your side. The cosmos wants you to succeed. Have faith the universe."

"I will put my faith in God. But thank you just the same. Listen, before I go, I wanted to thank you and your sister for everything you done. Give me one full day. It's afternoon right now. Figure this-if I am not back twenty-four hours, I'm dead. Maya's dead. And your uncle is probably dead. You need to leave so that no one finds you waiting here. Can you promise me that?"

They both nodded in despair. Eric hugged them and headed up the mountain towards Hitler's lair.

Chapter Thirty-Six

1944
Eagle's Nest, Germany

The ground shook so hard that at times it seemed as if we were flying. With each shake, our bodies were pulled toward the elevator. It was as if a force was helping us escape. I looked back and saw the Reptilians gaining ground as they slithered after us.

The elevator door was open just as we left it. Josef and I ran through the water, ignoring the teal metallic fish as they nipped at our feet. Josef was right behind me. We both lunged toward the elevator. I didn't understand the buttons, but Josef did. He quickly pressed the bottom one, and the door closed. We were ascending back up to the Eagle's Nest at a speed so fast that my ears began to pop.

As we rose, I looked at Josef and said, "Now what do we do?"

He smiled. "If there are no guards down there, we are safe. They keep the cars in the back with the keys on the front seat. I will send you back this time. I promise. And I really am sorry for all of this. It wasn't meant to go this far."

His voice sounded so far away. I yawned and my ears popped. I could now hear clearly. "But Hitler knows where you live. Your life could be in danger. Your family's life…"

"I am very valuable to him right now as a geneticist. There will be a price, but right now I serve a purpose.

"And if there are guards?" I asked. The elevator was slowing down.

"I don't know anymore. They tried to rape you, kill you, and then study you. Who knows what will happen. But they will think of something. They always do. Again, I serve a purpose and that purpose might be to torture you. I apologize in advance. Think positively. No guards."

A few minutes of silence went by. I remembered the Gray alien who I thought had communicated to me. *He is coming to save you.* Who was he? Could it be Eric? But how? Only hybrids and Advanced Beings can time travel. Jay was dead. Nothing made sense anymore.

The elevator's speed abruptly decreased to a stop. I was tossed to the other side of the car. The doors opened.

"Do we get out? Or do we go up another floor?" I whispered.

Josef shook his head. "It doesn't go any higher than the basement. And you don't want to go back down."

We tiptoed out of the elevator. The basement appeared to be empty, but then we heard some chatter in the far corner. I could see two soldiers talking about the human bones and ripped up clothes of the soldiers I had killed and then the Reptilians had eaten. Josef waved me forward. We had almost made it to the hallway until one of the soldiers yelled, "*Da sind sie!*"

We ran towards the hallway.

We were almost by the exit door. A third guard came out of nowhere and blocked our path. The other two had caught up. We were cornered.

The guards cuffed both of us and pushed us back towards the elevator. I wanted to scream. Again, back to where we started. I was never going home. This is where I would die-in a lab, poked and prodded by Nazi scientists until they figured out a way to kill me. I thought of Jay again. He died by drowning. Maybe I should just cut through all of their experiments and tell them to waterboard me.

The three guards seemed to gloat over our capture. I couldn't understand them, but their smug faces said it all. We stood around for several minutes as they seemed to blow smoke up each other's asses. I looked at Josef and he looked at me. We were waiting for something as we stood by that elevator. I hoped it wasn't Zykedo and Hensa to catch up with us.

Out of nowhere I heard a voice yell something in German. The three soldiers looked confused. Around the corner a fourth Nazi appeared. This one looked much more distinguished than the other three. His uniform bore all kinds of medals and pins. There was something familiar about him. I looked at his face. He had an uncanny resemblance to Eric. The soldier said something again in German. I knew that voice, even with the German accent. That was Eric. But how? Couldn't be.

The soldiers responded to his commands. One of them stayed back with me and Josef while the other two disappeared down the hallway. The fourth soldier looked at me and winked. Either Eric was trying to save us, or I had completely become delusional. I knew that Eric took German in high school, but never heard him speak it. I still wasn't fully convinced that this was a rescue mission and the man who looked like Eric was actually him.

The Eric look-a-like seemed to know his way around this basement. I was definitely losing it. He took us to the back parking lot that was attached to the basement. Once through, I saw a few dozen German cars from many decades ago.

As soon as we exited the Eagle's Nest, the Eric look-a-like kicked the other soldier in the groin and took his gun. Two shots were fired, one in the man's head and then one in the torso.

"Eric! It's really you? Am I seeing things? I don't understand. How on earth did you-"

"Maya, I will explain all of this later. Right now, we don't have the time. I got a getaway ride about a mile down this mountain. We are far from being out of the woods. Those soldiers I got rid of are probably upstairs telling Hitler right now that I came to take you and Josef back to Berlin under his orders. Soon this whole building will be after us." Eric bent down, took the keys out of the dead Nazi's pocket, and uncuffed us.

"If I may, Eric, most of the cars will be open. The keys will be on the front seat. My car is right over there," Josef said as he pointed to the black car only yards away.

We walked up to Josef's car and saw the keys. Seconds later, Josef got in the driver's side and started up the car. Eric quickly pushed him to the passenger side.

"If I may, I will drive us out of here. Your niece and nephew are waiting for us, and quite frankly, I don't trust you."

"Alright," said Josef. "My uniform fits you perfectly."

Eric sneered at Josef. I could tell he didn't like him, but still needed him. I felt the same way. We plowed through the flimsy barricade and headed down the mountain. There was a guard inside of a shack that saw us. We had a maximum of a three minute start.

"Shit!" Eric yelled. He quickly slowed down and honked his horn.

I saw a tan Volkswagen Beetle emerge from the tall grass. Instantly, I recognized the driver. It was Gretchen. Heinrich sat next to her in the front seat.

Eric rolled down the window and yelled, "Meet you back at the farm! We got your Uncle Josef!" Eric pointed to him in the passenger seat. "Stay hidden for ten or fifteen more minutes! We will soon have company! Wait until they pass!" Eric rolled the window back up and hit the gas. "Josef, I haven't driven a stick shift in years. Can't believe I still remember. These cars go so slow."

"Tell me what they are like in 2017," Josef said as Eric drove like a maniac away from the Eagle's Nest. The car jolted as he shifted gears.

"Maybe you will live to see for yourself. They go a hell of a lot faster than this. Most cars don't use this bullshit manual transmission. Do Hitler's cars go faster than this?"

"No, but they know about my farm. They know about my time machine. It's how you got here, correct?" Josef asked.

Eric nodded as he turned down the curvy road. "Your nephew showed me how to work it. If you could help? Maybe get us the hell out of here before the Nazis invade your farm?"

Josef nodded and then said, "Maya is a phenomenal woman. I wish I would have met her under better circumstances. For the record, I know that we lose the war, and I don't want to live in South America with the others. All I ever wanted to be was a scientist."

I touched Josef's shoulder from the back seat. "Maybe America will take you back with them after they win the war. They do that, you know. They take back many scientists and use them for their knowledge."

"Whatever you do, please take care of Gretchen and Heinrich. They told me that you are all they have. They are the reason I was able to pull this off. They got me here with your uniform and gave me a secondhand layout of the place from what you have told them."

"I am surprised that they told you their personal business. Their father was shot down in France and their mother, my sister, was weak. She killed herself shortly afterwards. I was the one who took them in. Do not lecture me about my parenting."

I could see Josef's face tighten. His little family was a very sore subject that needed to be changed. "Eric, Josef and I have been through...well you'll never believe what we have been through. Jay and Glenn once said that they had proof of Advanced Beings landing here and maybe even living here on planet Earth. They never even scratched the surface. Right under our feet, probably a few miles down inside of the earth, they live and they wait. They are here and have been here for a long time, and now they decided to stay. I have so much to tell you. Whoever engineered Jay and me are not part of this Hollow Earth. Something big is about to happen."

I told Eric the condensed version of everything in the last week and he told me how Doctor Blacksmith had modified his DNA so that he could come here and bring me home. I wanted nothing more than to jump this man's bones right there in the car regardless of Josef's presence, but my desires and appreciation for this prince, my Prince Eric, would have to wait.

Josef turned around and looked at me in the cramped backseat of the car. "Maya, do you remember that book you were thumbing through when you waited for me in that tiny library back at the farm?" I nodded. "You know that it's a sequel of sorts to Hitler's *Mein Kampf.* Only this version will never get published."

I remembered the book vividly. The German language, the equations, all of it was a mystery to me. "I saw it and didn't understand it."

Josef grinned. "I do not fully understand it either. There are codes of DNA that are probably from Advanced Beings. You know that I am a doctor. These Advanced Beings have given me an edge on the world when it comes to genetics. But other parts of the book I am not familiar with. I want you to take the book and show it to someone who can figure it out. There is a map in the book that outlines Hitler's escape plan. It might be of some use in 2017. There are some other diagrams that might be maps to other portals or openings for the Reptilians. Copies of this book were only meant for high-ranking officials. I stole a general's copy. I was jealous for not being included. Maybe you can decipher it or figure out what those lizards want from us, from the world. They used all of Germany. We were the dress rehearsal for what is to come. Soon enough all of humanity will become extinct."

Josef rambled on for another ten minutes with the intensity of a psychopath. Eric kindly nodded and then snuck me a look of concern. I hooded my eyes just enough to let him know I got his message.

What Eric still did not fully comprehend was the reasons Josef had for all of this madness. Our stay at Hitler's lair was not some kind of hallucination. Josef's manic rant had some clarity. He wanted me to go back and somehow change the world if not all together save it. I assured him that I would do what I could, but had no intentions of sticking my neck again. I was just one person, actually one hybrid. What could I do about a few races that were living inside of the globe? They wanted to rule the world, how could I or anyone stop them from doing that? All I cared about was living out my days as Mrs. Eric O'Reilly. My science fiction seemed more like a horror memoir. From now on I would write about happy things such as romance or young adult stories or fantasies with dragons. Anything but sci-fi. I wanted nothing to do with reality.

"We are only a few kilometers from the farm. So far, I have not seen anyone tailing us. I hope Heinrich and Gretchen left after Hitler's men," Josef said.

Josef directed us to turn onto a gravelly road. About a mile up from the main road I saw the barn, some of the out-buildings, and the old white farmhouse. Eric pulled up to the front door. Josef jumped out of the car and ran inside, returning with the book in his hand.

"Hurry. If I am right, and they are on their way here, we have about five or six minutes to get you in that capsule," Josef said.

Eric peeled down the gravel and stopped outside of the barn. I took the book from Josef's hand and followed Eric to the inside of the barn. He moved the barrel and disappeared down the hole. I followed. He kept saying something about knobs and switches over and over as he turned everything on.

"Okay, Maya, everything is ready to go. It should kick on any minute. Let's go strap ourselves inside of the capsule. Still got the book? It might not go through."

"I think it will. Glenn gave me coins to take here and they passed," I said as we climbed back up the ladder. I could hear Josef screaming. "Hey, I think we have some company. The Nazis must be here."

I heard lots of yelling going on outside of the barn, all in German. Eric and I squeezed into the tube and strapped ourselves against the glass. Another car pulled up. I could hear a woman's voice and a child's voice amidst the yelling. It had to be Gretchen and Heinrich. *Damn! They were supposed to wait until the coast was clear!*

Through the capsule's glass, I could see a sliver of the barn's entrance. Nazis were now inside of the barn and looking for the capsule. Eric and I started to shake. We needed to start spinning immediately. Any second now. Three Nazi soldiers had heard the motor and were only steps away from finding us. They were screaming at Josef and Heinrich. One of the guards had just moved the barrel. He looked me straight in the eyes. Heinrich threw himself in front of the soldier. We started to spin. I heard a gunshot. I saw both Eric's and my limbs dissolve into flakes. A peaceful floating feeling came over me as it did before. I could think of nothing, not even the little boy who lay dead on the barn floor.

Chapter Thirty-Seven

Late 1980's
Los Angeles, California

A long pause turned awkward during Lori's and Jay's conversation. Both of them were deep in thought. Jay was the first to speak. "Okay, Lori, I am willing to help you in any capacity. Your father gave me truth and kept me from complete insanity. This is the very least that I can do for him."

Lori cried even more, wiping away her tears of gratitude. "I guess the first step would be to check my apartment. If no one knows that I am his daughter, then I can go on living my life, business as usual. We have different last names. He never adopted me or left a will with my name on it."

"But then you said you were involved in kidnapping babies. You also said that you flew to Las Vegas and he flew to Los Angeles frequently to visit each other. You both called each other a lot. There are records of a relationship. Someone could want to kill you as well. And by someone, it could be the top brass of the U.S. military, the president, or the group of elites who are in on this hybrid baby scheme."

Lori nodded in defeat. "Will you check my apartment out?"

"Let's go."

A half an hour later, Lori pulled into her high-rise building in the middle of Los Angeles. Her building had a small parking lot in the front for visitors. She found a spot that would allow her to watch the front entrance yet stay camouflaged from people going in and out of the building.

"Wow, nice place. This must cost a fortune in rent," Jay said as Lori parked.

"I am a doctor, so I can afford it. I was actually thinking of buying a place with …. never mind." Lori thought of Belinda and how they could have bought a home outside of the city. Her dreams were now on hold. "Here's my key. The doorman just glances at the key. There's no sign in. I kept everything inside of a Christmas tree box inside of my crawl. Go to my closet in the master bedroom. I packed artificial branches around everything to hide all of the slides and paperwork."

Once Jay left, Lori sat in her car for over an hour, letting the battery run as she listened to radio news. No more was said about the explosion. She watched her doorman from the car. He was reading a book in between watching people who came and went from the building. Jay was still gone. She became increasingly nervous. Something was wrong.

Several more minutes went by. Lori turned off the car and contemplated going inside of the building. She saw a shock of flaxen hair through the front windows. It was Belinda. She carried a large shopping bag as she exited the elevator. Lori could see her dialing a number on her cell phone. Lori didn't know how she got inside of the building. She wanted to give Belinda a key, but never did.

Belinda walked outside, and Lori slumped to the floor of her car. She listened for cars leaving the parking lot. Several minutes later she popped back up in her seat. Belinda had to be gone. Jay was now in the lobby saying something to the doorman. Lori unlocked the doors and he got back in the car.

"Go," Jay said. "Now." He looked worried.

Lori ran over the curb as she raced out of the complex.

Once they were a few blocks away, Jay was more relaxed. "You are in some deep shit, Lori. How deep, who knows. There was quite a party going on in your apartment. I gave the doorman some bullshit concerned neighbor crap and told him you hadn't been home. I told him that there were people inside of your apartment who didn't belong and gave him a description. Two men and a woman. He's calling the police and pulling the camera tapes. He said that two men flashed a key around 5:45 AM, a few minutes after he clocked in. A woman came later, an hour or so later."

"What about my files?" Lori asked.

"Gone. I stood in the hallway for a long time and listened through the walls. I couldn't hear what they were saying, but I could hear them moving your furniture around. The men left before the woman. She came out around twenty minutes later with a bag. She then locked the door with key."

Belinda. "So, how do you know my files are gone?"

"I went in. Stupid, I know. Someone else could have been there, waiting. Waiting with a gun. The men had that government agency look about them. The woman, not sure. She was a looker. Blonde. I went straight to your crawl space. Empty. Your Christmas tree box had nothing in it but a few artificial tree branches. Listen, Lori, you're going to stay with me for a while."

"Oh no. I caused you enough trouble for one day. Your fiancé is not going to like an English girl who is hunted by the global elite living in your house. Don't worry about me. I have money. The general planned for this. He kept all of his money in a safety deposit box, which I emptied."

Jay shook his head. He said, "You can't go too far. I have to help you. Your dad did so much for me, and now it's my turn. I have a good friend, a lawyer. Fan turned friend kind of thing. I've known him for years. He's my personal lawyer. He believes that aliens exist. He just started a TV show. It's kind of like a documentary about alien stories that were brushed off by the mainstream media for unknown reasons. His name is…"

"Glenn Lucasek," Lori interrupted. "I love the show. The mainstream media won't talk about any of this. Normal people who claim abduction or see UFOs, even photograph and film them, apparently isn't real news. Bollocks. They are bought and paid for by the elite."

"Exactly. He and I have a vision. Something that is much bigger than my novels or his TV show. We started a little museum. It's in the early stages, but we plan on growing it. We are dedicated to documenting activity that involves UFOs, aliens, and the steps that are taken in keeping them a secret. It's not open to the public yet. We have all kinds of news clippings, footage, pieces of extraterrestrial crystal and metal, telescopes, and some archeological findings. We have donors!" Jay's face lit up like a Christmas tree as he talked. "I can talk about this all day. Anyway, what kind of doctor are you?"

"I specialize in genetics. The slides that were taken from me would have been a hell of an exhibit for your museum. They were taken from the Advanced Beings that my father and his team had held in captivity. There were tissue samples from the hybrid babies that were born inside of the underground lab of Broom Lake. I had a slide of your tissue."

"I can give you another sample. It's not over."

Lori said, "Funny, huh? My parents' lifework, gone-blown up or taken. It would have been perfect for your museum." Lori pulled the car over and broke down in hysterics.

Jay clumsily put his arm around her. "Sorry, I'm not the best at comforting beautiful, mysterious doctors in a time of crisis. It is not all gone. Don't you see? This is fate, predestination, a causal loop, or whatever you want to call it. You still have those papers your father hid. You have your education as well as genetic information that has yet to be discovered. You have your memories. Write down everything you remember. And you have me." He smiled at her and she nodded. "Listen, I want you to work for me. It's only part-time for now. You are the only one who is qualified for this."

"Your charity is noble, but I just couldn't do that to you. The Government is looking for me…"

Jay held her arms and shook them. "Fuck Big Brother! I will get you a new name, new life. All of that's easy when you have money. No one has to know, not even Glenn. You will get a new set of credentials, degrees, references, you name it."

"You won't tell anyone who I really am?"

"Are you nuts? I kept your father a secret and promise you all the way to my grave that I will keep you a secret. Lori Parker, Lori Gaston, Lori Blacksmith…"

"Blacksmith. I like it."

"Then Doctor Lori Blacksmith it is."

"Jay, one more thing. The blonde you saw, she was my friend. No, that's a lie. She was my lover." Lori looked into his green eyes and saw no judgment. "I was in love with her. We worked together at the university. She is also a geneticist."

Jay shrugged his shoulders. "Ain't love grand, huh? Lori, I've had my heart broken dozens of times. My fiancé will be wife number three. To be honest, I don't think it will last. People can disappoint. I promise not to sell you out."

"Good. I don't think I could take it." Lori wiped her tears. "Jay, why do you think the elites of the world want hybrids?"

"That I don't know. A guess would be they want us to evolve."

Lori started the car back up and proceeded to drive. She asked, "And those who don't evolve?"

"They will serve the wants and the needs of their master race."

Chapter Thirty-Eight

Present Day
Ruby Mountains, Nevada

Glenn watched Eric disappear in disbelief. Everything he and his team had worked for was finally achieved. This was the biggest advancement in history and would surely change the world.

Glenn raced back to the adjoining room and brought up the footage on the computer screen. He replayed Eric's launch four times. Chuck and Lori stood behind him and watched.

Mercedes stuck her head in the room and said, "Congratulations. That boy and Maya better make it back or all of this was for nothing."

"We need champagne. This is worth a big celebration. Maybe I should gather everyone here and show the tape…" Glenn said.

Mercedes face turned red. "Yes, show everyone the tape. Everyone except Paula. She risked her life in trying to get an exact location of Maya's whereabouts, or have you already forgotten? I am on my way to check on her." She turned towards the door, but then walked back over to Glenn. "Who are you, Glenn Lucasek? You used to be my friend, Paula's friend." She left the round room in anger.

Chuck put his hand on Glenn's arm. "She will get over it. We did it. We figured out a way to send human beings through time, through space. The possibilities are limitless. Sooner or later, we will figure out how to get to other planets, different eras, maybe even different universes. I saw a few bottles of champagne in the kitchen. I'll go…"

"No, Chuck. I'll go. Doctor Blacksmith, please join me. I want you to check on Paula. I need Chuck to watch the capsule like a hawk in case something goes wrong."

Glenn and Lori walked through the maze of hallways in silence. When they got to the main reception area, Glenn stopped to fiddle with the security cameras. He said, "Lori, Doctor Blacksmith, Lori Osbourne, or whoever you are, we need to talk privately. I shut off the cameras in the library. See?" Lori looked at the control. Her hazel eyes showed nothing. She nodded. They walked down the main hallway of the institute to the library. The room was empty. Glenn locked the door.

"Sit. I have questions that you need to answer."

Lori sat at one of the wooden tables in the middle of the room. "Okay, then. It's about time we cleared the air."

Glenn sat across from her and said, "I have kept my mouth shut for over a year. This information gave rise to a set of new questions. As you can imagine, I learned that your entire work history is a lie. You are hiding behind the accomplishments of others. Why? We all know you are brilliant. You are obviously trained in science. Jay refused to explain when I brought it up to him. He trusted me with everything except you. Why? What makes you so special?"

"I'm nobody special. My parents were the special ones, together, and then apart. They risked everything…" Lori's stoic face could no longer hold. A few tears streamed down her cheek. She took a moment and then said, "They died for this, whatever it is. Jay never told you anything about me because that's who he was-a loyal friend."

Glenn was not about to slow down his line of questioning. "Listen, you are obviously a doctor. You came here with knowledge about A.B.s that no one else has. You gave Chuck mathematical equations that helped him build the time capsule. You know everything about this institute. I'm all by myself now. No Jay to help. Maya may never come back. So, who are you?"

"I don't know much about astrophysics. The equations came from my father. They were given to him from a Nazi doctor before his base was blown up. Jay helped me understand what they were for."

"Who's your father? Was he a Nazi?"

"No. He was a general in the U.S. Army. He and my mother had information, top secret files, A.B. slides, so much. I kept it in a big box, a Christmas tree box. That box was stolen from me, just like my life. I found an envelope in my father's apartment. The envelope was all I had left. It's where I got the math equations. It also contained DNA codes. I showed Jay all of it. He went through a few of his novels and figured out that genetics and time travel worked hand in hand."

"I remember that. He never mentioned anything about the formulas. He pretended that Chuck figured it out," Glenn said.

"Chuck is certainly smart enough to figure it out, but it would have taken years, even decades. Jay gave him one hell of a head start. I guess Chuck has earned his glory. Now the world will change because of it. Maybe not for the better."

Glenn had enough of her theatrical sense of morality as well as her self-righteousness. He wanted to slap her and scream, *Wake Up! The world doesn't work in your impossible set of ideals!* But there was something so sincere about her both now and since he first met her.

He carefully chose his words and said, "That's not fair. Doctor Chuck Wu has a real resume with real credentials. We recruited him from the top university in China. He also has inside knowledge of A.B.s, which is why he got involved in astrophysics. He told me his story.

Now how about you telling me yours? I am tired of the bits and the pieces you throw me."

"Alright. I owe you a summary of my past. We did just make history together."

Lori began with her upbringing in England and then meeting her father. She told him how her mother was murdered and then years later her father was murdered. She gave him strands of information about the U.S. government's Operation Chrome, even telling him that was how Jay was conceived. She left out names, dates, and places, but Glenn had been given everything.

"So, Jay was my last resort. I knew who he was because of my father's interest in him. He was one of the first hybrids created. I thought they might have ended the operation, but Maya is living proof that the operation lives on. She's what? Twenty-two now? She has a necklace, the same kind that Jay once had. Whoever stole her is copying my father, copying Michael."

"Do you know where the new baby manufacturing plant even is?"

Lori shook her head. "That was another life ago. Maya is an updated version of Jay. I can tell by her work. She writes more clearly, fills in more gaps. Jay's codes were never complete, and not always consistent either. Both Maya and Jay have unique genes that humans do not have. I don't know why or what these genes are for. There is much more research to be done."

Glenn tapped his fingers on the table. He believed her. He also needed her if T.A.H. was to continue its work. He said, "It's amazing she was stolen and spared, just like Jay. I wish I knew who. That's something we need to follow up on."

"Absolutely. Boy, could we talk some shop. Imagine someone picking up where we left off so long ago. What are the odds? There must be something inside of us, maybe it's a gene, something that is in our DNA that makes us want freedom…"

"Let me stop you right now," Glenn interrupted. "It's not a gene. Never was. It is our soul. It's the one thing those A.B.s do not have. I never understood that more than I do at this particular moment, talking with you. Creating hybrid infants inside of a laboratory for rich and powerful people is a form of oppression. You and your family knew that. The new hybrid kidnapper also knew that. Murder is also wrong, even when it's in the name of science. But you already knew that too. I guess I did too, but I chose not to listen. Jay was always the one who knew how to reign me in when I started talking big. Right before he died, he started talking more and more about the soul and how it must relate to God. I ignored him. I thought Paula and Mercedes were getting to him. Maybe it's our soul that makes us special. That's why the A.B.s don't want to destroy us, they want to improve us."

"Ah, our soul. That's the one thing I cannot find inside of our DNA. Someday…I am glad that you and I have cleared the air. When Maya gets back, and I know she will, I will tell her everything as well. She is now the new boss and deserves the truth. Let's go see how Paula is doing. I want to examine her," Lori said. Glenn nodded. They both got up and pushed in their chairs.

They walked to the other side of the institute which was still undergoing construction. The tape and the cones made Glenn think of the recent expansion plans that he and Jay made right before his death. They shared so many dreams. Both wanted more doctors, more dorms, more labs, and more telescopes. They longed for the kind of evidence that would allow the world to see the truth. They could accept other A.B.s as friendly visitors or prepare for war. They thought they could promote change for the better. When Jay died, so did their idealism. Glenn got sucked into the power of advancement instead. This should have been his and Jay's proudest moment. Was Jay watching over him like an angel?

They entered the small room and saw Mercedes sitting at Paula's side as she sat up and drank a bottle of 7-Up. Devon sat in the corner, preoccupied with his phone. This was the first time the newly built room was used.

Everything hit him at once as he watched Lori examine Paula. He should have been riding high after what had just happened in the round room, but instead he worried about Chuck. The doctor had computer access and video feed of Eric going through time. Did Lori leave her gene gun there? He wasn't stupid. Chuck had a wealth of information to steal.

"Glenn, Earth to Glenn," Mercedes said. "Where are you?"

"Oh, sorry Mercedes. I have a lot on my mind. You were saying?"

"She was saying that I am fine, Glenn. No more fussing. Doc, I appreciate all of this, but this has happened before. Sometimes spiritual communication will knock me out for a spell. Now please, enough," said Paula. She sounded ornerier than ever.

Glenn smiled and then said, "Glad you have made a recovery. Has Devon told you what has just happened?"

"Yes, and congratulations. But we are not out of the woods. Glenn, I talked to Jay. I know it was Jay. But then something happened. Interference. It's hard to explain," Paula said.

"You think you talked to Jay. It could have been another spirit..."

Mercedes cut him off. "I have just about had it with you! I was there. This was no wishful séance. Jay spoke to us. You said he spoke to you in your dream. What does it take, Glenn, for you to believe? If that little snake in the grass Chuck told you he spoke with Jay, you'd believe him."

"I do not know about that. Chuck is in the round room, waiting for us to return with some champagne. I told him to watch the capsule in case Eric saved Maya in record time. I know you do not trust him…"

"Trust? I hate him," Mercedes said. Lori smiled. "And you hate him too? Admit it, Doc!"

Lori shook her head. "I do not know him that well. Something about him…I took my gene gun back up to the lab. I get the same kind of intuition that Mercedes and Paula get. I try to be careful around him. But I have no proof of any misdoings. On the other hand, he is brilliant and invaluable to this institute."

Glenn looked at Devon who sat in the corner by the computer. "Is that computer hooked up to our security cameras?" Devon nodded and immediately faced the screen and started typing. The security software came up. "Click over to the round room. I want to know what Chuck is doing right now…"

"You already know. He's selling information to the highest bidder. Human time travel could probably fetch him a few billion or so…" Mercedes said.

Lori interrupted her. "He only has part of it. He has no idea how or where I inserted the time travel gene into Eric. I keep that information under lock and key. I will never sell it off."

Devon got the security cameras in the round room to work. Chuck was emailing someone with a Chinese name. Devon zoomed in. The email had a video file attached to it. "I am guessing it's the video you took of Eric disappearing inside of the capsule. Mercedes, you are right."

"What do you think of him, Devon?" Glenn asked.

"The ladies have it right. He is very secretive. I get a sense that he might be selling off information. No proof. Just private phone calls, the computer is quickly shut down if I walk in the room, that kind of thing. This time travel triumph gives him quite a bit of leverage. He has seen his time capsule work three times. You want me to get rid of him? Or do you still need him?" Devon asked.

"I don't have an answer for you right now. Too many other problems to contend with," Glenn said.

"There are other ways to find out about time travel. I think I know a way to get us to the next level with or without Chuck," Lori said.

"Love to hear any of your ideas," Glenn said.

"It was something that I found in Maya's book. I think it's a warning of some kind. My timing is probably off. Should I…"

Paula stood up from the bed and stretched. "Please Doctor, bring it on."

"Well, to make a long story short, I have firsthand information that Leonardo Lansatti is a hybrid. He and Jay were from the same litter of test tubes and A-wombs," Lori announced.

"How do you know?" Mercedes questioned.

"Trust me! Someday we will have some wine and I will bare my soul as I did with Jay, and now Glenn," Lori said. Glenn nodded for her to continue. "The Lansatti family runs VYA Energy. Leonardo Lansatti is in charge of the corporation. He also has a seat on the U.N. Security Council, follow?" Everyone nodded. "You might know they recently got a big, fat contract from the UN to look for energy in Antarctica."

"But what does this have to do with Maya's book?" asked Paula. Glen shot her a nasty look for interrupting.

"I'm getting there. Please, let me finish. I don't know what they are looking for, but it is not bloody oil. I think I know exactly where they are, and it's not the right spot. Again, to make a long story short, my father left me some papers. There were equations, DNA sequences, and there were some maps. I could never figure them out until now," Lori said.

"You think they are maps of Antarctica?" Devon asked.

"One of them. The others might be escape routes to Argentina after the war ended. I'd like to concentrate on the Antarctica map for now."

"What does Antarctica have to do with anything?" Glenn asked.

Paula smiled and then said, "Ah, something that I know and you don't. Hitler went to Antarctica in the '30s. Some kind of exploration. No one is really sure why or what he found. After the war, the U.S. went to the same spot. They called it Operation High Jump. An admiral reported that the earth might be hollow. Maybe technology back then wasn't advanced enough to get through the ice, but now... VYA is an energy company. They drill for oil all of the time."

Lori added, "Maybe this is an attempt to prove the earth is hollow. I can tell you this: Maya gave us the coordinates in her sequel."

"What?" Glenn asked. "How? Why would Maya..."

"Please, let me explain. It was Claude who gave me the idea. He was the one who mentioned Lansatti's Antarctica exploration. I know Antarctica is huge. When I went back to my lab to run some tests on Eric's DNA, I picked up my iPad and pulled up a map. The shape of my drawing matched the western half of the continent. I looked up the longitudes and latitudes of Antarctica, and then narrowed it down to the ones that encompassed my drawing.

"Well, I started scanning through pages sixty through one hundred, looking for something that had to do with Lansatti. On page ninety-one, there it was, another series of words that spelled out Lansatti."

"Was that the longitude or latitude?" Glenn asked.

"I am guessing that it's the longitude, west. The only other page that I found within my realm of possibilities was eighty-five, which I am assuming to be the latitude, south. Lansatti is also encoded on that page. This seems to be just west of the South Pole. Is that where Lansatti is drilling?"

"I have no idea. Is this the same spot where Hitler went back in the '30s?" asked Paula.

"It is in the same vicinity as was Operation High Jump."

"Lori, what do you really think they are looking for?" Glenn asked.

"I wish we could talk to Leonardo Lansatti ourselves and just ask him. Lay our cards on the table already. Maybe he can help us take the next step in time travel. I want to call him."

"What would you say?" Mercedes asked.

"Devon, please find the phone number for VYA Energy." Devon looked on the website and then made the first of many more calls to come. Several minutes went by. Glenn had radioed Chuck that he would soon be there with some champagne. He thought of all of the emails and phone calls Chuck was probably making and winced.

Devon finally got Leonardo Lansatti's secretary. "Hello there. I am Devon Newberry, head of security at T.A.H. I am calling for Doctor Lori Blacksmith. She has something very important to tell Mister Lansatti."

Devon paused and then said, "This is confidential and personal, maybe even life-saving… Yes, I know he is a busy man…Please…"

Lori whispered "Atlantis."

Devon then said into the receiver, "Atlantis."

Within a minute, Leonardo Lansatti was on the phone. Devon handed the receiver to Lori.

In front of the room, Lori said into the phone, "My father was there when you were born. He was in command of the air base where you were created. Were you told about the team of Nazi doctors or the murdered prostitutes? Did you ever see the A.B.s that gave you your unique DNA? I do not pretend to know all of it, but I do know that one of their genes allows for time travel. Do I have your attention?" There was a pause. "I thought so. There are many people who believe you are here to help your race of aliens takeover..."

Lori paused. "So, it's not a takeover? I am crazy, huh? Give me a second to show you how crazy I really am." Lori nodded to Devon who had the day's videos up on the computer screen. He sent Lansatti's secretary the footage of Eric disappearing into space. "Your secretary has an email. Get it from her quickly if you don't want her to see it." There was another pause. A minute or two later Lori nodded at her little audience once the man was back on the line. "Yes, it's real. One more thing, Sir. How is your Antarctica exploration for energy going? Is that what you are looking for? Or are you looking for Atlantis?" Another long pause. "Are you looking in the right place? Antarctica is huge. I might be able to help you with the coordinates... Wait, I am not threatening you! Don't hang up..." Lori shook her head as she hung up the phone.

"Threatening you?" Paula asked.

"He sounded spooked once I brought up Antarctica. I bet they have not found anything yet. Give him some time. Now let's get some champagne and join Chuck. I do not want to miss Maya's and Eric's return flight."

The little group exited the newly built dorm room. They briefly went their separate ways, and then one by one returned to the round room. Glenn grabbed several bottles of champagne and a stack of Styrofoam coffee cups. He was the last to enter the room.

"Anything happen, Chuck?" Glenn asked with a smile.

"Nothing. Quiet as a morgue in here. Glad to see that Paula is doing alright," Chuck said. He was still seated in front of the computer. It appeared as if he was reading about different kinds of centrifuges. Glenn thought this was all for show, but didn't say anything. He passed out cups and then poured the champagne.

"I would like to make a toast. To the beginnings of time travel, available to all." Glenn looked at Mercedes and Paula and then rolled his eyes as if to suggest this was all for show. "I could not have done this without Jay. Wherever you are, dear old friend, I hope I can join you when the time comes. May you oversee Eric's and Maya's journey back home. I want to give credit to all of our staff, especially Doctors Chuck Wu and Lori Blacksmith. Without their brilliance and creativity, this would have never been possible. I want to thank Mercedes Garcia and Paula Linquist in their spiritual beliefs that gave Eric the direction needed for his rescue." He paused and gave Mercedes and Paula another eye roll. They looked back at him and shrugged.

"I need a drink already. Could you please get on with it?" Paula said. Everyone laughed.

"Yes, of course. But one last thing. I want to talk about what the future of all of this means. We could open this up to the world's most wealthy people on the planet and send them on the wildest vacations. We could travel back ourselves and check to see if history was in fact correct. Maybe even go as far back as the beginning of when this planet was formed. We could team up with NASA or some other country's space program and perfect where our capsule lands. We could somehow use this technology and meet A.B.s, maybe learn from them. Hell, what can't we do? We could be kings and queens of the world!" Glenn looked at the women again. This time they knew where he was going. "So, drink up. Cheers! We will soon be running the world!"

Chuck especially seemed to enjoy Glenn's words. He smiled in approval as he guzzled down the champagne. He was very relaxed.

"Oh crap! I forgot the cheese tray! I saw some caviar in the fridge. With everything that has happened, I forgot all about food. Chuck, would you mind? I want to watch the capsule for a little while."

Chuck reluctantly nodded and then shut down his computer. "Alright. I understand. You had errands to make and now you want to watch. This is so damn exciting! I will be back in a flash."

Once Chuck had left the room, Glenn looked at Devon and then the computer. He immediately sat down and thumbed through his phone.

"How do you know his password?" Glenn asked.

"I don't. Here is the footage of him signing onto the computer earlier. Watch his fingers. AZ2464VCqst. Bingo!" Devon said as he logged on. "He has his email set on memory." A couple of clicks later, Devon had pulled eight emails onto the screen. All of them were clips of the time capsule. All of them were offering the technology for sale. The doctor was clear that he wanted to continue his work, but was willing to share it. Three billion was the starting price and he would go to the highest bidder.

"How can he do that to us?" Glenn said.

"He doesn't have the gene or its sequence," Lori offered.

"He has Maya's novels. He will have other brilliant geneticists at his disposal. It can be done," Glenn said.

"China already responded. Three-point-five billion, and a laboratory staffed with as many doctors as he needs," Devon said. "You are the boss, Glenn. Tell me what to do."

"I cannot speak for all of us, but this is high treason. He broke every condition of his contract," Lori said.

The beeps and clicks of the doors broke up their conversation as Chuck stood outside of the door with an armload of food. Glenn could see him from the camera. He was leaning in for the final retina scan.

"Be cool. Devon, take my lead." Glenn walked into the round room and paced the floor like he was anxiously awaiting Eric's and Maya's landing. This wasn't entirely an act. He wanted them back more than ever. Glenn didn't want to accept the reality of never seeing them again. It made him too sad to think about. Besides, he had other fish to fry.

"Ah, food! I am starving," Glen said.

Glenn helped him carry the food to the back room where he and Mercedes set everything up. He munched on some crackers and made small talk with everyone. An hour went by as they watched for the capsule to spin. Glenn remembered when Jay disappeared for an hour. Jay thought he was gone for half of a day. The minutes back in time were not the same as the minutes in the present.

Slowly and carefully, Glenn said, "Chuck, you would never quit on me, would you? You know, work for a government or an industry? Sell off what we accomplished?"

The look on Chuck's face said it all. "You looked through my emails! The food errand was a wild goose chase!" Chuck ran to the door.

"Devon, we have no other option," Glenn said as he tried to block Chuck from leaving.

Devon lunged at Chuck as he opened the first door. Glenn dashed to the phone and ordered a lock-down for the entire institute. Chuck should have been dead, but Devon's take-down turned into a brawl. Chuck was not going down easily. His expertise in the martial arts held the big Aussie at bay. The doctor managed to kick Devon's gun away. The women screamed, but the noise of the centrifuge drowned them out.

The floor shook. The capsule moved sideways and then spun. The distraction allowed Chuck to grab the gun that had been kicked over to the corner.

Chuck pointed it at Devon. "I will kill him and all of you if you don't let me out of this place right now. Cancel the lockdown."

Glenn went to the nearest phone and made the call.

Chapter Thirty-Nine

Present Day
Ruby Mountains, Nevada

A little boy was shot in front of my eyes as my body dissolved into a million pieces. Eric's body was still intact. I began to worry. The speed of the spinning capsule got faster. I felt Nazi blue eyes hovering over us. Finally, Eric's body began to disappear. We made it. Would Heinrich survive? I couldn't feel guilty. I was too numb. Eric and I floated as one. We were bound together for what seemed like eternity. I emptied my head and enjoyed the ride.

Then I could see my extremities. My body was rebuilding itself. I still wore the white nightgown from the Eagle's Nest. It was filthy. Where was Eric? I stood alone in the spinning capsule. The speed was decelerating. I could see the round room. Eric? Please… I could see his arm, and then torso, and then face. He was still wearing the Nazi uniform. His body was complete before the spinning had stopped.

"Oh, Eric, I was worried. I thought you weren't going to transform."

"I just take a little bit longer than you. Look! What the hell is going on? That's Devon, the head of security. And Chuck's pointing a gun at him."

Eric had both of our straps undone. He kicked out the door panel. We both jumped out of the capsule while it still moved. I jumped on Chuck's back. He dropped the gun which Eric retrieved. Chuck threw me on the floor like a rag doll and headed for the door.

Shouts of 'stop him', 'he's got my technology', and 'he's getting away' were heard in spite of the thunderous sounds of the centrifuge. Chuck was fiddling with the door. Eric pointed the gun and fired. Doctor Wu slumped to the floor. Blood soon puddled beneath him. I thought of Heinrich, the little boy who died for me, for Eric. We left 1944 with death and returned to the present with death. Was it symbolism or a warning to what time travel had to offer?

I couldn't think of that now. Time was moving too fast. The security man was on the phone. Instantly, a small team of men took Chuck's body away. One of the men stayed back and mopped up the mess. I thought of Hitler and the Eagle's Nest and my attempted rapists. But this was different. At least, that's what I told myself. Chuck didn't exactly have a stellar reputation among the T.A.H. Institute's board of directors.

Everyone in the room seemed unfazed. There would be no swanky funeral for Chuck. His contributions were already forgotten. Eric and I received hugs and tears, all wanting our story. Mercedes handed both of us two Styrofoam cups filled with champagne.

Glenn stood in the middle of the room and announced, "Listen up, I want all of us to move this party into the library. We will give our legendary time astronauts the floor."

"And one more request. Eric, please change your clothes. I never want to see Nazi regalia again," I said. He agreed. I also needed to get out of my disgusting hospital gown.

The location change was a smart move. The round room gave me chills. We packed up the champagne and snacks. On the short walk, I was told all about Chuck's attempt to walk away with T.A.H.'s discoveries. I now understood what had to be done. Devon stayed back from our little party. Glenn ordered him to run a fine-toothed comb through all of Chuck's communications. He needed to know about any potential leaks.

Glenn rearranged the room so that Eric and I sat next to each other in the comfortable leather chairs and Paula, Glenn, Doctor Blacksmith, and Mercedes sat at a long table that faced us. Eric and I changed into T.A.H. sweatshirts and sweatpants from the gift shop. I began with my story before Eric came to my rescue. I told them about Hitler and Josef, the Eagle's Nest, Maria Orsic, and Martin Bormann. I told them how Jay might have played a role in keeping me alive.

Paula said, "This will be my only interruption, Maya. But Jay was working for you on this end as well. That's how Eric knew how to find you. Believe me now, Glenn?"

She gave Glenn a look that would kill. I had to laugh. It was so good to see their faces. I didn't think I would ever see them again. I continued with my story, telling them about the Hollowed Earth, the Reptilians, their council and community, and their New World Order plans. I told them about their underground construction, the Grays, and how I suspected slavery. Once again, I was interrupted, this time by Doctor Blacksmith.

"I used to have photos of the Reptilians. They made contact with some of the British chaps. My mum took the photo. But that was a long time ago. Did you see any Atlanteans?"

I was surprised that she brought the race of aliens up. "No, but they talked about them. They ruled Earth thousands of years ago. Most of them died from the Great Flood, but many believe some escaped. Thousands of their bodies are inside of the earth, sleeping. Hitler believed they started the Aryan race."

"What do you think of the Atlanteans?" the doctor pressed.

"No one has any clear answers. Their dead bodies show up every now and then. They were once regarded as peaceful and advanced. I might even be one according to the Reptilians," I answered.

I could see by Doctor Blacksmith's face that she had many more questions, but held back. She seemed to drift off in thought. I knew she was not asking me out of sheer curiosity. I finished up with my trip to 1944.

Eric's turn. He told them all about the farm and Heinrich and Gretchen. He told them how he borrowed the Nazi uniform and somehow remembered much of what he learned in high school German class. The story finished with poor little Heinrich who died for us during our takeoff. "He saved our lives and somehow I will think of a way to honor him. I love you, Maya. I have come to love all of you. But I think my time traveling days are over. I want to take it easy from now on."

I kissed him on the mouth in front of everyone. Lots of "ooohhhs!" filled the room. I was in love. Claude was completely out of my mind. I had even forgotten about how he tried to kill me.

"Oh, I almost forgot," Eric said as he pulled the book out of his jogging pants pocket. "We brought back a souvenir. It's Hitler's sequel to *Mein Kampf*. It's copied, but handwritten by the *Fuehrer* himself. This has got to be worth something."

The book changed hands several times until it was Doctor Blacksmith's turn. She slowly turned page after page. I thought she might even speak German.

"I will be right back." She returned with a stack of papers in her hand a few minutes later. She placed her stack next to the book and compared page to paper. "This is it." Everyone in the room stopped talking. She looked to be in a state of shock. Once the doctor gained control of her emotions, she said, "Eric, this is a gift. You do not know how valuable. Thank you. Thank you for validating my father's work, my work. I cannot thank you enough." The doctor started to sob.

"Are you German, Doctor Blacksmith? Is there something in that book that matches your papers?" I asked.

"Oh, that's only part of it. Maya, your German doctor, the one you call Josef, is my father's German doctor, Doctor Karl Jaeger. He was a brilliant geneticist."

I couldn't believe what I was hearing. "He told me that was his area of expertise. But he was also quite the physicist. He had his own time machine. The Nazis probably took it after Eric and I left. Please, tell me more about him. He really put me in harm's way, yet still managed to keep me alive. Complicated man."

Lori told me all that she knew. She then said, "He must have written down all that he could remember once he gave Eric the book. He carried a lot of secrets around with him. Listen, I have to show you something." The doctor held out the page with the maps and then her paper with a hand-drawn map. "I think this one is Antarctica. Did you know that you encoded Lansatti several times throughout your sequel? Don't you see? You don't even know who he is. A force is calling on you to act. You were meant to save them. Don't you get it? You wrote about Reptilians taking over the world and then you meet them seventy years before your book is written. This is not fiction, Maya. You were chosen to be a prophet."

My sequel was the last thing on my mind. I barely remembered the name Lansatti, but it supposedly had significance. Doctor Blacksmith connected the dots. Lansatti, Atlantis. VYA Energy. Antarctica.

"Wait, he owns VYA Energy? Now you are scaring me. Vril-ya, that's what it stands for. Vril-ya is the energy used down below. It powers the Hollow Earth. The Nazis were tapped into it," I said.

Was the doctor right? Was this my true purpose? To help my hybrid siblings find our long-lost ancestors? I thought I could wash my hands of all of this.

"Glenn, is Devon free? I need him to get me Lansatti's number again," Lori said.

Glenn radioed Devon. He was in the library in less than a minute.

"I am so sorry. Lansatti left a voicemail on T.A.H.'s main number an hour ago. I got so busy... No one is at the reception desk today. I just checked it. Here." Devon passed a torn piece of paper to Lori.

"Devon, thank you so much. Send him the new video of Maya and Eric returning from their journey. We got him. Okay, here we go. May my negotiation skills be on point today. It's ringing." She looked at everyone in the room and made a gesture with her hands to let us know that he answered. "Mister Lansatti, nice that we are playing some telephone tag. I am assuming my video got your attention. Another one is on the way. I know you want to save your people buried in the ice." There was a pause. He sounded angry. "Please, Sir. We do not bid you harm. We want to help you." There was another long pause. "I understand this all sounds crazy. We believe... What's that sound? I hear helicopter blades. I can barely hear you..."

Devon was on the radio and flashed Glenn a nervous look. "A helicopter just landed on top of the institute. I've got my men armed, and ready to fire if this guy is going to break in."

"How the hell did he know where we are?" Glenn asked. "Lori, keep him on the line if possible."

My hands began to shake. Lansatti had found us? Were we a threat to him?

"I am getting some intel that you are already here. Do you want to continue this conversation? Good. Your guards cannot enter the institute. Just you, and our security will make sure you are unarmed. Do you follow?"

Doctor Blacksmith was one amazing woman. She seemed so in control, always knowing what to say-cool as Antarctic ice. I was about to crap my pants. I listened to her give Lansatti directions and then listened to Devon whisper to Glenn. Lansatti came with a whole Navy Seal team, ready to rumble. He must have really needed those coordinates.

Two men who worked under Devon escorted Leonardo Lansatti into the library. He was clearly in his sixties, thinning hair that was both blonde and light gray. He wore a black suit and a red tie. His face was chiseled, lined, and lacked emotion. He looked at all of us with his glacier blue eyes and said, "I have no idea how any of you know this. And I don't have the time to find out. As you seem to know, my exploration is not going anywhere. I am not surprised. It didn't go very far for Hitler, or the U.S. My company has been there for over two months and found nothing. If you have any information for me, then I would greatly appreciate it. My people will be here very soon. They want to take their ancestors back home."

I looked at Doctor Blacksmith and Glenn, not sure what to say. Lori broke the silence.

"Maya is your sister. Your people are also her people. You both are hybrids, but I am going to guess you had different mothers. She was raised very differently than you were. She was never told the truth."

"I did not come here for a lecture," Lansatti said.

"I know you didn't. My point is this-she, without any guidance, has given the world your DNA code through her fiction. With a little help from me, she has identified one of your genes as the time travel gene. And finally, this modern day Wonder Woman has also told me through her encoded fiction how to modify human beings for the same kind of travel. In her sequel, your name comes up several times, in code, but we found it. Lansatti. Also spells out Atlantis. Nice family name. I believe the pages and positioning of where she inserts her code are the coordinates that you need. But that's not all. I have a map from my father. And Eric took a book that Hitler wrote which contains the same map. The coordinates mesh with the maps."

"Your father? Was he part of Operation Chrome? He might have placed me. General Andreas I was told ran the base…"

"Yes, that was him," Lori said.

"I guess this would be six degrees of separation undone. Now what do you want out of all of this?" asked Lansatti. "You have my full attention." Lansatti crossed his legs and looked at everyone in the room.

Lori was silent for a long moment. I doubt she wanted anything, but would not waste this opportunity.

I couldn't take the tension and then said, "If I may, Sir, I went back in time. 1944 Germany to be exact. I saw them, those things."

"The Reptilians. Yes. You must have been underground. They have been looking for our ancestors for centuries. They found some, a few thousand that we cannot get to at this point. I am betting they will one day use them as prisoners of war. But there are so many more, an entire civilization. The Reptilians dig their tunnels and build their cities, but still cannot find them. They like to tout peace and tolerance, yet they want our race exterminated."

I slammed my hands on the library table. "Mister Lansatti, how do you know that your ancestors are alive? The flood happened thousands of years ago. I was told by the Reptilians that they all were wiped out."

"We know this through our dreams. You know this through your writing. They are asleep, waiting for someone to save them. They have that ability to hold onto life when frozen, as do you and I. They need someone to thaw them out, take them home. They are deep under the ice. It's very dangerous and very expensive to look for them. I have already lost three men. Now please, name your price. As you know, I am very rich."

I smiled as I remembered that I, too, was very rich. "I am not looking for money. I get the sense that you do not like the Reptilians, right?" He nodded. "They are a threat to the world right now."

"Absolutely. Do you know that they can shapeshift? Only for short periods, hours, maybe a day. They want to overthrow the world."

I nodded. "Then you need to seal up all of their portals. Can you do that?"

He nodded. "Yes, seal them in so they cannot get out. That will work for now. It's a temporary fix, but will give us time...Wait, we could blow them up. But then the Earth's crust would take a hit."

"Can you rescue the Grays? They are using them as slaves." I suggested.

"That would be a full declaration of war. I cannot do that. If I tell those in the Gray Government, then they will come down here. Another potential war. The Grays are a casualty that cannot be helped. They brashly and stupidly took on the Reptilians centuries ago. One day we will be better equipped to help them, but not now," Lansatti said.

I didn't like his answer. Was he being honest, or did he not want to get involved? I had to respect him for not making a promise he couldn't keep.

"Alright. Glenn and I run this place. It's an institute dedicated to extraterrestrial research. We just figured out how to travel through time, but we still have so many questions. Can you can give Glenn some direction in going back to specific times and places of the past?" Lansatti nodded. "He needs more information in general relativity.

He wants to visit the future. His best physicist just…quit. He needs…"

"Will you give me one of your men for this trip? You know, for insurance. So that you are not sending me on a wild goose chase."

Glenn inserted himself into the conversation. He quickly responded,

"I will send you two men with the coordinates. They will join you in the expedition. They can even join you in sealing up the portals that the Reptilians use."

I looked at Glenn with questions in my mind. He winked at me.

"Alright then. We have a deal." Lansatti extended his hand.

"One more request. I want photographs and footage. I promise not to put it up on a website or YouTube. It would be part of T.A.H.'s research. I would have them here, in the library, for only our visitors to see."

"Alright. I guess it is time to be a little more transparent about other intelligent species. Give me a notepad, and I will write out the equations step by step. I don't have it all memorized, but you can call my company for the details. Sorry to tell you that you are not the first to figure this out, but you are one of the few who didn't have certain advantages."

"Our time travel program must be elementary to you," Glenn said.

"It's definitely in the early stages, but you jumped over the first and hardest hurdle. Once everything is said and done, I would love to be part of your experiment. T.A.H. has done some very important work. I hope I can come here as a visitor and friend."

Glenn handed Lansatti a blank journal that sat on the table. The energy tycoon scribbled down several pages within minutes.

Glenn said, "I will be back shortly with your two men." He returned several minutes later, about the same time Lansatti was finished writing up his formulas. He went over each equation with Lori who had a general understanding of how math related to time travel. Their conversation was over my head.

Glenn walked back into the room with my husband and Sam. I almost fainted. If I had a gun in my hand, I might have pulled the trigger. It had been a week since Claude had tried to kill me.

"It's alright," Eric whispered. He held my hand that started to tremble. "Lots to catch up on. I think Glenn has the perfect solution to getting rid of these two while giving them exactly what they deserve."

Glenn handed me an envelope and then said, "Mister Lansatti, these two men are my employees, Sam Marshall and Claude Kazinsky. They each have a copy of Doctor Blacksmith's maps as well as the coordinates found within Maya's novel. I gave them a printout of Maya's unpublished novel. All of her codes are highlighted. If you have questions, you can also call me or any of us here. They have cameras in their bags. Claude and Sam have agreed to help you in your exploration. Once their mission is complete, please drop them off…"

"Argentina," Claude said. "That's somewhat close to Antarctica."

Glenn nodded and then said, "Argentina. I will pay them for their services."

Leonardo Lansatti looked at his very expensive gold watch. "We need to leave. I have a pilot to meet in San Diego and then we will be off to join the rest of the crew. I hope we both are happy with this agreement. Thank you all. And Maya, I would like to know you better. You are my sister. In due time." He waved to us and then followed Devon, Claude, and Sam out of the library. Fifteen minutes later I heard the propellers. They were gone.

I looked inside of the envelope that Glenn had just given me. Signed divorce papers. I laughed a laugh of gratitude and then threw my arms around Glenn. "I am ready to go home."

Epilogue

One Year Later

Doctor Lori Blacksmith greeted Eric and me on T.A.H.'s helipad. "Come, I have much to show you."

Eric and I eagerly followed her down the stairs to the lab. She took us into one of the newly built laboratories. We lovingly looked into the artificial womb. There it was. Our baby.

"It's a boy," Doctor Blacksmith said. "He's about five months old now. I can take him out around month eight. Start getting the nursery ready in your favorite shade of blue."

When my gynecologist back in Las Vegas told me I was unable to have children, I spiraled into depression. After everything I had been through, all I wanted was to marry Eric and have children. I got the first part of my dream to come true. Our wedding was small. The ceremony and reception consisted of a church service and then an all-you-can-eat buffet. Eric's parents, his book store employees, and our new friends at T.A.H. attended. We couldn't have been happier.

I sold my Vegas mansion and bought a decent sized ranch with Eric not too far off of the strip. We occasionally made use of the mammoth home that Jay left me. Every few weeks we would fly in and hang out with Paula, Mercedes, and Glenn. I occasionally made it to T.A.H., usually to sign paperwork involving the institute. Glenn ran the institute without me, but I promised to get more involved in the near future.

The second part of my dream required some creativity. My uterus was malformed. Having children was out of the question. I shared my problem with Doctor Blacksmith and hoped she could direct me to a good orphanage. I liked the idea of adoption. Maybe I could save someone from the nightmare that I went through. The doctor admired me for wanting to adopt, but knew of another way.

"It is not exactly traditional, and might not even be legal. A test tube will get things started and then we can transfer the embryo into an artificial womb, also called an A-womb. You don't even need a surrogate."

We were thrilled with the doctor's idea.

"He looks like you," Eric said as he lovingly looked at our baby boy floating in the giant clear bowl.

"Oh right. You can't tell what he will look like. I just hope he is healthy and normal."

"What are you going to name him?" the doctor asked as we gushed over the machine.

Eric shrugged. "We hadn't discussed a name."

I slowly answered. "Well, Doc, if it is alright with Eric, I would like to name him Jay."

"It's more than alright."

Glenn interrupted us with a large suitcase in hand. We agreed to run an errand for him. He gave Eric the suitcase. "Two million U.S. for our favorite friends, Claude and Sam. They are waiting in Argentina. A deal is a deal. They will be out of your life forever."

"I saw the footage they took. No one will ever believe this. For weeks, hundreds of giant saucers landed in the western part of the continent. Body after body was just lifted inside of the crafts. It looked like a Hollywood movie. Claude told us that none of them were awake and he doubted that they were even alive. He took lots of photos. He was fascinated by their uniforms. They were like spandex but with swirls of color moving through the material. There was a swastika on their sleeves. I asked him if this was why Hitler picked it as his symbol," I said. "He didn't know, but would ask Lansatti."

"'Great question. You should ask Lansatti yourself. He is your brother, you know. I hope he calls and you two have some kind of relationship," Glenn said. "The plane is ready whenever you are. Are you sure you want to go with?"

I nodded. "We are bringing Devon in case Claude tries something. Lori is also on board."

Lori said, "I have had this map of Argentina for decades. I was just curious. It's just a couple of hours out of the way. I want to know why my father got a hold of it. It's the same map in Hitler's sequel."

The plane trip took several hours. We landed in Rio Gallegos, a town on the southern tip of the country. Claude and Sam waited with one of the air traffic controllers in the small airport. Eric hopped out of the plane and then came back a few minutes later with a stack of photos and a flash-drive.

"What did he say?" I asked, still not even close to reaching a state of forgiveness.

Eric handed me the photos and said, "He wanted to give you these. Just you. It's in addition to the footage he sent. A truce offering. You can show them to Glenn or whoever you want, or keep them to yourself." He looked over at Lori who had her earbuds on and was taking notes, completely disconnected to the conversation. Devon was watching a movie, also in his own world.

I went through the stack of photos. Hundreds of lifeless bodies of Reptilians and Grays lain inside of the ice tunnel where the Atlanteans were found. They looked more like casualties of war rather than a crew of A.B.s who died during an exploration. "Were they dead before Lansatti drilled underneath the ice?"

"No. They had some company. Claude said that Lansatti had armed everyone in his crew with laser guns before they entered the cave and drilled. He also said it was the thrill of his life. He and Sam thought they killed a few dozen Reptilians. They were offered full time work with Lansatti, huge salaries and lots of time off in between explorations. They were going help seal up some portals. I think Claude has found his niche," Eric said.

I smiled. "What's that? Killing aliens? Everyone has a place in this world. As long as he sticks to killing Reptilians. Eric, do you think Lansatti just wanted to send the Atlanteans back home?"

"What do you mean, Maya?"

"I mean, what if they are the real enemy? Remember that Hitler worshipped them. He claimed that all pure Germans were their descendants. After seeing those Nazis face to face, they were so evil. How could the Atlanteans be good? What if they really are the Master Race and they want Atlantis and the entire planet back? What if they wanted hybrids in place to help them run this planet?"

"I thought you said the Reptilians were the biggest threat?"

"Yes, Eric, I did. Yes, they are. But evil has many layers."

"Maya, you're part Atlantean, and you are good. I believe that all life has free will. A race isn't all evil, they only choose to follow it."

Maybe he was right. I didn't want to think of it. I had no reason to fear the Altanteans. They had shown Lori's father and his airbase nothing but technology secrets. Almost all of them were drowned. They were the victims, not the aggressors. I had a baby on the way and a new life with Eric, but I still doubted everything good that was in my life.

After the "Claude" stop, we flew into Bariloche, a town in Argentina that seemed to be marked in both Lori's father's papers and Hitler's sequel. Lori just wanted to get off of the plane, walk around the town, and maybe have lunch. Curious.

Bariloche was in the southwestern part of Argentina, right on the foothills of the Andes Mountains. Lori had read that it was a tourist area known for skiing. As we landed, I looked around and admired the town's beauty. There were snow-capped mountains and a lake. The town looked like a quaint Alpine village from a movie.

The pilot landed the plane nearby the ski lodge. A taxi took us into town. We walked through the shops. I bought some baby's clothes and Eric bought a wooden toy set of Noah's Ark. We went inside a pottery shop and looked around.

Eric saw a man behind the counter and asked, "Sir, can you recommend a good place to eat German food?" He seemed to understand English.

"Oh yes. Go to the end of the block and turn right. A few blocks down is a place called *House of Heinrich.*"

The restaurant was as charming as the village. It was a large place built in a European chalet style. Devon chose to stand guard outside of the restaurant and the rest of us went inside. We ordered sausage and sauerkraut from an older waitress. As we waited for our food, we walked around and looked at the photographs on the wall. There were no pictures of Hitler, but I recognized one of Bormann. Above the fireplace, was a picture of a beautiful blonde woman who used to own the place. I recognized her at once.

"Eric, isn't that…"

"Yes, it is! Gretchen, Josef's niece. Small world," he said.

"So, this is where they all came after the war. I suspected, but it's nice to see," Lori said.

The waitress tapped us on the shoulder. With a thick, heavy Argentinian accent, she said, "Your food is ready. Do you know her? She died many years ago, probably before you were born." We sat down back at the table.

"I know of her. She and her brother, Heinrich, were very brave," I said.

"Yes, they were. Heinrich Handel died when he was a little boy. Got in the middle of gunfire during war," the waitress said. "Gretchen Handel owned this restaurant. She moved away from Germany right after the war. Her relatives were Nazis and she was scared. She came here with nothing. The only thing she knew how to do was cook. She built this place, and it's one of the most successful restaurants in southern Argentina. I am sorry, I am talking too much. Would you like anything else? More to drink? More bread?"

The woman looked so familiar. She had dark hair, streaked with gray, dark skin, and large dark eyes. She was very short and slightly plump. I liked her more than I ever liked a waitress. I didn't want her to walk away so I asked, "You sound like you loved her."

"I did very much. She was my mother." The waitress smiled and walked away.

Eric looked at Lori and Lori looked at Eric. Finally, he said, "That woman looks like you as an old woman. Is it possible?"

I didn't say anything, but it was more than possible. I remembered waking up with my pants removed in the basement of Eagle's Nest. As I ate my lunch, I looked around the restaurant for more pictures. There was one of Gretchen and her daughter at the park. She was probably seven or eight years old. Then there was a picture of Gretchen and her daughter at the zoo. The girl was around twelve. A photo of the two of them by a car. The girl was now sixteen. I was afraid to look. The next picture was of Gretchen and her daughter, now a young woman, with a young man dressed up in front of a church. There were no pictures with the waitress and her father. I couldn't deny that I looked just like her. Did Hitler escape with my eggs and clone me?

The waitress returned with a pot of coffee and the check. She smiled and put her hand on my shoulder. "You remind me of me when I was young."

The moment was like a déjà vu on steroids. We couldn't get out of the country fast enough. I never wanted to go to Argentina again.

Three months later, I sat at the kitchen table in our Vegas home and rocked my son's cradle with my left hand and wrote my next novel with my right hand in a notebook. I planned on cleaning it up and typing it into my laptop once Jay was asleep. Writing was my passion, but science fiction had become too real. I decided to try romance. Life with Eric gave me a taste of it on a daily basis.

"Eric, when you got a chance, what do you think of my last chapter?" I yelled. He was in the baby's room stenciling the baby's name on the wall.

"Got it up. Jay in dark blue. It looks great against the baby blue paint. You go look at my masterpiece and I'll look at yours. I got up and walked over to his room. Eric was right. The room was a masterpiece. He wanted an astronaut theme despite my protests. I gave in. There were rockets and spaceships all over the wall. The ceiling fan was shaped like a flying saucer. Underneath Jay's name, was an astronaut decal of a little boy with reddish hair. It was a very cool room.

I walked back into the kitchen and saw Eric smiling as he read my last chapter. "You are something else. You're kidding? Right?"

"I am not sure what you are talking about? You don't like the ending?"

"That has nothing to do with it. Listen to me. You are still encoding A.B. information! Let me read it to you:

At the lighthouse, Andrea nervously took Ian's sapphire ring. 'Ian, somehow eternity survives.' Really?"

I shrugged my shoulders. "Too cheesy? I am new at this romance novel stuff."

Eric walked away laughing.

Atlantis Rises

Author's Notes:

Hope you enjoyed both volumes of *The Best Seller* and *The Sequel*. Below is an informal list of conspiracy theories and history trivia that inspired my story.

Operation Paperclip: A governmental program that took German doctors from Germany and had them work for the U.S. The goal was to advance American technology. These Germans were exonerated from all war crimes.

Broom Lake: A literary version of Groom Lake also known as Area 51, the famous Nevada base involved in alien and UFO conspiracy.

Utah air base: The 'new' Area 51.

Reptilian/Reptoid aliens: David Icke most famously coined this race. They are associated with the elite powers of the West and want to take over the world.

Eagle's Nest: One of Hitler's hideouts. Martin Bormann had it built for Hitler's 50th birthday.

Vril Society: A secret society that used mediums such as Maria Orsic to channel aliens. According to conspiracy theory, Maria disappeared in a space ship after Germany lost the war.

The Coming Race by Edward Bulwar-Lytton: A famous book about Vril energy controlled by Vril-ya in the hollow earth.

Thule/Hyperborea: Part of the history of the Aryan race. Their origins reach back to Atlantis. This was used in an occult associated with Hitler.

Zweites Buch: Hitler's sequel. Mainly about foreign policy.

Hitler's escape: Many conspiracy theories arose after his "death". Most believe that if he did escape, he lived out the rest of his days in Argentina or Brazil.

About Dina Rae

Dina Rae has written seven novels. She lives with her husband, two daughters, and two dogs outside of Dallas. She is a Christian, avid tennis player, movie buff, teacher, and self-proclaimed expert on several conspiracy theories. She has been interviewed numerous times on blogs, newspapers, and syndicated radio programs. She enjoys reading about religion, UFOs, New World Order, government conspiracies, political intrigue, and other cultures. The Sequel, Volume 2 of The Best Seller series, will soon be released by Solstice Publishing.

Social Media Links

Blog: https://dinaraeswritestuff.blogspot.com/

Twitter: https://twitter.com/HalooftheDamned

Facebook: https://www.facebook.com/DinaRaeBooks/?ref=bookmarks

Trailer: https://www.youtube.com/watch?v=ZAMlurlxPZs&t=3s

Goodreads: https://www.goodreads.com/author/show/5747496.Dina_Rae

Amazon Page: https://www.amazon.com/Dina-Rae/e/B0085348DY/ref=sr_ntt_srch_lnk_1?qid=1508029892&sr=8-1

Acknowledgements

To Mike, my soulmate and biggest cheerleader! Love, Dina

If you enjoyed this story, check out these other Solstice Publishing books by Dina Rae:

The Best Seller

When Maya Smock writes her first novel, everything seems to go her way. Her book practically writes itself. She marries her gorgeous agent. Her name is on all of the best seller lists. Billionaire author Jay McCallister takes an interest in her meteoric rise to fame and invites her into his world of alien-believing celebrities. Her life changes forever when he tells her that they were both created inside of a laboratory. These authors are embedding an alien genetic code within the pages of their novels that originated from Nazi Germany because...

The time has come. They are here.

https://bookgoodies.com/a/B01G2AKGMS